LUKEWARM

Angela Marie Holmes

ACKNOWLEDGMENTS

Lord you gave me a vision and made it reality. You gave me the title Lukewarm and never let it die. May my testimony direct those who are lukewarm to choose whom they shall serve? I thank you Lord for all your guidance and instruction when I wanted to give up. I thank you for your faithfulness, direction and your favor over my life. May this book be a blessing to everyone you intended to read it.

To Teri and Brooke You two saved my life. Brooke who knew you would be the calm one in a crisis. Thank you both for protecting me when I couldn't protect myself. I will love and cherish our friendship forever. Teri you are my best friend forever. What a dear sweet friendship we have! Thank you for always being there for me as a sister and a friend. We have experienced a lot in our lives. Thank you for allowing me to be family. I love you. Thank you Jessica for all the talks we've had to get IT off our chest, whatever IT was, for the shoulder to cry on and all the hugs. Thank you for letting us love unconditionally. Thank you ladies for always having my back and my front. I cherish the three of you!

To all my friends who supported me along this seven-year journey! Can we say completion! Special thanks to Kim Livingston, Brenda Barnes, Rene Porter, Alexandra Barbosa- Deas for that amazing synopsis, Tammy Bishop for all your encouraging words, and especially Sunni Harley withthe Princess Book Club!

ANGELA

DEDICATION

This book is dedicated to my parents,
Glenn Holmes and Ella Holmes-Belle

See what God can do! He was making my life a living testimony. He knew his plan for my life when no one else did. I thank you both for your continued support in the midst of my trials and tribulations. I never meant to break your hearts or make you cry. Just know that God is truly amazing and let tomorrow worry about itself.

Love your daughter,
Angela

To my sisters, Shera and Sheila

Thank you for believing in me and all the endless talks over the phone, when I had another story to tell.

Shera

You showed me how to accept the shades of gray when I didn't want to. You have so much class and style I look up to you and always want the very best for you.

Sheila

Girl, you have always been everyones favorite. You always make me laugh and keep it real. You are such a sweetie pie and I thank you for always telling me how beautiful I was inside and out. You saw this book in your dream and encouraged me to keep writing, for that I am grateful.

To my younger BIG brother, Walter Hollis, aka (Hollis)

I love you man. Look at you! You have inspired me to reach for the stars as you sit amongst them. I can never express my appreciation and gratitude to you for being my big brother! Good lookin' out!

To my brother, Don, aka (Donnie Holmes)

I am thankful for the love you have always shown me since my birth. You have been there to protect me and teach me whatever it was I needed to know. I love you and wish the best for you. God always answers my prayer concerning you and this you know. Continue to seek His will for your life. I love you.

To the two most beautiful ladies in my world, my cousins, Dede and Stacey

You two have been with me through all my mess. Thank you for not judging me and always standing with me in the end. I love you two more than you will ever know, we are not just cousins we are sisters, through the good and bad times, family first.

Lastly I would like to acknowledge my children, Aricka, Kumari and Caleb

I pray the road you travel will not be the one I chose. I pray continuously for God's hand over your lives, His guidance and instruction. May His grace be sufficient and His mercy endure. I love you all individually, each one of you are special and unique. Always put God first and He will take care of you. I love you with all my heart, Mom.

TABLE OF CONTENTS

CHAPTER ONE

What have I done? This has got to be a nightmare, her voice whispered over and over in her head. *I feel like the movies I've seen where your body is numb and you just sit as the water runs down your face, except this was no dream.*

As I squeezed the wash cloth over my head and water ran down my face, I knew I couldn't sit in the tub for long. The door opened.

"I put your clothes in bag and threw them in a dumpster. Here is another shirt and some shorts."

"Okay," I whispered.

It was time to get out of the tub, but where would I go? I needed to find out what was going on.

"Take me to 33rd."

When we pulled up, the front door was open and everyone was standing around. As I walked through the door, my cousin Steve yelled.

"Man! What happened at Aunt Nora's? It's police everywhere, and they have yellow tape blocking the house off!"

"Oh shit! Does that mean somebody's *dead?*"

"I don't know? That's what it looks like to me."

"She *stabbed* that girl!" That was my cousin Monique jumping in the converstion.

"What the fuck you *do* that for?"

"I don't *know?* We got in a fight, and I stabbed her."

1

"Let me go back down there and see what the hell is goin on!" You stay yo ass here. I'll be back."

Everyone sat around in a daze. We could hear the crickets on the steps by the front door. The phone rang.

"It's for you."

"Hello?"

"Baby, are you okay?" "Yes."

"Everyone's over your mother's. You need to go over there.

Daddy's on his way."

"Okay," I whispered and hung up the phone. "Everyone's at my moms. My dad wants me to go over there."

When we pulled around the corner, in front of my mother's house, I felt sick. My heart was pounding as I walked up the walkway approaching the door. As I opened the door, I saw that everyone was in the den and the kitchen. All my mom's sisters were there waiting. How did they find out? How did everyone get over there so fast? What would they say?

A voice sounded from the kitchen.

"What happened?" My Aunt Chellie asked as she approached the doorway of the den.

"I got in a fight." "Over some *man*?" "No."

"Then what happened?"

"I just got in a fight, she had a knife... and I took it and stabbed her."

"Did you have to *kill* her?" "She's dead?"

"That's what they said." "Your uncle Carl says half the city police are looking for you."

Uncle Carl just happened to be the chief of homicide for the police department and Aunt Chellie's ex-husband.

"Mommy!" A little voice echoed from the hallway.

I reached down and picked up one-year-old Nadia. My aunt Jean walked into the room.

"This reminds me of the night your Aunt Liz died." "Everyone was at the house in the middle of the night, and Dawn was Nadia's age, walking around, not knowing what was going on."

Dawn was my oldest girl cousin. Her mother passed away when she was just two years old. She was my mom's oldest sister.

"What were you *thinking*?" My mom said as she snatched Nadia from my arms. "You're going to *jail*!"

My mother went to the living room and began rocking Nadia in one of the chairs. I couldn't bear to look at her. She was upset, beyond upset. I could feel her stare piercing through my body.

When the front door opened, it was my father. He didn't say much. He just stood there and made an announcement to everyone in the room.

"I've talked to Carl. He has agreed not to make an arrest tonight if I promise to bring her downtown in the morning."

"Daddy, I have to go to *jail*? I didn't mean to *kill* her!" "We'll figure it all out in the morning."

"I'll be here in the morning at seven to take you downtown," my dad said as he kissed me on my forehead.

"Okay."

That night I slept on the couch with Nadia in my arms.

"Your father is on his way."

Nadia was sound asleep. It was morning. I sat up on the couch, staring out the window.

When my father pulled up my mom opened the door watching him come up the walkway. I stood up and walked toward the door.

"You ready?

"Yes."

"Take off all your jewelry." "Oh, okay."

I took off my earrings and all my rings. First, it was my pinky diamond ring I got from Santana or "Stan" as they now called him. The other pinky diamond ring I got from Juelz. Then I took the gold ring with the queen symbol that I got from Bernard from my ring finger, and the one-third karat ring from my index finger that I got from my sister Shelise, and finally the other diamond crafted ring, which I also had got from Juelz. I handed the rings to my mom.

"Let's go."

My mom grabbed me, crying with sorrow. "I'll be okay Mama, don't cry."

My mom strained and covered her mouth, trying to hold back the tears. I walked to the truck. As I climbed in, I looked back at my mom, then I looked ahead as we drove off.

CHAPTER TWO

"**S**tate your full name." "Danielle Kimberly Manning." "State your date of birth." "April 24, 1970." "I will now read you your rights. You have the right to remain silent, anything you say can and will be used against you in a court of law, and you have the right for an attorney to be present..."

Oh no! I am being arrested for murder? Where are they going to take me? Am I gonna get to go home? Where's my dad? Did he just leave me here? Where's my uncle Carl? Is he gonna come talk to me?

After the policeman left me in his office by myself, some lady came in, pretending to empty the trash.

"What they got you for?"

I acted as if I didn't hear her. I remember my father telling me not to talk to anyone.

"Don't answer any questions until you go before the judge."

"You'll be all right. I know you're scared."

"Single file ladies. You'll need to undress, remove your panties and bras. You will be issued clothing from the holding tank. Remove all items from your hair and run your fingers through it. Manning you're going to need to take your braids out before processing. We'll place you in the holding tank until you take all your braids out."

Damn! Ain't this a bitch? Juelz just paid a hundred dollars for these damn braids and I got to take them out? How am I gonna comb my hair? My hair's gonna be all over my head! Not to mention the three rows of braids that bitch pulled out from my scalp! How am I supposed to take these braids out with these nails and no comb? This some fucked up shit! I wonder if we're allowed to use this phone.

There was a phone on the wall.

"Can we use this phone?"

"Yeah go ahead. They'll cut you off after two minutes, so you better talk fast."

"Oh!" Who should I call? Who else, but my best friend Candi. I gotta tell her what happened.

I met Candi the summer before our freshman year at Sac High. Since I had a boyfriend at the time, we didn't hang too much. I was still close to my other friend Rochelle, who I met the previous summer through one of my cousins.

Candi and I found out that my brother Dennis was good friends with her older sisters and brothers. She was the last born of twelve children, six boys and six girls. She had a sister named Star, who was two years older than us.

"We can start walking to school together and dressing alike."

"Yeah, that would be *fun*."

Candi already had her group of childhood friends. I moved to Oak Park with my mom after living with my dad for seventh and eighth grade. We had moved from College Greens when my parents divorced, so I was the new booty on the block, but it seemed that Candi and I had the most in common. We were the same age, born in the same month, ten days apart. We wore the same size clothes and same size shoes.

She was light, and I was dark in complexion, so we balanced each other. When I wanted to do something crazy, she would always act as my conscience, and when she was afraid to do something, I would be the one to push her to "just do it!"

Whoever knew my best friend was just on the other side of town, in the hood. We were a perfect match, and we were pretty too! When you saw Candi, you saw me. We were together so much that you couldn't call out one name without saying the other. It was *Danielle and Candi*.

****

"You are *where*?" "In jail!"

"Girl, quit playing."

"I'm not *playing*! I got in a fight last night, stabbed a girl, and she died."

"What?"

"Yeah."

"Oh shit! You serious!"

"Hell *yeah*! It's on the news right now. Turn to channel three." It was on the news all right.

"That *you*?"

"Yeah."

"She must have been fuckin with you, huh? I mean, we know you didn't mean to kill her, but sometimes you have to do what you have to do, right?"

"No comment."

From that moment on, it was as if I was a celebrity. *How could they think that way? Someone was dead, and I killed her. It was unreal.* For the next few hours, the other girls helped me take my braids out. They wanted to hear what happened. They wanted my tragedy to be their entertainment.

"Manning. Come this way."

"Stay up, home girl. You'll be alright, baby."

The girls wished me well, if that's what you wanna call it. "Remove all your clothing and undergarments."

Undergarments? My bra and panties? I removed my clothes. I had heard about the routine, the bend over and cough. For real? Oh my God!

"Bend forward and run your fingers through your hair... Now, spread your butt cheeks and cough three times."

I couldn't believe this was happening!

"Okay, step to the table... Here put this on. You'll be placed in solitary confinement. You'll be able to come out one hour each day...you'll eat all your meals in your cell. Breakfast is at five thirty in the morning, lunch is at eleven, and dinner is at four thirty in the evening."

Damn! Who wakes up to eat at five thirty in the morning? Shit, I'm not eating a damn thing. Fuck that! What they give me to put on? Smells like old hospital sheets. And who had this bra before I did? At least the panties are new.

Two weeks had gone by, I hadn't eaten a thing.

"You gotta eat baby girl." "At least drink the milk."

"I don't want nothing," I said from underneath the blanket.

I had been charged with involuntary manslaughter. Bail was set at five hundred thousand dollars. No one would take Juelz's money. Juelz was my man. I had been with him for almost a year by that time. Yep, I loved me some him, and he loved me. They had me listed as a flight risk, but why? Where would I go? Something wasn't right. Why would they say that?

****

"What can I do for you? What are you saying? Are you sure? Where would she try to go? She doesn't have that type of money does she? Well I'll take your word for it. I assured Danielle's father that we would make sure she got out... I'll let the others know."

That was Cal, a lawyer working with the bail agents to get me out on bond. That call would change the fate of my release. That phone call had come from my mother.

"I don't know if bailing Danielle out is a good idea." "She is very headstrong and I think she would try to leave the state. Who knows where she might go? Her boyfriend has money. I believe he would take her somewhere and hide her. I really don't trust her. She can't be thinking of the seriousness of this situation!"

No one was going to bail me out. My dad himself was a bondsman, the first black one in the city of Sacramento. He must have let all of them know not to bail me out. My dad was well respected in the city. Everyone knew my dad, and after this incident, they knew who I was. I never thought of it like that. It was not a good thought.

I told Juelz exactly what I wanted to eat. Corndog and fries from Keith's Patio, a chicken leg from KFC original recipe, with a strawberry parfait, and a beef burrito with extra cheese from Jimboy's. I was so hungry that I could taste the food! My mouth was watering at the thought of it.

We were on the phone for that hour, waiting to hear my name called to bail out. They hadn't called me. *What's going on?* "Are they gonna keep me locked up?" I could barely get my words out of my mouth as I began to cry.

"Don't worry, Mama, you gonna get out, it just take so fuckin long. Don't trip, baby."

"But it's almost time for them to lock us down."

"I'll be waiting outside for you. I'll be right there, baby!"

"Okay. Maybe they'll call at like, two in the morning. I'm going to call my uncle again, and see what he says."

I had bugged my uncle Simon to death. He was my dad's brother, and my father had left him in charge of everything when he left for his vacation.

When I woke up, I realized I had slept all night. That time never came. I could see daylight in the sky from the tiny window near the ceiling. They had never called for me to bail out. All I could do was cry. It must have been eleven o'clock that morning.

They let us out early that day. The door clicked. It was unlocked for me to come out when I was ready. I had to call Juelz. I was hoping I could find something out about my bail.

"You have a collect call from the Sacramento County Jail..." "What happened, baby?"

"I don't know. No one ever called me."

"Shit, my ass was waiting outside till four in the morning. And then I told myself, shit, they ain't letting my baby out. Your daddy a sucka' man. That's real talk!"

I didn't know what to think. My uncle stopped accepting my collect calls. My dad was gone; he left me in there and didn't tell me anything.

I realized I wasn't going home and started to cry. Juelz tried to calm me down, but there really was not anything he could say. It was the weekend—no court until Monday. The next step was to try to get a bail reduction.

I was going crazy not knowing what was going on, on the outside. I was on the seventh floor and all I could see from my tiny window was the other side of the jail.

"Manning you have a visitor. Push the button when you're ready."

Who could it be? I had been telling Juelz to get his driver's license. You can't visit without a valid ID, and that was something he never had. I pushed the button. "I'm ready."

I went down the stairs and out the door to the visitation booths. As I approached the stairs to walk up, I saw my father and my stepmother. I immediately started to cry and run back up the stairs.

He was back, but he had turned his back so I wouldn't see him crying. It was just too much. My father hated seeing me behind that glass; he couldn't bear to see me that way. My stepmother had sat down and had picked up the phone.

I was crying uncontrollably, so I had to calm myself down in order to speak.

"How are they treating you?" "Okay."

"What are they were feeding you? Have you eaten?" "No!"

I hadn't eaten a thing in three weeks. *Who could eat at a time like this? I may not ever get out of this place!*

"What?" "You've been here three weeks and you haven't eaten anything?"

"Baby, you have to eat."

"I can't eat anything. I just want to go home. Why can't you bail me out?"

My dad heard that much behind the glass. He put the phone to his ear.

"We'll see what we can do. We're trying to get your bail reduced. We have to get you on the calendar to go before the judge."

I knew he wasn't going to bail me out. Juelz told me that my father had given the fifty thousand dollars back, when he could have easily bailed me out. He wasn't the only one Juelz went to for help. He wanted me out just as bad as I wanted to be home. At the end of our visit, I promised my stepmother I would eat something only if it looked eatable and didn't smell funny.

That afternoon, they placed my tray through the flap in the door.

"Here, baby girl you need to eat something. It ain't that bad.

Just try it."

It was baked chicken, cabbage and a carton of milk. That was actually my favorite, but of course, it wasn't my mother's. Boy, it might have been bland, but in my mind, it had all the flavor I needed. I could not believe it: just when I promised to eat, I had gotten my favorite dish.

Weeks went by, I tried to sleep most of my days away. It was the only way not to go crazy in this tiny cell. Early that morning, I noticed an envelope under my door. It was a letter of some kind. When I picked it up it, I saw it was from my mother. I could barely open the letter fast enough. There were pictures enclosed.

Once I saw the pictures of my daughter, I burst into tears. I missed her so much and I couldn't take being in that cell, not knowing what was going on. Was my daughter asking, "Where is my mommy?" Was she crying? I hadn't talked to my mother at all. During the times I got to come out to use the phone, my mother was unable to receive my collect calls at the Care Home where she worked for my Aunt Chellie. We had discussed earlier who would keep the baby. I had insisted she stay with Juelz, at our apartment.

"Are you crazy?"

"Mom, that's her dad. He can keep her."

"That is not her father, and she ain't staying with him. I can't *believe* you!"

I had talked to Juelz about my welfare checks. He was cashing my checks at Oak Park Market, since we didn't know when and if I would be getting out. I told him to just give the money to my mom for the baby.

Nadia was turning two years old. I had been locked up for two months. I called my cousins to arrange a birthday party for her at McDonald's. I gave my cousins Evelyn and Moná a list of things to do and people to call over the phone.

They were maybe a year apart. They were as close cousins as me and LeAnn. We were six months apart, and we were inseparable growing up. We were all extremely close. Our mothers were sisters. We knew Evelyn was the prettiest of the four of us and everybody loved her.

It wasn't until Evelyn came of age that we were all able to hang out together. She had two older brothers, and she was sweet and quiet, petite with a big ol booty, nice pretty skin, hair with never a strand out of place. She was the *fashionista* of the group, her man kept her with dollars in her pocket, not to mention draped with necklaces and rings on most of her fingers. Yep, he was a D boy. There was nothing Evelyn wanted that he didn't get for her. That was Marquisee. She had been dating that boy since she was twelve. She was sixteen when I was arrested, four years younger than LeAnn and me.

I made sure Juelz got Nadia her first tricycle. I tried to make a good day out of a bad situation. I wrote a letter, to be read by Mona' at the party, apologizing for my absence. I even went as far as calling my mother and having her to call on a three-way to the McDonalds to make sure the party started on time and everyone was there.

I felt so helpless. I just wanted Nadia's birthday to be a good one, even if I was not there. I didn't know when I would see my baby again. I definitely didn't want her to visit me in jail. Seeing her from behind the glass and not being able to touch her would be something I could not handle. At such a young age, would she remember that her mommy went away for a long time?

Juelz got his ID, so he was finally able to visit me. He asked if Nadia could come to see me. I began to think maybe it would be a good idea. I just didn't know how she would react, not being able to touch me or even sit in my lap. We were allowed only two visits a week. The visitation cycle began on Sunday, so he would come see me on Friday, Saturday, and Sunday. Then we would talk the whole week on the phone and start over on Friday.

I didn't want anyone coming to mess up my visits, not even my dad. I told him not to come see me, because it was hard knowing that I would not be getting out. One thing about those visits that is all you have. We talked on the phone every chance we got, and we always had *something* to talk about.

Just as I had become somewhat used to being in the cell by myself, I went before the judge for a bail reduction. It was actually my second appearance. During my first appearance, which they called an arraignment, I didn't know what to expect. As I approached the courtroom, I saw my family there to support me. Well, it was my mother, father and my oldest sister Krishna.

When I glanced up, all I saw was that same look on my mother's face. Her face was still so full of sorrow. It was as if her eyes had turned black as coal. There was no emotion, no feeling; she was merely existing.

Juelz was also there with all his folks. They were all sitting on the opposite side of the courtroom. The district attorney called Juelz to the stand and asked a series of questions regarding events about that fatal night. His answer remained the same, "I can't recall."

After seeing my mother's face, I never once again looked up. I sat right next to my public defender. It seemed he was the only one they called to the stand.

I knew he was nervous.

"How well do you know the defendant?"

"I know her."

"Would you say she was your girlfriend?" "Yes."

"Do you and the defendant live together?" "No."

"How long has the defendant been quote unquote, your girlfriend?"

"About six or seven months."

"Which is it, six months or seven months?" "Seven months."

"And how well did you know the victim?"

"I knew her."

"Was there any reason for the defendant to be jealous or envious of the victim?"

"Possibly, but Baby didn't have to kill her though..."

I couldn't look at him, I was too embarrassed. I kept my head down while Juelz was on the stand.

I was in and out so fast that I didn't really know what happened. I only knew I wasn't going home. It took forever to get back to my cell, but Juelz was there waiting for me. As soon as I stepped into go to my POD, I heard, "Manning you have a visitor."

It was Juelz, waiting for me at our same booth. I saw that white tee and his tall stature under the lights. He was standing, looking down the stairs as I walked up. I was so happy to see him that I didn't mention anything that was said in court. He didn't have any good news to tell.

They had reduced the bail to $250,000, and still no one would bail me out. My father had said, "God told me He took a life to save a life and she'll be safer in jail than on the streets." That was a done deal. I was not going home, not bailing out.

After that, I was reclassified to general population. That meant I would be moving to another POD with everyone else. I was really nervous about facing all those ladies in the POD, which was what they called each block of rooms. PODS held about twenty-five rooms, with two inmates per cell. I didn't speak to anyone, but everyone knew who I was. They knew about my case, and they knew who Juelz was. Every time I stepped out of my cell, they crowded around me like I was a celebrity.

"Come on over here, girl! You play spades?"

Her name was Dee. She said I knew her brother, Darwin, from the streets and he told her to look out for me once I came through. *Man! What a relief.* They gave me food and put me on the card game. They wanted to hear my story, and I told them what I wanted them to know. They let me know everything that was going on, what not to do, what to do and how the police were in there.

I told them they had me across the way, in the other POD, in protective custody.

"Why the fuck they had you over there with that crazy lady that killed all those people? Yeah, girl buried them and kept they social security checks? You would have been cool over here with us. You cool."

There were only three phones in the POD, and they gave us 15 minutes per call, unless no one wanted to use it. There was one phone next to a table by the window, which was the phone I always used to talk to Juelz. The ladies were so cool that they let everybody know it was my phone and let me talk as long as I wanted. I would stay on the phone with Juelz for an hour at a time. We missed each other so much.

I met with the public defender. Although he was a public defender, he was a friend of my father, so I thought at least he would try to have my back as much as possible. The next court date would be my sentencing.

I made the best of the next few months, as I didn't know when I would be put on the calendar for sentencing. He told me it could be six months from then. *Wow! That long?*

Then he said that "transportation" would come pick me up to take me to prison. *You mean I have to go someplace else after this?* I had gotten so comfortable that I didn't want to go anywhere else. I was scared.

During the course of the next few months, I became close to two ladies. One was my cellmate, Strawberry. She was locked up for a drug charge related to her husband and couldn't bail out. She cried the whole time most nights, wanting to go home. I felt sorry for her. I knew how she felt, wanting to go home. Every day was a new day to get some money up. She said her husband promised her he was trying, and that as soon as he got the money, she would get out.

The other girl was Sabrina, same type of case, except that she and her husband were in together. They had already been in for a minute. I had to make the best of it, and about then, everything seemed to be on my side. When the holiday season came, I had old boyfriends putting money on my books.

I got letters from people I didn't even know. The guards even showed me favor. The officers made me and Sabrina trustees of the POD. That meant that while the other inmates were in their cells, we would be out cleaning and preparing trays. I didn't know that she would become an important person in my life for the rest of my life.

I guess you could say I never thought of being down with my man, where we would get caught up and we would *both* go to jail. I guess that *could* have been my case. Juelz kept the dope away from our house for the most part. He made sure he used them dumb hoes that wanted to seem down to hold his dope at their houses.

Sabrina was a pretty lady. She was light-skinned with long, thick jet-black hair. She looked like them old-school, yellow girls all the niggas liked back in the day, with the light mustache on their lip. You know what *that* meant. Yeah, I had hair on my lip, too.

Sabrina had a skinny frame. I didn't know if she was thin because of our situations or if it was her natural weight. Usually, when you're in the county, you *gain* weight, but not our asses. We were skin and bones, stressed the hell out, on top of trying to get used to that nasty food.

Sabrina was from St. Louis, and she had the accent to go with it. We spent many of days talking about everything under the sun. Our third wheel, Strawberry, had bailed out. The two of us, Sabrina and I, we were all each other had. We had each other's back in that joint. Whatever I didn't have she gave me and vice versa. I couldn't imagine us being separated, but I knew my day was coming sooner or later.

As days, weeks and months went by, I started reading the Bible. I was trying to see if God would visit me in jail. Considering I had gone to Catholic school since the first grade that's basically all I had to go on when it came to the Lord. I *did* get baptized at fifteen at Saint Paul Baptist Church, under Dr. Ephraim Williams. My father taught me principles and morals for life and for being a respectful young woman. At some point I think I ignored those morals when I met Juelz.

I had sincere feelings for others, and I also cared about how others felt toward me. The ladies and I became close. It was as if they had respect for me. I even convinced some of them to join me for bible study. We had a Chaplain to come in and conduct bible study during the week. If anything, it gave them a chance to get out of their cells. At least it got them there. One thing I did believe in was prayer. As I looked around at those ladies, I saw that incarceration was not for me. I almost felt sorry for some who knew nothing else.

Lights went out at eleven. On one particular night, after I had gone to sleep, I began to dream of the incident, all over again.

This time, I was the victim, looking at myself. It was as real as if it was actually happening all over again. I was having the altercation with myself. I felt something pierce my chest, although I didn't know what it was. I kept fighting until someone pulled me off of myself. I had braids wrapped in my clenched fist as they pulled us apart.

All of a sudden I was losing my breath. I couldn't gasp for air. I heard splashes of water as if someone turned on the water hose on a cement porch.

As I looked down, I realized it was me. Blood was pouring out from my chest. I was dying. Oh Jesus, I couldn't breathe!

I fell, awakened, sitting straight up in my bed before I hit the ground. I was clinching my chest, grasping for air. I was crying. I was so scared that it felt like my heart was pounding out of my chest.

Oh God! Forgive me, Lord! Please forgive me, I didn't mean to do it. I didn't mean for her to die. Oh Lord, what did I do? I'm so sorry, Lord, I am so sorry!

I couldn't shake that feeling. I cried until there were no more tears left. I looked around at my surroundings from a jail cell. What had I done? I believe God wanted me to feel exactly what my victim felt. I never meant to kill her.

I thought about her children. They were Nadia's age, if I remember correctly. She was only twenty-four-years-old. What would their lives be without their mother? Christmas was coming. How would her family handle the holiday without her? So many questions raced through my mind. Then I believe God spoke to me as he did my father, saying he took a life to save one, and as time went on, I would understand. I felt I would still have to live with being judged for my actions if I ever got out. It was just too much to think about. All I could do was take one day at a time.

If we were watching a show, the guards would always cut the television off right before the end. I thought that was wrong of them. I talked to the ladies one night and asked them if we could turn the television off before they did and end our night with prayer. Would you believe they agreed? I led the prayer for the group for most of the nights before the lights went out. I felt proud! So did the guards. They started treating the ladies better after that, and that made our days better.

"Manning you have an attorney visit."

Attorney visit? I wondered what he had to tell me. *Was I going to get to go home?* I quickly got ready. I was directed up a different flight of stairs to a small, dark room.

"How are you holding up since our last appearance?"

"Okay, I guess. Just ready to get on with my time."

"Well, the DA has offered a plea bargain. Since there is no self- defense law in California, they want to offer you a charge of involuntary manslaughter. This charge holds a four, six and maximum twelve-year sentence. If you accept the deal, they are willing to offer you the less of the three."

"Okay."

"If you want to go to trial, you can and not take the deal. You have a little time to think about it, but I am submitting the paperwork to get you on the schedule for sentencing. I'll let you discuss it with whomever and I will be in touch."

I called Juelz to tell him I met with the public defender. "Fuck that! You going to trial!"

"No! I don't want to go to trial." "Why not?"

"I just want this to be over, so I can do my time and get out." "Bullshit!" You ain't takin' no mothafuckin' deal. You gonna go to trial and get yo black ass *out!*"

There was no arguing with him. I just sat on the phone and began to cry.

"I'll be down there baby!" "Okay."

Juelz didn't come visit me until after dinner, at around seven.

We sat down at our same booth and began to talk.

I immediately noticed lipstick on the shoulder of that famous white tee. My mind was spinning so fast that I got dizzy for a second.

"What took you so long?"

"I had shit to do and I didn't want to be rushing baby. I wanted to make sure I had as much time with you as possible.

"Is that right?" "Fa sho mama."

"Then whose lipstick is that on your shirt?" "What lipstick?"

"That *lipstick* on your shirt!"

He tried to look puzzled.

"Oh! That must have been from my mama when she hugged me."

"Yo *mama*? Oh, okay."

This lying mothafucka! Guess he didn't expect that slip up to happen.

"So, you going to trial?"

"No, I don't want to go through all that. I just want to do my time and get out."

"By the time you go to trial and shit you'll have timed served!" "Not if they find me guilty."

"Guilty of *what* shit? You was defending yourself!" I gave him a look like, *Man please!*

"There is no guarantee that will happen. People go to jail all day long and be innocent. I don't want to talk about it, and I feel real sick right about now so I'm going to go back to my cell. I don't have much to say, I'll call you."

I stood up, hung the phone up, turned and walked away, leaving him standing right there. I didn't call him anymore. As I returned to my cell, I wondered if he was fuckin around on me already. *Damn! What the fuck?* But maybe it *was* his mom's lipstick. I just kept playing what he said over and over in my head. I tried not to let the tears fall, but so much for that not happening!

As I laid down, one tear fell from one eye into the other and onto the pillow. *What the hell have I done?*

A few days later, the officers called me out of my cell early to come up to their watch booth to talk. These two particular officers worked the same shift together most days. One guard was hella cool. She was short, Filipino, with long hair. She kept her hair pulled up most of the time.

The other guard was white. She was the officer that the others said was mean and prejudiced, but from my point of view, she had to be that way in order to maintain respect and to keep the inmates from fucking with her. She was tall and thick, still feminine, but she looked strong. She had long hair as well, but she had bangs and kept her hair behind her ears. She tried to treat me mean at first, but I just kept being nice until she was cool with me.

"Manning what the hell did you *do*? What happened? You don't look like someone who would have your charge."

"I know."

"We see you don't belong here, so what the hell did you get yourself into, girl?"

I couldn't say much. It was all like a dream for me, and I was just waiting for someone to wake me up. I didn't have an answer. *Things in our lives happen for a reason, and that this might be the biggest lesson I might learn in life.*

"We see that big old man that comes to see you. That's your man, huh?"

"Yes, it is."

"Well, just be prepared to do your time by yourself."

"Yeah. We have seen so many women start out with their man coming to visit, and then they just stop coming."

"Yes, I don't advise anyone to take any relationship seriously.

"You have children?"

"Yes. She just turned two."

"See that is tough by itself, being without your kid."

Boy! I had no idea what was in store for me, but I would soon find out. They wished me well in my future and let me know I would be going up for sentencing, and then I would be leaving that next morning.

"Are you serious? I am finally leaving?"

****

"Does the DA have any last minute incriminating statements or request before the sentence is rendered for the defendant?"

"No, your Honor. We would just like to state to the court that the defendant had been a model citizen up until this unfortunate altercation, and that we are aware that this has been the defendant's first offense."

Oh my God! Did you hear that? The district attorney had that to say on my behalf. I thought they were the ones who were against you and your public defender. God must be in this place!

"The court has heard and has taken those statements under consideration."

My Dad had told me to stand with my arms folded directly in front of me, with my hands extended across my arms, not tucked. It was a sign of humility.

"Does the defendant have any last remarks?" "No, sir."

"Very well, then. You have been charged with involuntary manslaughter. You will serve a four-year sentence. This is your first offense and since you are obviously not prison material, you will be placed for the remainder of your time in the California Youth Authority. This charge also holds a six, and twelve-year maximum sentence. You have received the lesser sentence of the charge. If I see your face in my courtroom ever again, you will receive the maximum sentence for this charge to run concurrent with your present sentence. Do you understand?"

"Yes, sir."

My public defender explained the deal they were giving me. I was over the initial shock of the four-year sentence, but I was just hoping they would change their mind at the last minute and let me go home. As I understood it, I was to do half the time of my sentence. Two years seemed like a long time. I had already been in the county jail for six months. Who knew it would be another six months waiting for transportation.

CHAPTER THREE

"**M**anning, roll 'em up!"
The loud voice sounded through the intercom in my room. "Sabrina!"

"Danielle, you *leaving* me?"

The guards popped the lock on Sabrina's cell so she could come and say goodbye. When she got to my door, they popped my lock. Sabrina's face was red and she was in tears.

"I'm gonna miss you friend," as she always called me. "Don't you forget me? You gonna write me once you get settled in and tell me how it is?"

"Yes, I promise."

We hugged each other before I ran down the stairs. All the ladies were banging on their doors, telling me good-bye.

"Hold it down baby girl! You gonna be alright!"

I was on the bus just like they said, except this bus was going to the Rio Consumnes Correctional Center in Elk Grove. This is where you either serve a short-term sentence or wait for transportation to pick you up and take you to prison. Usually transportation only takes two weeks. That was not the case for me. *What were they waiting for? That place was awful!*

I constantly called home, asking if my father knew what was going on. What was taking so long? He promised to talk to the judge to find out more information on my transportation, but it was not fast enough. Then he had gone on vacation earlier, leaving me in jail for weeks without bailing me out. *I don't know what's going on, and they taking their time? What the fuck? I'm ready to go and get my time started. They say your time here is "dead time."*

It seemed as if everybody had forgotten about me. I couldn't come out of my cell. With the smoked glass windows down the hall, I could never tell if it was day or night. There was just a row of cells, side by side, with plastic glass fronts, facing a cement wall.

The food was awful! *Really* awful! I had shrunk to a size five from a size ten. I didn't even remember *ever* being that skinny. I hadn't looked in a mirror in months. In the county jail, they only had a piece of plastic to *resemble* a mirror. I had to hold it close to my face to see any type of vague reflection. And my hair? What in the world did *that* look like?

The lady in my cell braided it for me soon as I got there. She was cool, I guess. *If she could only stop farting? Damn! She stank. She said it was the milk.*

"Well, don't you think you should drink water? Shit!"

I was wrapped up in wondering what Juelz was doing. I called all day, every day and never got an answer.

The guards had given out the phone early for some reason. *Maybe I can catch him before he hit the streets.* The phone was ringing...

"You have a collect call from Danielle..."

"Hello?" A woman's voice sounded on the other end. I had to take a double-take at the receiver.

"Hello? Who is this?" "Yvette."

"Where is Juelz? And what the fuck are you doing answering my mothafuckin phone?"

"He's not here right now, but I will let him know you called." "Bitch! I don't need you to let him know a mothafuckin thing!" "I..."

"I don't give a fuck about what you think you doing, but I promise you I don't care if I don't get out for five mothafuckin' years bitch! I'm gonna beat yo ass on sight! That's a mothafuckin' promise on my mama, bitch! I'm gonna beat yo ass! You don't answer my mothafuckin' phone bitch!"

Click! *Shit! What the fuck just happened. Who was that bitch? Oh my fuckin' God!* I was so damn mad I started jumping up and down in my cell and kicked the seat at the little table they had. *Damn! That hurt! Shit!* I forgot it was nailed to the floor. *Damn! I almost broke my foot. Shit! Oh, my God! Wait till I talk to his ass!* I thought my head was going to fly off my body!

He used to sit by the phone, waiting for me to call. Lately, it was as if everyone went on with their lives, and I was stuck not knowing when I was leaving, or where I was going.

I couldn't receive money and I had to eat what they gave us. I passed on the shit. I only ate the fruit and desserts they had.

Sometimes I wished I was back downtown with the ladies. It was torture beyond belief. I stayed in that metal box for six months. I could only shower one day a week. It was so nasty I hated for my things to touch the walls or the floor. I basically had to dress wet. I used my dry towel to stand on in the shower.

I got in a routine of sleeping all day, missing breakfast and lunch, waking up for dinner and watching television all night. *Soul Train* came on at one o'clock in the morning. I looked forward to that. The night guard would leave the television on for me. She would also bring the phone and leave it at my door. Favor again. It was an old-school dial phone on a pole. That was crazy. It had a long cord, so I was able to sit on the edge of my hard metal bed and talk.

Once, I got a hold of Juelz and cussed his ass out! Who the fuck was that bitch that answered my mothafuckin' phone?"

"When?"

"When I called my mothafuckin' house and some bitch named Yvette answered the fuckin' phone and said you weren't there! What the fuck, man? That's how you doing it now?"

"No, baby. That's Jamie's bitch!"

"Stop mothafuckin' lyin'! That bitch ain't just let me cuss her out for nothin'!"

"Real talk mama, you think I'm gonna have some other bitch answer my phone?"

"What they doing there anyway?"

"I already told Jamie about that shit! I been told him to check that bitch!"

"Whateva, nigga!"

Click! I hung the phone up. A lot of good that does hell it ain't like he can call me back. Damn it!"

Officer Blue was cool peoples. Her name matched her contact lenses. We talked a little, but she didn't want anyone to think she was being nice to me. I couldn't come out of the cell at all. She told me to write her if I liked to let her know how I was doing whenever I *did* leave.

I started calling Juelz every night at eleven and we would talk until midnight, sometimes even until one o'clock in the morning, when she would leave the phone that long. She would always act as if she forgot I had it, and I would be the last to use it. So I could talk the longest.

I was so in love with this man that it was unreal. I missed him so much. I never even thought he was out there fuckin' around with other females. "So you been fuckin' around on me already, huh?" "Not at all, I'm waiting on you mama. I love yo black ass.

Everybody knows you my woman. All I do is jack-off to your picture every night."

I knew he would not tell me the truth. I started to think realistically by then. I just wanted to enjoy our conversation while I had the chance. Once I was sent off I was certain our relationship would have plenty of holes to fill.

CHAPTER FOUR

My father finally got in touch with the judge. They had my paperwork filed with one of the new Women's State Prison in Chowchilla, and I wasn't even *going* there. *Man! Damn! I waited there for six months, when all my dad had to do was find that out in the first place!* So they sent my paperwork to the correct facility and transportation was on their way to get me.

That was Wednesday. They picked me up Friday morning. *You've got to be kidding! Two days! And I waited six months for that?* I was pissed. I had no control over my life in there. I could only depend on people to do exactly what I told them to do, when they got ready to do it. *Yes, I said that.*

I got credit for those six months I did downtown, so I only had to do two years, meaning I would get out sometime after August the next year. *Damn!* That was better than a twelve-year sentence. Officer Blue wished me well. She let me know they would be buying me something to eat for lunch that they usually stop at Burger King. I was hoping they would get me a whopper with cheese. I can't eat a hamburger without cheese.

When they picked me up, I had to ride in a van with six dudes. They put me in the back, with a cage wall between us. Might as well say I was in the trunk, shackled and handcuffed for an eight-hour ride. What if we got in an accident? What if a Mack truck hit us from the back? That's me back here. *Hello! I'm crushed and in one position, smashed!* As cars passed by, I was thinking, damn! They knew where we were going. I wondered if they knew what I did. I felt so ashamed.

I thought anyone who saw me knew I was in jail for murder. I tried to go to sleep, but it was not happening. I just dazed out on the highway, watching the lines pass, one by one. It made me dizzy, so I just looked into the sky, wondering where I was going, and what would it be like once I got there?

My new celly had braided my hair again, going back, before I left, so at least it wasn't all over my head. I hadn't seen myself in a mirror in a year. I didn't know what I looked like. My father had told me my skin was clear when he saw me. No makeup, no Radiant Red lipstick. You know Fashion Fair cosmetics? I probably looked like one of these dudes in the van. "Manning this is your stop."

We pulled up to what looked like a library or a school of some sort. There were pretty green trees and a big blue sky. Everything looked so clear. The warmth of the sun shining on my face was nice. I hadn't been outside in over a year. I forgot how green the trees and the grass were, and the shackles came off, along with the handcuffs. I thought my arms were gonna fall off not to mention my ass on that hard floor for eight hours! I had to feel to see if my bones were there. As a size five, there was no cushion what so ever back there, and I never *really* had any ass as a size ten.

They brought me into processing. By the time they were done, they sent me to a building they called a cottage. It was like a big teen center with a big TV mounted on the wall. I was just in time for dinner. I sat in a room full of girls, young girls at that. I wondered if I was the oldest. I had turned twenty-one while I was in the County Jail. Just think one of the most exciting birthday's a girl could have, besides her sweet sixteen and tuning eighteen, and I was in jail. I can always say that will be a birthday I would not forget.

That night they sent me and another girl to a different cottage to sleep until they found us a permanent room. Morning came so fast. It felt like I was away at camp, looking out the window into the trees. There was the smell of morning air, and the birds were chirping. They unlocked our door and told us to go back to the other cottage.

I had no idea how to get back there. I just followed the girl I was with. She seemed to be familiar with everything. I never asked her name. I had been deep in thought, nervous about this new place, and had drifted off to sleep pretty quickly. It was seven in the morning. There was no washing my face or brushing my teeth. I didn't want anyone to see me without my face being washed that early in the morning. The dayroom was full of chatter. Saturday morning cartoons were on.

After breakfast, I got to use the phone. I called Juelz first. "He better be home."

Before I got arrested, we lived together in a one-bedroom apartment. He was still living there with everything I owned for that matter. Of course, Nadia was with my mother, but Juelz had wanted to keep her. I had just been with him since Nadia was one year old. Her real father lived around the corner from my mama's and had only seen Nadia maybe three times in her first year of life. His name was Chase, and little did I know he and Juelz had a past.

What better way to get back at your baby's daddy than to start messin' around with someone he had funked wit? Juelz had shot Chase back in the day. I had no idea to that extent though. Chase dogged me out once I started showing. He was seeing other bitches, and they came out of the woodwork in my face. I didn't really know too much about dealing with an older cat.

I had lost my virginity to a fourth cousin the summer I turned thirteen. It was not fun, but at least I could say I wasn't a virgin, to myself that is. After it actually happened, I didn't tell a soul. I may have even blocked it out of my mind. I started dating a guy named John when I was in the eighth grade. He was a senior at the high school up the block from the Catholic school I went to on the corner.

Everyday, I would watch him and my best friend at the time, Rochelle and her boyfriend, who was his best friend, walk to Kentucky Fried Chicken for lunch. My desk was right next to the window and it was always open, rain or shine. My teacher was going through the change and she frequently had personal summers. They went the same time every day, so Rochelle would always look up at my classroom window and secretly wave to me as they walked by.

Every Friday, I went over Rochelle's house to stay for the weekend. My father thought it was fine, because they went to church on Sunday. Friday and Saturday nights, we walked around town until two in the morning. I would always feel John's penis on my thigh as we kissed. By the time the kissing was over there was always a wet spot in his jeans. I didn't know what that was then. I just knew it happened every time we kissed.

That fall, I started ninth grade at the high school where John had just finished. I had to tell him the truth, the closer we got. He had a lot of respect for me. That year, he gave me a ride to school every morning and picked me up. Rochelle had broken up with John's friend, so we began our relationship one on one. He was my first real boyfriend. He took me on dates, to the movies, and to football games. We really enjoyed each other and had begun to fall in love. At least that's what I thought at the time.

On my fifteenth birthday, John thought it was time to take our relationship to the next level. Yes, the big "S" word. Sex. Was I ready for that? I never told him about my previous experience. I didn't think I liked it that much, but that one night before my birthday, he wanted to be the first one to wish me happy birthday with a gift. My room had a back door that led to the back yard, and we always went in and out the back gate. My mom never wanted my company to walk on her shiny, waxed hardwood floors, and it was more convenient for me to sneak in and out anyway.

That night, he came through the door. He said he had come to give me my birthday present. I was already in the bed, he lied down next to me and we started kissing.

He layed on top of me and asked me to take off my pajama bottoms. As he tried to take them off for me, I objected.

"I don't want to." "Come on. Just relax."

Although I kept saying "no" my hands ended up above my head. He held them with one hand while he pulled my pajamas down with the other hand.

"No, John! I don't want to!" "Be still!" he said. "Just relax!"

"No, John! Get off of me! STOP!"

He took my legs and kept them spread apart with his legs and put his dick inside of me. I lay there, looking toward the wall as a tear rolled down my face, I couldn't believe he was doing this to me.

"Don't you *like* it?"

He whispered the words in my ear as he tried to kiss my face. He was enjoying it all by himself fucking me, taking his time, grinding in and out of me with no regard to my non-participation. When he got up, there was slimy stuff inside me, dripping between my thighs. He thought it was funny, laughing to disguise his shame for taking advantage of me.

I was pissed. I asked him to leave. I was so mad. I couldn't believe what had just happened. He tried to talk me out of being upset, but I was past upset. I didn't even think I ever wanted to see him again. I told him to just leave.

When I returned to school that next day, a balloon attached to "Garfield" was delivered to the office. Garfield was John's favorite cartoon character. The words on the balloon read, *Happy Birthday!*

CHAPTER FIVE

I t had been two months, eight whole weeks and I hadn't talked to John or even seen him. I had been sleeping a lot and eating potatoes and cheese eggs everyday, while watching *Days of Our Lives.*

That was my favorite Soap. I had noticed my stomach looking a certain kind of way, and even at night when I would normally lay on my stomach to sleep, I no longer could. I called my sister Shelise. I wanted her to see it. *What a way to spend your summer!* I didn't exactly know what was going on, but I knew my stomach had grown in the past months.

"Can you come by after you get off?" "Why? What's up?"

"I need you to come by. I have to show you something, and it's really important."

"Okay. I get off at three thirty."

My sister arrived after work. I greeted her at the door and she followed me into the kitchen.

"What's going on?" I lifted up my shirt.

"Danielle, you're *pregnant*! Does your mother know?" "Hell no! Are you sure I'm pregnant?" I asked.

"Hell, ya *think*?" Blinking her eyes out of shock. "Yes, you are definitely pregnant."

"I'm taking you to Planned Parenthood. What time does your mother get off work?"

"Five."

"Go put on some clothes so we can go. You've been walking *around* like that?"

"No, I try to leave before she gets home, and then I come home by like ten, and go straight to my room."

"Girl, hurry up! When was the last time you had a period?"

"I don't remember. I haven't had one in a few months though, maybe like April?"

"Oh Lord! Your ass is plenty pregnant. It's July now!"

My sister took me to Planned Parenthood. She filled out the papers for me and I went in and peed in a cup. They took a blood test to determine how far along I was in the pregnancy. The lady came back in the room.

"The rabbit died. You are pregnant all right. Let's wait for the blood test to determine how far along you are. According to your last cycle, you may be almost two months, give or take a few weeks. Wait here. I'll be back."

"Girl, what you gonna do?"

I didn't have much to say, I didn't even want to tell my sister how the whole shit happened.

The nurse returned to the room. "You are nine weeks."

"Nine weeks? That's like two months?"

"Yes, give or take a week. I'll give you a list of doctors to follow up care with whatever you may decide to do."

My sister thanked the lady for her assistance and accepted the list of doctors and the information regarding teen pregnancy. As we left the building, neither of us said a word. I didn't know what to think. I was actually pregnant.

"So what are you going to do Danielle?"

"I don't know, but I'm not telling my mama. Remember she said she'd kick us out of the house if any of us ever got pregnant."

"What about John? Where his mothafuckin ass at?"

"I haven't talked to him since my birthday. That's how I got in this situation. He raped me."

"Raped you? What the hell do you mean, raped you?"
"Well, I kept telling him to stop, and he wouldn't." "Girl, I just can't believe this shit! I need a drink."

We arrived back at the house.

"I'll call you later. You want me to drop you off somewhere?" "No, my friends will come pick me up."

"Keep me posted. If you need anything, let me know."

"You don't have much time to decide what you going to do." "I'll call you."

"Okay."

When I walked through the front door, the first thing I did was call my friend Sharon to tell her just what had happened.

"I'm going to call Darwin to come and pick you up. So get dressed so you can be ready."

"I'm already dressed." "Okay."

By that time I had had a whole new group of friends all John's friends, but no John. I stayed around their families to keep my pregnancy from my mother. I even stayed in touch with John's dad, who begged me to keep his grandbaby. The rumor was out that John was dating another girl. How could he have done that to me? Two years we dated, and that is how he did me?

Once I found out about the other girl I realized I loved him, not to mention the fact that I was carrying his baby. At that point he didn't know but they set it up so that we would be at the house at the same time. I was showing all right and I started wearing Darwin's football shorts because they were draw-string, the big T-shirts to cover up so my mother wouldn't find out.

She got off work and came home at five o'clock I was headed out the door. I would be home all day and had intentionally arranged for my friends to pick me up every day at five o'clock. That way I wouldn't have any time to spend with my her.

Sharon and I decided to go swimming over Amanda's house. Amanda was Darwin's sister. They told me that they had invited John over to go swimming, but they didn't tell him that I was going to be there. They had already told him that I was pregnant and that he needed to talk to me. They had told me he was seeing some girl named Kim who lived in the north area by his dad.

When he arrived I was in the pool by myself. When I noticed him coming out the sliding glass door into the backyard my heart sank. My anger instantly became anxiety! I was anxious to share what had been going on with me that summer, anxious to hear how he felt about the baby, to know if he still loved me.

As he walked toward the pool, I got out hoping he would notice my stomach without me saying anything.

"What's up?"

I looked at my stomach, "Well what does it *look* like?"

John looked at my stomach. *Oh, damn!* He thought to himself. "Do you mind getting dressed, and then we can go somewhere to sit and talk?"

"Okay."

I grabbed a towel to start drying off. It was dark by the time I was dressed. We left and went to the park. We found a spot away from traffic and we lied on the grass. I was so happy to be beside him. I had missed him. We made love under the stars. I felt so free being with him again. The night was pitch black. The headlights from the cars far off looked like twinkles of light.

"I have missed you." "I've missed you too." He was still so quiet.

"So they told you about Kim, huh?"

"Yes, but I'm not trippin. I'm just happy to see you and talk to you about the baby."

"What's wrong?"

"Nothing, I just have a lot on my mind."

"Well, do you want to talk about it? Is it the baby? That I'm pregnant?"

"No."

"Then what is it?"

"I have somewhere to go tonight."

"Okay, no problem. You can come see me tomorrow?" "No, I won't be back."

I sat up.

"Where are you going?"

"I'm going to Reno tonight. Kim and I are getting married."

"Married! Why are you marrying *her*?"

"I don't want to marry her." "Then why *are* you?"

"Her mom's *making* me marry her." "Why?"

"She's five months pregnant." "She's pregnant?"

My heart stopped. I just knew it dropped to my stomach. I thought for sure my baby would fall out. I was so hurt. All I could do was cry and scream but no sound would come out. I was in shock.

"We better go."

I couldn't move. I couldn't say a word. I didn't want to let him go. I clutched his shirt in my fists.

"No! Please don't marry her. I love you. We were together first!"

"I know. I love you too, but I just don't have a choice. I'm sorry."

I got up and did not say another word to him. For the next few weeks I was angry. Everyone was invited to John and Kim's reception and I was going. Darwin's mom, sister and Sharon took me shopping. They spent all day trying to find something for me to wear. I was even bigger by then. I couldn't find anything to fit me. I hadn't realized I was showing so much. Darwin's mother Janice and I had become close. She did everything for me.

They asked me if I wanted to move in with them to keep the pregnancy from my mom. I told them I wasn't for sure, but probably so. We discussed living arrangements and taking me to apply for food stamps to contribute to the household. It was all too much to think about. I just wanted to take one day at a time.

That night was a disaster. I knew what they were doing and I was all for it. I wanted to see who Kim was. I wanted her to see my belly. The reception would be at her mother's house where they were actually living. We entered through the side door, directly into the kitchen where everyone was gathered around the cake for the toast. We walked in just in time. It seemed as if Kim knew exactly who I was and I didn't care. I was standing so close I could have slapped her.

She kept sneaking peaks at me, trying to make out that shape of my belly. As they cut the cake and did their toast I just glared at them as if I could send a piercing ray that would shatter their champagne glasses. Kim couldn't take it anymore. She ran out the kitchen into the room. John followed behind her.

"What the fuck is *up* John?" "What do you mean?"

"You know what I mean."

"Danielle! I know that's *her*, and she is in my mama's house and she pregnant. How the hell did that happen? Thought you said you hadn't *seen* her John?"

"I haven't." "It wasn't like that. I haven't slept with that girl since May. I haven't even seen her or talked to her since then."

"If you haven't talked to her then why is she here?"

"I don't know. Man she came with Darwin's mom and Amanda." "I don't even want to look at you right now! Get her out of here."

John's ex-girlfriend was at the reception in her mother's house and pregnant too! The party was over! He stood on the porch with Darwin. I kept trying to get him to talk to me, but he wouldn't. He wouldn't even look at me.

His father walked me down the street to talk about the whole messy situation. He said that John did not love Kim and he told John not to marry her, but he wouldn't listen.

"Her mother is making that boy marry that girl because she's pregnant."

"They told me your mama was going to kick you out."

"Yeah."

"Does she know?"

"No, and I am not telling her."

"Well, looks like she's gonna find out sooner or later. Look at you poking out there girl! Keep my grandbaby. I will help you with whatever you need. I will get you an apartment and help you take care of the baby."

I told him I would keep in touch and that we better leave. Amanda and Janice were coming out of the house, cussing everybody out. It was time to go! Once we got home, we stayed up all night, talking about whose face was looking like what, and who was looking at me and who was looking at John.

I slept in Darwin's room with him, he had the bigger bed. He tried his best to comfort me regarding his best friend. I layed with my head at the foot of the bed and he layed with his head at the top. He and Sharon were the closest people to me during the time of my pregnancy. I was grateful for them. It was actually rather funny, but sad at the same time. They were married...

CHAPTER SIX

I woke up everyday at three o'clock to eat bacon and eggs with French fries while watching *Days of our Lives*. I had been keeping up with Peter and Jennifer, a young couple in love. They remind me of me and John.

By that time, I was lovesick. I missed him. I wanted to talk to him. After I ate I always had Maple Nut ice cream as I watched Oprah Winfrey. Eating Maple Nut ice cream while watching Oprah had become a ritual for me. Oprah's show ended at five o'clock but my mother came home early that day.

I had to run to the back to make up my bed. I didn't want her to think I was sleeping all day or even at home for that matter. I had run back up to the kitchen to put my cup of ice cream in the freezer when she came through the side door from the laundry room. She immediately noticed my stomach.

"Are you pregnant?" *Damn!* I froze. "No!"

I threw the cup in the freezer, slammed the door and quickly, yet nonchalant, walked back to my room. I looked at my side view in the mirror. I was big! I forgot I was wearing Darwin's half jersey with his drawstring shorts tied around my belly. I quickly picked up the phone to dial his number.

"Where are you? Hurry up and come pick me up. My mother saw my stomach and asked me if I was pregnant?"

"What you say?" "I said no!"

"Oh shit! I'm on my way."

My mother never came back to my room to confront me. I just sat in my room tapping my foot, wishing Darwin would hurry up and pick me up. When I looked up, he was coming through my door.

"Thank God. Let's go!"

I raced past the kitchen.

"Bye Mama! See you later. Going to Sharon's house." I yelled as I ran out the front door.

I hopped on the back of Darwin's moped and we rode over to Sharon's.

I didn't know what to do. How could I have forgotten to cover up? I was doing so good at hiding my stomach. I had not wanted my mother to know I was pregnant. Because one thing I knew I was *not* getting an abortion.

My father had promised me and my friends a trip to *Great America* later that month. Sharon, Amanda and I went shopping for matching outfits. My friends were paired off with each other and I was with my dad.

I kept the pregnancy from him as well, and I spent that day with him while my friends rode the rides and walked around. All I wanted to do was eat corn dogs and ice cream. My dad never questioned why I wasn't going on the rides with my friends. I told him I was scared of roller coasters.

"I don't blame you! I never cared for those rides either. For one, I'm claustrophobic and two I'm scared of heights."

We continued to sit and eat, and then when he was ready to take a nap, I met up with my friends. We had a good time that day. My father paid for everything, as always. Everyone passed out on the way back home.

CHAPTER SEVEN

My mother ended up confronting me one more time about being pregnant. I had no choice but to tell the truth. She was so upset that all she could do was go into the bathroom and cry. The sound of her crying tore me up.

I sat on the couch in our formal living room. It was a white room with red and black decor. There was a white sectional with two matching chairs, a red rug and thick luxurious red velvet curtains that hung from the top of the ceiling to the floor. Artwork, containing black accents were placed over the white-bricked fireplace and on the glass and chrome coffee table. Behind the sectional, there was the great window with large panes the kind that white people have, that let people look straight into their house, to see everything they are doing, that kind, except we had curtains and high bushes off the porch.

I saw a reflection of parking lights through the bushes. My brother Dennis and his girlfriend came through the front door.

"What's wrong with you?" "Nothin'."

As my brother walked down the hall to the bathroom, he heard my mother crying.

"Mama, what are you crying for?" "Your sister's *pregnant!*"

Her cries got louder. His girlfriend was in the living room with me.

"What's going on?"

I looked at her as my brother walked back into the living room. "You're pregnant?"

All I did was lift up my shirt. They both looked amazed at my stomach. I was pregnant all right.

"Damn! Why you tell her?" He whispered. "I didn't. She saw my stomach."

"Mama is trippin'. We need to get you out the house." "She's not going to let me go nowhere."

"She'll let you go with us, fuck that! We're going to the movies."

He went back into the bathroom and told our mother that he was going to take me with them while she cooled off. She agreed to let me go.

"Let's bounce before she changes her mind."

I was already dressed and ready to go. I ran out the door without saying a word and hopped in the back seat. I always loved to ride around town with my brother and his girlfriend. She was always so sweet to me. I just loved her to death. Her name is Gina, she was a pretty white girl with a black girl shape. Hella cool, but proper. My brother had been dating her since I was in the fourth grade.

During the movie, I was pretty uncomfortable in the back seat. I had to sit with my legs open. For the first time, I felt my baby move.

"Oh my God! My baby is moving!" "Are you serious?"

"Yes, Gina feel it."

She put her hand on my stomach, and sure enough she felt something. It startled her so much that she jerked her hand back.

"Oh my God, Danielle! How many months are you?" "I think by now, three. I'm like twelve weeks."

"Oh my gosh! You're three *months*?" "Does John know?" My brother asked.

"Yes, he knows."

"What he say?" Gina asked. "Nothin. He got married."

"You're kidding?" Dennis replied. "And she's *five* months pregnant." "I should kick his *ass*."

42

"No, you don't have to do that. I still love him."

"Well I should kick your ass because you a fool." He laughed. "Shut up!"

"I'm kidding, Sis. I know you feel fucked up!" "I'm alright."

CHAPTER EIGHT

I had gone over to Aunt Chellie's with my mom. We always went over there to eat or just chill out. I didn't think anything of the visit. I was so comfortable at that point that it never dawned on me that I was still showing.

"You're pregnant!"

My heart dropped. *Damn!*

"No, I am not."

"Yes you are. I can see it in your throat. And look how you're standing. You're resting your arms on your stomach. I know I had your cousin at fifteen. Does your mother know?"

"Yes."

"Girl, you can't fool me." "Your great-grandmother got me the same way. That heartbeat right there tells it all."

She walked up to me and pointed it out.

"I'm not going to say anything. I'll wait and see if she tells me."

****

My mother had scheduled an appointment for me to see a doctor. My aunt Chellie told her about a doctor's office downtown, so I guess that meant somebody said something. They did an ultrasound to determine the size of the baby. I looked at the screen amazed. *Was that my baby?* It was a little baby all right. The tech didn't say much and I didn't ask any questions. It was so tiny, but it was just kicking its little feet.

I knew that was a sign for me to keep my baby. I watched it kicking his feet back and forth. *Wow! That's a boy*, I said to myself. I couldn't wait to tell John. I had been talking to him when he was away from home or at his dad's.

I didn't have a way to contact him, but he always called before he went home for the night. I hadn't seen him, but I understood why. They gave me a urine test after the ultrasound. My urine was so dark they thought I might test positive for hepatitis, so they scheduled me to come back in two weeks. I would be fifteen weeks at that appointment.

Shelise took me to my next appointment. Once we got to the back, the nurse started pulling out all kind of needles and tubes.

"What are they doing?" I asked Shelise in a whisper. She approached the nurse.

"Hold up. What are you doing?"

"The procedure has been scheduled for today." "What procedure? I'm confused."

"To terminate the pregnancy. It's already been paid for."

"Wait a minute! My sister is only fifteen years old and we need to talk about this. She doesn't know anything about what's going on. I need to talk to my little sister in private."

The nurse stepped out of the room. "What do you want to do Danielle?" "I don't know."

"What you mean you don't know? It's up to you. You don't have to do anything you don't want to do."

"You know what mama said. If I come back home still pregnant she is going to kill me."

"She might be a bit upset, but she is not going to kill you. So what you decide?"

"Well I guess I'll do it. Mama is going to be mad if I come home pregnant, and she said it's already paid for."

"Are you sure?"

"I don't know. I guess so?"

"Okay. If you say so, but like I said, it's your decision. You have to live with it."

I never had time to really think about what I was about to do. How could my mom have tricked me like that? I didn't want to get rid of my baby. I wished John was there to tell me what to do.

I thought that was the worst day of my life. I had to have sea weed injected into my cervix to make me dilate or something, and then they told me to come back in three hours. I cried the whole time. Shelise took me over to Krishna's house for the three hours. I didn't want to give up my baby. I was well into my fourth month. I laid my head in Shelise's mother's lap and cried for the entire three hours.

Shelise and Krishna had the same mother, but we had the same father. Their mother held me in her arms the whole time. As I cried, she rubbed my hair, trying to comfort me the best she could. It was a sad day in that house, their little sister having to go through something so tragic that she really didn't understand.

After my procedure, all I could think about was the fact that I *killed* my baby. I knew I'd made a mistake. I was mad at my mom. I wanted my baby back. My body felt different. I felt like my old self, just with something missing. Now I could eat whatever I wanted. Nothing made me nauseous. Nothing made me sick, except the thought of my baby being gone.

Shelise and I went around the corner, where my brother worked at the car wash. Shelise explained to Dennis what happened, so when he came to the car and asked me if I was okay. I started to cry. Dennis opened the car door and gave me a hug.

"You want something to eat? Are you hungry?"

"Yes, I can eat."

"I got you! Come on in, and I'll have my homeboy cook you whatever you want."

I was surprised at my appetite, once I smelled the food. I had ordered a bacon cheeseburger, fries and a strawberry shake. My body felt back to normal, but not my heart.

When I arrived at the care home, Aunt Chellie was there waiting. She told me I was going to stay with her for few weeks until everything smoothed over. At that point, I felt like I hated both of them for making me have the abortion. They set me up. The office manager had explained to Shelise that the procedure was scheduled and paid for by a Chellie Assad. That was my aunt.

I returned home once it was time for school to start. I was a sophomore in high school, and couldn't bear to be in my bedroom. The last time I laid in my bed, I had my baby inside me. Who knew if the whole school would know what I did that summer? My breasts were leaking in class, so I had to leave early to go home. I was so embarrassed. I hated even going back to school.

Sharon and Amanda came over to check on me. They told me that it was nobody's business what happened that summer and that if they heard anybody talk about it, they was going to kick they ass. It made me feel better that my friends were on my side, working to convince me to go back to school even though I was only out for a week.

Janice bought me some breast pads that I was supposed to wear in my bra until my milk dried up. As the months went by, all the gossip and rumors stopped. Everything was back to normal but it took a long time to get John somewhat out of my system. Everything reminded me of him.

CHAPTER NINE

Fall was in the air. I ran into Will one day at school. I hadn't seen him since the second grade, but I never forgot him. I taught his ass how to read. He was so mannish back then. He was the same boy who used to pull up my skirt, always ready to rub and feel on you. He and Rochelle's brother were up there, hanging out.

After seeing him I didn't give him much thought until he mysteriously started hanging out at Rochelle's house. Will looked the same, just taller. He always had a skinny frame with peanut butter brown skin. He was actually very handsome, a slender face with light brown eyes, sort of slanted-almond shaped. I noticed how his eyes lit up as he looked at me. I could tell he was anticipating one day tasting my lips.

He starred at me so intensely as I spoke, and I picked up on our chemistry. He slid his way into my arms to say his goodbye after we exchanged numbers, and then we started talking on the phone until wee hours in the morning. It seemed as we were long lost friends playing the catch up game over the phone. Soon we visited each other after school.

I was sort of shy and not used to him yet. I had my driving permit, so I would sneak over to his house when my mom sent me to the grocery store or on an errand. He wasn't serious about dating only one girl. When I would pop up, he was always outside talking to another girl, or girls would call the house while

I was there. After a while, his mom made it clear he was to only have one girlfriend at a time, so he chose me.

By spring we had grown closer. I had gotten a little four-door yellow Datsun from my dad. He taught me how to drive a stick shift, and when it got close to me turning sixteen, he let me have the car early to drive back and forth to school. I started taking longer visits at Will's. With all the kissing, bumping and grinding me and Will were doing, we might as well have be doing the real thing and so we did.

We talked every night on the phone, but our visits were strictly for sexing. Will's mom worked at night, so we would always be alone in the apartment. When his sister was home, she made sure all clothes were still intact and there was plenty of distance between the two of us. We would look at each other and laugh, because by the time she got there, we had already did it about three times.

I would be turning sixteen. It was time for me and Candi to step it up a notch and have a Sweet Sixteen party! I was in graphic design, so I came up with a flyer for the party. I printed out two hundred flyers and we passed them out all over town, inviting people we didn't even know. We didn't care, because we were ready to party and our homeboy from school was a DJ. He offered to DJ the party for fifty bucks.

When the party was underway, people came from everywhere and the music was crackin. Candi had gone out front.

"There's cars everywhere bitch! We got it going on!" I ran down the driveway to see.

"God damn, its hella people out here!"

We went in back and the party was on. Will had arrived. *Computer Love* by Roger Troutman and Zapp was playing, and we started dancing. I *loved* that song. That was our song! As I turned, Darwin and John walked through the gate. I was feeling so good that the sight of him did not faze me. I gloated about my bomb party and my boyfriend. I went and mingled for a little bit after we finished dancing.

"Have you seen Will?"

"I thought I saw him walking down the driveway."

I went to see if, by chance, he was outside the gate. I lived right on the busy street, and it was common to stand on the sidewalk and watch whoever drove by. No sign of him though. Where did he go?

"So that's your *girl's* party. Yeah, that's a friend of mine. What's up with you?"

Will had run into the neighborhood hoe. She was one of those short, chocolate girls with a big ass, she was a slut and everyone knew it.

"You stay around here? Yeah, I live around the block by the green market. I wouldn't mind showing you my room if your girl ain't gonna miss you."

"Naw, she cool, she has plenty of things to do at the party."

They started walking toward her house.

"It's dark enough right here. Why make the trip to your house? That car over there is right next to some bushes. I'm down, baby, if you down."

They snuck behind the car. Will had already pulled his pants down and had pulled up her skirt.

"You got some rubbers?"

"No, I ain't trippin, baby. Just pull it out and nut on my ass." "For sure, I'm down with that!"

He bent her over and slid his dick in from the back. Will never made it back to the party.

I continued to mingle with all my friends, ones I knew and ones I didn't know. By eleven o'clock, the party had gotten out of hand. The party was so packed that there were people everywhere, drinking and smoking. We tried to get them to stay behind the gate, but no such luck. The cops came, five cars deep. They opened up the gate and my mom told everyone to leave.

"Get out! Get out now! You guys are crazy!"

I was so embarrassed. We all looked at each other in disbelief. "Oh my God, for real?"

My mom was yelling and the cops were escorting everyone out the backyard. The music stopped playing.

"The party is over folks. Let's go home." The policeman announced.

I ran into the house.

"Why did you do that? They were staying behind the gate. Why did you even open it?"

"Do you see all those people out there? Do you even know half of them? They are crazy, drinking and smoking."

Someone had actually knocked over the main pipe to the water. They had leaned on it and it came out of the ground. Water was shooting everywhere up between the bushes.

Candi and I sat dumbfounded in my room. "Man, yo mama crazy!"

"Don't remind me. She ruined my party."

My mother walked in and saw our somber faces.

"I'm sorry, but what did you want me to do? Those people where going to tear up my yard. They were crazy." I didn't say a word. I just shook my head.

That next morning, the backyard did look like a recycle field for beer bottles. There were Old English forty-ounce bottles everywhere, next to cigarette butts and joint roaches. Candi looked at me.

"Maybe your mama was right, girl. It's all kinds of trash, and look at all these Forties."

I looked in agreement.

"Oohwee! That's a shame. We didn't know half them Negros at the party."

Candi and I fell out laughing,

"But it was crackin for them two hours, huh?"

We got bags and more bags and picked up all the bottles and trash. My mom stood at my bedroom door.

"Sorry mama. You were right."

"Look at all this trash, I told ya'll those people were idiots."

"Where did you two meet those people?"

We looked at each other.

"We didn't."

"What do you mean, *you didn't*?"

We passed out two hundred flyers all over Sacramento.

"Are you crazy? No wonder! You can't do that. That is just not acceptable. You don't know who those people are."

"I know, but it was still crackin. We had it going on! They gonna be talking about this party for the rest of the summer."

CHAPTER TEN

B y the fourth of July, I was definitely on fire. Will had confided in me about the issue he was having. He even showed me some pills he had to take.

"It burns when I pee."

"For real? What is that from?"

"I don't know, my grand-pops took me to the doctor and they gave me these pills to take."

Will and I were young and didn't know what we were doing. I thought nothing of it. We had both gotten summer jobs. I picked Will and his older brother up from work on the days I was off. I was working at *FunderLand*, an amusement park for little kids under the age of ten. We always found a way to be together. Will's mom said I was always welcome to come over, but I had to go home by ten every night.

His sister decided she wanted all of us to go to the lake one Saturday. We all rode up to Miller's park. I loved spending time with his family. I loved Will. I hated being away from him. As we waded in the water, I couldn't keep my hands off of him. I was horny and wanted to kiss and feel on him.

"Knock it off, kids." His sister yelled from the sand bank. Will took off running.

"That's Danny acting all freaky." "Shut up! I was not."

"Quit, girl! My Johnson gonna get hard." He whispered in my ear.

I laughed and left him alone. When we got home, I went to my house to grab some dry clothes. Then I went back over to

Will's so we could shower together while his sister went to her own place down the walkway. When we got out the shower, we went straight to the bed for a quickie. While I was getting dressed, I dropped my shirt on the floor next to the nightstand. When I picked it up, I saw some Polaroid pictures of that hoe that was at my party.

"What are you doing with pictures of her? And you have a few.

This is why you disappeared from my party isn't it?" "Naw, girl! I met her a long time ago."

"I have never seen any pictures of her in your room before, and when did you have time to meet her? Where you met her at? You know she's a slut."

I threw the pictures in the trash.

"You let me find out you been messing around. I better not catch her over here."

"You ain't gonna catch nobody over here." I was beyond heated.

"Bye, Will!"

"Wait, Danny."

"No, I'm leaving. You left my party with that hoe. I remember seeing her there and the next thing I know you were gone. Leave me alone!"

I stormed down the stairs, got in my car and left. I was so mad that I left town for my family reunion for the Fourth of July without bothering to call Will to let him know.

At my grandmother's, I was in so much pain. I didn't know what was wrong. She kept giving me Pepto-Bismol, Alka-Seltzer and even ginger ale. Nothing was working. I stayed balled up on the couch the whole weekend. When I returned home, my mom scheduled me an appointment with the doctor.

My father took me and said he would wait in the lobby to give me some privacy. I did the usual pee in the cup and waited for the Dr. to come in.

"So how are we doing, young lady?" "Okay, I guess."

"What seems to be the problem?" I explained my symptoms.

"Let's have a look."

After I got undressed, the doctor returned to the room. "Okay, lie back for me and just relax."

He proceeded to give me an exam. "Do you have a boyfriend?"

"Yes." I said with a grin.

"Well, it seems you aren't the *only* one. Is he the only one you have been active with?"

"Active?"

"Having *sex* with?" "Oh yes!"

How did he know I was having sex?

"Well, it seems your boyfriend is sexually active with someone else, and has passed you an STD.

"STD?"

"A sexually transmitted disease. Let me go take a look. I will be right back..."

The doctor returned his face serious.

"I am going to give you a shot. Don't worry. I'll also prescribe you some pills to take for two weeks. Take them with food and you cannot engage in sexual activity of any kind. If you decide to have sex again with your boyfriend, you can give it right back to him and the cycle will continue."

When the Dr. left the room, I thought back to those pills Will had to take. *He wasn't supposed to have sex either, because he had an STD, and he gave this shit to me!* The Dr. informed me I had contracted gonorrhea.

I didn't understand, but I understood I was *past* pissed at Will. Once I got home, I packed up everything he ever gave me, pictures and all. When I drove over his house, he wasn't there, but his sister was. I immediately told her what happened. Then I went in Will's room and took everything I saw that belonged to me and everything I ever gave him.

I made it clear to his sister that I didn't ever want to see or speak to Will again, and I left her the slip of paper from the doctor's office with my test results. Weeks went by. Months went by, and I never talked to Will ever again. His mother called several times, begging me to just call and talk to him.

"He is crying himself to sleep at night."

I still refused. After that relationship, I was free once again.

I had recovered from my hurts, and I decided to enjoy the fact that I was young and free to enjoy what was left of my summer. At the park I ran into Keith, one of John's friends. Keith had gone into the Army after graduation. We exchanged numbers and agreed to keep in touch. We thought we might visit with each other when he came home on leave during the Holidays.

CHAPTER ELEVEN

C hase came along during the fall of my senior year. He and the other dudes in the hood watched me grow up through high school, waiting until I turned eighteen so they could pounce on me, like a cat on a mouse. But no not Chase. He wanted me for himself.

That nigga said he wasn't waiting for me to turn eighteen. He just waited for me to become a senior in high school. When Candi and I walked home from school, he was always waiting at the end of the walkway of the park. The first time, we almost ran into him as he stood there.

"Hello, can I talk with you for a minute?" "Me?"

"Yes, if you don't mind."

I looked at Candi, puzzled.

"Bye." She kept walking, leaving me behind.

"So, how you doing?"

"Fine."

"I'm Chase."

"Yeah, I know who you are."

"I see you and Candi walking home from school every day, and thought I would take a chance and speak."

"Take a *chance*?"

"Yes, I didn't want your boyfriend to get upset or anything or jump out the bushes on me."

"I don't have a boyfriend." I laughed. "Oh, that's even *better*!"

We talked and he walked me to the corner near my house. I wrote his number on one of my books and told him I would call. I thanked him for walking me almost home.

I returned to school after Spring Break and ran into Stan, he had been in juvenile hall for most of the school year. I had never been interested in him before, but for some reason, he had become so cute to me. He had been lifting weights, he spoke different and that just changed his whole demeanor.

Since Chase had other interests, Stan and I started seeing each other. He really liked me, even with my belly. Yes, I was almost five months pregnant by Chase. I learned to keep my affairs private, and I didn't tell a soul until it was too late to even think about an abortion. My play brother, Ricky, hooked us up.

"Man, you know my sis like you?"

"She do?"

"Yeah, man."

"She told you that?" "Yeah, nigga."

"Then I can take it from here."

He took an interest in me. He would always make sure I had a ride home, something to eat and he took me shopping when I didn't have any maternity clothes. I couldn't believe he actually wanted to be with me. After I graduated, six months pregnant, we spent the summer together. He would always come to pick me up and drive me over to Candi's.

Stan was nothing other than a gentleman, and he was overprotective of me. If things got too rowdy or he felt like there was going to be some fighting or shootings, he would be like, "It's time for you to go home." I needed that. He treated me real good.

The word had got out that Stan and I were seeing each other. Chase told me that if he found out, he was going to kick my ass. After all the dirt he was doing, he found a way to confront me and question me about what he had heard. *Whatever Negro!*

I denied it of course, but he still told me if he found out I was lying, he was going to jump on me. I didn't take kindly to threats, and I remembered my cousin, Evelyn's older brother told me Chase beat women.

So when Chase confronted me, we were down the street from Candi's house, but closer to 33rd. I took off on him, right in his face, belly and all. We were fighting. Chase wouldn't hit me, but he was more or less trying to block me from hitting him. The guys on the corner came running over, once they saw what was going on.

"Man, come on! Man, you can't be hittin' on that girl!" "I wasn't! I was just trying to hold her."

Chase had actually slammed me into the fence, trying to hem me up to keep me from swinging. The guys broke it up and walked me in the opposite direction, then I walked home. Someone must have told Evelyn's other brother Ronnie what happened because he paid Chase a visit at his mama's house.

A few days before, I couldn't get in touch with Stan to tell him what Chase had told me. I decided to walk to Candi's brother's house, where they were hanging out. When I arrived, they were outside blasting MC Hammer. I still loved to dance. Stan had come by, seeing us outside, he called me to the car.

"Are you okay?"

"Yes, I'm alright. Where have you been?"

"In the North, taking care of some business. I just wanted to check on you because I know I haven't seen you in a few days. Are you going to be over here for a minute?"

"Yes."

"Have you had anything to eat?" "No."

"Well, when I come back, we can go get something." "But I... okay, I have something I want to tell you." "What is that?"

"Chase asked me was we messing around and I told him no." "What you tell him that for?"

"Because he said he heard that we were together and if he found out that it was true he was going to kick my ass. That's why we got into it. I took off on him before he got me first."

"You can't be fighting no man! And you pregnant even if you *ain't* pregnant! He ain't gonna touch you."

"Well, that's what he said, so I just told him it wasn't true."
"Well, we'll see about that. I'm gonna touch that nigga. He's not going to lay a finger on you."

"Just please don't say anything to him."

"Oh, I'm going to *say* something to him all right, and like I said, *he ain't going to touch you because I'm gonna beat his ass.*"

At that point, I was really worried that it was going to be a big commotion about me and Stan. I told Candi what he said.

"He is not going to do anything. He full of shit." "I don't think so. He seemed pretty mad."

Stan never came back to get me. I really didn't want to go anywhere with him in public after Chase found out we were messing around.

Summer ended. I had six weeks left to go in my pregnancy. I had become good friends with another cousin's wife, Nieci. We were actually pregnant at the same time. She started spending more time with me to show me what to do and how to prepare for my new baby.

Nieci was cool. She was the type of woman I wanted to be. I still looked so much like a teenager. I hadn't quite acquired my woman tendencies yet. I never carried a purse, I wore tennis shoes, and I always had on an athletic jacket of some sort.

Nieci was pretty, always dressed in cute outfits, shades and a cute purse. She had her "grown woman" on. We had a six-year age difference. She was twenty four, but she seemed so much more mature. She told me it would come naturally when I became a mother. She had a caramel skin color and she was shorter than me. She wore a cute haircut in a leisure curl, colored with golden auburn tones.

She was soft spoken, but she loved to talk. She was always full of advice, sharing things with me about relationships, and she was a good listener. I tried to absorb all I could. She didn't know how I ended up with Chase, but she knew he was no good.

Candi had told me about her sister getting a county check for having kids. Nieci explained to me exactly what I needed to do to apply for aid.

"You go downtown to the main welfare office, but you have to go first thing in the morning because it be packed full of people. You can get like, eight hundred dollars, just for having her baby."

"Are you serious?"

"Yeah, girl. You could have been getting checks every month on the first."

I got dropped off downtown and followed her instructions. She told me what to say and what not to say so that I could get the full amount and some food stamps. After my appointment, the lady informed me that I should be receiving a check in less than 30 days. Nieci explained to me that I would also get back pay because they start your aid once you reach six months of pregnancy. I ended up getting three months' worth of back pay, which turned out to be almost $1,200.

I couldn't believe it when I saw that check in the mail.

It actually came within two and a half weeks. I called Nieci to tell her, and she said she was going to take me shopping to get the baby stuff. I spent a lot of time with her after she gave birth to her son. I got to get in some practice. She showed me how to prepare bottles, change diapers, give the baby a bath and how to watch for the cord to fall off.

She made a list for me of all the things I would need for the baby. I bought a bassinet and Disney everything. When I got everything home, I looked at my room and thought, *this doesn't look like a mother's room.* I decided to change it around to make it look like, shall I say, more mature? I took down all the collages and all the posters that I had on the walls. I asked my stepdad to paint the room, and then I bought a new comforter set to match the sofa set I bought from Nieci.

I had fixed it up really nice. My mother started a hope chest, because she knew, sooner or later, I would want to have my own place. She ordered dishes, glasses, and a red cordless phone from Spiegel. Everything I would need for my apartment whenever I did move out. It seemed like every week, the UPS truck was pulling up to my house and a cute black guy was the driver. We become very well acquainted, and wouldn't you know his name was Chase too! *Damn!*

My pregnancy didn't seem to bother him. He always took time to talk to me on his route and even came back after his route was over. What was it with guys and pregnant women? He was real handsome. I hadn't really seen Stan much.

I started feeling really uncomfortable during the next few weeks. With the baby due any day, I talked to Chase more often. I was just really irritable and my stomach hurt. For some reason, I wanted to be around him. I decided to go to his mama's house, because I thought I was having contractions. I didn't know why I called Chase and not Stan, but there I was, on his mama's couch.

Wouldn't you know it? Just when I really needed him, he left me alone with my contractions so he could run with his boys. I had gone to his room to lie down when he came flying into the room.

"You been fuckin' with that nigga, Stan?" My heart was ready to beat out of my chest. "No!"

He slapped me in the mouth.

"*That's* for lyin'! Me and that nigga just got into it at the Big park. When my company leave, I'm kickin' yo ass!"

While Chase was out, Stan ran up on him. He had been standing up at the front of the park with the rest of the homies.

"Oh, you gonna kick my woman's ass, huh?"

Before Chase knew it, Stan had jumped on him like he stole something. Them niggas just watched in shock, as it all happened so fast. To top it off, Stan took Chase's hat and took it to Steve on 33rd and warned him.

"Tell your boy if he lay a hand on Danielle, I'm gonna get him again."

Leann was there. She immediately called to Chase's house for me. I sat on the bed, scared to move. My contractions got harder, and then the phone rang. Chase's mom came to the door.

"The phone is for you. I'm going to walk to the store. I'll be back."

I picked up the phone. "Hello."

LeAnn started to tell the story, full of laughter. I told her I already knew, that Chase slapped me in the mouth and that he was gonna kick my ass.

"I'm on my way!"

When I looked up, there she was. *Damn! That was fast.* We both hurried out the house to the porch.

"Hey baby, where you going?" "To get something to eat."

"Bring me back an orange soda." "Okay."

I got in the car.

"I won't be coming back to this mothafucka!"

Once we drove off, LeAnn and Monique screamed in laughter about what happened, but I was in labor, so wasn't shit funny. We went to 33rd. After about thirty minutes of pain, I walked to my mom's job around the corner.

"What happened to your mouth?"

My mom asked as she cupped my face in her hand.

"Nothing, I opened the door too fast and knocked myself in the face."

"Girl, you are so clumsy!" "Yeah, I know."

I just couldn't get comfortable and had to pee. I went to the bathroom and when I wiped I saw the plug.

"It's time!" I screamed, calling my mom into the bathroom. "I saw the mucous thing."

"Really?"

My uncle drove me, LeAnn, and Evelyn to the hospital. LeAnn had called Stan. They almost arrived before we did. I was scared. I did not want Stan and Chase to be at the hospital at the same time.

Stan and his friends hung around my side in the hospital. "What happen to your lip?"

"Chase slapped me after you jumped on him. I went to his house when I couldn't get in touch with you because I was having contractions."

Stan had a mean look on his face, his nose flared up and his jaw muscle flexed. He just stared at me. I definitely didn't want them bumping heads again at the hospital, with all this going on. I was scared of Chase.

"I'm hungry. Can you sneak me something? I'm starving?" "You can't eat."

"No, she know she can't have anything to eat." LeAnn said. "But I am starving!"

I was so hungry, but I couldn't eat anything! Evelyn was leaning over my bed, sucking on an apple blow pop. I looked and snatched it out of her hand and chewed it up so fast. She looked at me like I was crazy and fell out laughing. It was so good too.

Hours went by. It turned out I was in false labor, so they sent me home.

Stan and his friends decided to leave and meet me back at the house. It was gonna take a minute for them to discharge me. Within a matter of ten minutes, Chase walked into my room. I couldn't figure out how he found out I had gone to the hospital. LeAnn spoke to him.

"You gonna take her home, because they're discharging her?" "Yes, I'm here now. I can take her home."

I gave LeAnn that look like, "don't leave me!" I was scared to be alone with him. As we sat in the room he glanced at my busted lip. "Did I do that?" He asked softly.

I nodded my head as I looked down, fidgeting with my fingers. He apologized for slapping me.

"Baby, I didn't mean to put my hands on you." I did not reply.

For some reason, even though I was afraid of him, I still wanted him around. Maybe it was his slick charm. By the time we got back to the house, my labor contractions started again. He dropped me off at home and went home himself.

"It looks like it's going to be a long night."

My mother didn't have any idea what had transpired that day, as she spoke to Chase.

"Go home and get some rest, and come back in a few hours so we can take turns while she's having contractions."

"I'm not going back to the hospital until I am about to give birth, because I don't want to go out there again and they send me back home."

Within the next hour, I called Chase to let him know that the contractions had started getting closer and closer. He said he would be on his way. It seemed like the contractions were coming every five minutes. I couldn't take the pain. I was screaming, hot and sweaty. My only relief was lying on the cold, waxed floor between contractions, which didn't last long, but they were coming one after another.

The phone rang, it was Evelyn's mom, calling to check on me.

"What is all that noise?"

"The girl's in labor and this child is going crazy. She doesn't want to go to the hospital because the already sent her home." "Well keep me posted. I'll let you go deal with that, okay?" Chase finally arrived.

"Great! Now *you* can take over the show. She's crazy!" They both laughed.

"It's not *funny*! God, I want to die Jesus!"

Chase tried to get me to lie down in the bed, but I was too uncomfortable for that.

"Whatever you do, just don't cry." He whispered.

"If you got to squeeze my hand, squeeze my hand."

How the hell can you tell someone in labor not to cry? He was no help at all. It was three o'clock in the morning. I was so tired that I was falling asleep between contractions. What a fight, every two minutes, to fall asleep until another contraction hit. That lasted till five o'clock that morning and then I just couldn't take it anymore.

When I called Labor and Delivery to let them know how far along the contractions were, they advised me to come to the hospital. My mother let Chase drive her car. When we arrived at the hospital, it was too late to give me an epidural. I didn't want one anyway, after hearing rumors that paralysis could result from the procedure.

At each contraction, I started to cry. Chase sat in the chair, telling me to stop crying. He gave me a disgusted look, kind of the same look he gave me when we were riding in the car with Nieci and my cousin. I started singing out loud. I was so embarrassed by the look he gave me. Guess that wasn't a mature thing to do.

Why was Chase there? I thought he should have just stayed at home? Where was Stan anyway? He hadn't come back to check on me. I was in too much pain to care, but the thought crossed my mind. Chase was becoming impatient. He was falling asleep in the chair.

"I'm about to leave. Have them call me when you about to have the baby."

They hooked me up to the monitor and an IV and gave me a shot of something to relax me. I could no longer feel the contractions. Soon after that, I felt like I had to go to the bathroom. I looked around for the call button. Luckily, the nurse placed it at the head of my bed. I pushed the button. After a few minutes, a sweet voice rang through the speaker on the wall.

"May we help you?"

"I think I have to go to the bathroom."

"Number one or number two?"

"Number two."

The nurse came in to check to see how far I had dilated.

"Okay, sweetheart looks like you are ready to have a precious bundle. I will call the doctor. It may feel like you have to have a bowel movement, but don't push okay? It is very important that you don't push."

I couldn't feel the contractions, but I did feel the pressure. A team of nurses entered the room. They broke the bed down and prepared the room for my delivery. Within minutes, the doctor came into the room.

"Okay, darling you ready for this little angel to come out?"

I smiled and shook my head yes. They scooted me down to the edge of the bed. The nurses held my legs up and instructed me when I should push. I pushed once during a contraction. They instructed me to push again as hard as I could, and then the baby was born. That's all it took two pushes!

They were trying to wake the baby up. She must have gotten some of what they gave me for the contractions. They rubbed and rubbed, telling her to wake up. I was getting worried. Was my baby breathing?

"Is she okay?"

"She's fine. She's just being a little sleepy head."

The baby stretched out from her little ball and opened her eyes. She didn't even cry.

"There we go. Come on, sweetie."

They placed her on my chest. She was so cute and tiny, blinking up at me with a little frown while trying to focus her eyes, they looked like little black buttons.

She was so pretty.

"I guess Daddy *just* missed you being born."

"Yes, I guess he did."

I stayed in the hospital for three days. No one came to visit me, except Krishna and my nephew, Jamal. She called before she came and asked if there was anything I needed. I told her I wanted a whopper.

"I forgot to tell her with cheese."

I was holding the baby when she came into the room.

"She is so cute! Oh my goodness, look at her! You see her Jamal? Isn't she beautiful?"

"I haven't ever seen a baby that just comes out cute."

Their visit was brief, so I spent the rest of the day resting with the baby. Chase arrived that evening for a short visit. He brought his friend, Rod, with him. Rod was real cool. Never wanted to see me dogged out by Chase, but it wasn't his place to tell me what I didn't need to know. He would always just remind me how cool I was and that any man would be lucky to have me. He held Nadia and told me how pretty she was. They didn't stay long.

The nurses took the baby at night and brought her back first thing in the morning for a feeding. I would be going home the next day and wouldn't you know, it was only my father there to pick me up. No Chase, no Stan.

CHAPTER TWELVE

My six weeks was up. Stan and I got together with Evelyn, LeAnn and Ricky to attend the high school's homecoming game at Hugh's Stadium.

When they arrived at the house to pick me up, I had taken my braids out and relaxed my hair.

"Dang, Sis! You look like a college girl for real, like a grown woman."

"I *am* grown."

"You lookin' good." Stan said as he slapped me on my butt. "Thank you!"

My mom kept the baby. We had a great time that night. I even had a few drinks to celebrate. They were teasing me and Stan about my six weeks being up. Stan did end up staying over most nights. He was a big help with Nadia. He fed her, while I would make the bed or fix us breakfast. My mom was always gone to work by that time, so we were always home alone.

He had got the big head from all the talk about him jumping on Chase over me. We started seeing less of each other, but that was fine. Chase acted like he owned me, even when he was with other women. He would take me to his mama's house and leave me there with the baby. He'd say he'd be back and wouldn't return until morning. I got smart though. I started hanging out on the south side again with Nieci.

The more I spent time over there, the more time I spent with her brother-in-law, Leander. He was tall and skinny, with a fair complexion the same color as Shemar Amor, almost as fine but not quite. He was cute though. He had the cutest smirk on his face when he laughed.

He always seemed to tell jokes and he talked so fast. Half the time I was asking him to repeat himself. He seemed to adore Nadia. Who could resist a newborn. They sleep all the time and don't make any noise, and they *smell* good. I ended up staying there over the weekends.

Before long Chase figured out where I had been. There was a knock at the door. We were lying on a pallet in the living room with Nadia and Nieci was in her room with his brother. Leander got up and opened the door. It was Chase. He came in and told me to pack my stuff and that he was taking me home. Leander stepped to the bathroom and fingered for me to follow.

Chase couldn't tell from the front door which way we went, if we went down the hall or into a room.

"You know you don't have to leave, right?"

"I know that. It's okay. He's just going to take me home and leave anyway, so I'll be back."

"If you need a ride back, just call and I'll come pick you up. But that really doesn't make any sense for you to have to go home. He don't own you."

I told Leander I would be back and not to cause a scene. Chase didn't need to know what was really going on. Leander tried to persuade me, but I wasn't really into him. He seemed like he liked me too much and wasn't much of a challenge. I would be starting school winter quarter. I wanted to focus on the future for me and my baby.

CHAPTER THIRTEEN

Winter semester came and I enrolled in college. Star and I decided to go together. I had math, English, psychology and dance just to start. My first day, I was waiting for my math class to start. Another class was in session, and when it was over, a fine brother walked out. We locked eyes every day for about a month.

As I was waiting for the bus across the street from the college, a new black Maxima pulled up.

"Are you going to wait for the bus? Or are you going to let me give you a ride home?"

I smiled my famous smile. "Sure!" I hopped in.

"Where about you stay?"

"Straight down this main street." "My name is TJ, by the way."

"Nice to meet you TJ. My name is Danielle."

Once we arrived in front of my house, we exchanged numbers and talked for a while. I didn't tell him about Nadia. I didn't know how he'd feel about a three month old, so I decided to wait.

We began to see each other every day. We talked between classes and met up afterwards. The neighborhood was small, so everyone was curious about the black Maxima in front of my mom's house every day.

One night TJ called and said he wanted to stop by after class. I agreed and told him I had someone for him to meet.

"Oh, your *mom's* home?" "No."

When he arrived, I invited him in. Nadia was in her swing. He had no response when he saw the baby. That made me nervous. I went to the back to get a diaper and when I returned, I saw him playing with the baby. I thought that was so cute. When he realized I had come back in the room, he jumped back on the couch.

"You're fine."

"I didn't know? Some people don't like you to touch their kids." "No, you're fine. That was sweet. At first I thought you didn't like her."

"No, no, she's a cutie. Can I hold her?" "Sure."

After three months went by, I mentioned to my mom that I wanted to move into my own place.

"What do you know about living by yourself? How would you pay your bills?"

I tried to explain I would have enough money if I had a roommate, but my mother didn't like that idea. When I talked it over with TJ, he told me everything I would have to do.

"All you need to do is get money orders when you get your check to pay your bills. You and your roommate can split the rent. You should only have your SMUD bill. That's for your electricity and your phone bill."

He even created a budget for me, adding up my check and food stamps I received every month.

"I'll be there to help you if you ever need any money."

That's all I needed to hear. It was settled. I mentioned my plan to Evelyn.

"Becky is looking to move too." "Who is Becky?"

"She used to go with Adonté."

I actually went with him a few years back. He was Marquisee's best friend. Evelyn called Becky on the three-way and introduced us over the phone. Becky said she could meet me over Evelyn's to talk in person. She seemed cool over the phone. She was staying at her mom's and had a two year old daughter.

Becky arrived at Evelyn's.

"Oh my God, Becky! You pregnant?" "Yes, Evelyn. I'm six months."

"Who you pregnant by?"

"You already know. That asshole Adonté." She said with a goofy laugh.

"You must be Evelyn's cousin, Danielle?" "Yes, how are you?"

"Where he at?" Evelyn asked.

"I left his ass in Detroit, he started beating me and shit, and you know I don't play that. Me and my baby got the hell up out of there! He probably don't even know I'm gone. I left his ass. I been staying at my mama's, trying to find me a place. I don't think he knows I'm even in Sacramento."

"Shit! How did you get back?" "On the bus."

"You caught the bus all the way from Detroit?" "Hell yeah!"

"Well, shit! Then ya'll cool to get a place together?" "Cool with me. You down, Danielle?"

"Yep!"

We sat and talked about when we could go and look for some apartments to rent.

"I get eight hundred and forty dollars a month, plus my food stamps."

"And I get twelve hundred plus food stamps."

We spent that next day looking for apartments. I met Becky's mom, she drove us around the South Area looking for some place nice. We settled on some new apartments on Mack Road with a move-in special. Two hundred dollars off the first month's rent with a year lease. The apartment complex was right next to a grocery store and around the corner from G-Parkway.

"Is this you ladies first apartment?" "Yes."

"Okay. So you don't have any rental history?" "No ma'am."

"They both get aid."

We both gave her our income verification and she agreed to rent to us.

"Make sure you pay the rent on time. It is due on the first and late after the third."

"Yes, ma'am, we will."

A brand-new apartment, two bedroom, two bath. It had a bathroom in each bedroom. Each bedroom was off the living room on opposite sides, with a dining area next to the kitchen. I chose the bedroom with the shower, and Becky got the bedroom with the bathtub, since she had a little girl. The rent was four hundred forty dollars a month. We would split the rent and, of course, buy groceries with our stamps.

Over the next few months, everything was good in school. Change was good, life was good. Chase never found out where I moved, and I never really went to visit my mom. We just talked every day over the phone.

Me and Becky started hanging out on Saturday nights. We would alternate on weekends to watch the babies. TJ had mentioned a club that he and his brother frequented. He invited me and my friend Kim to meet him up there on one particular night. I was not too much of a clubber, but that night, dancing sounded good. When we arrived at the club, it was nice. There were tables and chairs in one area, across from the dance floor. The music was good.

TJ spotted me as soon as I walked in. He greeted Kim and me and whispered in my ear.

"My baby's mother is here. Her ass followed us to the club. She don't ever come out. Her ass just wanted to be nosy."

TJ had mentioned the situation to me earlier.

They had been broken up for a few months because she was such a liar and a sneak. After they broke up, she kept the pregnancy from him and waited until she was six months to tell him. Hell, he wasn't even sure if it was his. I told him it was cool. I didn't want anyone to cause a scene.

So we could talk as he danced with his sister and I danced with his brother. TJ was a good guy, always nice and considerate, a real gentleman. I wasn't used to dating a real man, responsible with credit cards and with his own place, not to mention with a nice ride. I loved his Maximum, with its tinted windows! And he looked good in it, too.

He was the complete package, with a big body that looked like he played football. In fact, he played until he messed up his knee. His dark features against his caramel skin were sexy too. And he was a good kisser. Those juicy lips and mustache! He was nothing like Chase. This was a man with a job.

I should have listened while I was hanging out, but no! I just *had* to get pregnant! I was gonna show *them*. I didn't tell anyone until I was too far along for me to get rid of it. I was keeping my baby. She was gonna be all mine.

We got ready to leave the club. TJ had already made it to the car and was coming out the parking lot while me and Kim were walking to her car.

"Hey sexy." It was TJ passing by in his car.

"I'll meet you at your house after I drop these guys off."

"Okay." I said as I leaned into in his window to give him one of those soft kisses.

"Who is she?" A voice yelled through the passenger side window.

"A friend of mine, I'll see you later."

"Okay." I stood up and walked toward the car. Kim was standing behind it talking with some friends.

As we were all talking, a short, pregnant girl walked up to me. "Excuse me, can I talk to you?"

I never looked at her when she was at TJ's car. I just walked away. When I turned around to see her face, I couldn't believe it.

"Keri?" "Danielle?"

It was my classmate from the seventh grade. We were good friends and we hung out for the entire year. Yeah, Keri and I were tight that year, and then I never saw her again. For a split second, we forgot the situation at hand, because we were so happy to see each other again. We even wanted to hug each other, but reality quickly brought us back.

"Are you pregnant?" "Yeah, girl. Six months,"

"Oh, you look so cute. I didn't know you were pregnant."
"So what's up with you and TJ?"

"Nothin', we go to City together. He didn't tell me he was with anyone."

"I bet he didn't. We're together. I'm just staying at my mother's for a minute."

Kim's car pulled up beside me. "You ready?"

"Yeah!" I turned back to Keri. "It was good to see you again."

I hopped in the car.

"You too girl."

"Can you believe that shit?" "Who was that bitch?"

"That girl is pregnant by TJ. We used to be friends in junior high. I sure missed her. I had forgotten all about her."

When I got home TJ was right on schedule, he called to say he was on his way.

"Okay."

TJ knocked on my bedroom window. I had dozed off waiting on him to get there. I went to the front door and let him in. My room was right off the living room, by the front door. Once we closed the bedroom door we both knew what time it was. We took off our clothes and headed for the shower.

I was comfortable being naked in front of TJ. I had never felt so comfortable with anybody else. Hell, I was embarrassed for Chase to lift up my shirt to see how big my belly was getting. We always had sex with half my clothes on. I only took off my panties whenever he pulled them off to eat my pussy.

That night TJ and I talked about what had happened. "I know Keri from junior high."

"Get *out* of here! Boy, this is a small mother fuckin' world!"

We continued to see each other and Keri continued to call me to see if TJ was at my house. She took it upon herself to move back in and TJ took it upon himself to spend all of his nights with me. He decided he had enough of Keri's lies and put her out for good. He told her he would take care of the baby if it was his.

One morning, I woke up and got ready to go to school. When I went to unlock my car door, I noticed my tire was flat. I never thought to ask anyone what to do. So my car stayed in the parking lot on a flat. TJ had left to visit his mom in Detroit for a month, so I dropped out of school and my car just sat in the parking lot.

Becky and I would sometimes hang out in G-Parkway on Saturdays. We would get our babies dressed and packed up their strollers and we would be out of there. One day back then, Becky set me up on a blind date with this dude named Shyran, who wore a do-rag. He was dark-skinned, with sparkling brown eyes and had a little hint of a mustache and a goatee. We were both nineteen.

We hit it off pretty quickly, talking over the phone in the first week. His voice, over the phone, did something to me. Just the way he said my name when he called was so sexy and alluring in my ear. Not to mention, he left a visual impression on my mind. He was a handsome, chocolate Casanova. He said things that made him sound like he was well over nineteen. He moistened his lips before he spoke, with a slight twitch. That was sexy in itself. We agreed to meet up again on the weekend.

He stayed with his mom, so I offered for him to come over to my apartment. When he got there I told him to come into my room. He looked as if to say, *Oh yeah, I'm about to get some pussy!* I had my same waterbed centered under my bedroom window. Nadia's crib was alongside the wall next to left of my bed, with the night stand on the right side. I had a five-drawer dresser in the opposite corner, next to my bathroom. My 19-inch television sat on top of it.

When he entered my room, I could feel his nervousness hiding behind his suave demeanor. What did he think was going to happen?

"You can lay on my bed." I said as I turned on the TV.

As I sat on the bed, the wave of the waterbed made me fall back. I ended up underneath him, and he was able to pin me down long enough to steal a kiss. The smell of him enticed me to want to discover all he had behind that kiss. His lips were so juicy and the way he caressed my tongue in his mouth made me so wet.

I wanted to take my clothes off before he even put his hand between my legs. His hands made their way under my shirt, rubbing on my breasts. He was real smooth, unhooking my bra with one hand. He paused as we looked into each other's eyes.

"I really feel the need to fuck you right now!" He said as he pulled my shirt over my head.

We began to kiss again. He led my hand to his penis. Oh my! I thought to myself. I could not resist his invitation at that point. As he stood up and began to take off his pants, I didn't actually know what to feel. I was nervous as he stood there naked, with his socks on.

He assisted me with my shorts and began to kiss my breasts. He was so aggressive that I thought I was making a mistake in giving it up so fast, but my anxiety quickly left as I received his directions. His body language showed me he had everything under control.

As he took me through several positions, our bodies began to sweat.

"It's hot in here!"

I didn't know if it was me or the room that was so hot, even with the A/C blaring at sixty-five degrees. I needed to stop, but I couldn't. He wouldn't let me. He wanted me at the mercy of his dick.

"I'm not finished with you yet."

By the way he grabbed my hair, I knew he wanted me to feel all he had. When I woke up, I realized another two hours had passed. After that day, I cut all ties. The way my walls were throbbing, I thought I had had enough dick to last me a lifetime. Boy was I wrong!

CHAPTER FOURTEEN

Ricky ended up coming over one day. "Sis, what's wrong with your car."

"It has a flat."

"You don't have a spare?" "No."

"You should have a one in the trunk." "Oh!"

I didn't know anything about that. Sure enough, there was a spare. Ricky changed the tire in a matter of minutes.

"That's a damn shame. That's all I needed to do? We back rolling! Thanks, bro."

I went into the apartment to tell Becky,

"Girl, Ricky fixed the flat. Let's hit the streets.

"Aw shit! Let's get the hell out of here!" Becky exclaimed, with that goofy laugh of hers.

We got dressed and found someplace to go.

Becky baby daddy had showed up and tried to break in. We called the police, but he kept coming back. One day, he caught her coming home and jumped on her. She was still pregnant. *Oh my goodness!* That became an ongoing thing. He would beat her up, and then the next thing I knew, they were fucking again. I got tired of calling the police, only to have him end up right back in her bed two days later.

There finally was a "last straw" for me. I was in my room watching TV and my door flew open. As Becky was running from him, she tried to run into my bathroom, but she couldn't move fast enough with her belly. He caught her and knocked her in my shower. Then he hit her upside the head so many times that all her beads from her braids went flying everywhere. I pulled him off her, cussing and screaming at the same time.

"This is *enough* of this shit! You got to get the fuck up *out* of here!"

He went to act like he was pulling a knife out and I went to grab it out his hand and sliced my own hand. Blood was everywhere. I ended up going to the emergency room to get stitches.

I told Becky I wasn't fucking around with them anymore. I said that if she kept fucking with him, I was done trying to help her stupid ass! That night, when I returned from the hospital, there he was. They were in the kitchen cooking. He tried to apologize to me, but I wasn't trying to hear that shit! My hand stayed wrapped up for almost three weeks.

When TJ returned, I told him everything that had gone on while he was gone. *Well, not everything.* I also told my mom.

"Pack your stuff and move with me or to your mom's. I don't want you involved in any of that foolishness. Someone could really get hurt."

I chose my mother's, and she was glad to have me back. The lease for the apartment was up that next month, so I moved out and left them there. We were on bad terms and weren't even speaking.

The more time TJ and I spent together, the more he wanted me and Nadia to stay nights at his house. It was fine at first. I really felt like I was a part of his family. His sister stayed with him too. Things were good. The attention was just what I needed. We went for a nice walk one night and decided to spend some time in the Jacuzzi. I really enjoyed how caring and romantic TJ was toward me.

Nine months into our relationship, he declared how much he cared about me. I thought it was sweet and I felt real comfortable about our future, until he told me that he wanted to have more kids.

"Yes, that would be nice."

"With you." He said. "And soon."

I looked at him as if he had slapped me in my face.

"You kidding, right? You want to have kids now? Nadia is not even a year-old yet."

"I know, I just want you to know how much I want to be with you."

That night, I was assured that TJ was not who I wanted, after all. More kids? I was only 19. The last thing on my mind was to have more kids. I had just started going to technical college to become a medical assistant. I wanted to go to a training school that would lead to a job. I could always go back to college. I needed a career. Having more children was not on my agenda.

The next morning, TJ kissed me and Nadia goodbye. He was working the day shift that week. He was my alarm clock. Once he left, I knew to get up and get me and Nadia ready for school. I walked in TJ's closet and ran my hands over his row of shirts. I touched one of the shirts and put it to my face, smelling its scent. He always smelled so good.

I realized in that moment that I did have a good thing with TJ. Maybe the kids could wait, though. I was looking at all the tennis shoes he had. He had everything, movies and chests full of cassette tapes. He knew everyone he had. I couldn't even think of taking one without asking. That's one thing he didn't play with. Love or no love, *don't mess with his movies or his music.*

As it was quite chilly that morning, I needed to warm up the car. The cold, crisp air hit me in the face as the sun shined in my eyes. I saw my breath evaporate in the wind. I rushed down the stairs, but when I got to the bottom, my car was gone.

"What the fuck? I know I parked my car in this parking space!"

There was another car in its place. I looked to the left then to the right again. *I know I parked there!* I ran back up the stairs into the apartment and turned back to look over the parking lot.

"I must be trippin?"

I went to wake his sister. "My car is gone."

"What you mean?"

"I went outside to start the car, and it's gone." "Where's TJ?"

"He left for work already. I'm going to be late for school!"
"Let me call him for you."

Vette called TJ and told him what happened. "Let me speak to Danielle."

"What happened baby? Where is your car?"

"I don't know. It's gone and I need to go to school." "Did you call the police?"

"No.

"Call them and report it as stolen." "Who would steal that bucket?"

"Man, it's a car and it runs. Hell, some youngster probably took it."

"Okay."

I called the police and filed a report, and then I called my school and Nadia's daycare to tell them what happened and that I wouldn't be in. TJ didn't get off until two-thirty. He said he would come straight home after work and we would find out what happened. So I hung out with his sister.

"I know who got your car." "What you mean?"

"Keri had your shit towed." "You are lying!"

"I bet you money on it. That girl crazy!"

"She called last night and heard me playing with Nadia."

"When she asked who's baby was over here, I told her your baby. So yeah, she probably mad."

The police called back and reported that the car had been towed and that it was at some tow yard on the West Side.

"I told you! I knew it! That bitch had your shit towed." Yvette called TJ and told him.

"Tell Danielle to be ready and we can go get her car. Call the place and see how much it costs. I'll put it on my credit card."

When he got home he honked the horn. I was ready. He was pissed. Not at me, but at Keri.

"*See* why I don't fuck with her? She is bad news, man. She's done way more shit than this too. She is crazy.

"You okay?" "Yeah, I'm fine."

We finally made it to the tow yard after driving around trying to find the place. I followed TJ back to the house to get

Nadia and the rest of my things. That was the last time I spent the night at TJs. Nadia's first birthday was coming up. I stopped talking to TJ so much. Guess you could say I lost interest after that conversation about wanting more kids and the whole Keri thing with the car.

CHAPTER FIFTEEN

My days consisted of going to school and coming home after picking up Nadia from my mom at the care home. I planned for Nadia's birthday party at my father's house. He lived in a big two-story house in the South Area.

JP was dating one of my close friends from high school. He was ballin' out of control. He had picked up all the kids from the P in his Astro Van and brought them to the party. He paid for all the decorations for the party. TJ missed the birthday party, but that night he had brought over ten outfits for Nadia.

"Yvette picked them out." "Thank you! They are so cute!

"What is that baby going to do with all those clothes? She has more clothes than I do." My mom laughed.

TJ didn't stay long. He had to be to work that night. Someone had called out and he had to replace them.

"Let me get on out of here and get to the job." "Okay, baby. Let me walk you out."

"You know I wanted to get me some tonight. I was hoping you would come home with me but you safe, them folks called me in and you know what it is when I get home, straight to the pillow."

"Baby, just let me know, you know you got this wheneva'..." "Give me some sugga then, so I can go. I'll come pick you up tomorrow after I wake up and shit." "Okay."

He came to pick me and Nadia up like he said. I had left Nadia's car seat in the house.

"Here take her while I run in the house."

A car pulled up across the street. Chase jumped out the car like the police. Whoever dropped him off drove off and left him.

"Hey, let me see my baby."

TJ was giving Nadia to Chase as I came out of the house. "What's up?"

TJ had gotten in the car as I placed the car seat in the back seat.

"If I catch another nigga holding my baby, I am going to beat your ass and his ass too." He whispered trying not to make a scene.

"Oh really? Like you beat Stan's ass?"

My mother walked from the doorway. "Give me my damn baby!"

I took Nadia and put her in the car seat.

"You heard what I said!" Chase yelled back as he was walking back around the corner.

"I'm not holding Nadia in public no more." "Why? This is *my* baby!"

"I don't want no shit jumping off like it could have right then." "That nigga live right around the corner and he ain't seen her but maybe twice." "No shit?"

"For real, he stay at his mama house. He stopped fucking with me when I started showin'."

"Damn, that's fucked up! Hell, better for me."

CHAPTER SIXTEEN

My cousin Monique had come by one night to see the baby. "I got somebody I want you to meet."

"Who?"

"He's outside. Come meet him."

I walked outside to see some tall yellow nigga with some braids that looked as if they needed to be redone and a full thick mustache and beard, looking like Jesus. This man had to be at least 30 years old. He stood about six foot two inches. Why my cousin wanted me to meet him, I did not know.

"Girl, that man is too old for me!" "He's the same age as Chase." "Well, he don't look like it."

"Girl, you better get with him. He has a gang of money and all them females be trying to get at him."

"So he is not my type."

He ended up giving me his pager number and I never used it.

After a few weeks went by, I was hanging out with Candi and a few of our other friends. We went up to the liquor store. I only drank on my birthday, but they wanted something before we went to the club down the street.

Just as we pulled up I noticed the same man coming out of the store. He noticed me right away.

"I ain't heard from you. What's up?" "Oh, nothin."

When I looked at him, he didn't look the same. His hair was freshly braided. He had on a lot of jewelry and he smelled good, with a clean shave. He wore a crisp white tee, a pair of Levi's and some fresh white Nike Cortez tennis shoes. He was looking pretty good. I didn't know everybody knew him, but me. I got the 411 on him. His name was Juelz. I never met anyone with that name before.

Everyone was telling me I better get with him. He leaned over in the car.

"What everybody drinking? "I don't drink."

"That's cool mama. You want a soda?" "No, I'm good."

He bought everyone their own bottle, I was impressed.

I didn't know what it was but after that a spark lit in my heart and I saw that twinkle in his eyes. I saw this man every day after that.

I talked to Evelyn on the phone after school and like clockwork, he was pulling up at four o'clock, with that loud music playing Heavy D, Somebody For Me. It soon became my favorite song.

Days turned into weeks, or more like months. I was starting to get annoyed that he came over every day. When I got home from school, Evelyn and I stayed on the phone until he arrived. If she wasn't calling me, I was calling her. We stayed on the phone just to keep each other company. We would even watch television together over the phone. I wasn't the type to run the streets with Nadia. I basically stayed home every night. Once I met Juelz, I stopped seeing TJ, and he stopped calling.

It was fall and it was starting to get pretty cold. I tried to have him out of the house by six before my mom got home. He would always call me once I put Nadia to bed and ask me to come outside to sit in the car and talk. We talked about everything. I moved back into the same room I had in high school with the back door. Juelz used to sneak in my room after my mom went to work. She had started working the grave yard shift. He would never ask me could he stay. He would just show up drunk when he figured my mom was gone. One night he was so lit he was snoring like a bear. I just knew my stepdad would hear him. He was so nosey I couldn't stand him half the time.

"You gotta go you snoring too loud!"

As I shook him. I still had my same waterbed, which made it impossible to move around. This nigga was every bit of two hundred eighty pounds.

"My stepdad is going to hear you."

I wouldn't dare fall asleep, just a few more hours and my mom would be home. Juelz barely heard anything I said.

"Get up, man, come on!"

"Okay, baby, okay! I think I'm still drunk. Shit!"

He sat on the side of my waterbed for another fifteen minutes. "Please get up and go! My mom is going to kill us if she finds you in here."

He finally stood up. I tried to open the screen door slowly so it would not squeak. I always forgot to get the WD40. He was finally gone. All I had left to bear was hearing his loud ass car start up with those duel pipes.

"Oh my God!"

They were ten times as loud at five in the morning. He finally drove off.

"Whew."

I buried my head under the covers. I could finally get some sleep in peace. His drinking was so unattractive, and it damn sure wasn't worth getting busted in my mother's house. As soon as I was in a deep sleep, my bedroom door went flying open.

"Get up!"

My heart jumped out of my chest.

"What for?" I asked sitting straight up in my bed. "Oh! Never mind. Go back to sleep."

"What?"

I flopped back on my pillow and covered my head with the blanket. Once I heard the door closed I laughed to myself.

"Oh shit!"

My stepdad must have told her someone was in the room. Thank God! I got him out when I did. Wait 'till I tell him. That shit was crazy!

He always wanted me to come and take a ride with him. I had told him that I never went out at night with the baby, and that we didn't have any coats.

"What? That's cool. Let's go to the mall and buy you and your baby a coat."

"Oh! Okay."

I got Nadia and we went to the mall. I picked out a brown suede jacket with wool lining and a hood. He picked Nadia out some type of Eskimo onesie suit. It had a hood, gloves, and footsies that attached with snaps. He pulled it out and asked if I liked it? I didn't look at the price until I held it in my arms. Ninety-five dollars.

"Oh my God! This is almost one hundred dollars! You know how many outfits I could have gotten with one hundred dollars. I hated to sound so shallow, but after that, I was in love.

My mom got annoyed at the fact that Juelz was coming over every day. One night, when he knocked on the front door and my mom questioned him as she let him in.

"How old are you?" "Twenty-four."

"You look older than that."

They both laughed. He was actually 26. He lied, just like Chase. They were the same age. It had only been a few weeks, a month at the most, and Thanksgiving was approaching. My mom started flipping out the more Juelz came over. If I went out the door just to sit outside she would lock me out.

"What is that?"

"What's the problem with me going outside to talk? I go to school, I'm at home, I don't drink, I don't smoke and I don't go out to the club and Nadia is asleep.

"What's the problem?"

I began to think my mom was somewhat jealous. I go outside and she'd lock me out. The last time it happened, Juelz was in the car watching me knock on the door. He called me later that night.

"Was your mom trippin?" "Yes."

"You want to come stay with me?" "Stay with you?"

"Yeah, I got a spot. You can come stay with me. I'll send someone over tomorrow with a U-Haul to come get your stuff and put it in storage."

"Okay!"

"I'll see you tomorrow around eleven."

I was out of school for the holidays. He was there at eleven, with a big U-Haul truck, just like he said. I didn't really believe him, so I never packed. I didn't have much, most of my stuff from the apartment was still in boxes. We packed while my mom was at work. My stepdad was there, wondering where I was going. I told him I was moving in with Juelz. He understood why.

"I know your mom overreacts at times."

"Well I'm tired of it and I'm gone. Hope she's happy now. When she comes home, I won't be here."

"If you need anything, give me a call. I'll talk to your mom."

"Okay."

While they were loading the truck, some girl pulled over and gets out of the car. Juelz went to talk to her. I asked him who she was?

"My wife." "Your wife?"

"Yeah, but we ain't together. I married her in jail." "In jail? What?"

"I'll tell you about it later. Here, I got something for you."

It was a beautiful diamond ring. It was almost like a custom- made ring, with twenty diamonds in a setting.

"Where did you get it from?" "I took it back from her."

"I want you to have it and don't lose it." "Okay, I won't."

It was a nice ring, and it fit right on my ring finger. Of course I wore it on my right hand not the left. By the end of the day, we went to his apartment. It was really nice. I was surprised and a little intimidated at the same time. His wife's picture was on one of the end tables. She looked like a woman much older than me. The apartment was a cozy one-bedroom with a fireplace.

Juelz put my things in the bedroom. All his wife's things were gone alright. The drawers were empty. He told me to make myself at home. He lit the fireplace and he put Nadia in the bed. That night we made love in the front of the fire. He kissed with so much passion. As he lied on top of me, he was so heavy that I couldn't breathe. He put me on top of him. He was so strong. He controlled my body with every thrust as he was inside of me.

90

I felt as if I was on top of a mountain of ecstasy. As he held my waist, he guided my body up and down, front to back, in an out. It was heaven. No one had ever felt that way inside me, nor had anyone made me feel that way. I was falling deeper in love with this man. I never had to ask for anything. He kept money in my pocket. He told me that I should always keep at least fifty dollars in my pocket every day.

That next morning, his cousins came knocking on the front door. He let them in. They were cool. They treated me like family. We cooked breakfast together, ate and got dressed. It felt so good to spend the whole day with him. I got to meet his friends. I could see that he was popular and very giving, or was it that he hung around people who didn't have as much as he did? Either way, I felt comfortable with him. He was always smiling at me. Telling me how much he was digging me. I guess he was. We stayed in his apartment over the holidays.

I hadn't been back over to my mother's, but I saw her on Thanksgiving at my Aunt Chellie's. We always spent the holidays over there. After Christmas, Juelz let his wife move back into the apartment. He moved out and we stayed at a motel until we found our own apartment. We ended up getting an apartment close to my school. After school, we hung up at the Big park and went home about nine every night.

I would hang out at my mom's and give the baby a bath and get her ready for bed. By the time we made it home, Nadia would already be sleep when we put her in her crib. I loved the fact that we slept together every night. I loved Juelz, and even more, I loved how he made me feel in and out of bed. I didn't know what oral sex was until he introduced me to that world of lovemaking.

I had never imagined going down on a man. That was just nasty.

"Come on baby, kiss it," he would say as he guided me with full instructions on how to suck his dick.

The noises he made gave me more incentive. Every time I sucked his dick, he would make this same funny noise and his toes would curl up and get stuck.

"My toes, my toes, god damn it!"

I thought that was too funny. He was busting a fat nut! What was I supposed to do with that shit? It made me gag. I even threw up the first few times. He laughed at me and told me to swallow it.

"Are you crazy? It tastes like salt!"

I wanted to taste every inch of his body, but damn! I had more fun with Juelz than I had ever had. He always made it home by midnight on the weekends. He would always call when he was on his way. I loved when we lied in the bed all day, but I came to realize that he spent that time with me so he could be gone most of the night.

I became more and more attached to him as the months went by. He introduced me to selling dope, drinking and cussin'. I picked up quick on the cussin, and so did Nadia. Cursing seemed to be the way we naturally communicated. I went everywhere with Juelz, once I got out of school. If we didn't meet in the park, we were hanging out together in the club. Everyone knew he was my man, but that still didn't stop them bitches from trying it behind my back. If I even thought a bitch was trying to be slick, I'd cuss him out and tell him he better save them hoes from an ass whoopin. He would laugh and tell me to chill out and say that he wasn't paying them bitches no attention.

The weekend came again, and I made it home first, waiting for Juelz to show up right behind me. When I made it home, I always checked my answering machine. This time, there was a message I didn't want to hear. Juelz was in jail.

"Jail? What the hell?"

He left me instructions to go down to his parole officer to see if they would lift what they called a parole hold. I didn't know anything about parole and going to jail stuff, but I didn't want to seem like a punk or that I couldn't handle his business.

I did what I had to do till he got out. I started writing him letters late at night before I went to bed. I really missed him. I ended up moving out of our apartment. My mother said it didn't make sense for me to waste money paying rent when I could stay with her while going to school.

I was happy to move back home again, I could save money that way. Juelz had always paid for everything. He had a 90-day parole violation. That would be three long months. I wasn't able to visit and was actually scared to. All of it was unfamiliar. It scared me, but I learned quickly when it came to his money.

He had left some dope in the freezer. I counted it out. It was five hundred dollars' worth, already cut up. I remembered him always selling twenty pieces, and sometimes, when those annoying crack heads only had ten dollars, he would break them in half. I let them know I had it and I started serving out of my bedroom window at my moms.

I moved back in my old bedroom with the back door, so there was easy access to my window. All they had to do was walk down the drive way to the last window on the side of the house. I would start to hear tapping on my window at one o'clock in the morning, and sometimes the tapping lasted until four. Man if these damn Negroes don't go to sleep. God damn! And I had to get up for school. I warned them.

"Don't knock on my damn window with twelve dollars, and I'm not breaking no dubs in half."

I needed all my money. One night, they got me. One dude came with his money balled up and that morning, when I opened it, it was only five dollars. That pissed me off. I couldn't get home fast enough. Once they saw me coming down 33rd, they flagged me from the corner. I got rid of it all pretty quick. I wasn't used to having money in my pocket every day. I sold about sixty to eighty bucks on a good day. I tried not to spend it as soon as I made it.

My main objective was to be able to buy my lunch at school every day. I was even able to treat when my classmates and I went to lunch together. I grew close to one classmate and confided in her. We found out that our men had been locked up together back in the day, except her man was a smoker and Juelz was the supplier, as she called it. We started hanging tight through school.

The release day came, and I was excited. I had to drive two and a half hours to pick up Juelz. When I arrived, I waited at least one hour. I left early to make sure I would not get lost or be late picking him up. I was nervous. I fell in love between the phone calls and letters. I felt we had become even closer. When he came out, I didn't know if I should run and jump on him, like Whitney did Bobby Brown or wait in the car.

I drove my dad's white '63 classic model Volkswagen bug. I had blown out the engine in the bucket that I bought back when I had Nadia. I forgot to put oil in it. On the way home from school one day, it just cut out on the freeway. It was my third car.

I had also had a '78, yellow Volkswagen, with a sunroof during my junior year. With every car I had, I forgot to put in oil and burned up the engines. So this time, I promised him I would keep oil in it. He couldn't let me be without a car, with the baby, while I was still in school. It was almost time for me to start my externship before graduating as a medical assistant.

Juelz walked out the gate. He hurried to the car so fast and put a passionate I can't wait to fuck you kiss on me.

"Let's get the hell out of this motherfucka!"

He handed me his gate money. It was $120 more than I had in my pocket. I finally got to tell him about the dope he left in the freezer.

"Is that right? Damn, where you put it?" "I sold it!"

"Nigga, you shittin me?"

"For real. I told that one smoker dude you always served to that I had it and he helped me get rid of it."

He was tickled to death.

"So where my money at, Nigga?" "I spent it."

"You what?" "I spent it."

"How much was it?"

"Like two hundred dollars"

"Awe shit! That's chump change. You cool, mama."

"Baby say she sold that shit." He repated laughing out loud. I would be keeping the amount a little secret.

When we made it back to town, Juelz told me to go to some apartments. I wondered who lived there, but I just did as he asked. We got out of the car and looked for an apartment number. When we found it, he told me to knock on the door for him.

"Who lives here?"

"My wife, but if she know I was out here, she ain't gonna open the door. She spent all my money and supposed to be fucking with some square."

Oh shit! What is he about to do?

I knocked on the door and she opened it slightly to see who I was.

When she did, Juelz came from around the side and pushed his way into the apartment. She ran to the back, causing some guy sitting on the couch to jump up. Juelz threw him out the house, grabbed him and punched him in the face. I stood there in shock. I had never seen two men fight. After Juelz punched him again, he had a big knot on his forehead. Then the man ran off. Juelz's wife was standing in the doorway, holding a baby and screaming at the top of her lungs.

"Stop!"

He grabbed her by her hair and dragged her from room to room.

"Bitch, where my mothafuckin money?"

I was so scared for her. I tried to pry the baby out of her arms. "Give me the baby?"

I pleaded with her to give me the baby. I guess holding the baby was saving her ass and I was right. I didn't know what to do, but by that time she was on the floor and he had his foot on her neck. I had to say something. I put the baby down on the couch.

"Juelz let her up! Stop! Get off of her! Someone is going to call the police!"

Once we left, I just looked at him in disappointment and shook my head.

"I was wrong, wasn't I?" "Hell yes!"

"Man, I just get so mad and I go ta flashin! Hell, my ass scared now! She gonna call my parole officer. Drop me off at the Big park."

"Take off your shirt and just wear your T-shirt."

At the park, everybody was hanging out and happy to see he was home. I went to the mall to buy him another outfit. Nothing came of the incident. The camera guy in the park took our picture, and we enjoyed hanging out that day.

I found an apartment for us to stay in around the corner from where he and his wife used to stay. The place wouldn't be ready until the following week, so my mom agreed to let Juelz stay at the house until we could move in. All I had to move was my mattress and my floor model TV I had bought with my school money. I was hoping he would buy me some new furniture, and he did.

"Go pick out something you like and I'll get it for you."

****

The next month was my birthday. I would be turning twenty. I never showed Juelz my drivers' license. He didn't know I was only 19, but he soon would find out.

"What do you want to do for your birthday?"

"I don't know, maybe just invite friends over to go swimming and barbeque."

"I'll have my uncle grill up some meat."

"Okay, and everybody else can bring side dishes."

A week before my birthday, as I was getting ready for work, Juelz had asked me to iron his shirt and I told him I couldn't because I was gonna be late for work. He walked up on me in the bathroom while I was getting dressed.

"Bitch! Iron my mothafuckin shirt!"

Now you know those are fighting words, but he wasn't some girl. I slung my Louise Vuitton bag off the counter and hit him right in the face! Then he slapped me so hard that he knocked me into the bathtub. I tried to catch my balance by grabbing the towel rack, but it broke. I flew into the shower curtain and it ended up on the top of my head.

He just stared at me as I tried to get my balance to get out of the tub. By the time I got up, I looked in the mirror, my lips were busted in four places, and I had blood all over my white lab coat. I immediately began to cry.

Juelz tried to apologize, but I pushed past him, grabbed Nadia and raced down the stairs. I couldn't believe he hit me. I couldn't go to work with my face like that. I had nowhere to go, but I had to tell my worksite I couldn't come in. I wasn't taking

Nadia to daycare. I couldn't, not looking like that. After thinking, I realized I had to go to my job. I couldn't just *not* show up.

When I got there, I went in the back way, hoping to speak to my office manager, Ella. She was such a sweet lady and I trusted her. When I got Ella's attention, I asked if we could talk in private outside. Ella had yet to see my face. I held my head down and talked with my hand over my face. I tried to explain but nothing would come out. I just burst into tears as she saw my face.

"Oh no, baby! What happened? Come let me get you cleaned up."

"No, I can't! I have to go. I just came to tell you I couldn't come in today."

"Please come in, Danielle. Let us help you, sweetheart!"
"No! I have to go."

As I got in my car, Ella ran back into the office.

"Dr. Marsh, Danielle just left. Her boyfriend has beaten her. Her face is all busted up. Her mouth and clothes were full of blood! I tried to convince her to come in and let you take a look at her, but she just ran back to her car."

"Oh my word! What is with these young girls today, letting these grown men abuse them? She's living with my niece's husband."

"What?"

"He beat her too, but they are separated. You know my sister's daughter Kim?"

"Yes."

"She's still married to him. He's been in and out of jail since they've been together. As a matter of fact, the last time he came home from prison, he found out where she was living with another man and he broke in her house and damn near killed her."

"Let me call Chellie. She may know how to get in touch with her."

"Hello. Hi Chellie. This is Regina. How are you doing?" "Oh I'm fine, Regina. How have you been?"

"Just fine Chellie. Just fine. Your niece, Danielle, is doing her externship in my office."

"So she did get in? Great. I told her I knew you and that I would talk to you."

"Yes. She's been here almost a month now." "Well good."

"Chellie, the reason I'm calling is because Danielle came into the office this morning, and apparently that boyfriend of hers has beaten her up. My office manager tried to convince her to come in to let me take a look at her. It seems her face was in bad shape."

"You've got to be kidding me! Let me call her mother! She works at my Care Home."

"Okay, I just thought you needed to know. I'll give you a call if she happens to show back up."

"Okay, thank you and you take care." "Okay good-bye."

"Well, she said she was going to call Danielle's mother. She thinks she may have gone to see her. She works at Chellie's care home. "Poor child. I hope she'll be okay." "Anna, have you seen Danielle?" "No, not yet."

"Well Dr. Marsh just called me. Danielle works in her office and she said Danielle came to work with her face all busted up and bloody. That boy has jumped on that girl. They don't know where she went. She didn't stay at work. I figured she might have come over there with you."

"No, she's not going to come over here because she knows I don't approve of any of that mess. She's probably too embarrassed." "You know she doesn't listen to anything you say about that man. Maybe she'll show up."

I didn't know where to go. Since I had the baby and her lunch box, I decided to go to the park. There was a pretty grassy area on the other side of the park that was very peaceful and I figured I could get my thoughts together and soak up the sun. *I can't believe he hit me!* Tears rolled down my face as Nadia sat in my lap. She turned and was wiping my face.

"Don't cry."She kissed me on my lips.

Ouch! I felt so stupid. *Why did I hit him with my bag? What was I supposed to do after he called me a bitch? It was like a reflex. He had never called me that before.*

I fell asleep in the park. The baby had played a little and she ate her lunch after our nap, it was almost three o'clock. I wanted to go home, but I didn't know if Juelz would be there. When I got to the stop sign, my heart started pounding. As I turned into my apartment complex, I thought, *please don't let him be home!*

We stayed right in front, so I could easily see if he was in our parking spot. He wasn't. The baby and I made our way up the stairs and went inside. I didn't know what to think or do. I plopped on the couch, turned on the television and dozed off.

"Man, you talk to Danielle today?"

"No, that's why we riding to the house. I called her job and the smart ass bitch Ella said she didn't come into work today. Probably stayed at her boyfriend's all day. I called her a bitch and she hit me dead in my face with her damn purse. Man, before I knew it I slapped the shit out her."

"Danielle ain't no joke, Nigga!"

That was Jamal, Juelz's cousin. He had been hanging out with us the last few weeks. He just got out of jail himself and was tryin to put in some work.

"Yeah, I know, but she gonna get her wig twisted she keep fuckin wit me."

"Nigga, you crazy. What you call her a bitch for?"

"Her punk ass got smart when I told her to iron my shirt before she went to work. Talkin bout, *iron it yourself, it's gonna make me late.* I told her, 'Bitch, if you don't iron my mothafuckin shirt, I know somethin!'"

He laughed at the thought of me slappin him with the bag. "That shit funny now, but it wasn't funny then. She fucked me up. Her punk ass home." He said as they pulled in the parking lot.

I was asleep on the couch when they came up the stairs. Hearing the key in the lock, I jumped up and ran to the bedroom and tried to lock the door, but he caught me before I could shut it all the way.

"Come on, baby! I'm sorry!" I was too embarrassed to let him see my face. I tried to keep my head turned the other way.

"Let me see, baby? Let me see."

"See what you did, you bastard!"

"Damn! Baby, I didn't mean to. When you hit me, I just snapped. I don't know why you be fuckin with me?"

"You called me a *bitch*!"

"Bitch please!" I immediately went to hit him.

"I'm sorry baby damn!" He laughed as he grabbed me. We fell onto the bed while he was kissing my face,

"I'm sorry."

"What am I supposed to do about my face man?"

"Fuck em! If they say something, tell them you ran into a door or some shit."

"Yeah right, Nigga."

Jamal came to the bedroom door. "You two love birds all right in here?" I turned to Jamal,

"What you think?" "Damn!"

"Shut up, Nigga!"

"Man, Juelz she must have slapped the shit out of you." "Shut up!"

We walked back into the living room. Nadia was still sleep on the couch. Juelz picked her up.

"My little nigga knocked out."

He kissed her and took her to the room.

"So Danielle, what you gonna do for your birthday?" "Hell, I ain't doin shit if my face still look like this."

It took almost two weeks for the swelling to go down in my lips. I could see both top and bottom teeth imprints on the inside. It hurt to even eat.

Evelyn called and invited me to their high school talent show that Friday.

"You should come up here. We having a talent show and Kim and those guys are performing. Kim was one of Evelyn's many friends that would come with her to my house to kick it after school. They liked hanging over there, listening to all my drama while they were out trying to be fast.

"Okay, I guess I will come, but I'm telling you now don't say nothing, and don't stare at me."

"Why? What happened, and what are you talking about?"

"You'll see when I get there. I'll be up there."

"Okay."

I went to the school and boldly walked into the gym. Evelyn spotted me and Nadia.

"Oh my God, Evelyn! What happen? Look her face! Damn! Did Juelz do that?"

"She told me not to say anything, but damn! Don't say nothing ya'll, and don't stare. Shit!"

We climbed the bleachers to where they were sitting. I barely made eye contact, just long enough to give Evelyn a look at what he did to me.

Nobody said anything, but I knew they were thinking it. I was glad the focus was on the performance, and the way we were sitting, they didn't have full view of my face. I stuck it out.

Evelyn never asked and I never told her until later on, when I could speak about it without crying from embarrassment.

CHAPTER SEVENTEEN

I didn't return to work until the swelling went down. Dr. Marsh made me so nervous. I didn't feel comfortable any longer. I eventually requested to be sent to another site for my externship. So until they found me something else, I stayed home and just hung out. Our days consisted of hangin on the hoe corner or the market serving.

Juelz was the ghetto superstar (don't you just love those kind?) I was his girl and everybody knew it. I was everywhere he was. When you saw him, you saw me. That summer, we were closer than we'd ever been. I had completed my externship and was trying to find a full-time job. Juelz paid the rent and bills and let me keep my welfare check to do whatever I wanted to do with it.

I did not cook, because we went out to eat every day. The only thing I knew how to cook was breakfast. A broiled T-bone steak for Juelz, bacon, scrambled eggs with cheese, with smothered potatoes.

August was so hot that everyone hung out until one, two in the morning. I met a girl from Oakland who braided hair in that new style, going back, with the gold-tie wrapped around the ends. I was dying to get my hair done in that style. That way, it could grow it out and I wouldn't have to fool with it in the morning when I did get a job. With some cute earrings, I would look professional.

I was in the car with my cousin Tarsha, and her girlfriend Kiki, all day. I saw Juelz at the market. The girl charged a hundred for my hair, and I needed to get some money from him.

"Hey mama! What's up, baby?"As he kissed my lips.

"I need the money for my hair."

"Oh, you bout to go get it done?" "Yeah."

"How much is it?" "A hundred."

"Here go one twenty." Counting out six twenties. "You eat yet?'

"No."

"Well get you something to eat and save my change, Nigga." "Whateva, Nigga!"

"Damn, baby! I don't get no sugga?"

I went back and gave him a kiss on the lips. I loved that shit, and yes, I loved that man. It took about five hours for her to finish my hair. I called Tarsha and Kiki to come pick me up. I couldn't find Juelz, and it seemed as if no one else had seen him either.

That was strange. It was eleven o'clock at night, and the streets were empty. The Market was closed. I told Tarsha to take me to my mom's to pick up Nadia. She stayed over there while I got my hair braided.

When I pulled up at the house, I saw Juelz, across the street, using the pay phone.

"There he goes, right there."

We pulled off and headed across the street. "He must have not known I was in the car." "Follow them."

They headed down the street to my grandmother's house. When we pulled up beside them, I hopped out the car to show him my hair. When I looked in the car, some woman was driving, and they took off.

I hopped back in the car.

"Who the fuck was that? Catch them!"

What was he doing? Who was that bitch? They wouldn't stop. I was honking the horn for them to stop. She kept bending corners.

"Hurry up! Catch them! Go faster, speed up!" I said as I banged on the dashboard.

Who the fuck is that bitch? We could not catch up to them before they hopped on the freeway. I was pissed! Yelling and screaming at the top of my lungs.

"Take me home to get his car!"

When we got to my apartment, I ran up the stairs to get the keys to his "Drop."

"Oh, I'm gonna fuck him up!"

When I tried to start the car, the battery was dead. "Damn! Take me back to pick up Nadia."

Soon as we got back to the neighborhood there they were at the light, making a left.

"Yeah, there they go. They going to Aunt Nora's. Take me over there."

Just like I thought, the car was parked right in front. When I got out of the car, Juelz was walking up from the back of the house.

"What the fuck you think you doing? Who's that bitch?"
"Calm down."

"No! Fuck that! Who is she? You fuckin her or something?" Juelz tried to calm me down.

"No, let me go! Who the fuck *is* she Juelz? Oh, you ain't gonna tell me? *Fuck* you then!"

The girl was walking toward the front door. "Who the fuck are you, Bitch..."

"Come on man! You don't need to be out here fighting.

Danielle, let's go! Get in the car!" Tarsha yelled. As they pushed me in the car, I was yelling. "Fuck you, Nigga. Fuck you!"

In the back of my mind, I thought I heard water running. The same sound you hear when you are washing off your porch or sidewalk with a hose. I didn't want to look back. I didn't want to see what I thought I may have done.

CHAPTER EIGHTEEN

"Y ou have a collect call from, Danielle, do you accept?" "Hell yeah!" Juelz yelled through the phone.

"What's up, baby!"

"Hi! I made it."

"Where they take you?"

"I don't know. I'm near Los Angeles." "How long it take you to get there?"

"All day! We left at around 7 o'clock and got here at about 4 o'clock."

"What it look like? Are you hungry?"

"No, but they're about to call breakfast. I'm in some building they call a cottage. It looks like a teen center or something."

"That's the day room."

"Yeah, I guess. It has a big television you can watch. It's a bunch of young girls here. At least on this side. On the other side I believe are the college girls. They look more my age."

"What do you need? I'll give LeAnn some money and she can go get your box ready."

"Okay. I have to get a list to find out what I am allowed to have."

I paused.

"Well, let me call my mom and let her know I made it. We have to sign up for the phone, so I don't know if I can call you back."

"Okay mama!"

"Stay up and let me know what you need." "I will."

"Okay, I miss you mama." "I miss you too. Love you." "Love you too. Bye-bye."

They assigned a counselor who I was supposed to talk to on a daily basis. There was a man in the breakfast hall. I was hoping he would be nice, since I was new. I didn't eat because I was too nervous. He walked by and spoke.

"Breakfast is almost over, and you won't eat again until three o'clock."

"I'm not hungry." I said as I looked up over my shoulder. He was tall and slender, but damn was he handsome! *Man, and he has to see me like this!* I was so embarrassed.

They put me in a room with a girl named Lisa. She was white, with long blonde hair, hazel eyes, and she was pregnant. That must have been an awful feeling to be pregnant and in jail. She looked to be six or seven months. She was pretty big. I thought she may have been a little uneasy, but she was actually nice. We started talking about our lives and what brought us in the situation.

She had got caught in a dope case with her baby daddy, who was black. He was locked up too, she had not been in contact with him since. I asked her was she going to get to go home before the baby was due. She said his mom was going to get the baby and she would be sent to prison once she turned twenty-six.

She had a television and a Walkman. "Will I be able to have a television?"

"Yeah girl, you can have almost everything you need."

The only things we couldn't have were glass containers and mirrors in the make-up compact. They allowed us only white tennis shoes and two pair of blue jeans, our own under clothes and pajamas. I asked her about hair stuff. She said friends outside could send me a boxed perm and toiletries, so I started my list.

Lisa was a college student, so she was at school all day. They would let me out before all the other girls came home, and I would hang out in the dayroom to give her space after a long day at school. I called Juelz the next day to let him know what I needed.

So that first week, I mostly stayed in Lisa's room while the other girls went to school. The man from breakfast the other day was a counselor named Chris. He would always let me and Lisa shower first. That was the program. You come home from school and everyone would take showers before dinner.

"He must like you because he has never spoken to me before, and he always started showers from the other end of the hall. I would always be last.

"Girl, no he doesn't."

"I actually thought he was mean, because he rarely spoke to any of the girls, but now you're here."

Hmmm. He *was* handsome.

We were called out for dinner. While we were eating, Lisa noticed Chris was staring at me. "You have an admirer." "What?"

"He keeps staring at you." "Oh, I am so embarrassed."

If he thought I was half-way cute, wait until my package gets here. I can't wait to perm my hair!

The next week, they put me in my own cell. The day counselor Perez asked me if I wanted to get out of my cell during the day by mopping and waxing the floors and cleaning up.

"Sure!"

"Then when you're done, you can hang out in the day room and watch television."

"Okay."

They called everyone by their last name as if it was your first name. Perez yelled, "Manning they want you up in receiving right away".

"What for?"

"I don't know. Just get there quick."

I didn't know where I was going. No one told me where it was. I walked to the tower and asked the officers in the window. They told me I had a package and that I could go pick it up.

"Oh! My package is here already?"

107

"Manning? Yes, you have a package. How long have you been here?"

"I got here last Saturday."

"And you have a package already? Most wards don't receive packages when they're still on the receiving cottage. Your man must love you, girl!"

That was an officer who worked in packaging named Jesse. He said that everybody called him by his first name because he was so cool. He was nice, by the book, but nice. We went through my package together, so in case there was anything I couldn't have, he would let me know why. I got my thirteen-inch television, but I couldn't have the remote. I don't know why. They sent me some cassette tapes, makeup and my Radiant Red lipstick. They knew I couldn't live without that.

There were jeans, shoes, and a cute pink t-shirt gown with a matching silk robe and slippers. I was in! I couldn't wait to get back and fix myself up before everyone got home from school, especially Chris. I couldn't wait to see the look on his face.

Jesse broke my makeup compact in half.

"You aren't allowed to have the glass mirror."

"What kind of sense did that make? Who would pop the mirror out to use it to cut somebody?"

"You'd be surprised girl. It's some crazy kids in here."

Well, I got a cart to haul all my stuff back to my cottage. When I got back, Perez said I could go into the shampoo room. That is a room they have were you could use blow dryers and curling irons to do your hair.

I put all my stuff up in my room. LeAnn even sent a picture of me and Juelz we took in the park that day he got out. I put it right on my door so you could see it when you opened it.

It was about two-thirty in the afternoon and time for Chris to come in. He always peeked in the little window and let me out first for showers, before the other girls come in from school movement. This time he had to take a double-take. He looked through the window, and then he looked again before opening my door.

"Manning is that you?" "Yes, it's me."

"Boy, you sure clean up well!" "Thank you."

"Who is this, your man?" "Yes."

"He sent you your package already?" "Yeah. That was fast, huh?"

"No one ever gets a package on receiving."

"That's what I heard. They know I needed my stuff. I haven't had my hair done in how long? I couldn't stand looking like a boy another day."

"Well, you look good. That's for damn sure..."

CHAPTER NINETEEN

Over the next few months, I settled in well. I mostly bonded with the camp-side girls. Those were the girls over 18 years of age who worked in the fire fighters program. The staff had made the effort to get me in the program, but because of my offense, I was unable to leave off the grounds to work. Every ward was assigned a counselor and had to have a number of sessions per week.

I looked forward to my weekly sessions with Chris. I knew he was attracted to me and I became attracted to him. We talked about so many things. I could share anything with him. I wished we were anywhere but where we were. I wanted to feel his lips against mine. The way he looked at me, sometimes I knew he felt the same way. The chemistry was undeniable. We continued to express our feelings toward one another without saying a word. I felt it and I know he felt it too. I also knew acting upon it could jeopardize his livelihood. Therefore, all I had to go on were my dreams.

I dreamed about Chris every night, especially during the weekends when we wasn't around. I hated the weekends when he was off. Any opportunity I had to show him affection, I took it, especially when he came to my door. I would always try to entice him in some type of way. I would leave my robe untied or one button undone. He had expressed to me that he could clearly see I was a woman amongst girls that he saw I just got caught up being sprung off some guy who called himself a pimp.

Through our sessions, Chris tried to get me to see the man I loved meant me no good. He thought I should wake up and face the reality of him moving on and being with other women. I didn't like that at all. I felt that Juelz really loved me and that Chris did not understand our relationship. When it came to Juelz, no one could really tell me anything. So I definitely would not be listening to someone who didn't even know him.

The more we talked, I began to realize that Chris was right. After receiving that first package, I never heard from Juelz, nor did he send me any money. Wow! I had really been stupid.

The conversations between me and Chris became intense. Our feelings for each other became more evident. My first roommate, Lisa, talked to me about it. She let me know it was very evident that Chris had feelings for me and I should be careful, because most of the inmates knew that he had been seeing the camp leader for quite some time.

They had just tried to keep their relationship private. Once I was told about their relationship, it kind of made sense. The camp leader had always looked at me differently, and she had not been friendly when I sat around the dayroom with the camp girls.

Her name was Ms. Joy. She acted as if she knew I had no business in the facility and that if I was on the streets, she may have a run for her money. She was not that attractive. She was a bit top heavy, with no shapely figure and long legs. She and Chris were actually the same height, which was tall for a woman.

"Manning you need to shower?" Chris said as he stood at my door.

"No, I need *you*." I said as I moved closer to touch his face. He was leaning in my cell while the door and the wall blocked his body from entering. Our lips met, but only for a mere second just enough to know that if allowed, it would be the softest, sweetest kiss he'd ever had.

"You know I can't."

"I know." I whispered.

"Come out when you're ready." "Okay."

I held the door as he walked down the hall. If only we were on the streets. I wanted that man, and I wanted him bad.

I started writing him letters saying all that I couldn't say in person. While being locked up, my mind took me all the places I couldn't go. Putting all my energy on paper was just as amazing as the real thing.

CHAPTER TWENTY

The weekend had finally come. I would get to see my family on my first visit. "Manning visit. Be on your door in five minutes to unlock."

I was already ready. Those five minutes seemed as long as the time I had already done.

"Okay." I was on my way out the door. As I walked down the long walkway across the grounds, I spotted Nadia and my father. I tried not to run. I walked really fast, but when I got closer, Nadia recognized me right away.

"Danielle! Danielle!" Nadia's little voice cried with her arms stretched out wide.

I ran to my little girl and cried. Just to hold her again after so long. My mind was spinning. Was I really locked up and away from my daughter? Everyone couldn't wait to hug me. I carried my baby with me to the guard tower to check in.

My mother, sisters and even my brother had come along with our father to come see me. I enjoyed that visit. I shared everything that had gone on since I arrived and what my daily routine was. Several cottages were out on movements, so I pointed out some of the people I had come to know.

We had a long day. The visit started at nine and didn't end until four-thirty. It was a very special day. I was able to apologize to my family and share my regrets about my actions. I wanted to communicate to my mother that I appreciated her for taking on the responsibility of caring for my child.

It never even occurred to me that if I didn't have them, my child could have been abandoned and put in the system. I was thankful she was safe and my family did not judge me. They supported me has much as they could, emotionally. The entire situation seemed unreal. I had entered into a new society of people I never even knew existed.

For that first year, they tried to bring Nadia to see me almost every three months. However, the trips became more difficult to make. The eight-hour drive and the hotels weren't very inviting. I understood and appreciated the visits, but I didn't want to burden my mother with that drive and expenses.

What I couldn't understand was why my sister Shelise never came to visit. She was the closest one to me, residing in Los Angeles. I wrote her a letter telling her how upset and frustrated I was that she would let me be locked up so close and not even take the time to come see me. This made me feel more alone and unimportant, especially coming from my favorite sister.

She sent that shit right back to me and said she was not allowing me to make her feel guilty for not coming to visit. The letter read,

"You can talk to me when you have a better outlook on your situation and you are not going to put the blame on me for being locked up. I didn't tell you to make that decision..."

I later came to realize that when you're incarcerated, the whole world forgets about you. As the days of their lives on the outside go by fast, they go twice as slow when you're locked up. Everyone was caught up in their own everyday affairs and struggles. It was easy to forget about the society that doesn't have anything to do but time.

CHAPTER TWENTY-ONE

"Manning pack up your stuff. You're going to be placed on Montecito."

"Why!"

"They can't place you in the camp program, so you'll have to enroll in school and go to the cottage with your age group."

I didn't like that. I didn't want to move. I was comfortable where I was. I didn't know anyone over there, and what was Chris going to say? I was actually scared. I had a great roommate, but who would they stick me with over there?

Once I got moved, all the girls were in the day room. The new cottage was really dark, and the whole set-up was different. As I sat in the dayroom, I found myself crying.

"Why are you crying?"

A girl came over and sat by me.

"You okay? You'll get used to it over here. We're cool over here."

I didn't care. Every chance I got, I would ask Chris to send for me. I missed him. I would stay up late at night, writing him letters so that when he called me over for those brief sessions, I could leave him with something to put on his mind.

We had grown careless as months went by, or shall I say Chris did. Apparently, Ms. Joy noticed all the sessions we were having and began to ask questions and Chris could not call me over to the cottage anymore. So I started sending letters by my old roommate. One day, another counselor got a hold of the letter. They placed Chris under investigation and moved him to a male cottage. He was able to fill me in on the situation.

"I can't be caught talking to you at all. They are moving me to work on the male cottages. I'm not going to be allowed to work on the women cottages."

"I feel terrible!"

"Don't worry about it. It's not totally your fault." "But I feel so bad."

"Don't. It was my mistake, and it won't happen again." "*What* won't ? Me?"

"Anybody."

I could tell he resented me for manipulating him. He never spoke to me again. I was so hurt. It was months before I saw him again.

My roommate came running down the hall.

"Girl, guess who's working on *our* cottage tonight?" "Ladies, get ready for showers. B hall will be first!"

I knew the voice. It was Chris! I couldn't wait to see him. I was so excited that he had to come unlock my door to let my roommate in. He didn't know it was my cell too. As soon as he unlocked the door, he saw me.

"Hi Chris!"

He didn't say a word. He didn't even look at me. I was so hurt. "Ooh."

"Guess he ain't foolin witcho ass no more."

"I guess not. You think he's mad at me still?"

"No, that motha fucka ain't mad, he just don't want to lose his job over a piece a pussy."

"I guess not, huh?" "I *know* not, shit!"

We laughed. I had told her the whole story. "Oh well," I voiced.

"Oh well, hell!"

"What can you do? Next!"

We laughed about the whole situation.

CHAPTER TWENTY-TWO

I t had been six months now that I was there. I was still seen as a woman amongst girls. I started the fall semester of college. I became the favorite of most counselors, and made two close friends, Claudia and Tiffany. Claudia was of Muslim faith and Tiffany was a member of a gang. Tiffany was my roommate. Both lived and committed their crimes in South Central LA. That was the year of the Rodney King beating, when the acquittal of the four officers involved sparked the LA riots.

The movie, *Boys in the Hood*, was our movie night pick. When I saw that film, I couldn't believe it was true. Most of the girls locked up were from the streets of LA, and all they saw was real-life to them.

I stayed in occasional contact with Juelz. I called him once every three months or so. I would get pissed off when I broke down and would ask him to send money, and then I would never receive it. He would say he gave LeAnn or Evelyn two-hundred dollars and they would say he never gave them nothing. It was ridiculous. The last time I called, Ricky just happened to be over there.

"Hey Sis! What's up? How you doing down there?" "I'm good. How are you doing?"

"Oh, you know. Just doing what it do." "Cool. That's good!"

"Everybody just been chillin, man waiting for you to come home."

"I know that's right. I am *too* ready!"

"Well, let me get off the phone. I was just calling checking on what Juelz was up to."

"Okay Sis. It's almost over. I'll see you when you get home. We gonna kick it blood!"

"Okay. I love you." "Love you too, Sis!"

I was really in no mood to chit chat, I just needed some money, but of course, nobody cared about that!

Over the course of my sentence, I became very comfortable with my surroundings. The guys on my list consisted of two plumbers. They always had very little supervision and were able to come to my cell. Devin sent me the most beautiful letters confessing his undying love for me. Then there was also Tim.

I shared a special bond with him. Our relationship was more of a grown puppy love. I felt the need to give him all the emotional attention he needed to make it through the rest of his sentence. He had been locked up since he was fifteen and he was about to be twenty-six. Both his parents had died when he was a child and his grandparents raised him. He was going to be released a few weeks before me.

We made arrangements to see each other once we got out. I would be staying my first night with Shelise. Toward the end of my time, I had somewhat fallen in lust with one of the plumbers. He had money and connections to get me things from the outside. Not to mention the one thing we shared so intimately. Sex!

We would make any excuse to get to be alone and enjoy what little stolen time we had to feel each other. The kisses we shared during class only made our bodies yearn for each other. I would love to make a rise in his jeans. A touch of my hand on his dick would have wet warmness spilling over onto it and the rest in his boxers. *It was worth it*, he'd always say.

Once we got the opportunity to be alone, Devin couldn't wait to taste my breasts. He squeezed them so gently, with his tongue massaging each one. I would quickly get him out his pants to feel him inside me. It was as if our bodies were made for each other. I often wondered what it would be like to be on the outside and to have a whole night with him. We also made plans to see each other once we got out. Tim resented Devin for being able to see me whenever he wanted.

Classes got cancelled and I couldn't stand not being able to see Devin for that long. The weekend was bad enough. He had sent me a message to clog up the toilet in my cell and it would shut down my whole bank. Then they would be able to spend at least four days on our cottage. It would shut down showers and they would have to service each room on my hall.

When it was our turn, we could enjoy several quickies in my cell. The door in the next cell would block a visual to my room. So while they were working on each side of my cell, Devin would slip into my cell without anyone knowing. The lust was so strong between us. We were like magnets.

During the last sixty days of my sentence, Tim and Devin were released within a weeks time of each other and sent to the same halfway house. They fought over my attention from the outside. Each would get their counselors to call to my cottage so they could talk to me. That was one of many favors I received from my counselors.

While they were at each other over me, I spent my last days secretly getting to know Cedric. Yes, another officer. He was gorgeous. He was just my type of man. Smooth caramel skin, chubby build and nice natural curly hair cut in a fade. I had never given him the time of day, no matter how hard he tried to flirt. Too many of the girls were infatuated by him and he knew it. I paid him no attention on purpose, but for some reason he was assigned to my cottage for overtime the last sixty days.

I received a card from Charlene Campbell. That was Ricky's mom. *Oh how sweet!* I thought. Ricky must have told her he talked to me. She was sweet to me. I spent a lot of time over her house with Ricky and his girlfriend. I was anxious to read her card. When I opened the envelope, it was an obituary. When I looked at the picture, it was Ricky (they called him YB for Young

Blood). My eyes filled with tears. I couldn't open the letter fast enough. It read:

My dear sweet Danielle,

As you may have heard, they killed my boy. Ricky is no longer with us, and I just thought I would send you his obituary, since you could not attend his funeral. It was a lovely homegoing service. I never knew my son had so many friends. I was deeply touched by all the thoughtful gestures from all the boys. Ricky was doing so well with his music and whatever else he had going on. His death was such a shock because I knew he was on the right track. Baby, all I can say is when you come home get your life together because these streets don't love nobody. I love you like a daughter.

May God bless you, Love Charlene

He was shot at the club and died. I couldn't believe it, knowing I just talked to him a couple months earlier. I felt bad that I had rushed off the phone with him. You never know when your last day is going to be. Vanessa Williams' song, *Save The Best For Last*, had just come out. For some reason, that song reminded me of him. The melody of the song made me cry. I felt bad. We had become so close since high school. We were the only two out of all our friends who graduated and walked the stage together.

He had been in love with Candi since junior high, but he was always so short that she paid him no attention. It wasn't until after we graduated that he shot up to be six feet tall. He had a curl and his hair had grown out so long. That boy could rock some bangin Shirley's! His hair made it past his shoulders, he was fine! He was so cool.

I hate to remember the time we went to a party in the South. It was me, Evelyn, him and Becky. Evelyn had snuck out of the house and popped up at our apartment with Becky. When I asked her what she was doing out, she said she wanted to go to the party. I told her, "Okay, but I'm going to take you home before it gets too late."

We all were cool, and before you know it Ricky had got into some funk with them Detroit niggas. It was crazy. The next thing it was five on one, and Ricky was the one. They were kicking him in the head and beating him with bats. I tried to jump in.

"Get off of him! Stop! What the fuck are you doing?"

I just kept trying to jump in to help him, but I couldn't. They were all over him. I just started pushing them off of him and screaming to the top of my lungs. I yelled for Becky to help me get him to the car and I rushed him to the Medical Center. I was hysterical.

"Ricky, hold on! Can you hear me?"

He just kept moaning. Blood was everywhere his head had swollen up so fast. I was speeding down the freeway with my hazard lights on. When we got to the hospital, I jumped out and ran for help. They brought out a wheelchair and transferred him to a gurney. They pushed him into the hallway and never came back.

What the hell? He could have brain damage. He could start hemorrhaging, anything!

"Somebody do something!" I screamed.

We sat there until five o'clock in the morning. I stood by his side the whole time, waiting for someone to see him. It was just ridiculous! The sun was coming up, and Evelyn was still with me. I never thought to have Becky drop her off because I was so consumed with Ricky. We finally were able to leave, and I took Evelyn home. We tried to sneak back into her sliding glass door that she always snuck out from. When she went to open it, it was locked. Oh shit! That was not a good sign. You could only imagine what happened after that...

I'm going to miss my brother. He was my dogg in the end. I'm just glad I got to be close to him while he was here on earth.

My roommate, Tiffany, moved out of the cell. We all wanted to take turns in the single bed cells. They were much cooler to stay in, and since I was going home soon, it was perfect time for her to move into it. She did not want some crazy broad to be put in the room with her. She was hella picky.

121

Since I had no cellmate, it was easy for Cedric to talk to me through my window during his late night grounds checks? We began to have deep conversations about life and the choices we make. He told me to go on movements he supervised for the cottage so he and I could talk more.

His eyes and lips made me wet every time he gave me that look. It was as if I knew, if given the opportunity, he would snatch my clothes off and give me all that he thought I was missing until our bodies were weak.

The night before my release, we had another movie night in the day room. When he came to my cell to unlock my door, he asked me to give him my sister's address and phone number, along with my flight information. I didn't hesitate. I slipped him a note with the information he requested. He asked me if he could take me out on a date, and I said *yes*.

That night, I requested for Claudia to stay the night in my cell so we could stay up all night talking and share inspiring plans, encouraging each other on how to make our lives whole again. I was so excited to be going home that I knew I wouldn't be able to sleep. I shared my plans with Claudia concerning Cedric.

"I am so happy for you."

"I'm going to miss you girl. Promise me we are going to stay in touch and never lose contact with each other?"

As Claudia listened to all my plans, we didn't realize we had fallen asleep until my cell door clicked when they unlocked it for breakfast.

CHAPTER TWENTY-THREE

M y day came. November 2, 1992. I was going home. My sister would pick me up. I had told her what type of outfits to get me from the styles I saw on television. Everyone had gone on the school movement, but Vanessa stayed in that day. Vanessa was my Mexican friend. She was pretty, with long beautiful hair.

Since I couldn't go back to college fall semester, Vanessa had gotten me a job with her instead. We rode on a truck, delivering the meal trays to all the cottages. It was just the two of us, working with a Mexican guy from the outside. He was real cool. He treated us like he would treat his nieces.

He never asked us any personal questions, but he always would drop hints of advice through his life experiences. The mornings we did breakfast, we had to be up by five in the morning. I hated those days. We had become close, really close.

At one point, Vanessa had acted as if she had a crush on me. That made me uncomfortable, but flattered at the same time. We had an understanding, but it didn't stop me from being even a bit curious. She would love to touch my breasts and put her hands between my legs. She more or less did it on purpose, knowing that I would tell her to stop.

Vanessa soon found a boyfriend, but made sure I knew she would always prefer me. She was beating down the door to get the counselor's attention so she could see me for the last time. I almost left without saying good-bye. When I made it down to her cell, she was cussing me out, she had an accent so it was funny to hear her talk.

"Bitch, what the fuck is your problem? So you were gonna fuckin leave and not say shit to me, you fuckin bitch. That's how you do me? Open this fuckin door!"

I knew that was her way of fighting her feelings of about me leaving.

Vanessa had grown to depend on our friendship, especially the time she would have me all to herself those few hours in the day when we worked. I stepped in the cell.

"Calm down, girl. I'm not going to forget you." "You promise, bitch?"

She walked toward me, and before I knew it, she kissed me. She grabbed my arms and slipped her tongue in my mouth. It was a soft sweet kiss. She touched the side of my face. I stared at her in amazement. She stared back and just sat on her bunk, looking at the floor.

A shout came from down the hall. "Manning let's go!"

"It's time for me to go." She didn't look up.

"I love you. I'm going to miss you."

She didn't reply. I stepped out, just as my counselor was there to lock the door.

I ran down the hall,

"I love you! I love you!"

She was beating and kicking on the door. "I love you!"

I looked at my counselor,

"She'll be fine. You better get out of here, girl." "Yeah."

I headed to the tower. I tried not to run, but then, what the hell! I was finally going home. I took one last look at the grounds. I couldn't believe this day had finally come, and my sister was waiting on the other side of the door! I couldn't change my clothes fast enough.

I said my last goodbye and greeted my favorite sister in the parking lot. I jumped in the car and she gave me the biggest hug. She couldn't stop kissing my cheek.

"You're home! You're home! Let's get out of here! So what do you want to do? Are you hungry?"

"No. I need my hair done."

"Well, I can give you a relaxer. What you want to do tonight." "Girl, this officer in there wants to take me to dinner and a movie."

"What! Shut up! I don't believe it. Are you serious?" "Girl, yes! I got some stories for your ass!"

"I gave him your phone number. He said he would call me as soon as he thought I'd made it to your house. He took the day off."

"Oh my God! Okay, we can go by the store and I can put your relaxer in."

"Okay!"

Once we made it to my sister's, Cedric had called three times already.

"Ah, this is Cedric calling for Danielle. I'll try calling back."

After my sister put in my relaxer, she ran me a bubble bath with candles, in her garden tub.

"Just relax, baby sista'. Soak and clear your mind. You home now.

Just relax!"

I had never been in a tub so big, let alone with the bubbles and the candles. I thought I was dreaming.

"Come pinch me. I'm scared I'm going to wake up and be back in jail."

"It's not a dream, girl. You home and it's for real."

I leaned back and closed my eyes. The water felt so good and silky to my skin. The phone rang.

"Hey Cedric." Shelise said as she walked into the bathroom. "Yes, she's right here. I ran her a bubble bath with some candles and shit. Here she is."

"Hello?"

"Damn! You even sound different. You're in the tub huh?" "Yes."

"I can't wait to see you! What time you want me to pick you up?"

"Where are we going?"

"I figure we can go to a movie, like I said, and get a bite to eat. Have you eaten?"

"No, I was saving it for tonight."

"Okay, I'll pick you up around six and we can go to eat first then go to the movies."

"That sounds cool."

"It's already four o'clock." "I'll be ready."

"Where does your sister live?"

"I don't know. Let me let her give you directions. Shelise, can you give him directions?"

"Yea, where are you coming from brotha?"

I started to get nervous. He was coming to pick me up. I was even scared! What if he wanted some pussy? I didn't know him like that. I mean he was fine and all, but he was a grown man. I was only twenty-two. Cedric was almost ten years older than I was.

"Oh no! Did I make a mistake?" I told my sister how I felt.

"Naw! Don't be chicken now, witcha hot ass. I'm sure he'll be okay. Let him take you out. He sounds like he really likes you. Hell the nigga den left three messages for yo ass. He wants some pussy!" Shelise said as she started laughing.

"Girl, he is not gettin anything! Hmm."

Cedric knocked on the door. "Come in!" Shelise yelled.

Cedric was his first name. His last name was Thomas. They always call officers by their last name, as well as the inmates. As he walked up the steps, I was standing there, waiting for him to get to the top. As he looked up, he didn't even recognize me. I had my hair in bob style. It was long on one side, covering my left eye.

I had bought some more make-up, arched my eye brows with some hair remover, and of course, I had my radiant red lipstick and mascara to make my lashes extra-long. Shelise stood by, watching the whole scene, play-by-play, with the biggest grin on her face.

"She looks good, doesn't she?"

"Man, you are fine! I didn't even recognize you." Cedric grabbed me and squeezed me tight.

"Boy! You look good! This sho beat them navy blues you was wearing. God *damn!*"

I was laughing at Cedric's reaction. "Okay already!"

"No, don't get me wrong. You were cute and all, but now you just look like a woman. Girl, you are beautiful! And I get to be the first dude to take you out. You ready to go?"

"Yes."

"Take care of my little sister. Don't have her out too late." "Shit, I might not bring her back!"

"What?"

"Just kiddin, Shelise. I can call you Shelise, right?"

"Yeah, you two have fun. Don't do anything I wouldn't do. Oh shit! That don't leave much. I take that back." She said laughing.

"Bye you two, have fun!"

He opened the door for me. Then he ran around the car so fast. "Calm down Cedric."

"Okay, okay. Hell, I'm kind of nervous."

"Nervous? You? Not with all that shit you was talking." "I'm really a shy guy."

"Yeah, right."

"I am. I am, seriously. I just want to show you a good time. You want to go eat first?"

"Sure."

"We'll go to FRIDAYS. You ever been there?" "No."

"The movie theatre is over that way too. You like scary movies?"

"Not really. What's playing?" "Candyman."

"Candyman? Oh yeah, we can go see that."

"Good. That will give you a reason to grab on me." "Whatever man, you crazy."

"I'm serious or me grabbing on you?" "Yeah I'm sure that's how it will go down."

We both laughed. As we pulled up to the restaurant, I began to get nervous again.

Juelz had never taken me out to eat. Keith's Patio on the boulevard did not count. FRIDAYS was a nice place. I looked at all the people sitting down. We sat at the bar first, waiting for the hostess to seat us.

"You want a drink?" "A drink?"

"Yeah."

"I don't drink."

"I'll get you something fruity so you can't taste the alcohol." "Okay."

"I'm going to get you a Georgia Peach." "What's that?"

"It's good! It has peach Schnapps, orange juice, cranberry juice and gin. Gin don't make you sin, do it?"

"Not at all!" "Damn!"

"What you mean, *damn*?" I laughed.

"I was hoping to get you drunk and take advantage of you." "Shut up. I bet you were."

"No. No, I'm just kidding."

"Seriously, I have a lot of respect for you. You carried yourself like a lady the whole time you were locked up. Oh, I was watching you acting all stuck up."

"No, I wasn't. I just heard all those stories about you. I wasn't going to be on that list. I waited. I knew you wanted me the whole time."

"Yeah, you knew *right* too. Those girls were jealous of you, boy."

"For real?"

"Hell yeah, that's why I didn't want any of them in our business. They would have started fuckin' with you."

"Oh well."

"Are you done with your drink already? Damn baby, you got to sip on it."

"It tastes so good. You sure there's alcohol in it?"

"Yes, that shits going to creep up on you too. You want another one?"

"Yep!"

"Okay, but it's a two-drink limit. I don't want to have to carry you out of here. We still have to eat and catch the movie."

"Let's just go to the movie. We can grab a hamburger afterwards."

"You sure?"

"Yeah, I can't eat around a lot of people like this." "Okay, let's go. We can catch the next showing." As we got up to leave, I kept giggling.

"Oh shit! It's hittin you now."

"I think so. Ooh, I feel *good!*" I said, hanging onto Cedric's arm.

We made it to the movies. Once we settled in the seat, I felt like I was floating. I laid my head on his shoulder. He took advantage of all that touching. The first scary scene in the movie, he grabbed me. Once I laughed, he went in for the kill. He grabbed my face and turned it toward his, and then he leaned over and placed his lips on mine. All I felt was tongue. He was kissing me like he lost something in my throat. I pulled back.

"Watch the movie!" I whispered.

I was almost embarrassed that he kissed me in public. I allowed him to kiss me a few more times after I got comfortable. The movie was actually scary with a few jumpy scenes. He kept his arm around me and felt me up with the other. When the movie was over, we headed back to my sister's place.

I hadn't realized how late it was. It was pitch black. Shelise had left the door open for us. It was so dark that we tripped over each other and started laughing on the way up the stairs. I couldn't see a thing. I thought for sure we would wake up Shelise. So far so good!

We settled in on the floor with some pillows from the couch. He didn't waste any time. He had me butt naked in a matter of two minutes. We were both on our knees, kissing like crazy as he unbuttoned my two top buttons of my blouse with his teeth, finding my breast with his tongue.

As we knelt there naked, he sucked my breasts so gently while slipping his hand between my thighs. He rubbed my clit and felt the warmth and wetness of my walls on his fingers. As he laid me down and spread my legs open, his tongue caressed my outer lips, gently sampling my juices. His tongue was so soft. It

129

felt like heaven. I never imagined he would have done that. I guess he figured I hadn't been touched in almost three years. Are you kidding me? He thought he was doing me a favor. *What the hell? Let him enjoy it!* He acted like he was eating the Last Supper.

"Danielle?" Shelise whispered in the dark. We both jumped. He froze between my legs.

"We're home."

"Oh, sorry!" Shelise said as she closed the door.

Her apartment was so small her bedroom was the next room on the other side of the living room.

"Damn!"

"She scared the hell out of me!" "Sorry!" I giggled as I kissed his lips.

"Come on, baby."

As we kissed, I could smell me on his lips.

He slid his dick inside of me. It didn't penetrate as smoothly as planned. He held my legs on his shoulders and gently forced himself inside me. I felt so good. The thought of receiving all of him was over whelming. He was a screamer. I put my hand over his mouth as our bodies moved in a motion uncontrolled.

"Baby, don't stop!"

It felt so good, I couldn't get enough of him. We kissed and licked on each other. It was getting to good to him, and he was making more noise than I was. *Dang!* He buried his face in the pillow, next to my head. Then he whispered in my ear.

"Damn you feel good! What the hell am I going to do now?"

He got on his knees and grabbed my thighs. His thrusts were so hard and we felt so good to each other that I thought for sure Shelise would hear us. I had heard music coming from her room so maybe she couldn't.

He had my body sliding back and forth. He took control of my pussy and was fucking the shit out of me. It felt so damn good I wanted to scream. My eyes where shut, they were closed so tight. When I opened them, I thought I was seeing stars.

"Don't cum in me!" "Too late."

"What?"

"I have on a rubber."

"When did you put that on? Oh you're good. It felt so wet, I didn't even know.

"Yeah, I didn't want to kill the mood." "Oh my gosh!"

"You feel so good, girl. You ain't going to be able to get rid of me."

"You promise?"

"Keep talking. I'm gonna bring my ass to Sacramento." We sat and talked in a whisper.

"What time does your flight leave?"

"Not until eight o'clock tomorrow night. We're going to go shopping and out to eat before I go."

I didn't want to tell him Tim would be coming over first thing in the morning. He had gotten released from the half-way house before Devin.

"Can we keep in touch?" "Sure."

"I'm serious. I'm taking some time off, and maybe I can come see you in Sacramento."

"Are you serious?"

"Hell yes! I want to finish what I started. I really *like* you. I wouldn't mind having a long distance relationship with you."

"Okay, if you say so." "I would like that."

No way could he come to Sacramento. Juelz would kill me, not to mention him too.

"Well, I better go. I'll give you a call tomorrow, before your plane leaves."

"Okay, I'd like that."

I walked him down the stairs and we stood outside for one more goodbye kiss. He hugged me tight. Maybe he really *did* have feelings for me.

Well I was not thinking about all that right then. I wanted to get home to see Juelz and Nadia. He didn't know what day I was coming home. I hadn't told him anything. I had wanted to surprise him.

The next morning Tim just popped up at Shelise's house. "Oh my God!"

He had remembered her address from the letters. As he walked in the door, he whistled as he came up the stairs. It startled me. We couldn't believe we were standing face to face. There was no one to say, "No contact!"

Tim walked up to me, grabbed my face, he kissed me gently. "Hey you two what's up?"

Shelise had scared him. He jumped back. "I'm sorry. Did I scare you?"

"Hell, yeah!"

"I'm sorry. You must be Tim." "And you must be Shelise."

"That's me. You are a cutie pie. Danielle, he's cute." "Yes, I am, aren't I?"

Tim hung around until I got dressed. He had his own car, and he had wanted to join us for lunch. I wasn't feeling him like that at all. I just wanted to spend time with my sister and go home.

"Where are you guys going to eat?"

"I don't know. We might go to the mall first." I said as I put my things in the car.

"Ask him to come with us." Shelise whispered. "No, I don't want him to." I whispered back.

"Awe. That's cold. Look at him he wants you to ask him to come with us."

"I don't care. No, I don't feel like being bothered." I turned back to him.

"I'll see you later. I'll call you before my plane leaves." "Okay, you do that then."

He hopped in his car and drove off.

I had no intention on calling him. I just wanted to enjoy my day and get home to Nadia.

CHAPTER TWENTY-FOUR

T *hank you for flying Delta. We hope you enjoyed your flight, and please, fly with us again!*

I was finally home! I made my way through the airport. It was a little after ten that evening. As I made my way down the escalator, I could see my father and Nadia. I only had a carry-on bag, so I went straight to the front were they were.

"Mommy!"

When Nadia ran to me, I picked her up. She couldn't stop staring at me. We were full of smiles, from cheek to cheek. My dad picked me up in the Porsche, so Nadia had to sit in my lap on the way to my mother's.

The city still looked the same. I couldn't believe I was home. We pulled up in front of my mother's house. I ran up to the door and went in. It was just like the night I left. All my aunts were in the kitchen, waiting for me to arrive. As I walked through the living room, my pictures were everywhere. It was like a shrine. It was as if I had died. I guess in my mother's eyes I had.

Everyone joined me around the table. Nadia sat on my lap the entire time. Evelyn and Yolanda were on their way over. I didn't want to hold any grudges with all the people who didn't write or send money while I was away. Evelyn always wrote me and sent pictures of her and her crew. I had missed those girls. They would walk over to my apartment to hang out, *wit they fast tails.* They were glad I was home. I hadn't told Juelz when I was coming back. That's who was on my mind.

Once Evelyn and Yolanda arrived, they were ready to hit the streets.

"You talk to Juelz?" "No."

"When you going to let him know you home?" "I don't know."

"You know he been blowin up my phone. He might be over Aunt Nora's. You want to go around there?"

I felt a knot come in my stomach.

"Yeah, might as well get it over with. I need some money anyway." "He better break you off. You just coming home too!" "Mama, I'm gonna ride with them for a minute." "Okay."

"We'll be right back. Come on, Nadia, you gonna go with me."

Nadia hopped out the seat and ran to get her jacket. She wasn't letting me out of her sight.

"So bitch, I know you hella happy to be home." "Hell yeah! I can't believe it!"

"Dang Danielle! How long was you gone?"

"Too *damn* long! Two years, two months, and two days."

We pulled up at Aunt Nora's. There they were. Juelz, his brother Jamie and some other homeboys I didn't recognize. I was excited. I got out the car and walked up behind Juelz.

"What's up, Nigga?"

"Oh shit! What's up baby?" Juelz said as he turned around in surprise. He hugged me so tight it was as if he didn't ever want to let me go.

I began to cry. I had missed him so much. He grabbed my face to wipe my tears, and then he pressed his lips against mine for that kiss we had waited two years to share.

A voice came from behind. It was Jamie. He hadn't recognized me at first.

"What's *up*, baby girl? When you get out?" "Two days ago."

"What, Nigga? And you just *now* coming to see me? Ain't that a bitch?"

"Naw, I stayed in LA with my sister." "Who? Shelise?"

"Yes."

"Oh, okay. You still could have called a nigga!" We all went inside.

Nadia hadn't really spoken to Juelz.

"What's up baby! Come give me a hug nigga." Juelz grabbed Nadia and squeezed her.

"You happy to see yo mama?" "Yes."

Jamie had run outside.

"There them marks go, Nigga!"

All we could hear after that was gunshots. Jamie was running down the street shooting at the car.

"What the fuck!"

"Mommy! Mommy!" Nadia screamed. "Come here, baby! It's all right." Evelyn and Yolanda went to laughing. "You can tell she been with yo mama."

"Hell, my baby ain't supposed to be used to no gunshots!" "What the fuck is you doin man!" Juelz yelled. "Fuckin' idiot."

He slapped Jamie upside his head and they started fighting outside. "Let's go! Shit!"

We hopped in the car. I didn't even say *bye*. We went back at my moms.

"What the *matter*?"

Nadia was still crying she ran to my mom. "They dumb behinds over there shootin." "Over where?"

I knew I shouldn't have gone over there. I ain't gonna be able to stay here. They do the same stupid stuff."

I might have been over reacting, but for that moment, I wasn't comfortable.

While I was locked up, I sent in a letter requesting an interview to work the Christmas season at Target. I let them know I would be home from college and wanted a seasonal position. They replied by mail and had scheduled an interview with me that next week. Things weren't going like I had planned far as Juelz was concerned. *That nigga ain't gave me shit!*

Damn! Word was he had just bought a car for that other bitch he had been fucking with while I was locked up. I hadn't even bothered to see him that much. It took too much time to spend time with me and the other bitch.

Plus, I started working that next week. After my interview, they asked me to start as soon as possible. With me working until closing, I didn't have much time. Sure, he would make his way to the house late at night, but what good was that? I was used to going to bed early, plus I was chilling with Nadia. It would be midnight and he would send someone to knock on the door.

I would do most of my running' in the day and never see him. There was always someone coming to pick me up and take me around on my days off. Many of all my old boyfriends were coming out of the woodwork, mostly the ones from high school. What did they want? Once I had Nadia and got with Juelz, I paid no one else any attention not even TJ. There was *one* I had wondered about John. He showed up all right, and I had to admit, it was a pleasant surprise.

We started spending time together. I mainly needed a ride to work. He would always take me and pick me up when my father couldn't. Juelz even picked me up from work a few times, but he had other things going on. He hadn't even given me money to buy clothes or anything.

That kept me not fucking with him because soon as he said, I ain't got, I would curse him out. Hell! Didn't I just do two years, two months, and two days behind this nigga? And he couldn't give me no money and he didn't even buy me a car when I got home. Why should I even fuck with him? He left me for dea. The only person I could depend on was my mother.

CHAPTER TWENTY-FIVE

Cedric had come to see me a few weeks after Thanksgiving. He had an interview with Rio Cosumnes Correctional Center. I had no idea he had been making plans to move to Sacramento. My father picked me up from work that day.

I worked until four-thirty that week, and I met Cedric back at my mom's house. When we pulled up, there was a Red BMW parked in my mom's driveway. I didn't dare tell my dad who it was. He didn't bother to ask anyway. My mom was cooking dinner. They were in the kitchen talking when I walked through the door.

"Hey doll!" He said as he stood up and greeted me with a kiss on my cheek.

I gave him a big hug. I was happy to see him. We sat down and ate dinner. I got Nadia ready for bed and we left to go to Cedric's hotel. He was staying at the Residence Inn at Cal Expo. He had no idea where to make his reservation. We settled in the room and hopped in the shower together.

"I can't believe we are here together, *and* I am out of jail!"

Cedric kissed me and we rubbed on each other as the water ran over our bodies. I was digging that man right there. His caramel skin and curly hair, not to mention those dimples! I could kiss his fat lips all night.

I felt his dick get hard against my leg. I thought I'd give him a treat. I kissed his chest as I held onto his body. I licked down his stomach until I squatted in front of him and guided him in my mouth, rubbing on his chest as I looked up at him to watch his facial expressions. He held my head with both his hands and began a rhythm.

I wanted him to cum so I could taste every drop of him. He was screaming so loud that I knew my mouth was giving his dick all it needed. We were soaking wet from the shower. After he came, he leaned back as the water dripped down his face. I stood up and he grabbed me close and began to trace my lips with his tongue. We stood, kissing under the water.

"You gonna make a nigga fall in love, man!" He said to me. "Good! "Okay, that's what you say *now*."

I got the soap started washing his chest. We showered and continued what we started in the bed. He went into his bag and pulled out some edible body paste. He rubbed it on my breasts so gently, anticipating the taste against my moist skin. Watching his hands gently rubbing my breasts made my mouth water.

He caressed my breasts with his tongue, licking one breast then the other, inviting me to join in the taste, I licked my breast as our tongues met. The taste was sweet as I absorbed the juices from his mouth. Tracing his lips with my tongue, we engaged in the most intimate connection. He positioned his body against mine as his hand felt the wetness between my legs. He penetrated me with his fingers, as my body rose with every motion of his hand.

"Give it to me, baby." I whispered softly against his lips.

CHAPTER TWENTY-SIX

I worked through the Christmas season. There was a guy who I noticed rather quickly. His name was Lesley. He was tall, with a nice build and nice complexion, and looked to be around my age. We became friends quickly. He would call my register station to tell me how cute I looked that day or how he couldn't wait to kiss my pretty lips when we got off.

He had no car and he lived with his parents, so there was no need to pursue that. Nadia had chicken pox, which meant I couldn't return back to work. I didn't bother keeping in touch.

Juelz had other things going on. He and the bitch were fighting a dope case together. He had said she was going to say the dope was hers. He said she had five kids, and that was why he bought her the car. I went to his court dates with my cousins.

We were all sitting there, me on one side and the bitch on the other. I don't know why I was even there. Just wanted to feel a part of something I had already lost. He actually had two bitches and I wanted a piece of both of them, but I was on parole and I didn't know how that would fly. They sentenced him to six years and let the bitch walk with probation first offense.

How could he have wanted her to take the case? She had five kids! I missed him at first, then I told myself, *let them bitches deal with his ass! He didn't send me shit but one package. It was his turn to be left white around the mouth, like a Safeway chicken.*

My Aunt Chellie called me for a little talk over to Evelyn's mom's house. She got me there to chastise me, saying I was ungrateful and that my mom didn't have to keep my child. She said I hadn't shown my mom any appreciation.

"Don't you know that your mother took off two weeks from her job to spend time with you and you haven't even taken a minute of your time to spend time with her? You too busy running around behind that nigga you went to jail behind. I hired a PI when you were in jail, he had all kinds of girls at your apartment, when you hadn't been in jail a good month! And don't think I don't know you called me a bitch for not bailing you out. Oh, I heard about it!"

Where was all this coming from? I had said no such thing.

Juelz, on the other hand, had a lot to say about no one bailing me out or taking his money.

That one-sided conversation ended with Evelyn's mom running out the room, crying at the horrible things her sister was saying to me. She ended by apologizing and saying that she still loved and forgave me. Forgave me for what? I hadn't even *done* anything.

My mother was going through an emotional breakdown. I hadn't realized that she had taken two weeks off to spend some time with me. I was so busy catching up with my friends that I didn't even notice.

She couldn't take it anymore. She told me she hated to seem as if she was deserting me but that she needed a break and left to stay with a friend in Los Angeles. The house became crazy. Between my stepfather and his two teenage kids and their friends, it was even too much for me to deal with.

I had hooked up with an old girlfriend named Tamika. I hadn't seen in a while who told me that her apartment complex downtown had a vacancy. The manager was rather difficult, but she let me rent a one bedroom. I was thankful for that. Nadia and I settled in pretty well. My father picked Nadia up for pre-school and dropped her off. I still didn't have a car, so spending all day in that apartment wasn't going over too well for me.

I woke up to dress Nadia and lie right back on the couch, with my head under the covers all day. I didn't sleep in my bed, I let Nadia sleep there. I felt more comfortable on the couch. I slept all day in silence. I fell into a deep depression. Everything Nadia did got on my nerves. It seemed that Nadia was just some other little kid and not my daughter. The connection wasn't there.

I had left the most beautiful one year old and returned to a four year old kid. Nadia didn't understand my anger. How could she? She was just a child. All she knew was she was getting hit or yelled out for every little thing. I made sure she ate breakfast every morning. I got used to eating three meals a day. I would get Nadia dressed, comb her hair, and then fix her something to eat.

"Turn around, damn it!" I said.

"Didn't I say turn your goddamned head around?"

I had slapped her right in the face with the brush. I realized I was taking my frustrations out on my child.

One morning at breakfast, we were sitting at the table eating waffles, *Let go my Eggo waffles* which had come to be our favorite. I wasn't in a good mood.

"Quit smacking!" I yelled at the top of my lungs, with her sitting right across from me. That scared her so bad that she almost jumped out of her seat. Tears came rolling down her face.

"Finish your food and go wash your face before Papa comes."

I felt bad, but I couldn't bring myself to say I was sorry. I never showed her any type of affection no hugs, no kisses and no "*I love yous.*"

Nadia often said she wished she were a baby again.

I think she remembered when I did those things. My family loved Nadia. When she was a baby, I couldn't kiss her enough. I always dressed her so cute, and because I wasn't fond of the color pink, I put her in a light blue outfit for her first baby picture. *I believe I cursed her by not wearing pink.* She was such a good baby. The family just knew she would be one of those babies that would cry all night and my mother would be the one to have her all the time. Boy, were they wrong. Little Nadia never said a peep only when she was hungry.

CHAPTER TWENTY-SEVEN

T hat April, my dad bought me a car. One of my stepsister's husband's friends was selling it for six hundred dollars as a favor to them, knowing how badly I needed a car. I was thrilled! I could start living and getting out of the apartment. This was the sixth car I've had since I was fifteen. My first official car was a Datsun 210.

It was a little four-door car my friends called "a soapbox." We drove all around town piled in six-deep, all the time three in the front, and three in the back sometimes even seven, if it was one extra person that would be left out of the click. I would tell them to hop in and fit in the best they could. The car was a stick, but I had that mastered. I let a third person sit right in the middle and make her cross her legs so I could still shift the gears.

When I turned sixteen, I wanted a brand new car. I talked my mother into taking me to look for a car for my birthday. My dad said he would pay for it. My mother ended up paying the down payment on the car on her credit card if I agreed to make the payments. It was a brand new, red four door Hyundai, with just enough room for my friends.

I worked at *Funderland*. That was my first job. I had only made two payments before I got rammed at the light, crashed into two other vehicles and sailed right through the intersection into a field. After that, the insurance company dropped me from the policy and took me off as a driver, and I had no car.

By summer the next year, I had saw a Volkswagen bug in the paper for sale. I told my father, who was a sucker for a Volkswagen bugs. He loved those cars. So that Saturday, we took a ride to check it out. The family selling it was just leaving for vacation. Five minutes more, and they might have been gone. They were asking $900 for the car. My dad pulled seven hundred cash out of his briefcase.

"Sold! To the pretty girl in yellow, to match the car."

I kept my Volkswagen almost a year, and then I blew up the engine. I had never put any oil in it. I even had a personalized license plate made, it read 2Q4U. After it blew up, my dad put it in the shop and we never got it out. I had some good times in that car. Star and I were dating these guys from the football house at

Sac City College. We ended up being exclusive with these guys. We made several trips to San Francisco on Saturdays just to go to the movies or out to eat. That was between time of me getting over Will, when I was sixteen, and before running into Chase and getting pregnant at seventeen.

His name was Edwin Dutch. He had come on a scholarship from Texas. He left to go home on off season. He wrote a letter to me and sent it to Candi and Star's address, hoping it would reach me. He mentioned that he would love to resume our relationship and possibly drive me back to Texas to meet his mother.

I was flattered, but by the time he returned, I was a few weeks pregnant with Nadia. We hung out as long as we could then, but I was too wrapped up with Chase. He wished me well and I never saw him again until that math class I took in college where I met TJ. He was walking through the hall when he noticed me standing there, holding Nadia. He was with a female friend, but he immediately stopped to give me a hug and hold Nadia.

"So this is the princess, huh?" "Yes, this is she."
"She is beautiful just like her mama." "Thank you."

TJ came out of the class and walked up to join us. "Hey man, how's it going?"

"What's up?" Edwin answered as he handed Nadia back to me." "It was nice seeing you."

"You too."

When I thought about it I had so many good guys I've met in my life! But of course, I wanted all the creeps!

CHAPTER TWENTY-EIGHT

I decided to take the kids to the parks. When we arrived at Miller Park, the first crew I spotted was Juelz's brother and my cousins.

"Park!" They yelled as I drove by. "Okay."

Once I parked and started to walk over, I spotted Jamie talking to Juelz's bitch, Yvette the one he had caught the case with.

"What the fuck was *she* doing over here?" I asked Jamie while walking over to the others.

"What the fuck is she doing?"

"Don't know." Said Steve.

"You wit us. Don't sweat it." Just when he said that the bitch started to get loud.

"Fuck a bitch, I got something for that ass!"

"Who the fuck she think she talking to? I *know* that bitch ain't talking to me on the sly."

At the same time, she went to waving a pocketknife in the air. "Oh hell *no! That* bitch ain't disrespecting me? I'll be back. I'm gonna to fuck her up, you watch! You better tell her! I'm going to fuck her up!"

I was not about to fight in front of the kids. I went to Candi's to drop them off at the house and I was coming right back. Vanessa had just got off work. Vanessa was Candi's niece, but we were all actually the same age.

Vanessa was the cute, sassy one out the bunch. I think she loved men more than I did. She did her own thing. She was not feeling me back in the day, and was always ready for a fight, just so hostile all the time.

She was the closest to Candi, but it wasn't until I went to jail that she realized how important I was to all of them. Our circle became small. Other females might have drifted in and out, but we remained solid.

"What's up?"

"That bitch up at the park with my folks waving knives and shit, disrespecting me. I told them I was coming right back to fuck her ass up!"

"Let's go get that bitch. Move over. I'm driving." Vanessa said. She and Candi hopped in. When we got back up to the park everyone was gone.

"They must have gone to William Land Park."

We rode over there. Once we made it in the park, we rode until I spotted her.

"There that bitch go!"

I jumped out before Vanessa could even stop the car. She didn't know what hit her. She tried to pull her knife out.

I grabbed her arm and twisted it around and that bitch fell to the ground.

"Bitch! Remember I *told* you I was gonna whoop your mothafuckin ass for answering my mothafuckin phone while I was locked up, bitch! And then you trying to be half-ass slick! You bet not never try me, bitch! I bet not never see yo mothafuckin ass nowhere near where the fuck I'm at, bitch!"

Her cousin tried to jump in, but Vanessa pulled her off. While the crowd tried pulling me off, Steve managed to get me off of her. He walked me back to the car before the police came.

"I'm buying you dinner tonight!" He said, squeezing my shoulders.

As we walked to the car I got in, the bitch came out of nowhere, pounding on my passenger window, where I sat.

"Don't move!" Vanessa yelled. "Stay in the car. We got this!"

She and Candi jumped back out the car and approached them bitches, swinging a machete.

"You bitches sure you want some of this?"

The crowd screamed and backed the fuck up. I got in the driver seat and swooped around to pick them up. We left the park and went home. I felt bad for what I had done.

I shouldn't have done that, I thought.

A part of me was scared I would get in trouble with my parole officer, and another part of me was really regretful. I felt I had no right to ever put my hands on another human being, ever. That stunt at the park won me rave reviews. It wasn't 24 hours before Juelz heard what had happened and was on the phone, hot and heavy, yelling at me.

"What the hell did you jump on that girl for?" I had enough!

"How the fuck are you gonna question me over that bitch?

Fuck you and that bitch! Let her send yo ass money and accept yo mothafuckin phone calls. Fuck you, Nigga!"

I hung up the phone. From there on out I was done!

CHAPTER TWENTY-NINE

I ran into Darwin. Dee the one I was locked up with he was her brother. He's the one who told her to look out for me. He didn't remember me from years back, but we used to flirt with each other at the club before I got locked up. But back then, I was with Juelz.

"Seems like I've seen you before."

"You have, I'm Juelz's woman the one that went to jail."

"That's right! How long you been out?"

"I been out like six months now."

"Yeah, you the one who I caught on film fighting up at William Land? That *was* you?" He confirmed.

"You filmed me fighting? I'm so embarrassed."

"Don't be embarrassed. You was tappin that ass. Yeah! I need you on *my* team."

"No you don't. I am not in the least bit proud of my actions. I do want to thank you for telling your sister to look out for me, though. You forgot all about that, huh?"

"That's right. I did tell her that shit. I remember we used to flirt back in the day, too. You remember that shit?"

"Yeah, I remember. Juelz would have killed me, but it was funny to me."

"You always been fine to me, with yo chocolate ass! It's just something about you that has always made me smile. I like that your presence always made me feel good. Like now, my ass is cheesin' for no reason. Them big pretty ass lips of yours, all shiny and shit, just make me want to kiss you."

"You are so crazy! We are *not* going there." "Why not?"

"Nah man, I'm good."

"Okay, if you say so, but don't be surprised if the next time I see you, I just walk up to you and kiss yo ass." He said with a big old smile on his face.

"Whatever, man!"

I knew I could not go there with him. We had strong chemistry, but with him that would just be another mess for me. That would be one piece of wood I would just have to *pass* on!

CHAPTER THIRTY

I had to go to the Target on Broadway and Riverside to pick up a few things. I was always nervous about going into stores, worried about someone recognizing me and possibly talking about what I did, or asking, "when did you get out?"

That is the reason I chose to work at the Target way on the white side of town black people only go in the circumference of their surroundings.

"Danielle Manning?"

When I heard my name spoken in just that way, I turned to look into familiar brown eyes. As we stood there and took each other in, my heart raced. He examined me from head to toe, stopping me dead in my tracks. He wore gray slacks, a dress shirt and tie, and he was clean cut, with a mustache and a goatee.

"Hmm, hmmm, Shyran?" "How you doing?"

"I'm fine."

I thought I sounded cool and confident, but in actuality I was aroused at the thought of our last encounter four years earlier.

"When you get home?"

See what I mean?

"Last year November, about eight months ago." "Wow, girl you looking good!"

"You too, all grown!"

"Girl, I *been* grown. What you talking about?"

"Well, last I remember, you was wearing a do-rag and some Dickies."

But now he was looking twice as delicious with his grown man on.

"Funny that's not the last memory I have of you." He laughed. The look in his eyes said everything! "So you doing alright?"

"Yes, I'm fine."

After the small talk, he finally got around to asking me what he really wanted to know.

"So where you staying? At your mom's?" "No, I actually live downtown."

"Me too. Where about downtown?" "On O Street."

"I stay on Q Street."

"Oh, okay then."

All the while thinking, *Am I really going to give this man my number...? Yes!*

"If I give you my number will you call me?" "Sure."

As if for on second thought, he asked, "Wait are you *seeing* anyone?"

"Oh no. Not at all." "Okay. Call me.""Okay."

He grabbed a pen from his shirt pocket and wrote his number down on the back of an old receipt.

"It was nice seeing you." "You too!"

I knew I was going to end up seeing someone I knew. He was the last person I expected to see. He was still sexy, a grown man.

On the way back home, all I could think about was that dick. The anticipation of what I knew was going to happen put a smile on my face.

We talked over the phone. Even though we were catching up on lost time, I was waiting anxiously for him to ask when he could come over. As I sat there, holding my breath he began.

"Do you think I could stop by Sunday after church?"

Oh Lord! He goes to church?

"Church?"

"Dang girl! Why you say it like that?"

"No reason. I was just surprised you said 'church'." "Yeah, man. I'm *saved* now. No more of the old Shy." "Well, that's cool."

Inside I was screaming, *No, No, No! He changed more than his clothes!* While we continued talking, I tried to have a general conversation and ask the right questions and give the right answers. I just wanted to know 'why'?

"How old is your daughter now?" "She's four. Do you have any kids?"

"Yes, I have a two-year-old daughter. Her mom and I didn't share the same beliefs. She's a Jehovah's Witness and she did not want to join my church. I tried to work it out, but she wouldn't let me be the head."

Half-listening, I was still saying to myself, *Why, Shyran?*

And then he said the one thing I didn't want to hear.

"So, I'm trying to do my own thing as a man of God. I've been celibate for two years now."

"Oh, wow! Celibate? Are you serious? I'm impressed."

Shyran and I became pretty close, with him living around the corner. We started spending a lot of time together. We got to know each other as friends all over again, without the sex. I was still used to three meals a day, so I often invited him over for dinner after his hard day of work, or breakfast on Saturday morning. One morning, he brought his daughter over for me to comb her hair before church.

"Why don't you and Nadia join us?"

"Join you where? At Church? Hell nah! I'm not going to church!"

"Why not?"

"Because I don't want to!" "Why don't you want to?" "Because I don't, Shyran!"

"Okay, maybe I can convince you to join us another day." "Whatever."

We continued to keep each other company, I guess you could say. I invited him over for dinner by candle light. I wasn't trying to temp him. I just wanted him to know I cared about him and hoped he wasn't too offended that I wasn't willing to go to church with him. I made broiled T-bone steaks, baked potatoes and asparagus that was my specialty dish! After dinner, I put Nadia to bed and we relaxed on the couch.

"You mind if I take my shoes off and get comfortable?"

"Not at all. Let me help you. Can I give you a foot massage?"

I took his shoes off and went into the bathroom and got a dry towel, a hot towel and some lotion. I lit some candles and turned the lights down.

"Massage my feet? You're serious, aren't you?" "Of course I am. Look I have all my stuff."

I sat down in front of him, placing his feet on the dry towel, and I wrapped his feet with the hot towel. Once I saw his toes, I took it upon myself to give him a pedicure. He had pretty feet.

"Relax. Lay your head back and tell me your deepest desires for your life."

"My desires?"

"Yes. How do you vision your life five years from now?"

"I know I want to be financially stable, married with more children, and maybe even a deacon in my church."

"You want to be *married*?" "Yeah. I desire a wife."

"Why? So you can have sex?"

"No." He laughed.

"You're funny, Ms. Manning."

"I'm just asking."

As I continued to rub his feet, he began to watch me intensely, as if there was something else he desired or wanted to say.

"I better go. My mind is going to a place it doesn't need to be." "Really? Okay. No, we don't want that to happen. I just wanted you to be able to relax."

I finished up his foot massage and placed his socks back on his feet. He put on his shoes and grabbed his keys. I walked him out and we said another goodnight under the moonlight.

"Good night Danielle." He said, as he hugged me tight and gave me a big kiss on my cheek.

He felt so good, he wrapped his arms around my neck as my face melted into his chest. If I closed my eyes, I could still smell him.

Isaac. He had a best friend that he always confided in, named "Man, remember back in the day when we were living in G- parkway, and I got hooked up on that blind date with that girl, Danielle?"

"I remember you tellin me you ran into her at Target."
"Yeah, yeah, so I *did* tell you already."

"So, what's goin' on with that?"

"Man, it's a trip. We talk every night and she's been cooking dinner for me and she's invited me over for breakfast a few times. She's been over to my apartment. She's the one. She is so sweet, and she is good with my little girl."

"Are you serious? You haven't slept with her, have you?"

"Man dude, of course not. We already did that back in the day, and it was perfect then. I already know how that will be. After dinner, she massaged my feet."

"Your feet? What was *that* all about?"

"That's what I'm sayin. I have never seen a woman do the things she does. She can cook, she's clean and neat. She lights her candles and her apartment is immaculate, everything in its place. It's just one thing missing."

"What's that?"

"She won't go to church."

"To church? Well, is she saved?"

"I don't know. No, yeah she *is*, but she needs to rededicate. She was baptized when she was a teenager. If she would only come to church, God will touch her, and I promise you I will ask that girl to marry me."

"Man, you serious huh?" "I am. I love that girl!"

After that night, I didn't see Shyran for a while. I started to feel that I didn't want to see him. We continued to talk on the phone every night, without the house visits. He thought that would be the safest thing to do, with him being celibate and all. He asked me what my dreams were and about my heart's desires.

I let him know that I hadn't planned that far ahead and that my heart didn't have a desire just yet. I had recently come out of a depression related to the crime I had committed. Being back at home in society, I feared being judged and didn't know where to turn.

"*That's* why you should come to church with me! God has forgiven you, so you have to forgive yourself and ask Him to guide you. He will do it. I promise you."

I believed he would have, but I honestly hadn't even thought about it. I shared my experience in jail with Shyran, about leading the ladies in prayer and going to bible study. But since I got home, I couldn't remember if I even prayed.

We kept the same routine. I started getting out a little more. He would always catch me coming home from somewhere, headed up my walkway, just as I was putting the key in the door.

"Where you been, Ms. Manning?" "Over Candi's."

"What are *you* doing?" I asked as I entered my apartment. "Come on in."

"*That's* what you wore today?" "Yes."

"Don't you think those shorts are a little *too* short?" "No! Why?"

"I'm just saying."

I didn't know what he was trying to insinuate, but what the hell was he worried about my clothes for? We started going back and forth about my wardrobe. I guess I did wear short dresses and short shorts everything was always short. So what? He didn't hold back his opinions and still was insisting I go to church with him. That really started to get on my nerves!

If I was in the Big park, he always made his way to drive through there, and if he saw me standing on the hoe corner, or posted on the sidewalk at the Big park, he would always stop, park, get out and come over to talk to me, no matter who I was talking to.

What was he doing stalking me? The minute I spotted him, I turned and acted as if I didn't see him. That didn't stop him. He would still walk right up to me and ask me what was I doing and why I had on whatever outfit I was wearing. By the time I made it home, he was right there. We continued to have the same discussions, and he continued to ask me to go to church. I always declined.

Sunday afternoon, Tamika came over to see what I was doing.

She was all dressed up.

"Where you going?" I asked her.

"Oh, I just came from church with Shyran. Mind you, yes he was my friend, but she also knew him. I didn't say a word, but best believe when we had our nightly conversations, I jammed him up about it. By then, I could see his true colors.

"Well, you said you didn't want to go, so I asked Tamika."

"Okay, whatever."

I ended our phone call abruptly. I didn't hang up in his face. I just acted as if a call was coming in on the other line and told him I would call him back. After that little charade, I was done. I no longer wanted to communicate with him on any basis. At least when I had sexual desires, I couldn't see his faults.

CHAPTER THIRTY-ONE

There was something new in store for me. No one really knew about me or what I had been going through. No need to alarm anyone, *but this next one, Oh!* Sound the alarm!

"Who is that?"

"Oh, that's Juelz's woman, Danielle."

"Ain't that nigga locked up for a few years?" "Yeah."

"Then that ain't his woman den."

That was Lem. He had just gotten out of prison, sentenced for twenty-years. I noticed him sitting in the house as I walked through my grandmother's door. The way he looked at me, I knew he was asking questions. I announced that I was about to walk up to Oak Park Market.

By the time I got there, Lem was pulling up in his car.

Gotcha! I said as I smiled to myself. This guy was fine! Black chocolate like Wesley Snipes fine! He was 6'4, nice, athletic body frame not too skinny not too fat, just right! He had pretty white teeth, a low fade, and was dressed fresh to death! When I walked to the back to get a soda, he ended up on the next isle, getting water.

"What's up?"

"What's up?" I replied.

I walked to the register, paid for my soda and left. *Yeah, he'll be next.* I always knew when a guy wanted to holla at me and to what extent he would go to talk to me when I paid him no attention.

By the end of the week, I was standing up at the market chillin, as I read a magazine in the window. Lem walked through the door, taking me by surprise.

"What's up?"

"What's up?" I answered. "You."

"Me? What you mean by that?"

"You already knowin what it mean. What you doing posted up here for?"

"No reason. Just chillin." "What you doin later?" "Nothing."

"You want to go to the movies or go get something to eat?" "Yeah, sure."

"Where you stay?" "Downtown."

"You got your own place?"

"Of course. My mother stays across the street." "That's where your little girl is?"

"Yes."

How did he know I had a little girl? He must have really been asking questions.

"When you going home?" "In a minute."

"Well, give me your number and I'll call you for directions when I'm on my way."

"Okay."

When I made it home, I went right next door to see if Tamika would babysit.

"Got you a hot date huh?" Tamika's mom teased. "Yeah, with this dude named Lem."

"Oh! We know Lem." "You do?"

"Yeah he grew up with my sister's boys back in the day, before he went to prison for all those years."

Well damn?

Lem had arrived with no problem. Nadia fell asleep on the couch for the night.

"You got a baby sitter?"

"Yeah. Tamika lives next door. She says she knows you." As I went to pick up Nadia, Lem stopped me.

"Wait. Let me get her for you."

He picked up Nadia and carried her next door. Once they answered the door, they were happy to see him.

"Oh, look! He's carrying the baby."

He handed Tamika twenty dollars and thanked her for babysitting.

"No problem. We love the kids."

That night was wonderful. We went to the movies and saw *The Fugitive*. I wasn't too big on suspense movies, but I didn't mind, since that was what he liked. All the food places were closed by the time the movie was over. I couldn't eat if I wanted too. I was so excited to be on a date with someone new. That night we hit it off well.

On the way home, we talked about different things and about how it felt to be home. Out of nowhere he began.

"I don't ever want to be away from you, Danielle." I didn't know what to say...

While I made breakfast in his T shirt, I could smell us, which made me remember everything I did the night before. He brought out a passion I felt comfortable sharing with him. The way we touched, our lips, our hands, and everywhere felt uncontrollable.

I put my mouth on every inch of his body. The way he felt in my mouth made me want to eat him up. No chocolate has ever tasted so good! I had no idea what he had in store for me. I really felt that I was being made love to, and I knew I wanted to feel him inside me again, and again and again. This was someplace I needed to be.

Lem made love to me slowly and gently. As we kissed, it was if our bodies became one. I couldn't believe all the things we talked about in that one night. It was as if we poured all our hurts out to one another and promised to be there for each other, no matter what anyone said. We both knew people would start talking and hating the fact that they were fuckin around. He didn't owe Juelz anything, and neither did I.

We became inseparable. We spent most of our time outside the hood. We visited his mother often. They fell in love with

160

me and Nadia. He had four sisters. One of them was in prison too. They loved their brother, and his mother loved her son.

"If my son loves you, then I love you. He needs a good woman so he can give me some grandbabies."

I tried not to look shocked by that statement. By the fall, the word was out that we were together. Everyone was telling me I was wrong for being with Lem that I was breaking the code messing with someone from the same hood.

"Whatever! Them niggas wasn't saying that while Juelz had two bitches and left me for dead, doing my time."

I told Lem what was being said.

"Let me handle all of that. Don't even worry about it. Ain't nobody going to disrespect my woman while I'm around."

That morning, we woke up, looking into each other's eyes as we planned our day. Lem jumped in the shower. We ate breakfast, and then he ironed me and Nadia's clothes, while I took a shower. I got Nadia dressed first, and then myself. We dropped her off at my mom's for the day. My cousin, LeAnn, was having her baby shower. Lem took me to Mervyns' to pick out a gift. As we looked at baby clothes, we thought of us picking out our own baby clothes.

"You know you my woman, right?" "Yes, I know."

"You want to get married?" "Yes."

He grabbed me and kissed me. "I think we need to plan that."

We laughed to each other at the thought of really getting married.

I couldn't believe things were going so well between us. He was always home by eleven and he always called to let me know he was on his way. On one particular night, he didn't call. It was almost one o'clock in the morning and I hadn't heard from him. When I looked at the clock, I began to get nervous. He was too consistent. Something was definitely wrong!

I heard a knock on the door. It was Tamika, she had the cordless phone in her hand.

"Danielle, Lem on the phone. He's in jail." "Oh, damn! Hello?"

"Hey, baby."

"Hey baby! What happened? Are you okay?"

"Listen baby, I'm going to need you to come down and get my property and go get my car from Gene's house. I got a ride with him back to my car when the police pulled us over. He had a *gun* in the car. That's an automatic parole violation."

"So you can't get out?" "No."

"Damn, baby!"

"I know. Just make sure you come up here and get my property, so you can get my car before them niggas break into it."

"Okay, I will."

"I love you, baby. I'm sorry. I started to come home early and I didn't. I should have followed my first mind."

"I wish you would have. I knew something was wrong when you weren't home by eleven."

I had "collect calls" blocked on my phone so Juelz wouldn't think about calling me.

"I'll make sure I take the block off the phone in the morning." "Okay, baby. I gotta go. I love you."

"I love you too."

I hung up the phone and it felt like my whole world had sunk to the bottom of my stomach. Lem had got sentenced to six months. I thought that would be the longest six months of my life. I did just as he told me to. I went and got Candi and told her the bad news. I asked her to follow me downtown to get Lem's property. I told her to drop me off, take Nadia to school then come back and pick me up.

She pulled up just as I was walking out. She hopped in the passenger seat, and I drove to where Lem's car was parked, off Florin Road.

"You can have my car now." He told me to keep his car and drive it."

"For real?"

"Hell yeah, girl. I ain't trippin. You can have it." "Okay, shit! Somebody about to be mad as hell?"

She was talking about Rochelle's bother, CJ. She had three kids by him. She had just had a little boy, about six months. All they did was fight. They'd been knowing each other since elementary school. Hell, two of Candi's siblings married two of his siblings and they were following suit with all those kids. He had been best friends with her forever and now he wanted to show his ass! Didn't make no sense. They would actually fight. I hated to see that. He was hen-pecked, until she cussed him out and one of his friends told him to *beat* her.

You told Harpo to "beat" me!

Lord that is just what happened. It was a wrap. That nigga started staying out all night and all that shit. That summer, he started fucking around with some girl who drove a Jeep. Candi kept noticing this Jeep riding through the hood, but she never put two and two together. It wasn't until then that shit was getting ugly. She told me to ride with her somewhere.

"Where the hell we going?" I asked her.

She was up to something. Usually it was me plottin'. It was, like ten o'clock at night.

"I ain't seen CJ's ass all day and I bet you he at Marquisee's apartment they got over there off of third, where they be taking different bitches to. They were all friends. Evelyn's Marquise and CJ it was about four of them that hung tight.

"Pull up in this alley. They parking is in the back."

Damn! She wasn't lyin'!

"There go that Jeep. He in there with that bitch. Come on!"

We parked and went around the front to find the apartment number.

"I remember him saying the apartment number when he was meeting Marquise and those guys over here. Here it go number eight!"

When she put her ear to the door, she could hear him talking.

Candi started banging on the door. *Bam! Bam! Bam!*

"Open this mothafucka!" She yelled. She had had a pipe in her hand, she said she was gonna fuck him up. And there was that pocket knife she always carried. She was walking in circles, heated!

"What we gonna do?" I asked her.

163

"Kick the door in. This mothafucka think he slick. Kick the door in!"

"Are you sure?"

"Hell yeah! Kick that mothafucka!" "Okay, stand back." I told her.

I stepped back and propped my foot back to catch my balance, and then *BOOM!* I kicked the door. It moved a little.

"Kick it again!" She shouted.

I got my balance again, stepped back and *BOOM!* The door went flying open! Candi rushed up in that apartment. That nigga was sitting on the couch, like he wasn't doing anything.

"Where that bitch at? I know she in here! I seen her mothafuckin Jeep parked in the back! Where she at motha fucka?"

"Man, Cee! Ain't no *bitch up*in here."

"You's a mothafuckin lie." Candi protested as she looked in the bedroom. When she opened the closet door, the girl was hiding under some dirty clothes. Candi pulled the bitch out by her hair and drug her into the living room. I was weak.

"Oh? Ain't no bitch up in here, huh? Who the fuck is *this*, then?"

Candi kept slappin the girl in the face, while CJ tried to get Candi off of her. So they started fighting. She dropped her pipe. CJ had grabbed Candi by her hair, so I was trying to break them up. Candi had the girl by her hair in one hand while she socked CJ with the other. CJ had Candi's hair, trying to pull her down. I was trying to stop CJ from holding her hair while I was socking him and the bitch at the same time.

She finally let the girl's hair go and the girl ran out the apartment. Then I was punching CJ until he let Candi go. When he let her go, he tried to go out the door, but she grabbed her pipe and went to chasing him in the corridor.

She popped him with the pipe on his arm, and then she pulled her knife from her purse and went to poking him with the knife. She was popping' him with the pipe in one hand and poking him with the knife in the other. I kept trying to tell her to stop, but my ass was cracking up! That nigga was crying, flinching and shit every time she went to swing that pipe. She even thought it was funny and she started laughing.

"Man, this shit is crazy! Come on, girl you don't want to end up in jail like I did." I said. "Come on! Leave him alone. Let him go, Candi!"

She let up off him after a minute. We left and went back to her mom's. It set in after a while and she was mad all over again.

"Can we stay with you? I don't want to be nowhere near that mothafucka."

"Hell *yeah*. Don't trip."

She packed up her kids and piled them in the car. She made sure she had the car keys, and she hopped in my car with me.

We settled in at my place. I made them a pallet in the living room. I offered her my bed, but she said they were cool on the floor.

"Okay, make yourself at home."

I went in my bedroom. I left the door open a little, in case she needed something. Nadia was at my mom's, as usual. Through the night I could hear Candi crying. Oh! My God she was crying. I felt so bad, but I knew exactly how she felt. I always kept my tears to myself.

Everybody always thought I was solid, but after what I went through, I was shedding hella tears in my own closet. Morning came, and as we talked about what was happening, she began to cry again! *Damn! Stop that, please!* I didn't know what to do. I had never seen my friend cry before. *Damn it!* I was holding the baby, with his cute self.

"The only thing that would make her feel better was time, and that was some real shit. That shit gonna hurt for a minute but not forever."

"Girl, did you see that nigga's face?" Candi laughed.

"Girl, I thought you was gonna kill'em!" I responded laughing.

"No, bitch but you really kicked that motha fuckin *door* in!"
"Hahaha! I know, huh? Hell I got some skills. I know he was like, *What the fuck?*"

165

We laughed at that shit for a minute. She was going to be all right. The dust just had to settle.

CHAPTER THIRTY-TWO

L em and I got to know each other even better over all the phone calls and letters. It was the day after Thanksgiving. I called Tamika,

"You want to go shopping?"

It was Black Friday, the biggest shopping day of the year. "I don't have any money."

"Don't worry. I got you. How fast can you get dressed?"

"You ain't said nothin but a word. Let a nigga get her wig straight and I'll be ready!"

I spent five thousand dollars in three days, buying Christmas presents for Lem and Nadia and stocking my cabinets with toiletries. I went and scooped up Candi and took her shopping. We hit up a gang of stores in the mall and went to Victoria Secret and bought us some matching bra and panty sets.

I had had at least six months' worth of stuff to last us well after Lem came home. I took a picture of the Christmas tree to show Lem all the gifts that were under the tree for him and Nadia.

He told me to keep his car and drive it not to let any of his family members come get the car, because they weren't going to take care of it. He also told me not to let them borrow any money, because they would try to use me. Once he gave me those instructions, it was like they did everything he said they would do.

In that forth month, they started sending messages to Lem, telling him I was riding with some dude in his car. The "dude" in the car was my brother, who had moved around the corner. I told Lem I got a job at the new Super Wal-Mart.

"That's good, baby. I'm proud of you. That's the type of store you can grow with by you being one of their first employees."

I also let him know I moved to a two-bedroom apartment in Greenhaven. Once I moved, I put all his clothes in our walk-in closet. I wanted everything to be right when he came home. The more I tried, the more trouble came and even double the rumors. I had been faithful to Lem the whole four months.

I had even put a brand new CD player and speakers in his car. Then one day, while I was working, Lem's friend came by the store. I had remembered seeing him with Lem over my dad's. We had met up over my father's house on their wedding day, before they moved to Georgia.

I had let him know that I had moved and was getting my spot ready for Lem to come home. I made the mistake in telling him where I had moved. He offered to drop off a house-warming gift. I thought that was nice of him, so I gave him the phone number. I saw how he looked at me, but this was one I could not touch.

When he called that next week, I gave him the address and he said he would stop by one day. When that day came, it was unexpected. There was a knock at the door. I had just got out the shower when I answered.

I had become friends with the guy next door. He was very respectful, taking care of his two small children while his wife was away in the military. I thought it may have been him or my sister at the door, no big deal. When I opened the door, it was neither of the two. It was Lem's friend, Chase. Lord, another Chase damn! We were both shocked to see each other on either side of the door. He immediately turned his head.

"You straight come on in. I was just getting out the shower. I'll throw something on."

"I told you I would stop by to give you and my boy a house-warming gift. You never told me what you wanted."

"Yes, I did. I said a comforter set."

"You did say that, didn't you? Well, I'll give you the money and you can go pick it out yourself."

He pulled out a wad of money. That was all I needed to see two hundred dollars.

"Let me know if you need anything else. I'll look out for you while my homeboy gone."

"Okay."

We looked at each other, as if we knew what each other were thinking.

"I better go before I do something I won't regret." "Yes, I think you better."

He looked even better to me after I saw all that money. One night, he said he's was coming by to check on me. When he got there, it was late and all the lights were out down the walkway in the complex. As I opened the door, there was only light from the moon shining on the stairs.

He was on his motorcycle. It was huge and nice! He didn't waste any time. As soon as he stepped in, I closed the door, he pulled me to him and we began to kiss. I hadn't had sex in four months, and boy did his body feel good against mine!

"See what you do to me?"

He led my hand down his leg. We continued to kiss, down the hall to the bedroom, undressing each other until we made it to the bed. He pushed me down on my back and grabbed my legs. He spread them wide and put his face right in the middle of my thighs. Damn! He knew exactly what he was doing. It felt like that the room began to spin! I couldn't believe what I was doing! He kissed up my stomach on my neck and then my lips. He slipped his dick in so smooth and it was so good. Our bodies together could not be controlled.

We had to have been fucking nonstop for at least thirty to forty five minutes. Damn! How did he do that? I was out of breath and couldn't move a muscle. After he bit my ass cheek and said good night, he showed himself out. Every time he came by after that, we knew what it was. If we saw each other on the street, we knew to meet at the house that night. The more he gave me money and sex, it was as if I was forgetting all about Lem. Damn! How could I let things go this far? Sixty days away from the house?

Next thing I knew, Nadia's father had gotten out of jail, and I knew he was going to want to see Nadia. Somehow or another, he ended up coming over too. We were locked up during the same time. He hadn't even seen Nadia since she was one year old. I felt sorry for him. He pulled that same old sad story about missing me and wanting to be a family again. He was only saying that shit because Juelz was locked up.

Chase could never compete with Juelz, or anyone else for that matter. We were never really ever together. I was young, seventeen to be exact when he started running game on me.

That night with Nadia's father was like old times. Just the touch of that man sent me to another world. I had forgotten how persuasive he was with his words and how slick he was with his hands. He had me out of my clothes and he was out of his just as fast.

We were on the floor in my living room in the heat of passion. He went down between my legs so quick. I had forgotten how well he did that too. That was our favorite position. He always wanted me to get mine first, and boy did I every time! I felt my body explode. My heart was racing. Every inch of my body felt this orgasm, and he would always give it to me so hard that we would cum together during the next round. It was so intense.

That nigga knew how to eat some pussy. As he moved up on top of me, our lips met and we kissed as if we had never been apart. It was as if we belonged back together. By the morning, when we woke up, he went in to look at Nadia. I watched from the doorway as he admired his chocolate baby.

"She's my only chocolate baby, Dan."

That's what he called me for short. If he wasn't calling me Dan, he called me Slim.

"Are you going to bring her by moms later?" "Sure."

"We got a lot to talk about."

I didn't like the sound of that. What did he want to talk about? For sure he knew I was with Lem. If he didn't, he would soon find out from his uncle. He hated the fact that I was with his nephew. Lem had also told him that he better not disrespect me ever in front of him.

I did not take Nadia to his mom's. That was all I needed to hear. The next rumor out would be that I was getting back with my baby daddy, and that was definitely not the case.

Six weeks went by and I began to get sick. I worked in the bakery, by the middle of my shift I could barely stand up. I would have hot flashes and become short of breath. I would have to go and sit in the cooler. What was going on?

Different smells even made me sick. I couldn't even brush my teeth the toothpaste made me throw up. Damn! I was pregnant. Oh shit! Lem was coming home soon. The next question was, whose was it? I knew how potent my baby daddy could be, but I only slept with him one time. I had been with the other Chase too many times to count.

I told both of them the news. What did I do that for? I already knew what my baby daddy's response would be.

"Dang, Dan I never had two kids by the same mother. You will be the first. You know, if we move in together, you gonna have to get rid of all that furniture Juelz bought you. I ain't gonna be sitting on another nigga's shit."

Move in together? Hell no! Oh brother!

I told the other Chase about the pregnancy, and he responded. "I can't have no more babies. You gonna get rid of it?"

That bastard! I thought he would be somewhat thrilled. Not! For a minute I had forgotten the fact that he was Lem's friend. After that, he barely spoke to me anymore. He didn't touch me at all after that. It was just me and my stupid baby daddy now. I entertained him for a minute, but I couldn't go through with that shit! He made me sick!

I scheduled an abortion, but when I got there, I couldn't go through with it. I had gotten an ultrasound and saw this little figure of a baby just a kicking away. Oh my God! It's a formed baby! I called Chase when I got home. His response was not positive.

"Did you get rid of it?"

"No! Damn! I couldn't. They gave me an ultrasound, and it was moving around and everything I just left."

"I'll be over there tonight." "You promise?"

"Yeah, I promise."

All those nights I had waited for him to come through, and he never did. I had missed him, and boy, did I want some of his sex. He came through that night. I didn't know what to say, and as far as he was concerned, I didn't need to.

"Damn, I've missed you."

"I've missed you too. I guess I got scared. I don't want any more kids."

"I know, but you act like it's my fault. I told you I wasn't on any birth control when we started."

"Well at least we ain't got to worry about you gettin pregnant now."

"You are stupid" I said laughing. "Come here, girl!"

He grabbed me and pulled me on top of him.

"Damn you feel good, baby. You're so wet and warm." He felt so good inside me.

CHAPTER THIRTY-THREE

I had taken Lem's car to my uncle's mechanic, because it was over heating or something. He fixed it faster than I thought. It was still early, so I went to my mother's. The blinds weren't open yet, which meant she wasn't up. I sat in the car until I saw her open the blinds. I got out of the car, and a sharp pain hit me at the bottom of my stomach as I walked up to the door. I fell to my knees. I couldn't stand up. The pain was excruciating. I made it to the door, yelling for my mother to help me. She opened the door, "What happened?"

She helped me to the bed so I could lie down. It felt like something was coming out of my vagina. Was I bleeding? It felt like something stabbing me with sharp knives.

"What's wrong with you?"

"I'm pregnant. I think I'm having a miscarriage!" "I'm calling 911!"

"You're ultrasound doesn't look good. You will probably miscarry through the night. Go home, and keep your feet elevated." "At least you don't have to get an abortion." My mom said.

They released me from the hospital. I was scared to walk. Everyone met me back at the house. I positioned myself on the couch, with my feet elevated like the doctor said.

During the next few days, nothing happened. The last thing I could do was to have a baby. I suddenly missed Lem. What mess had I started? That next morning, when I woke up to go to the bathroom, the sharp pains came. I was having the miscarriage and had to be rushed to the hospital. As long as all this would be over before Lem came home, everything would be okay.

Nadia's father kept trying to hem me up. He was coming by the apartment late at night without calling, coming early in the morning, trying to spend time with me and Nadia. He had called one day, asking all these questions about the baby.

"What baby? What are you talking about? There is no baby!"

I hung up in his face and avoided the rest of his calls. I never told him what happened.

Lem came home. I couldn't even go pick him up. I had been let go from work after my miscarriage and I didn't have any money. There was no gas in the car, and I didn't tell him that I, sort of, bent his fender, and after putting in the new CD system, the car got broken into. I gave him directions to the apartment. I was still bleeding. I told him I was on my period. *Jesus!*

That next morning, I was in the shower, cramping and huge clots started dropping out of me. What was going on? I didn't want to wake Lem, so I called my girlfriend Amiria, and told her what was happening.

"I'll be right over to take you to the hospital. Does Lem know?" "No, he's still asleep. Hurry!"

I put some sweats on over the towel I had between my legs. "Baby? What you doing?"

"I'll be right back, baby. Amiria wants me to come over her house to help her do something."

"Oh, okay."

I leaned over the bed and gave him a kiss. When we got to her house, she immediately called the advice nurse at the hospital. They called an ambulance for me. I had lost a lot of blood. When I arrived at the hospital, they ordered an emergency ultrasound and found that I needed a D and C.

They hooked me up to an IV. I had become weak and dehydrated. Once they released me, I rested the remainder of the day at Amiria's. We talked about the whole situation I was in and tried to come up with a plan to get me out of it. I called Lem to let him know I was still over there.

"Okay, baby. I was wondering when you didn't come back, and I don't have her number, so I couldn't call."

"I'm sorry. I forgot to give it to you."

"Well I'm in the P, so I'll see you later on tonight." "Okay."

Everything seemed okay at first. I mean, we were home together for the next few weeks, so no one had time to spread any lies, but one morning fate had had its last word. Lem and I were having a beautiful morning. We laid around in bed nothing felt better.

As we were making plans for the day, his sister had called. She was still locked up. Lem thought of going to take some pictures so we could send them to her. I talked to her for a minute, and she said she couldn't wait to meet her new sister-in-law.

As Lem and I kissed each other passionately, he loved the feel of my breasts. He was squeezing and sucking on my nipples.

"What was that?" "What was *what?*"

Lem squeezed my breast, and milk had squirted out.

"Oh shit! What the fuck *was* that? I know that is not what I *think* it is."

"I don't know. Maybe it's from my birth control. I don't know?" "That's some bullshit. That was milk coming out your damn..." He couldn't even finish his sentence. He was not buying it.

Damn! It was over. Lem got up, got dressed and left the house without saying a word.

That weekend he didn't come home. He wouldn't answer my calls. I cried the whole weekend. When he finally called, he had said we needed to talk.

"I only did six months, and you couldn't even be faithful! That ain't cool. I can't *trust* you. I told you I wanted to marry you. You didn't even go around my *mom* while I was locked up."

"You told me *not* to." I cried.

"But damn! I didn't mean at all. That's my mom and you didn't even try to get to know her."

"I'm sorry. I wasn't thinking."

"You weren't thinking about me. That's for damn sure!" I couldn't say anything.

"I can't be with anyone I can't trust." He hung up the phone.

I figured it wouldn't have been as bad if Nadia's father's name had come up. I had a baby by him. Everybody would have expected that he would say he was fucking with me. And I thought for sure that the real secret wouldn't get out. Wrong!

Chase must have told him everything. He knew I cared about Lem, so he didn't care.

When I came home, all Lem's stuff was gone from his side of the closet. I had bought his clothes and he took all of them. My heart dropped. I plopped down on the bed and stared into the closet. Krishna came in and told me what happened.

"He came in with one of his girl cousins and she helped him get all his stuff. He did introduce me as his sister-in-law though, if that means anything."

Damn! He left me. I tried paging him, but he never answered my pages. I was sick. I cried every night for the next month. He didn't call. I had messed up with the only man who had fell in love with me and put me first, not caring what anybody said. He treated me so nice, and I fucked it up! He found comfort in my cousins, and they didn't even try to defend me or help the situation. *Bitches!*

All kind of rumors came out that weren't even true. I could deal with the truth, but all the added lies just made things worse. It was not right. I stayed away from everyone. I decided to start school for Office Technician. I found it hard to even go to school every day. I left school early on some days, because I just couldn't concentrate. I wanted to ride the bus and think about all my mistakes.

By my birthday, I had lost the baby fat. My body felt brand new, but my heart was heavier than it had ever been. Amiria thought I would feel better going out to the club to celebrate my birthday. She was right.

After a few too many drinks, the pain was gone. I felt even better when all eyes were on me especially when he walked through the door. I returned to the table from the dance floor.

"He's watching you girl." "Who?"

"Chase." "Where is he?"

"Don't turn around. He's starring at you right now. He's over by the bar."

I wanted him to see me having a good time, with a flat stomach. I returned to the dance floor, making sure he was watching my every move. After dancing, I made my way through the crowd to go outside. I felt him following me.

I walked a few feet down the street, stopped and turned around. There he was. My heartfelt heavy again. I wasn't over him. It had been a while since we spoke.

"So, how have you been?" "Like you *care*."

"I *do* care." "You didn't act like it when I was pregnant." "Come on! You *know* I can't have any more kids."

"You act like I wanted to keep it. I was scared. You could have come to check on me. I had a miscarriage, and they fired me from my job."

"I'm sorry. I just couldn't keep coming around you like that.

You know what effect you have on me." "Whatever, man. You're full of shit."

"Wait!" He said as he grabbed my arm. "Let me make it up to you. Let me come see you tonight, so we can talk."

"Hell no! Just keep acting like you've been acting not giving a fuck about me."

That night, I went home. My drinks had worn off and my heart was back heavy. As I sat outside, my neighbor came to join me. He was a really nice guy. We started leaning on each other for the comfort of good conversation.

"Would you like to come in?" "Yeah, the kids asleep?"

"Yeah, I saw your dude moving out." "Yeah. That was a big mess."

"Well, it's his loss no matter what happened." "No, I think this time, it *was* really all my fault."

"We are not perfect. We all make mistakes, and we learn from them. Then you won't make the same mistake with the next guy."

"What next guy?"

"What do you mean? You are a beautiful woman. There will be another."

"No time soon if I can help it. I lost him and I did that. I fucked it up all by myself."

I didn't want to cry, but the tears rolled down my face. He held me and told me time would heal the pain. As he wiped my tears, I looked into his eyes. I never realized what pretty brown eyes he had along with those eye lashes.

Gazing at me with compassion, he kissed me. I didn't want to kiss him back, but he continued to press his lips against mine, forcing his tongue in my mouth. *Oh shit!* I thought. *What the hell is he doing? What are we doing?* I knew he missed a woman's touch, but why *me*? Why now?

Once he started, I knew he wouldn't want to stop. He wanted to feel it to feel his body inside a warm, wet place.

"I can't."

"Please?" "No, I can't!"

"Please! I'm begging you. I *need* you."

He held on to me tightly as he unzipped his pants with the other hand.

"Please baby? Please don't make me stop." He had tears in his eyes.

"I'm lonely and I want you."

He kissed me once more, hoping that would convince me to let him have his way.

I didn't fight it. I enjoyed the fact that someone needed me. I longed for that passion he was giving me. His body was so hard. I couldn't resist. Our bodies moved together in an unheard of rhythm. We lied on the floor in each other's arms. Then I began to feel so dirty. Tears began to fall again.

"I'm sorry." He whispered.

"I'm sorry."

"I know. I better go."

"Don't go."

"No, I really need to."

I felt dirty. In this case, I wanted to wash away my shame. That next morning, he invited me to breakfast. It was an *I'm really sorry* gesture. He said he had been drinking wine all night and he couldn't help himself.

"Let's just forget it happened."

From that day forward, we developed a close relationship. We could talk about any and everything. He became my therapy. Just knowing that the sex was good, and if I said go, he would be there at the drop of a hat. That was better than the real thing friendship. I moved out of the apartment into a one bedroom in another building.

It was the memories of Lem being gone that were still too much to bear. Boys II Men had come out with a new CD. The whole CD seemed to sing about my whole situation. How did they do that? The very thing you are going through, a song came out about it. My favorite was *Water Runs Dry*.

I stayed up many of nights by the phone, hoping Lem would call. He never did. I knew I had to get over it. As I continued to go to school, the pain got easier. When I got paid on the first I called my uncle and asked him if he would take me around to help me find a car. He agreed.

"Pick me up over Candi's house when you are ready."

When I arrived at Candi's, I told her my uncle was coming to get me.

"Girl, where are you two going?"

"I'm going to find me a car, and I am not coming back until I do. I'm going to use my whole check. I don't care. When I come back, I will have me a car."

We rode around the whole day all over town with a newspaper going from place to place. No luck. By the end of the day, it was time to head back home. We took the downtown route to avoid the traffic on the freeway. Along the way, I spotted a "For Sale" sign on a blue Toyota Corolla. I couldn't believe it, it was in perfect condition, with no dents and a perfect interior, and it had a sign for $500 in the window.

"Let's call. I want it!"

When I walked around the car wouldn't you know it had a grey door.

"Dang!"

"You can paint that." My uncle said. "Sure can. I don't care."

We called the number and the owner, who was just getting off work, said he would meet us in five minutes. He was just around the corner building.

Wow! We had almost given up. Thank you, thank you!

I gave the man my whole check. I didn't even think about the gas in the car. There *was* none. I made it back to Candi's house, honking the horn.

"Oh my God! You bought this car?"

"Yep! I gave him my whole check. We just bought it from a guy downtown about thirty minutes ago."

"For real?"

"Yes! We rode around all day. We even went out to CarMax and saw nothing."

"You said you were going to buy a car, and you did."

It was a small Toyota, but it had great A/C. It was too hot to keep riding the bus back and forth to school. I rode through the hood hoping to see Lem. Each time I saw him, I tried to get his attention, tried to get him to talk to me. He just ignored me. I even pulled up next to him, but he would just drive off while I was talking. That was cold.

I stayed away from everyone, doing my own thing. Graduation was coming up. My friend April and I stuck it out and finally finished. I remember how we met.

"I'm going to be taking roll. All present say 'present' when you hear your name called." Several names had been called.

"April Dixon." "Present." "Lydia Goins." "Present."

"Margaret Lawson." "Present."

"Danielle Manning." "Present."

"What's your name?" April whispered to me. "Danielle Manning."

"*The* Danielle Manning? You're the Danielle that went to jail for murder?"

It took me by surprise. I was almost afraid to answer.

"Don't trip girl, everybody knows you didn't mean to do it. You did what you had to do, right?"

"Yeah."

After that, April became my close friend. I started working at Marshall's at night, for the holiday season. She had a little girl the same age as Nadia. We helped each other through school. She didn't have a car and was catching the bus. I let her keep my car while I went to work and she took the girls with her. Then when I got off at eleven, she would pick me up and I would take her back home. The girls would already have had their baths and be ready for bed. She was a big help to me.

The night of our graduation, Krishna left me a surprise gift. She had also moved in with me to the one bedroom until she could find a place of her own. The gift had a card attached to it.

Congratulations, baby sister! Wear this tonight and come out to the Radisson to celebrate at my friend's birthday party. Call once you're in the lobby.

Cool! I was up for a party. I showered and got dressed. The gift was a cute black skort and a classic white shirt with French cuffs and a pink and black tweed half-jacket to match. It was a real sexy, classy type of outfit. Krishna always had the best taste in clothes.

When I made it to the hotel, I joined my sister and her friends. She introduced me to everyone, and her boyfriend kept bringing me Shirley Temples.

I never knew that drink was just gin and cranberry juice. I drank so many, trying to loosen up, that they crept up on me.

A voice came from nowhere. "You're Krishna's sister?"

I turned around. "Yes."

"Well, you better slow down. I've been watching you. That's about your seventh drink."

"Yeah, I think I'm feelin it now." I said giggling.

"Yeah, looks to me that you are too. I didn't know Krishna had a sister. I've been knowing your sister for years. I'm Chase, by the way."

Oh no! Not another Chase! That would make it, what? Number three, or was it four?

"It's nice to meet you."

"They have this party every year, and I've never seen you." "No. This is my first time."

"Well, I'm glad you came." "Thanks."

I mingled a little more and then I caught up to my sister. "Girl, you is tipsy aren't you?"

"You know that's right. I'm feelin good." "I see you met Chase."

"Yeah. He's a cool brother." "Oh is he?"

Not long after that, Chase found me and asked if I wanted to go get some breakfast.

"Sure, let me tell my sister."

As we walked to the parking lot he spoke. "Are you in any shape to drive?"

"Sure I am." I giggled again.

"No, I don't' think you are. I'll drive your car and let my uncle know to follow us to the restaurant."

"Okay! If you insist." "I do."

We decided on Denny's. As we ate, I sobered up a little, but not much.

"Where do you live?" "In Greenhaven."

"Damn! That's on the other side of town. You're going to have to stay at my place."

"What?"

"Serious you can have my bed. I'll sleep on the couch. I can't let you drive home like that. I wouldn't be able to forgive myself if anything happened to you."

"Okay! If you insist." I laughed.

"You so silly girl! Let's get you to bed."

He gathered up everything and left the money on the table with a tip.

When we made it to his apartment, he was true to his word. He showed me to his room and where he would be sleeping on the couch in the living room. He gave me a shirt to put on. I felt bad for having him sleep on the couch.

"We're both adults you can sleep in your bed. I don't bite. I'll just draw a line down the middle."

"If you insist." He said laughing. "I insist."

I made it out of my top and jacket, and then I took off my skort. I didn't bother taking off my stockings I was too weak to move a muscle. We kept our word. I lied on one side, and he lied on the other. All of a sudden I was not sleepy, I was wondering how I ended up in this stranger's bed. He *was* a stranger, even if he did know my sister.

The next thing I knew our legs touched and we both rolled toward each other and began kissing. He was trying to get my stockings off so fast he ripped them right off of me. The shirt he gave me to put on, he pulled it right over my head. As he did that, he began sucking my breasts. He kissed me passionately.

I felt him inside me. He was big. None like I had felt before. He felt so so good. He pulled out and began to go down on me. *Oh shit! What was he doing?* Whatever it was, he knew what to do. He must have been a pro. He made me cum so hard, the damn room started spinning, but it might have been from all those drinks I had.

Damn! Where did he come from? A big dick, and he knew how to suck my pussy. He had me all over the bed, in all kinds of positions. He ran his hands through my hair as he kissed me. The next thing I knew, it was morning and all I had on was his t-shirt. Did I put that on? I couldn't remember. I looked over, and I was not dreaming. There he was, all bright-eyed and bushy-tailed.

"How did you sleep?" He asked, smiling from ear to ear with his head propped up on one hand.

"I slept good, thank you." "No, thank *you*."

"What time is it?" "Seven forty-eight." "I have to get home."

"Well, give me your phone number and take mine so I know you made it home safely."

"Okay."

I drove home quickly. Once I got there, I forgot to call the man. I had several messages on my answering machine.

"Danielle this is your sister, let me know you made it home safe. Call over to Mile's."

"*Beep.* Danielle where are you? You haven't called and no one knows where you are. Call us. We're getting worried."

"*Beep.* Danielle call us. We haven't heard from you." "Oh shit! Let me call this girl."

I called Krishna. After they cussed me out for not calling, they laughed at me for staying out all night.

"Where *were* you, slut?"

"I went to Chase's house."

"You did what? Are you crazy?"

She spent the night at Chase's house.

I could hear Krishna telling her boyfriend where I had been. He grabbed the phone.

"Girl, you must have been feelin really good?" "Yeah, somethin like that."

"Okay, you go girl!"

Krishna got back on the phone.

"Okay, we can all go back to sleep now." "Yes, especially me. Talk to you later." "Okay. Bye."

I hopped back in bed and slept until six that evening. When I woke up, I had several messages from Chase.

"Danielle this is Chase you didn't call me. I'm worried about you. Call me so I know you made it home safely."

As I lied in the bed, I star sixty-nined the phone, since he was the last caller.

"I apologize for not calling. I just woke up. I promise I will call you back."

I didn't think to take Chase too seriously. I didn't really know what to expect after my one-night stand. To my surprise, he kept calling. Two weeks went by before we saw each other again. We got along real well. I thought he was a nice guy. Weeks turned into months and when Valentine's Day rolled around, we agreed to exchange gifts.

I showed him the exact gift I wanted at the mall. We had learned each other pretty quick and the sex just made the relationship better. He loved to give oral sex, but he wasn't too fond of receiving it. That worked out very well, as far as I was concerned. He was rather large, and that was one thing I hadn't mastered.

"So *that's* all you want for Valentine's Day?" "Yes, that's all."

"Okay, I can work with that. Oh can you get me a ticket to the Ice Cube concert in April?"

"Ice Cube?"

"Yeah, me and my homegirls want to go." "Find out how much they cost."

I had already bought my ticket. I just wanted to see what he would say. He wasn't really the type to do that, but I guess he didn't want me to get an attitude if he told me *no.*

"You know I have to make sure I'm on my P's and Q's with you. You're spoiled ass will get an attitude, and you won't speak to a brotha for a week."

"No, I don't." I laughed. "Yes, the hell you do."

Valentine's Day finally arrived. April and I planned what I was going to do that night. We had gone to Pier 1 and purchased some candles and a red light bulb for his bedroom. April kept the girls that night and dropped me off at Chase's apartment. It was early in the evening. Chase had prepared a candlelight dinner.

When I walked inside the apartment, there were plates fixed and waiting on the table.

"Hey baby, Happy Valentine's." He said with a smile as he hugged me.

I always made him smile those cheesy grins. We loved how we made each other feel. When we kissed, Chase was real affectionate. I liked that.

He was a true man in every sense. That was something I had to get used to. He was in his mid-thirties almost ten years my senior. He wanted me to lose some of my hood rat mentality and always told me I was an *educated thug*, that I was a product of my environment.

"At some point, it's time to be more of a lady to set an example for Nadia."

Chase couldn't have any children, and he was also an only child. When he shared that, it broke my heart.

"I thought I was doing pretty good raising Nadia."

"You *are* doing a good job raising your daughter and everything. You're just a little rough around the edges. You'll cuss a nigga out in a minute. But I got love for you though Danielle, I really do."

I thought I was a pretty important part of Chase's life at this point.

"Did you want to exchange gifts now or later?" "Later would be fine."

"Okay, baby."

"You know I've never celebrated Valentine's. You special, girl! I usually get rid of a female before Valentine's and Christmas."

"That's a shame."

"Shoot ! What you talking about. You females get too attached and comfortable when a brotha buy you somethin'. The next thing ya know, she'll be trying to leave clothes at your pad. Then she'll want a key."

"You crazy!"

"I'm serious. So consider yourself lucky. I think you're a keeper."

The candles he had weren't burning brightly enough. I couldn't see my food.

"It's too dark. Can we turn the lights on?"

"It *is* kind of dark, ain't it?" We laughed together.

"I was trying to be romantic and yo thug ass, 'turn the lights on I can't see my food'." Chase said, shaking his head laughing at me.

After dinner it was time for dessert, as Chase would put it. *I* was his dessert. He loved to taste me. We went to the bedroom. "Don't you want to jump in the shower?"

"Yeah."

"I want you to kiss on my body tonight." He said, laughing.

I knew once he was in the bathroom, he would always lock the door, he would come out at the same time every time.

He always used the bathroom before he showered and he always unlocked the door before brushing his teeth. He didn't open the door until he did the mouthwash rinse. I had just enough time to put in the cassette tape I made with all his favorite slow songs.

I used his stereo one night at his apartment when he left and went to his bowling league. *Red Light Special* by TLC was the first song. I had to change into my lingerie and put in the red light bulb. He had unlocked the door. He turned the water off and I could hear him gargling.

I positioned myself across the bed and unpaused the play button. When the music began, he opened the bathroom door like clock-work. He couldn't believe what he saw. He had walked into the red room, with me waiting for him, with his present sitting in front of me.

"Damn, baby!"

I got up on my knees.

"You look so good." He said as he ran his hands over my body in amazement.

"Oh your gift, I need to put it on you."

He took the beautifully wrapped box, opened it and pulled out a gold herringbone necklace. He placed it around my neck.

"Thank you. Here's your gift."

I bought him a Calvin Klein gift set. I remembered him saying the scent smelled so good it turned *him* on. As we kissed, he laid me back on the bed. He pulled my lingerie off and went straight for his dessert. I was ready to feel him inside me.

"What's wrong?"

"I'm too excited. Feel my heart. I've never had anybody to do this for me. I'm in shock."

I laughed. "It's okay."

Everlasting Love by Chaka Khan was playing. That was his favorite song.

"When did you make that tape?"

"The night you left me here, while you went bowling."

"You pretty slick. I'm trippin. I'll never forget this Valentine's Day as long as I live. If I had a ring, I'd put it on your finger right now. Girl, you're special."

We talked a few hours to let the shock wear off. Then it was on. Whatever he had built up in his heart, he let it all out on my body... all ended well and I was pleased. We were knocked out.

Chase forgot he had to take me home. In the morning we jumped up, because both of us had to be at work. We arrived at my apartment and kissed our famous kiss goodbye. I ran up the stairs as Chase watched. I blew him one last good-bye kiss as I turned and waved.

Things were good between us. There were moments when I got an attitude for no reason or he did something I didn't like. I just had those moods where he got on my nerves. The clutch in my car had gone out, so he let me use his car while he was at work. I would drop him off at work and pick him up.

"I must really love you. I ain't never let a female drive my car.

What you doin to me, girl?"

One day, I had thought Nadia and I were going back to his place. Instead, he told me he had something to do and was dropping us off at my apartment. What did he say that for? I wondered.

"Why we have to go home?"

188

"I told you why."

I shut down. Every time I got upset, I would never express my feelings, I would just simply stop talking. I straight simply ignored anything he said.

"I hate when you do that shit, Danielle. I let you use my car. I do more for you than I've ever done for any woman, and you act so ungrateful. Damn! Danielle, you ain't right!"

I felt bad when he said all that, but I couldn't bring myself to speak or even apologize. When we got to my apartment, I got out the car, slammed the door and never looked back. I knew he would be calling as soon as he made it home. He did and I didn't answer. I waited for him to hang up and then I blocked his number to prevent his calls from coming through.

Anytime someone made me mad, I'd block they ass. We didn't speak for the next three weeks. It had gone into the next month. Chase was really sick of my attitude. He wished I would grow up, not to mention toning down my language. I didn't care! I did okay until I got mad and cursed him out. That's something he just couldn't stand from me. I toned it down all right, at least around him.

It was April. The Ice Cube Concert was coming up. I couldn't wait. "You get your ticket?"

"I did."

"Just making sure before you don't speak to a brother."

"There you go again. I got it, don't trip I would have felt bad asking you for the tickets after you got me my necklace on Valentine's Day..."

****

Somehow Chase had surfaced again. We hadn't started sleeping together though. We kept an agreement that this time it was business. I think I was rather offended that he didn't even try. He trusted me. He thought I had fallen in love with him, but it was more just lust. I kept his dope in my apartment, as well as huge stacks of something wrapped up like bricks that he told me not to "touch."

I respected his wishes, until one day they locked themselves up in my bedroom. I needed something and knocked on the door. When I peeked in, my bed was covered in money. That's what was wrapped up money! Oh my God! I had never seen so much money in my life. He left it again. By then, I was "touching" it whenever I needed to.

Would he know I was dippin into his money? He did trust me with all of it and I didn't want to give him the impression that I couldn't be trusted but there were things I needed and wanted and hell what was I to do.

"You off work today?"

"Yeah, why?" Vanessa replied.

"I'm about to come scoop you up. Get ready."

Vanessa was always down with me when I called. Let's go get the tickets to the concert. I got some more money from Chase.

"He gave it to you or you took it?" She asked.

"I *took* it, hell! He just gave me some money the other day. I forgot I had to buy three tickets for me you and Candi."

We went and got the tickets and stopped at the mall just to see if there was anything I needed.

Hell, it was the least he could do. I was cooking for them, all hours of the night. When Chase came by, he always wanted something to eat. So I made sure I had dinner ready and that there was enough for his brother or a homeboy he would bring.

"What you cook tonight, Sis?" His brother asked as he came through the door.

"I made some tacos, Spanish rice and some beans. You hungry?"

"Hell yeah!" He replied.

After I fixed their plates, they ate and went into my bedroom, as usual, to do their business. They left and this time Chase asked me to grab the bricks out of the closet that I had hid in a little crawl space with some type of door in the ceiling you could move.

For whatever next big transaction that would take place, he needed all that money. Damn! I wished I could've gotten a few more thousands. I must have spent ten thousand in the last month. I walked Chase out to the stairs. He grabbed my ass and gave me a kiss.

"Thank you baby." He said. "You're welcome." I replied.

I guess he didn't notice the money I had taken. It was so much money he probably didn't know how much he had to begin with. I didn't hear from Chase again. I would page him and he never called back. I had gotten pissed all over again.

****

"Mama, I've been seeing a lot of crows flying around lately.

Doesn't that mean something bad?" Vanessa asked. "It means death!" Her mom replied.

"Anytime you see a bunch of crows flying around at random, somebody is going to die, and if they don't die, something bad is gonna happen."

It was Saturday, the day of the concert, and it was time to go get our outfits. I called Vanessa and asked if she ready to go shopping.

"I'm not going. I been seeing crows flying around all this week and my mama said that means death. You know my scary ass don't play about that shit! Just give my ticket to Star. I ain't fuckin around at that concert, and it's Ice Cube too! I'm cool on that."

"Girl, you so crazy! Ain't nothing gonna happen at that concert, but okay let me go pick them up so we can go get our outfits. We'll tell you all about it! Bye."

I had gone to pick out a leather skort outfit for the concert. I bought a cute burgundy panty and bra set that was so cute. It was going to be my lucky set. The day of the concert I went over to Candi's, and we all got dressed over there.

Everyone was dressed and ready to go. I was driving Candi's brother's Chevy Caprice. It had more room and was cuter than my car. Candi's son came running out of the house, screaming for her not to go. We didn't know what that was all about. He'd never done that before.

"We'll be back, CJ. Go back into the house! Kiki!"

Candi called for her oldest daughter to come get him and take him into the house. He was kicking and screaming.

CHAPTER THIRTY-FIVE

"Park over there!"

"Way back *here*? You better remember where the car is." "There goes Steven and them."

"Oh, good! We'll park by them. We'll end up following them to the after party anyway."

"Yeah."

"What's up, Nigga?" "What's up witcha?"

We parked and got out the car... "Y'all look fly."

"You didn't know? You better ask somebody."

I was the biggest flirt of the three. I commanded attention wherever I went. Candi was so shy, but that's the one the niggas wanted, with her yellow ass! She was too scary. She wasn't going to talk to no niggas.

That was where I came in, always trying to hook her ass up with somebody. I just knew that night would be my lucky night. I was hoping to meet somebody I could creep with. My hair was fly just like Coko's in SWV. My china bangs were laid, my leather skort outfit was fitting my slim figure perfectly, with my long ass legs. They called me a stallion when I wore shorts. Yeah, I was cute that night.

The concert was the bomb. Everyone came out in the lobby. "Look at that bitch. She thank she cute, bitch."

I heard that remark as I walked by some bitches. Oh, that was Darwin's baby mamma. I didn't care.

"Bitch you just mad cause yo man wanna fuck me."

Somehow, she found out about me. She was just mad. Darwin was the furthest thing from my mind. We made it out to the parking lot. Just as I thought, I knew exactly where we parked by all the niggas hanging by the car.

"Where's the after party going to be?" I asked

"Down off Broadway. Y'all headin that way?" Steve asked. "Yeah."

"Come on. We ready." "We are following you!" "You buying breakfast?"

"Yeah whatever, Nigga."

I knew just the spot of the after party. We all hopped on the freeway, caravanning to the party, riding a good bit, passing the downtown area and connecting freeways. Star was in the back seat.

"Danielle, look who riding up on us." "Who is that?"

"Chase!"

"Look, look he wants you!"

"I ain't fuckin wit that nigga. Fuck him!" I sped up in order to pass him.

"He wants you, Danielle. Look he is really trying to get your attention."

Chase was on the passenger side. His brother was driving.

As we sped past each other, we went from one lane to the next. I meant what I said. I wanted nothing to do with him. I continued to refuse his calls and I wasn't about to let him get my attention that night. By that time, I was in the far left lane. He had no choice but to come up on my right side, since I cut him off.

"There goes the exit, don't forget to get off!" Candi yelled. "Oh, yeah!"

I was going ninety miles per hour. Everyone was basically left in the dust after our little chicken race with Chase and his brother. I sped up to cross over all five lanes. By that time I was floating, had to be going at least one hundred and ten. As I came up on the last lane, the car filled with reflections of lights.

"Oh shit! They shootin! Get down, y'all!"

"Oh shit! I'm about to wreck your brother's car!"

Once I spoke those words, everything went pitch black and everything was silent. It was as if my eyes were closed, but they were open in the midst of blackness. All I could feel was the weight of Candi's body on mine. That might have been the longest sixty seconds ever. We had hydroplaned off the divider. The car flipped five times and we ended up on the opposite side of the freeway. The traffic going west and the car was facing east. All of a sudden, we landed. It was if someone had turned on the lights. At the snap of a finger, cars were honking, and headlights were flashing. Bam! A car hit us head on.

"Are you guys all right? Everybody okay?" Candi looked at me. I appeared to be okay from Candi's view. "That motha fucka shot me." I said, as I lifted my hand to wipe whatever was dripping in my eyes.

Right then, Candi started screaming. When I wiped my brow, my whole cap was peeled. Blood was gushing down my face. Candi said she could see my skull, and that my right eye had collapsed.

"We got to get out of this car! Are you okay?" Star asked "Yeah, I'm okay." I replied.

"Can you move?" "Yeah, I can move."

In a daze, I proceeded to use the headlights to flash the oncoming traffic.

"I'll flash the lights. Then they'll know we're in the car."

I didn't know the front end of the car was smashed to the windshield. It had hit nose first, and then it landed on all four tires, which were flattened by the impact.

"All the doors are jammed!" Star yelled.

"See if yours will open. We have to get out of the car before someone hits us again."

Bam! We got hit again.

"We got to get out! We got to get out! Danielle just try to open your door?"

"Okay."

I opened the door. I leaned out and fell onto the ground, unconscious. The car was in the far left lane on the opposite side of the freeway, so they had to make it to the other side of the freeway. Candi and Star had to carry me. They were dodging the cars so we wouldn't get hit. The sounds were so loud the wind of the passing cars, the honking and the sound of the freeway. Candi was hysterical. She kept screaming!

"Take off your coat and cover Danielle up so she won't go into shock!"

Star placed one coat on the ground for them to put me on, and then they covered me up with the other. I lay on the ground shaking uncontrollably. I knew where I was. I just didn't know how serious the gunshot was.

"*Jesus, I accept you as my Lord and Savior. Jesus, I accept you as my Lord and Savior.*"

I kept repeating those words over and over. If I were to die that night I wanted to make sure I was saved and went to heaven. That was the only thing I could think about. Not my mama, not Nadia, nobody but to call on Jesus!

Candi kept running up and down the freeway trying to stop anyone to help. A car pulled over and two men got out.

"We saw the accident. Is everyone okay?" "No, she's been shot in the head!"

The two white men who approached Candi said they saw someone in a SUV shooting at us. They were able to follow the truck off the freeway to get the license plate number. Two black guys jumped out the truck and ran.

The man called 911 from his car. "Do you need to call someone?" "Yes. Call my sister, Jeane..."

"Hello may I speak to Jeane?" "This is she."

"Yes, I am calling for your sister Candi. There's been an accident. I'm here on the freeway and I stopped to help. The car has been hit several times and someone has been shot in the head and apparently didn't make it. The paramedics are on their way I just wanted to inform you of what's going on, your sister is not in any condition to talk."

"Okay, well thank you so much. Let me call my daughter and God bless you for stopping!"

Jeane immediately called Vanessa.

"There's been a bad accident with Candi. Danielle got shot, and she's dead."

Vanessa started screaming, "No! No!" "They're taking her to UCD."

"What about Candi and Star."

"They're okay?... I got to call Nivea to give me a ride, and I'll call you from the hospital." Vanessa hung up the phone.

"Nivea, there's been an accident with Candi and my mom said Danielle got shot and she's dead."

"Oh damn! Vanessa. I'm on my way!"

"Lord, is my friend gonna die? Please don't let my friend die, please."

Candi was crying as she ran up and down the side of the freeway, screaming.

"Is she alive?"

"Yes!" Star hollered.

"Oh shit! I thought she was dead! Okay, the paramedics should be on the way."

A man came to me.

"Do you know where you are?" "Yes."

"Do you know what day it is?" "Saturday."

"Do you know who the president is....?" "He's comin back! He's comin back!"

Candi screamed down the freeway. It was Chase. He was in the car, backing up the freeway ramp.

"He ain't gonna do nothing to us with this man standing here." Chase walked up to Star.

"You just shot at us, you shot Danielle, it was you!"

"It wasn't me! I saw the car flipping and I said, "Them peoples is dead!"

"No, it was you in that SUV." "No. I was in the black Camry."

"Well the police are coming, so you can tell them yourself." Chase turned and went back to his car and left. As he drove off, the ambulance and the fire trucks drove up. At the same time, Candi's brother drove up and got out.

"What happened? Who got shot?" "Danielle!"

"Is she going to be okay?"

"I think so. She's still talking and everything." "What hospital are they taking her to?" "UCD."

They put me on the stretcher and loaded me in the ambulance.

As we drove off, the car went up in flames. "I'll meet you at the hospital."

I was in and out of consciousness as the ambulance arrived at the hospital. I could feel them bust through the ER doors.

"We have a gunshot wound to the head!"

Star and Candi arrived at the hospital shortly after me. Everyone was waiting. Star began to cry when she looked up and saw her son's father.

"Who shot at y'all? Who did it? Do you know who did it?" Chase walked in.

"He did it!"

Everyone looked at him.

"I didn't do it! I just saw the accident from the freeway. Where's Danielle?" Chase asked.

"You ain't going to see her." everybody yelled.

"You shot her!" Chase kicked his shoes off.

"Arrest me then, arrest me. I'm telling you I didn't do it! I didn't shoot her!"

CHAPTER THIRTY-SIX

"We have to stop at Danielle's moms to let her know. Are you going to tell her she's dead?"

"Hell no!"

When they pulled up, Vanessa's heart was pounding! She ran to the door. *Bam! Bam! Bam!* My mom opened the door. She stared in astonishment.

"Danielle has been shot. They were in a real bad accident and they took her to UCD."

"Okay. I'll put some clothes on. I'm on my way now."

When Vanessa arrived at the ER, she went to find out where they took me. She found Star.

"Chase shot Danielle!" "Is she really dead?" "No!"

"Shit! What?" Vanessa yelled. "Where is Candi?"

"In triage 2."

"I'll be right back."

Vanessa saw Candi's father standing over her. She was describing what had happened. When she saw Vanessa, she began to cry.

"Chase shot at us, girl. Danielle got shot in the head." "Are you sure?" Vanessa asked.

"Yeah I'm sure! He was trying to get her attention on the freeway and she said she didn't have nothing to say to him so we was on the freeway switching lanes to get away from him. Next thing we know we go to get off on the exit and they shot in the car." Candi replied.

"Well you know that Danielle was taking money from him maybe that is why he's mad. She was keeping all his dope and money at her apartment. I remember she said she had been calling him and he wouldn't call her back so she thought maybe he knew and he was mad."

"Do you think that is why he shot her?" Candi questioned. "Why else would he shoot at y'all...where is she?" Vanessa asked.

"Where is she?" She asked a nurse, walking by.

"Where is Danielle Manning?" "In trauma 2."

"I was just in there that's not her. That's someone *else*." "No." The nurse stated.

"That's her."

Vanessa went back and walked behind the curtain, looking over me.

"That *is* her." She whispered to herself.

Vanessa started to cry. She didn't even recognize her friend. My face was so swollen and covered in blood. There was blood everywhere. Vanessa noticed the bullet holes on top of my head.

"Are you related?" "I'm her cousin."

"She's going to be all right. We have to shave her hair off to prep her for surgery. We're going to say this was a blessing. The bullet didn't penetrate through her skull. If it had, she would definitely have some type of brain damage."

"Thank you."

Vanessa was upset and returned back to the waiting room. As she came out, my mother was standing there. Vanessa was crying,

"Danielle is in trauma 2. she got shot in the head."

As my mother approached me, her heart raced. Her eyes skimmed over my body to get full comprehension of what she saw. She couldn't believe what had happened.

"Just pray." She said to me as she kissed my forehead.

"Okay, we're going to have to prep her for surgery. We're going to have to remove the bullet fragments. She will be placed in ICU after the surgery."

"Okay."

Vanessa was looking for family members to tell them what really happened. Candi's father, Earl, went back to confirm the story Vanessa told him. He returned to the waiting room, crying.

"I'm going to kill these mothafuckas! They shot at my babies!"

Chase was leaning against the wall with his brother, waiting to find out my condition.

"You mothafuckas shot at my daughters? You gonna to pay for this shit!"

Chase turned as they all walked outside. "I didn't shoot at them!" "Well how do you explain this shit? Star said it was *you* in the car."

"I was in the Camry."

"Then who was in the truck?" Earl left the crowd.

"I'm going to get my pistol."

Candi's brothers continued to try and get the truth out of them. Vanessa went to the pay phone to let her mother know what was going on. Candi and Star's brother's escorted Chase out of the hospital.

"Ya'll gotta get the fuck up out of here, man." "It wasn't me, man. I didn't shoot her."

Star thought they were going to kill him.

"How is Danielle doing?" Candi asked the doctor. "She's doing fine. She's in surgery."

My mother walked up to Star. "How are you guys doing?"

"We're doing fine. Where's Danielle?"

"She's going to surgery. She's going to be okay."

That next morning when I woke up, I was in a tiny room with a sliding glass door. I remember seeing my stepsister, Nell, standing at my door.

The nurses came in to clean out all the debris from my legs.

Glass had been lodged on the left side of my thighs and face. "Where was she? Where did all this debris and glass come from?"

I couldn't answer, but I could hear the two nurses discussing my wounds, as if I couldn't hear them. After a few days,

I was moved from ICU to a regular room. My sister, Krishna, was there, along with Bernard. She was standing over me in tears.

"Who gave anyone the right to do this? How can anybody just go around shooting people for no reason? Look what they've done!" I could see Bernard at the door and the look on his face. He looked as if he had been crying too. As he stared at me, he had to break the ice by cracking a joke.

"Man, what you looking like that for?" I mumbled.

"Man you lookin like the Predator. Shit! I don't know how you made it out that accident man. That was some crazy shit!"

I didn't pay him any attention. I didn't know what he was talking about. I felt as if I looked the same. My father arrived from Georgia. He sat in the chair facing the TV most of the time. It seemed everyone who came to visit me did the same thing. No one could look at me. My Aunt Norma came to visit. She was a nurse. She examined my sutures.

"How was your hair, in a freeze?" "No, that's the dried-up blood."

"Oh my! They have half of your head shaved off."

She didn't say too much else. I was going in and out of sleep. When I woke up, my room was dark. I was in the room with another patient. The curtain stayed drawn the whole time. My bed was the one closest to the door. They had me on a constant drip of morphine for the pain. The phone rang. It was LeAnn.

"Danielle, I have Juelz on the line. He wanted to speak to you." "Okay."

"Juelz, go ahead. She's on the phone, but don't talk too loud and too long, cause she can't sit up too good to hold the phone."

"Hey baby! How you doing?" I immediately began to cry.

"I'm okay. My head hurts really bad, and they shaved my hair off."

"Awe baby it will grow back, man you don't know how hard your boy finally prayed to the man upstairs. I told him please don't let my baby die, please!" "You my nigga man, I love you!"

"You hear me?" "Yes."

"You gonna be posted for a minute, huh?" "I guess so."

"They say that nigga Chase got at you." "I don't know who it was."

"Okay Juelz, Danielle we gonna hang up. Me and Evelyn will be up there later, you get some rest."

"Okay."

"I love you, mama." "I love you too."

I lied there in the bed and began to think of what actually took place. I was still alive. I hadn't heard the details of the accident, but I knew it had to be terrible. Just the fact that I got shot and I was the driver. God spared our lives.

My man Chase wanted to visit me in the hospital. I had forbidden him to come see me that way. However, I thought he would have come anyway, or he would have at least sent me flowers. He didn't.

CHAPTER THIRTY-SEVEN

Weeks went by. It was almost time for me to be released. "We're going to remove the catheter so we can get you to go to the bathroom. Make sure you call one of us when you have to use the bathroom."

I wasn't able to stand by myself. They took off the drip and started giving me Vicodin pills. They made me throw up. I had wondered what I looked like with no hair. Even though I was told not to, I crawled out of the bed to the bathroom to take a look in the mirror. When I held my head up to see my reflection, I couldn't believe what I saw.

"Oh my God!"

I stared at myself and began to cry. I touched my face in disbelief. My head and face was tripled in size. I remembered the film, *The Elephant Man*, and that's what I looked like. My eyes were slits in my face, with purple rings around them. And I was bald.

"Damn! What happened to me?"

My eyes were bloodshot. *Lord, please don't let me be cockeyed!* I already didn't have any hair. I wondered how long it will take to grow back.

I barely made it back to my bed. I was just about to faint when the nurse came in and caught me. I cried for the rest of the night and that made my pain worse. The pills made me sick. I had started throwing up again, but at the same time, the pills took the pain away, as if I was a peppermint, floating above the bed evaporating. I was sweating and my gown was soaked.

One last CT Scan before I could be released. I was so embarrassed about my looks that I covered my head and face as they wheeled me through the hospital to the radiology department. Everything seemed to be healing on schedule. I would be released from the hospital, as there was nothing more they could do. I would have to stay in bed the next few months to let my head heal.

I was still unable to stand or walk on my own. LeAnn and Evelyn came to pick me up. They helped me in the wheelchair. I covered my head again.

LeAnn had a minivan. I was able to lie down across the back seat. My head hurt so bad that I had to lie on my stomach with half my body off the seat to support my head. Every bump in the road felt like someone hitting me on the head with a hammer. When we arrived at my mother's, my brother was waiting on us outside the house. He opened the sliding door to get me out of the van. He had to pick me up slowly.

"Oh no! Look at my baby. Oh God, what did they do!"

He couldn't bear to see me that way. He carried me into the house into my old bedroom. My mom had it dark, with a lot of pillows for me to prop myself up. During the next month, my aunts and grandmother came to see me. They peaked in while I was in and out from the pain medication.

"I can't bear to look at her. Isn't it gross? My goodness! How long before the swelling goes down?"

"I don't know."

Nadia ran in the room to see me. I quickly put the covers over my head.

"Mama, don't let her in here! I don't want her to see me like this. If she sees me, she'll have this memory in her head for the rest of her life."

I couldn't do anything but sleep the pain away. My mom fed me Jell-O and apple juice for the next two months.

"Did you want to try and let me bathe you today?" My mother asked. "You got this room hummin, little girl."

"Oh, I'm sorry."

"No, baby don't be sorry we know you can't help it, but it's just time to get you a bath."

We made it to the tub. While I soaked in the tub, my mom changed the sheets on the bed and freshened up the room. I wasn't able to bathe myself. I just sat in the water and waited for my mother. Technically, I hadn't eaten any food for two months. I didn't realize how much weight I had lost.

The sounds were so unbearable. I had to put cotton in my ears to drown out the sound of the cars and the sirens from the busy street. I was still in so much pain. It was the worst headache anyone could imagine.

I moved into the other room across the hall. It was more towards the back of the house, a little bit better with the noise control. The noise from the other room traveled straight down the driveway. This room had a window that faced the backyard. "Juelz called again through LeAnn." "Hey, baby! So you home now, huh?" "Yes."

"I sure been worried about you." "I'm getting there."

"Say your boy starvin. You think you can shoot a nigga somethin?"

"What? No, I don't have anything to send you."

"Ain't that a bitch! Mothafucka what you *mean* you ain't got nothing to send me?"

"Juelz! What the hell are you talking about? That girl can't walk or even sit up still and you talkin crazy!"

"Sorry Danielle, I'll call you back later."

The phone hung up. *Did he just cuss me out for no reason?* He had lost his mind. That's all I needed on my brain right about then. My head hurt so bad I couldn't burry it far enough into the pillows. The cotton wasn't working anymore and that room became just as noisy as the other one.

After a few weeks, it was time for my last follow up appointment for a CT Scan at the hospital. When we arrived at the hospital, they had to send someone out with a wheelchair. He was cute! I was embarrassed. My swelling had somewhat gone down, but I was still bald. I wore a scarf on my head. He rolled me in the hospital and down the hall, to my room. It seemed like hours of waiting for the doctor, and I still had to go for the CT. My father was back in town. He was meeting us at the hospital.

A voice came from the hallway. His face appeared from behind the door.

"Where's my girl?" "Hi, daddy!"

"Hi baby. How are you feeling?" "I feel okay."

"Looks like you are coming along just fine." He said as he examined my sutures and my baldness.

When the appointment was over, everything checked out okay. My sutures healed well and they removed them. The same guy came back to wheel me back to the car. This time I recognized him, and he recognized my name from her chart.

"Danielle?"

It was Zack from the eighth grade. Boy, did he clean up well! He was tall and muscular. He was always shorter than me in school. He was a physical therapist. *Man, what a catch!*

"What happened to you?" "I got shot in the head."

"You are kidding? Are you going to be okay?"

"Looks like it. I'm just bald. They shaved my hair off." "It'll grow back."

"Well, it needs to hurry up."

We exchanged numbers and promised each other we would keep in touch. On the way home, I saw Chase's car at the café.

"Stop and let me out at H&B's."

I wanted to confront him. My mom had to go to the bank across the street, so she agreed to drop me off while she went to the bank. I stepped into the café slowly and saw Chase, sitting at one of the tables by the window, which meant he saw me get out of the car. I sat down at his table, right in front of him. He looked as if he had seen a ghost.

"Why haven't you called or come by?" I asked. "You don't care about me? Look at me!" I yelled as I snatched the scarf off my head.

He couldn't do anything but look down. He shoved his plate to the side, as if he was too upset to eat.

"What am I supposed to do? Am I supposed to walk around like this? I need some money. I'm going to have to wear wigs or hats or something. Can you pay to get my hair done? What are you going to do, Chase?"

He would not look up.

"That's what I thought. Fuck you! Don't you even look my way ever again! I hate I ever fucked with your ass!"

"I'll take care of it. I'll call the shop." "Yeah, whatever!"

I walked out as my mom was just pulling up. I was mad. My feelings were really hurt because, truth be told, I thought he cared about me, and for him to *do* me like that! He should have given me some money right *then*, and he didn't. He didn't care anything about me. That was fine. It was time to move on.

My friend, Amiria, picked me up. She was a beautician and she owned her own salon. She washed a pressed the little hair they didn't shave off in the back. As she wet my hair, I could smell the old blood in the steam of the hot water. My hair was smashed to my head. I would definitely have to wear a hat until I could get some type of weave. I guess they would have to glue the tresses to my scalp. My scalp felt better. It was itching like crazy, and the smell reminded me of the hospital bed and those sheets.

Bernard came by to see me. I was up and walking slowly. Any fast movements made me dizzy. I was ready to go visit the girls. Candi was still on crutches. Her ankles were severely swollen, but not broken. We rode around the corner.

"Slow *down*, man!"

My stomach dropped like I was on a roller coaster. After the accident, I was scared to ride in a car let alone a speeding one. When we made it to the house, I walked up the brick stairs to the porch. As I walked in, they were all in the kitchen.

"Hello!" I yelled through the house. "Is that Danielle?"

That was Mrs. Jones, Candi's mom. As usual, she was at the kitchen sink, washing dishes, cleaning up after preparing dinner, which is something she did every day. For anyone who was hungry, they could always eat. She always had enough for everybody.

"Yes, hey everybody!"

"How you feeling?" Candi's mom asked.

"I feel okay. As long as I walk slow, I won't get dizzy."

They started talking about the accident and what each of them felt.

"That was nothing but God to lift you girls up in the middle of all that flipping."

"What did you guys feel?" "Everything went black." "I know." Candi said.

"For me too." Star said.

"Everything went pitch black and it was quiet."

"Sure was." Candi said.

"All I could feel was your body leaning on mine."

"Me too! Oh my God! We all felt the *same* thing."

"That was the Lord. He lifted you up and held you there and kept you from harm." "Thank you for my dimple!" "Your what?"

"My dimple, see something hit me in my face and left me a dimple. The doctors said they don't know what it is. There is no metal in my face or nothing."

"Oh my goodness! You are crazy, girl!" "Did the police contact you?" Candi asked.

"No. No one came to my room or anything. Why? What happened?"

"The police said they asked you if you knew who could have shot you, and you told them *no*. Chase was at the hospital, and we told the police *he* shot you. He kicked off his shoes and shit talking about *Arrest me, then, if you think I did it. I'm telling you I didn't shoot that girl!*

So we thought you told them he didn't do it."

"I don't think he did it. The guys who shot at us was in a truck, remember. The lights were shining high into the car."

"He did that shit. I don't care what nobody say." Star said.

I didn't want to believe Chase shot me. Why would he? What did I do to him? I had a miscarriage. Was that a reason to kill me? For being pregnant? It just didn't add up.

My stepdad came into the room with a dozen roses. "Some guy came and dropped these off for you." "What guy?"

"I don't know. He left. He was in a gold old-school."

That was Chase give me a break! What was I going to do with some roses? I wanted to throw them in the trash.

He contacted Tavia, the baddest stylist in Sacramento, and scheduled an appointment for me. She called Evelyn to let her know he had paid for me to get a full weave. As I got back into the swing of things, more rumors started to surface. People were saying *that's what I get...*

I got shot because I stole Chase's dope. I got shot because I spent his money. The more people saw me, the more the rumors were made up. Hell, they even said I was dead. Boy! Black people will make up a story won't they?

Well, it was time to make my official appearance. It was Sunday, and everyone was going to the park. I was still staying at my mother's, so she could help me with Nadia. My daughter still went to Bret Harte, a school in her neighborhood, so that my mother could look after her when she got out of school. I put on her favorite jean short outfit.

Wow! Had I lost that much weight? The jean vest used to be so tight. I had to leave it unzipped under my breast. By that day, it zipped right up, and I had room for some more breasts. I must have lost two whole sizes. I was about a size seven-eight. I went ahead and put on a matching hat, hoping it wouldn't fall off.

I was still overprotective about my gun wound. I was scared something might hit me in the head again. It was still a sensitive spot. I didn't have any feeling at the top of my head. The bullet tore through all my nerves. They were dead. I never realized how many layers of skin covered the skull. Well, let's just say I have a major dent in my head.

I could only thank God. If I had been going any slower on that freeway, I might not be alive. That bullet would have gone straight through the side of my head and I would not be around to tell about it.

The car accident alone was a major miracle. God kept me around for a reason. I just had to figure out what that reason was. I always knew I was special. The ordeal showed me just how much my friends cared about me. For all the friendships I had, Candi really loved me. I know we have been with each other since we were thirteen, but now between me, her, Star and Vanessa, we had a bond.

I was thankful I was with them that night. Star said Candi was crying running up and down the freeway, praying that I wouldn't die. I was shocked to hear that. I never thought we had an emotional relationship, but I didn't know how important I was, until she named her daughter after me. They could have left me in the car, but instead, they saved my life. They made sure I was safe when I couldn't help myself.

When I was locked up, she had a baby girl, and she gave her my whole name, Danielle Marie. She was more than my best friend we were family. I wanted my next child to be named Candice, and I would call her Candi for short.

Yes, I thanked God for them. God's favor had always been on me all my life. I always tried to do the right thing, and I was raised to be honest and trustworthy. I attended Catholic school for eight years. I was honest enough to tell my father not to send me to Bishop Minogue, an all-girl Catholic high school. I was not going to get straight A's, so there was no sense in wasting his money. I wanted a taste of public school life.

All our older siblings and cousins went to Sac High.

Well not Shelise and Krishna they both went to Bishop Minogue, but that didn't mean I had to go. Once I got a taste of the hood, I loved it, but I still stood out from the rest, because that wasn't where I was from. My dad was wealthy and we lived in College Greens, which was like the Beverly Hills of Los Angeles, back then. Some of my best friends were white.

CHAPTER THIRTY-EIGHT

I got so many get-well messages on my answering machine and a bunch of sticky notes of calls at my mothers. Chase finally came to visit me at my mom's, and when I mentioned the fact that he hadn't come to see me at all in the hospital, he got all upset.

"Look Danielle I'm tired of dealing with you and all your moods and attitudes. You told me *not* to come see you, so I didn't. Now you fussin because I did what you asked me to do."

"Well you could have least called to check on me or something. I was just embarrassed of how I looked, but you could have reassured me that that didn't matter if you cared about me?"

"Man, I'm done. Have a good life!"

He got up, walked out and slammed the door. I just watched in amazement out of the window as he got in his car and drove off.

I didn't think any more about him. I moved back to my apartment. I was still on welfare, so my mother was keeping up with my bills and paying the rent. Jada started spending time with me. She was Bernard's sister. She was the sweetest person a skinny, dark chocolate, Barbie doll. We became real close.

Her nickname was Nana, and her mom gave her that nickname because she loved bananas as a baby. I shared my thoughts and concerns with her about my future. She was spiritual. Church was all she knew.

"I don't think I belong here anymore." "What do you mean?"

"I want to move away from here. I don't have any ties to anyone."

"Girl, you know Juelz will have a fit if he find out you gone and have moved out of state." She said, laughing.

"Please, he'll be alright, I'm sure."

"I don't know about that, Danielle. You know how them Negros be once you been with them, they think they own you."

I just laughed. I didn't care anything about that statement.

My father arrived in town and would be picking me up to attend church with him at St. Paul. The night before, I had a dream that I was being chased by demons. I mean, real scary, unimaginable beasts, with all sorts of crazy features. I ran, and when I looked up, the Lord was a ways ahead in my path. I started to scream.

"I'm running to you, Lord. Help me!"

I kept running as fast as I could, but it seemed as the Lord's silhouette never got any closer. That didn't stop me. I cried and continued to scream.

"I'm running to you, Lord. Save me!"

I was so scared that I woke up from my sleep. My heart was pounding. I was sweating and began to cry. When I looked around, it was daylight. Nadia stayed over my mom's, so I was alone in my apartment. I went in the living room and got my Bible from the table.

Oh Lord, please speak to me. Lord, the Devil was trying to get me, but I was calling on you, Lord.

When I opened the Bible, it rested in the book of Psalms. I read the first scripture I saw, Psalm 50:14.

Offer unto God thanksgiving: and pay thy vows unto the most High: And call upon me in the day of trouble: I will deliver thee, and thou shalt glorify me...

The Lord was with me. I anticipated telling my father about my dream. It was so real. I was still scared to death. I told my dad about my dream and he was so excited. He wanted me to share my testimony in front of the church. I wasn't trying to do all that.

When we got to church, one of the choir members was singing a solo, *Lord, I say yes!* That song ripped through my soul and I threw my hands up as tears rolled down my face. I cried out to the Lord.

As more time went by, I felt that there wasn't any more room for me in the hood. Too many questions unanswered. My close friends had shown me love, but not like I expected.

Chase shouldn't have been able to just walk around, and nothing happened to him. His brother, who once called me his sis- in-law when I cooked them dinner, couldn't even look me in the eye. Whenever I came around in public, like at the Big park, he would always leave.

I knew he was the one who shot me unknowingly, but nevertheless it was time for me to go. My sister always said I could come stay with her in Atlanta, Georgia. So I sold everything I had and bought two plane tickets for me and Nadia and didn't look back.

CHAPTER THIRTY-NINE

T he Chocolate City! Wow! I felt like I was in a dream. I never saw so many black people. They were working in the stores all through the airport, everyone was black.

"Hi Michelle!"

I hugged my sister as we met up. Michelle was actually my stepsister. She was the youngest of four girls on her mom's side, and I was the youngest of three on my dad's side. I adored Michelle. We were a year apart. I was introduced to my other sister, Nell, when I was fifteen. She was the daughter my father never knew he had. So, with her in the middle, she made up the fourth girl in each set of sisters, a total of seven sisters by my father's marriage to their mother. With that being said, I stuck like glue to Michelle. She was my favorite.

We had to take a train and a bus to get back to the front of the airport. That was new to me. It was like a subway in the airport.

"Is this *you*?"

"Yeah, this is my baby!" "It's cute."

Michelle had a cute black BMW with a kit on it. It fit her. Small and short, just like her 5'4" frame. She was cute and chocolate like me, kept her hair in braids (that she did herself), and stayed dressed, matching to the T. She was always smiling and she always went out of her way to give advice or help someone in need.

Michelle was real smart and read everything she could get her hands on. She served in Desert Storm while I was locked up. Our children were six months apart. We also were pregnant at the same time I was fifteen and she was sixteen. I had the abortion and God saw fit to take her son at three months old of SIDS. We weren't close during those times. We actually had just met. I didn't quite understand the magnitude of her loss. Once it all set in, I guess I blocked all the hurt out, for me and her.

We made it back to Michelle's apartment to put my things up. Then we took a ride through College Park. The radio station was off the hook, V103! They were playing songs I never even heard. I couldn't see much, since it was dark. Once daylight came, I saw the city was surrounded by pine trees, with no sidewalks. There was not even green grass.

Michelle's husband arrived home from work. It was my first time meeting him. I remembered my sister being glued to the phone until they got married. They met on a blind date. Mutual friends hooked them up. They made a cute couple. He looked just like a college guy light skinned, tall, slim, clean-cut with a nice fade. Yeah, they looked great together, and he seemed to be a nice guy.

They were in the process of moving to the second floor of the apartment building because the rain had flooded their apartment. I helped pack and move boxes while they were at work, so it wouldn't be much work on them when they got home. Michelle's son and Nadia were like two peas in a pod. You wouldn't see one without the other. We both hoped they would grow to be the best of cousins being Michelle and I were only a year and seventeen days apart.

Our birthdays were even in the same month. The move from the downstairs to upstairs put them right above an apartment full of guys. Yes! That was right up my alley. MEN! I loved them couldn't get enough of them. Every man was a new adventure, in my book. They made little comments as I walked up and down the stairs. Once settled in upstairs, I peeked out the blinds of the sliding glass door when I heard them hanging outside.

I was still shy at times, until I became comfortable in my surroundings. Every day, I would walk and pick the kids up from school, down the street. There was one guy who seemed to take a liking to me, and I liked him. Although we hadn't spoken, we held whole conversations with our eyes. I knew I had caught his eye and started hanging out on the balcony, while the kids played outside after school. It began to be like clockwork.

Everyone got home from work around the same time and they came outside to chill, talking about the day's events. I looked for that guy to come out once I stepped on the balcony. It was if they told him when I stepped out.

"Say, what yo name is? "What my name is?"

"Do you mean what *is* my name? "Yeah, yeah."

"My name is Danielle."

"Where you from?"

"California."

"That yo little boy?"

"No, that's my nephew. That's my daughter." "Oh, is that yo sister?"

"Yes. We see them coming in and out, coming from work and everything. They seem like cool peoples.

"She from California too?" "Yes."

"So you shy or something? Why you never come off the balcony?"

"I don't know, and what's your name?"

"Adonté. Adonté Lattimore. Come down so I can talk to you. I don't bite."

"Here I come."

I went inside and closed the sliding glass door. I ran into the bathroom and checked my hair and makeup.

"Okay. Here it goes."

I eased down the stairs. He was really cute. He had a different look light brown skin, kind of a thick, round, meaty bald head. He was just an inch taller than me, so that was short for a man in my eyes. He was thick and stalky, I guess you could say. He had no facial hair, or maybe it was because he had shaved. Oh, he did have a mustache just no beard. He was cuter than all the other guys, seeming to be the oldest, and he had a car.

We began to talk. He really seemed to like me. He started taking me out to eat no fancy restaurants, but at least it was food and it was free. Whenever we went, I made sure we took Nadia and my nephew. So when I did need some grown-up time, Michelle wouldn't have too much to say. She was pretty cool.

After a month of seeing each other every day, I really felt close to Adonté. It seemed as if we had known each other for years. He was so easy to talk to. We sat on the steps late night and shared our goals and dreams. I shared all my tragedies. He couldn't believe what I told him.

"Baby, you don't look like anything you went through. I hate to hear you had to go through all that. You could have been killed. You don't even look like you have been shot in the head. Just think? I would have never met you. God knew I'd been waiting to love a lady like you, and he sent me an angel all the way from California. I feel like I've been waiting for you all my life."

"Really?"

"I'm serious! Where you been all my life?" "In California." I replied with a smile.

"Well, you here now and I want you to be my lady." "Okay."

Adonté leaned into me and brushed his lips against mine. Dang! He could kiss too. I felt as if I just melted at his touch. The feeling he gave me went straight between my legs. I didn't want our night to end. I asked Adonté up to my sister's apartment, where I always slept on the floor in the living room.

We snuck in quietly and settled on the floor. I didn't want to make any noise, at the risk of waking up my sister or my brother-in- law. As we kissed, Adonté laid me down so smoothly I melted in his arms. When he got me out of my panties, I knew he had to have done this a few good times. He eased his way between my legs. I was so wet and he was the perfect fit. He loved me hard and fast. *When was the last time he got some?* Either he felt incredible inside me, or I just hadn't had any in a while. Whatever the case, I couldn't believe how he made me feel.

Was this really going to be mine whenever I wanted it? I was in another state on the other side of the world, and I had a man and some good sex. I was never going back to California. We were so excited, we forgot we were supposed to be sneaking a quickie. I hoped we weren't making any noise.

"Slow down! Don't wake up my sister. You're making the floor squeak or something."

"I'm sorry, baby. I just can't help myself."

I had to admit he felt like no other. I forgot all about a rubber.

"Oh no! Are you about to cum? Don't cum in me. Make sure you pull it out."

"I will, baby, don't worry."

The sex was so good and he was taking longer than I thought. The last thing I wanted was for anyone in the house to wake up and catch us on the floor. After we finished, I rushed Adonté out the door, I was scared because, as the door opened, it made noise. "Damn! Remind me to get your sister some WD-40."

"Shut up!"

He grabbed me just as I was trying to close the door and gave me one last kiss. He gave me butterflies with his kisses. My heart was pounding. I snuck back to the floor. I lay there scared to move. I didn't even go to the bathroom. I wanted to make sure I didn't make a sound. I just delighted myself in my thoughts of my last encounter and fell asleep with a smile on my face.

I looked forward to seeing Adonté. When he got off work, he made sure he checked on me, to see if we had eaten dinner or needed to go anywhere. Michelle didn't have a problem keeping Nadia. I got to know Adontés brothers and cousins who stayed in the apartment. Each night, I stayed late nights with him. Friday night, we lay looking out the window at the moon and listening to the radio.

"Man, I miss hearin all these songs. We don't have any radio stations like this in California."

We had so much chemistry between us that he couldn't resist me.

"You'll make a nigga kill over you, girl." "Well, we wouldn't want *that* to happen." "Oh my bad, baby you know what I mean. I'm crazy about you."

On the weekends I got to stay all night with Adonté. The way we made love every night was unreal. The long talks and plans to get a place together! There were so many guys in and out the house, you didn't know who lived there. But we always seem to get first dibs on the bedroom, because no one else had girls coming to the house, and they always stayed out late at the club.

I got a job at the mall, which was really far to travel. Michelle didn't tell me she wasn't on the bus line or nowhere near the Marta station. After a while, she started treating me funny, acting as if she didn't want me there. I had to catch rides to work. Michelle introduced me to her friend, Roxanne. They were all close in age, and Roxanne turned out to be a good friend to me.

So between her, my brother in-law and the guys downstairs, I was able to make it to work. Michelle had told me that her husband didn't like waking up on his days off to take me to work, so I should not ask him. I understood and tried not to ask him unless I absolutely couldn't find a ride. Adonté often went into work late to take me, but he always made sure he was there to pick me up.

I began to get real tired and hungry during the day, and I hadn't seen my period. On my next day off, Roxanne took me to a clinic for a pregnancy test. I was pregnant all right six weeks. Damn! I had to call back home and tell Candi. I didn't know what time was a good time to tell Adonté, but I was definitely telling him.

"Girl, what's going on with you?"

"Well for one yo man put the word out for me to tell you to please come back home."

"Who?"

"Juelz!"

"Shut up! You are lying. No, I ain't. He told Bernard he was about to get out and he wanted you back in Sac when he came home. He said please tell you he love you and you was his nigga."

"Oh Lord, ain't nobody studying him, and I am not coming back to California."

"Never?"

"Hell no! I'm six weeks pregnant!" "By who?"

"This dude I met girl. He lives in the apartment downstairs with a gang of niggas. You know I was like *whoop! whoop!* I been seeing him ever since I got here, and I just found out I was pregnant, so I had to call you."

I filled Candi in on all the ways of Georgia. I told her not to tell Juelz I was pregnant just that I was not coming back.

The closer we became, the more controlling and possessive Adonté got. I didn't understand it. He had started hanging out with the guys drinking, then he would call me down to fuck. He always seemed to start an argument for no reason. He went so far as to keep me from leaving the room, grabbing on me while he was yelling at me.

"What's wrong with you? Let me go!" I cried.

He pushed me into the closet door, and when it made a loud noise, his brother came rushing into the room to see what was going on. That was when I took it upon myself to walk out the door. By the time I made it out the apartment and up the first flight of stairs, he grabbed me and made me lose my balance, causing me to slide down the stairs. He caught me before I fell and Michelle came running out of her apartment. When she saw it was me she yelled,

"What the hell do you think you doing? You know she's pregnant. You are going to make her have a miscarriage."

She had such a big fucking mouth! I hadn't told him yet.

The nights got shorter, me and Adonté did a lot of talking over the phone, since I had more hours at work. One night, I heard a door slam from downstairs. Who could that have been at that time of night? I slept with the blinds open to let the moonlight shine through. When I peeked out the blinds, it was

Adonté walking down the parking lot. *Where is he going?* I stayed up all night, watching to see if he would return. He didn't. So where did he go?

The next few nights, I acted as if I was so tired that I wanted to go right to sleep. He didn't argue with me, like he usually would. He got right off the phone, and when he thought I was asleep, out the door he would slip. I would look out the window. *Where was he going?* He had to be going to someone else's apartment. Was he living with someone else? No one actually had assigned bedrooms in that apartment. Folks kind of just lied where they fell asleep. I stayed up all night again to see if he would return. He didn't.

Over the next few nights, Adonté repeated his routine after getting off the phone with me. Same pattern, he would wait until he thought I was fast asleep, and then head out down the parking lot. One day when I was off work, I hung out downstairs with the guys who were from the same town where my father was living. I found out who was with who, who was doing who, and I learned that Adonté shared an apartment with his girlfriend of two years. So that was it! Thanks for that information!

Men gossiped like women, although that time it was to my benefit. My plan was fool proof. I couldn't wait! I was going to tell Adonté I was so tired and that I wanted to go to sleep. So that way, I could catch him leaving. After getting off the phone, I posted in the stairwell of the third floor. I was dozing off. I was beginning to wonder if he was going home that night. *Did he find out that I knew his business?*

In the dark of night and just as I had planned, he tipped out about forty-five minutes later. I stood over the balcony.

"Where are you going?" Adonté jumped and turned to find me.

I headed down the stairs. My heart was racing.

"Where you think you going? Home to your girlfriend?" "I thought you were so sleepy?"

"Oh, I'm nowhere near sleepy, you liar." "Come here, baby."

"Don't touch me! So when do you think was going to be a good time to tell me you had a girlfriend and you lived together?"

"It's not what you think. We're like roommates."

"Man, who the fuck do you think you are *talking* to? I heard the whole story. Your friends can't hold water."

"I love you, baby. Let me explain."

"Don't bother and don't call me anymore. I don't want anything to do with you."

I ran up the stairs, but just as I got to the top, Adonté caught me by the arm.

"Don't do this to me, baby. I need you." "You don't need me. You have a woman." "Come on, baby."

"Don't come on baby me. Leave me alone, and don't call my sister's phone."

Adonté continued to call again and again, but I refused to speak to him.

"Dang girl, what you do to him? He's not taking no for an answer."

"He's a liar and I'm not fooling with him. I'm sorry he keeps calling your phone."

"Oh, it's okay. It's funny to me." Michelle said. "He knows how far to take it. He don't want me to act a fool."

Michelle had started acting funny again. *Why was she acting like that?* She was the one who asked me to move across the world. I made sure her apartment was always clean when she came home and before I had started working. I also made sure I didn't eat or cook any of their food.

The situation didn't get any better. Adonté continued trying to control me. He even became a bit physically abusive, grabbing on me when I chose to walk away and not listen to what he had to say. He watched me at work on his off days to see if I was talking to any dudes.

I had started getting a ride from the guy across the hall, and Adonté would sit in the parking lot, waiting for me to get home from work at night, trying to force me to talk to him.

By Thanksgiving, I felt my pregnancy full force. We drove down to my father's for dinner. I had never been there, nor had he been up to Atlanta to see me.

"Daddy lives in a little town, like Mayberry on Andy Griffith, you'll see." Michelle said laughing.

When we arrived, it was just like she said. We laughed with each other as we saw the little town, with one Winn Dixie. My dad wanted to take us around town and show us his office. I was not interested in taking a tour. I was just ready to eat. Soon as I ate, I went straight to sleep.

When I woke up, we sat and talked a while, and then it was time to head back to Atlanta. It was my turn to drive back. We had a nice visit. Michelle had already told them about Adonté and how he had abusive tendencies. *There she go, talking again!* I guess that's what big sisters do, but she ain't that big or that much older than me.

"Don't let me have to take a trip up there." "Okay, Daddy. I'll be fine."

"All right. Daddy has spoken."

He always said that when he gave us advice, when he didn't want to get involved.

My father just couldn't resist after that. He came up to Atlanta to co-sign on an apartment for me. I moved into the apartment complex Roxanne lived in, across the parking lot from Michelle. I was still receiving my welfare check from California. That would cover my rent, and I would use the money from working to pay my bills.

There was nothing in the apartment. Nadia and I were scared to lie on the floor. There were huge, flying roaches that came out of nowhere and end up dead in the middle of the floor. It was a Georgia thing. I never even saw roaches so big. They came from all the trees I guess, because these suckas had wings. I bought some RAID, so that helped a little. Michelle gave me a few blankets. We made our pallet on the floor. It was so cold that winter season that I kept the heater at ninety degrees so that we could just use a sheet as a blanket.

A few weeks went by, and Michelle's husband told me the hotel he was working at was giving furniture away in order to remodel. I came up on a king size mattress set with rails for one hundred dollars. We finally got off the floor. My back started to have a permanent ache. Michelle had never come to the apartment. Adonté didn't know we had moved. Of course, when he called, Michelle told him I didn't live there. He followed me and found out the location of my apartment. Then he would bang on my bedroom window until I let him in.

If I had already gone to bed, I would lie still in the bed until he went away, but when we were up, and our bedroom light was on, and I had no choice but to let him in, because he would not stop until I did. He constantly begged for me to take him back, for the sake of the baby. He would cry, kneeling in front of my stomach, kissing it and telling me how much he needed us and that he loved me. I didn't care. I had no intention on staying in Georgia.

"Can I speak to Chase?" "Just one minute." "Hello?"

"Hi. What are you doing?" "Danielle?"

"Yes, it's me."

"What's going on, slim?"

"Nothing. I'm coming home Thursday. Can you pick us up from the airport?"

"Sure. What happened? Decided you was home sick, huh?" "No. I'm pregnant."

"I knew you would come back to me. I just didn't know how." "Yeah. Well I'm coming home."

"Where's my chocolate baby?"

"She's in the apartment. I'm at the payphone down by my walkway."

I know he didn't think the baby I was carrying was his baby! I didn't say any different, but I definitely didn't tell him it was.

"You know, Bradley died. He got shot on the hoe corner by some Crips."

"Oh my God! For real?"

I instantly thought about the last conversation me and Brad had...

"Man, you know why that man shot you." "*What* man, Chase?"

"He knew he couldn't have you." "*Who* knew?"

"*Chase.* He knew he couldn't have you because you belong to Juelz."

"No way man."

"I'm serious girl. That's on the real. I'm a man. I know what's up, but you can trust me not to say anything. This conversation will stay between us. I know what I'm talking about now, believe what I say."

I always wondered if what he said was true. I mean, men always knew what other men were thinking and why they would do what they do.

"When is the funeral?" "Friday."

"Oh, okay I'll be back just in time."

My flight was scheduled for that Thursday morning. "So can you pick me up from the airport?"

"Of course. Just call me when you get in."

"My plane will be there at 10:30 in the morning." "Okay. Just call me."

I thought to myself: *What is the point in calling if I'm telling you when my plane arrives?*

"Okay. I'll call you when I get there." Okay, baby. You and my baby be safe." "We will.

"Love you. baby." "Love you too."

CHAPTER FORTY

When I returned to California, I was ten weeks pregnant. I quickly made an appointment at the doctor's office to have an abortion. I wanted it over with, so I wouldn't have to think about what I was doing or to have any regrets or guilty feelings. I was able to get right in. My mother knew something.

"Are you pregnant? You've been a lazy bones since you've been back."

Every time I ate, I lied on the couch and fell asleep,

"Nah... I'm just tired. I haven't gotten used to the time change from Georgia."

I couldn't think of any other excuse. This time, I wanted to keep the pregnancy to myself. I didn't want my mom knowing everything. I had just had a miscarriage the previous year.

I had to go to the mall to find some boots to wear to the funeral. I could always find a deal at Leeds, so I planned to go in and come right out. I already knew what I was wearing. I hoped I would not be showing too much through my dress. I couldn't fasten my jeans any longer.

The funeral was packed. I stood outside with Candi and Star. After the funeral, Chase walked right up to me, put his hands around my stomach and gave me a kiss. He looked so nice, but I did not want anyone to see my stomach, and it was already poking out. His hands landed on it just like a basketball.

Amiria gave me a ride to the clinic. "Will you be picking her up?"

"Yes." Amiria answered, as the nurse escorted me to the back. "We will need your name and number to contact you once she comes out of recovery."

I didn't think to ask if they were going to do an ultrasound, but I found it odd that they didn't.

They only confirmed the pregnancy with another test and prepped me for the procedure. I must have been given a local anesthesia. I could hear the doctor talking toward the end of the procedure. I could also feel a strong tugging from the suction. When would it to be over? *Should I be feeling that much pressure?* I tried to hold my breath, but I could only imagine the image in my mind. "Give me more suction." The doctor said. "Yeah, it's two of them."

Two? What did he mean, two? Was I carrying twins? Adonté was a twin. OH MY GOD! Did I really just hear him say that? I wanted to stop. I had always wanted twins! Why didn't they give me an ultrasound? Damn! I just wanted to block it out of my mind. The next thing I remembered, the nurse and Amiria were trying to wake me up.

I called to Chase's mom's house.

"Is it okay if I come over and lie down for a while? I don't feel so good."

I didn't want to go to my mom's.

"Oh, it's a house full of kids over here. They are having Keith's little girl's birthday party right now."

I couldn't go to Amiria's, because it was already late and she would have to bring me all the way back across town. I went across the street to Candi's moms. Candi lived with her mom, but she wasn't home at the time. Mrs. Jones always talked to me and gave me advice on life's situations, about things she saw or heard me and Candi were going through.

It was funny how she always knew our business. She would sit on the bed next to the window every day and just look out, from time to time watching who was walking or driving by, or who would be coming through the door. I could remember back when we were in high school. Candi's two brothers stayed in the rooms upstairs, which were right in front of Mrs. Jones bedroom door.

No girls were allowed up those stairs. I would always try to sneak up there to see Candi's brother, Travis. He was so fine to me.

I could remember him always saying, "You betta get out of here, Dennis Manning, before my mama catch you up here."

That's all he had to say, and I was right back down those stairs. Candi's older siblings always called me my brother's name, because my brother always talked about me as if I didn't have a name, and they claimed I looked just like him.

"So, you gonna keep the baby?" How did she know I was pregnant?

"I watched you around here since you've been back, eating and sleeping, hanging around Chase. Is it his?"

"No, I met someone in Atlanta, but I got an abortion today."

" Ask God to forgive you and move on. You girls just gonna mess up your lives, sleeping with all those no good niggas and having them babies. Get as much education as you can and keep your legs closed. Go back to school, Danielle. I try to tell your friend, but she don't wanna listen. I done been there and done that. I know what I'm talking about.

I stayed with the same man and had twelve children. That was my job. He took good care of me and my kids. We didn't want for nothin. You don't find many men like that these days. They want you to have all these babies and don't want to take care of them. I was with him until he died. That's when I met Candi's dad. I wasn't looking for no man, but he begged me to have Candi. He promised me I would never regret a day being with him if I had her, and I haven't."

CHAPTER FORTY-ONE

"**S**ome guy named Adonté called for you."
"What! Adonté? Did he leave a number?"

"No, he said to tell you that he called and that he would call you back."

How did he get the number? I didn't want to call to my sister's. After all, I left without even saying goodbye. Roxanne took us to the airport. I still had Michelle's key, so I took the blankets she let me have and left her key on the table.

She never once came to see about us. She didn't care how I got to work, even though I ended up quitting, because I couldn't get a ride to or home from work. Roxanne had started taking me and picking me up on her days off.

We were just better going back home. We had no food and no money. I had one pot, two glasses, two bowls and two plates. I never really settled in and I didn't want to be with Adonté. I became close to my neighbors upstairs. In the last few weeks, as I waited to leave for California, they fed us and we hung out with them every day. They were some real southern folk with great hospitality. I left them the king sized bed.

Before I got my own apartment, another relative of Michelle's came to live with them. Her name was Kendra. She had called me to check to make sure we made it home safe. I told her I was leaving. She also called to tell me she was the one that gave Adonté my number in California. She gave me the whole rundown on how Michelle and her husband were talking about me like a dog. She said she felt bad for me. I told her it was okay, that I didn't care and I was home safe and sound. I wished her well and told her to keep in touch.

I still received my welfare check, but it was only five hundred ninety five dollars. I needed a job. That was no money to raise a child for a month, even if I did live with my mother.

Jada came over to see me. "I need to find a job."

"Dedrick needs a receptionist at his studio." "What kind of studio?"

"A recording studio. You know he be dealing with all those rappers and that ghetto hip hop music."

"Yeah girl. He has C-Lo on his label."

"Girl, are you serious? You should have been told me that! Do you think he will hire me?"

"I don't see why not. Let me find out. I'll ask him when I see him."

"Call him now!"

"No? I'll hook you up. I'll let him know you just came back from Atlanta and need a job."

I was patient. I ended up having an interview with Dedrick. Jada had already told me he was going to hire me if I wanted the position. During the interview, I met the staff and Dedrick showed me what I would be doing. The pay would be nine dollars an hour. I wanted ten, but I guess that would have been pushing it. I was just thankful to have a job, and all I had to do was answer the phone.

Juelz found out that I was back. Somehow, he called on three- way to my mother's house.

"I'm going to be home in six months man. You still my nigga?" "Yes." I replied.

"If I put you down to come visit, do you think you can come see your boy?"

"Where are you?" "In Tracy."

"How far is that?"

"About an hour and a half." "I guess I could."

"Do you want to get a spot together? You find it and I'll pay the rent and shit."

"We can talk about it."

"Okay, mama. I'll try to get someone to call for me again, mama."

"Okay."

"I'm going to write you, so get at me soon as you get it." "Okay, I will."

"I love you man." "I love you too."

I didn't know what to think. Yeah, all I could think of was *I* was the one. He wanted to come home to me.

Over those next six months, I started driving down to Tracy.

When I wasn't going to visit him, I was writing him the most passionate love letters. I was in love all over again. I was so happy to have my man back. He had me to call on three-way to Yvette. His "drop" was parked at her house.

"Hey!"

"What's up?"

"I'm gonna have Jamie come tow that car, and have Danielle meet you for the keys. I don't want that nigga getting my keys. He might sell my shit for a piece of crack rock."

"You so stupid." "Who's on the phone?"

"Danielle." I said interrupting.

"Nigga, you got a lot of nerve. Yeah, tell Jamie hurry up and come get your shit from my house, Nigga."

Click.

She had hung up the phone.

"Why you had to say something, man?" "I thought the phone was on mute."

I knew what I was doing. I wanted that bitch to know exactly what was up. She may have had him then, but when it came down to it, *I* was his nigga now.

Evelyn and I decided take some Customer Service classes at the Urban League. It was a six-month course that certified students in Customer Service Training. At that time, Evelyn had moved in with Marquise. I remember Evelyn and Marquise together through high school. They would talk on the phone until five o'clock in the morning. It seemed like true love, even then. As he got older, he got into the dope game and he took that real serious. It was like it put him on some Top Notch shit. He made Evelyn into the lady she needed to be. He was her first and only. The difference between me and Evelyn was that Evelyn was the quiet and submissive type. I, on the other hand, would tell you what I was going to do, when and how, and I might even ask you if you had any questions!

That was the one thing Marquise hated about me. Wherever the party was, that's where Marquise was, without Evelyn, and I was always there, watching his every move so I could go back and report to my cousin. She found out that everyone was going to hang out at a restaurant called The Black Angus. It was like a night club on Friday and Saturday nights. I told Evelyn to come out with me. Marquise told her he was going out of town. When we got to the restaurant, it was packed.

As the night progressed, who did I see at the bar when we were coming from the bathroom?

"I thought you said Marquise was going to be out of town?" "He did *say* that."

"Well he's not anymore. He's at the bar."

We walked by and stood at the end of the bar, making sure that he saw us.

Wait! He didn't even speak to Evelyn. "What the hell? Who is that he's talking to?"

"That same girl he had been accused of messing with over the years."

"Nikiesha? No he didn't!"

As always, I had to be my ghetto self and confront him when I saw tears in my cousin's eyes.

"That's it!"

I walked up to Marquise.

"What the fuck you think you doin?" He didn't respond.

"Oh, Nigga, so you gonna act like your women who lives with you ain't standing at the end of this bar? You gonna *disrespect* my cousin?"

"Get out my face, girl."

"Naw, I want you to answer the question? Why you tell her you was going out of town. So she wouldn't know you was up here with the *next* bitch?"

"Man, you better get out my face."

"Or what? Nigga, what you gonna do to me?"

Before I knew it, I had slapped his drink out his hand and made it spill on his clothes.

"What you gonna do to me?"

By then everybody was grabbing me, pulling me away, in case Marquise felt the need to slap me. That would not have been good. I told Evelyn I would take her to her mama's house if she was ready. The fun was over! When we got in the parking lot, we spotted his car. The only red Chevy convertible with all white leather interior, sitting on some gold Daytons in Sac.

"Let's put his shit on flat!" I wanted to stab his tires.

"No, no girl. He'll really kill me then."

We found the caps to the air tube and unscrewed them all. "Yeah, now that nigga stuck like chuck." We laughed as we deflated them.

Boy, those days were crazy. That was the straw that broke the camel's back. After that stunt, Marquise showed up at Evelyn's window at about four in the morning, giving her whatever story he usually would tell her, but whatever he said, he made sure she was never to talk or to be around me again. When Evelyn told me that, she was like, "Fuck that!"

"How he gonna tell you not to talk to me?" "Girl, I ain't payin Marquise no mind."

I knew what that meant, she wouldn't be able to talk on the phone all night, like we always did, go shopping or out to eat. One thing I knew was that Evelyn did whatever he said. And that was exactly what happened.

So now that we were taking the class I got to be with my cousin every day. I never said anything. Who was I to come between black love? And believe me, if it was me in the same situation, I would have to choose the money, the car, and those clothes I suppose...

During those months of class, I drove Juelz's Buick Centurion convertible. I loved those days, when the sun was shining, me and Evelyn would both drive our drop tops and ride through the hood. She had a white convertible Mustang. That was the only time we got to hang out before Marquise would be calling for her to meet him somewhere and to go home. Like I said,

"It was cool I got whatever time I could take to spend with my cousin."

LeAnn had found out that Aaron had been fucking around with some girl named Charlene. Aaron was Juelz's cousin. This was the last time she was going to hear this chicks name. LeAnn made up in her mind that she was going to beat the bitch's ass. Of course she came and got me. It seemed that was what everybody did when it was about to go down.

"The bitch up at the big park right now. I don't need you to do nothing but make sure don't no other bitches jump in. I want this hoe all to myself."

"Okay."

Evelyn was on her way to meet up with us, but she had no idea what LeAnn had planned. We pulled up to the big park and parked on 33rd, across from the bakery. We walked across to the rock at the front of the park. There they were, her and her homegirls. LeAnn spotted her instantly and handed me the tiny backpack she had. When I grabbed it, it had a little weight to it.

"What the hell is in here?" I asked as I unzipped it.

It was a pistol. *Oh shit!* I made sure no one jumped in. When LeAnn walked up on Charlene, she didn't even say a word. She punched her right in her face, and it was on from there. LeAnn was beating that girl's ass! *And you know you got to give them hoes a speech like your mama used to do when you got a whoopin!*

"Bitch, didn't I *tell* you to stay yo ass away from my husband, bitch! I *gave* your ass a warnin!"

LeAnn was killing the girl. Oh snap! I don't know where her homegirls disappeared too.

"Now I'm going to take yo ass to Aaron and let him *know* I beat yo ass!"

LeAnn grabbed the girl by her hair and dragged her kicking and screaming all the way back across the park. By that time, Evelyn was walking toward us looking like, "what the fuck is she doing?"

LeAnn got to her car and was going to literally drag the girl down the street. Right when she was about to get in the car, Aaron pulled up. They must have called that nigga 911, because they came flying down the street. He screamed for LeAnn to let the girl go, trying to get her to calm down. Her friends pulled up behind Aaron, and once the bitch got out of LeAnn's grasp, she ran and jumped in the car.

I looked around, and everybody was at the park, trying to see just what the hell was going on. Vanessa had made it through the crowd.

"What the fuck happened?" She asked.

I filled her in and Aaron took her keys, so LeAnn couldn't drive her car.

LeAnn walked over to Evelyn, Vanessa and me.

"Who rollin? Evelyn, I'm driving your car." "Okay." She said.

"I'm down. Let's go get them bitches!" Vanessa yelled.

We hopped in Evelyn's convertible Mustang and rode down every street. We circled around and could not find them. So we ended up going down Stockton Boulevard to Fruitridge. *Damn! There they go!* They were stopped at a red light. LeAnn hopped out the car. When they saw her coming, they locked the door, but didn't roll up the windows.

Charlene was sitting in the back seat, on the driver's side. LeAnn started punching her in the face. She tried to pull the girl out the window. When the light turned green, cars started honking their horns. As soon as they were able to move, they tried to speed off, but they weren't trying to have the girl fly out the window. Leann was forced to let go. Vanessa got in the driver's seat.

"Come on. We gonna get them bitches!"

LeAnn jumped in the back with me. We chased them all the way down Fruitridge to 24th, and when the light turned red, they ran it.

"God damn it!" Vanessa yelled.

We looked at each other and fell out laughing. When the light turned green we busted a U-turn and headed back to 33rd.

"What the fuck was you doin?" Evelyn asked.

"You drug that girl all the way back across the park!" I replied. "Shut the fuck up!" Vanessa said, as she fell out laughing. "That bitch got her ass beat. Oh my God that shit was hilarious! And she had the nerve to give me the backpack with the pistol."

"Hell, you never know. You know they think we *crazy*, especially *yo* ass." LeAnn said.

"Yeah, and I don't like that shit either. Them bitches will really try to hurt me if they scared. They do think *my* ass is crazy."

"They do!" Vanessa replied. "Hell, you *is*!" Evelyn joined in.

"Both y'all mothafuckas is crazy, Evelyn added. "Shoot, you know I ain't gonna bust a grape with these nails. I ain't fighting no bitches. I don't *do* that shit. I'm too cute for that, and Marquise would fuck me up if he heard that shit. Oh shit! He's gonna find out about this shit. I'm gonna have to hear his damn mouth!"

"Drop me off at Candi's." Vanessa said.

We rode out to Evelyn's mom's house and sat around, talking about these niggas and these bitches. They know god damn well these Negro's got somebody, but they don't care!

"That's alright. I got something for his ass! I don't know what it is just yet, because my feelins' is hurt, but don't worry about nothing. My ass gonna think of something."

We couldn't help but laugh one last time at that shit.

That bitch should be scared to look at Aaron, hell!

CHAPTER FORTY-TWO

I t was baseball season. Candi's brothers started their softball games in the park. Their team was called the Black Sox. We all decided to ride in "the Drop" to the game. It was at the park on 47th Street. I still loved Candi's brother Travis, but he was off limits; he was married. It didn't hurt to look though.

So we were sitting in the car, not really paying too much attention to the game at that point. I was pouncing around on my way back to the car, and just as I looked to my left, there was a guy walking from the bathroom that caught my eye.

Tall, dark chocolate, 6'foot 4. Every inch of his body was filled out. He had a nice ass, chest and arms, with a perfectly-shaped head. His hair real low, almost bald but you could tell he had good hair by the way it laid against his skin. It was jet black, damn! He was fine! He had a wife beater on, and he had his shirt hanging out the back pocket of his Levi's, with this big ass smile on his face. I had to return the favor.

"Damn, you a cutie pie!"

"Thank you." He said smiling with a big, cheesy grin.

We didn't take our eyes off each other the whole time. I headed back to sit in the car.

"Damn he is *cute!* You guys see him?"

"He sure is, with his chocolate self. And he was checking you out girl." Cheryl said.

"He was, wasn't he?" "Look, he's coming back."

He was waving at the car to get my attention.

I got back out of the car to see just exactly how I could oblige. "What's up? Can I talk to you for a minute?" He asked.

"Why certainly! What's up?" I replied. "I'm Devin, and you are?"

"Danielle."

"I just wanted to know if what I just felt was the same way you felt."

"Yes, pretty much." "You are so sexy."

"And so are you. That's a trip, huh?"

"Yeah, I wanted to get your number and invite you to my godparents' anniversary dinner tonight."

"Tonight?"

"Yeah, I didn't want this day to end without spending some time with you."

"Wow! What time?"

"I'm not sure. Just be dressed about eight and I'll call you to give you directions."

"Okay."

We exchanged numbers and I had a smile on my face the rest of the day.

"What he say, what he say?" They yelled when I got back into the car.

"He said he wants me to go with him to his godparents' anniversary dinner."

"What? Okay!"

"Are you gonna go?"

"Hell yes! He said he would call me and to be dressed by eight and he would meet me."

Eight o'clock turned into ten o'clock. I felt weird about meeting him so late. I thought he wasn't going to call back at all. I had put on a summer dress with some high heel sandals. I didn't know what type of dinner it was. When I asked Devin, he told me to put on something simple and cute. So that was what I did, with a pair of cute thongs to match. You never know...

The first time he called, he wanted to make sure I was still going to meet him, and then he kept telling me he was going to call me right back to meet him, and he never did. Well, he finally called back and gave me directions. I followed them, and there he was, waiting outside the place for me. I felt nervous seeing him again alone, without my girls.

"Hey baby." He said.

Grabbing me he planted a big wet kiss on my cheek. He had some big lips. I hugged him back.

"Come inside so I can introduce you to everybody."

Oh my God! Is he for real? He must have told them he met the girl of his dreams.

Everyone acted as if they have known me for years.

"It's not often Devin brings females around. You must be pretty special."

Did they know this fool just met me a few hours ago? Devin introduced me to his god sister.

"Devin already told me all about you. You are pretty. It's nice to meet you."

"Thank you, you too."

I was hoping no one knew Juelz in the crowd. I was driving his car and everyone knew that car.

After we mingled a bit and laughed with his family, Devin leaned over to me.

"You ready to get out of here?"

It had only been about an hour since I arrived. "Where you want to go?"

"Are you hungry?" "No."

"You sure? I know you couldn't really get full off finger foods." "No, I'm cool."

"Let's go back to my buddy's house." "Where does he live?"

"Out off of Howe?" "Way out there?"

"It's not that far, we can take the back streets." "Can I ride with you?" He asked.

"No, I can follow you."

"Seems like I seen this car before."

Oh God, here it comes. "Is this some dude's car?" "Yeah."

"Your man's?"

"No, not exactly. He's locked up."

"And he trusts a female with his car? You know that's your man. You females ain't shit!"

"What you mean?"

"You know what I mean." "Hey, it's a long story."

"Whatever you say. Maybe you can tell me all about it one day." As he gave me a big grin.

"Let's go girl, follow me."

He got in a long, yellow Cadillac one of those long old school pimp rides. It did not fit him at all!

We arrived at his friend's house. No one was home. Imagine that. It was dark and he didn't even turn on the lights. We went straight to the room. Was this his room? Because he had a key. The next thing I knew, we were kissing like there was no tomorrow. His strong hands were rubbing all over my body. Damn! Of course, the next thing to go up was my dress, and he grabbed my ass and felt those thongs... I knew it. His pants were to his ankles and he was slipping on a rubber.

What the hell? Did I *miss* something? Was this discussed back at the party? Thank God for the rubber. I don't know if I could have stopped him. He was so big, it almost didn't fit. Dang! And he can kiss too.

In my mind, I felt like those commercials where they fall back into a pool, arms stretched out and douche into the water you go. It had been a minute, and I felt as if I was floating in that pool.

"I don't want to hurt you." He couldn't put it all in.

You mean to tell me there was more? Oh my God I've died and gone to heaven he felt so good!

I wanted it all. He grabbed my hair and was kissing me all over my face, neck, and then my breasts. Whew! What pleasure! That had to be going on for at least an hour, and we were dripping wet with sweat. So much for trying to look cute!

I didn't bring a purse, a comb or nothing, damn! Wait, what happened to the rubber? Did it fall off? All I knew was it was skin to skin and something was pretty slimy. After that he was dead, he rolled off me with his legs still wrapped around me.

Was he really asleep? Out like a light! What the...? I didn't know my way around the apartment and I couldn't see a damn thing!

I had to go to the bathroom. Where were my clothes? Main thing where was that rubber? I guessed it was in the bed somewhere? Ugh! I had no choice but to go to sleep. When I opened my eyes, it was just about daylight. What time was it? At least I could see my way around.

I looked over at him. He was still knocked out. As I made my way to the bathroom, I couldn't wait to pee. I looked around no toilet paper! Oh lord, it was really a guy's pad. There was a balled up towel in the corner of the bath tub. I looked underneath the sink nothing. There wasn't even a comb or a brush. It was some toothpaste and some beat up looking toothbrush. I had to wipe myself. No way could I just sit and drip dry.

"Oh well."

I used the empty toilet paper roll. I tiptoed back to the room, standing over him and staring while he slept. Not too cute, he was hanging off the side of the bed. Big lips hanging open and he was snoring.

I thought I may have made a big mistake. I tried to find my thongs and my sandals. Where were my keys? I was trying to get the hell out of there fast as I could. I didn't want him to see me like this and I didn't want anyone knowing I spent the night with some dude I didn't even know in Juelz's car.

You might as well say I was paranoid. I just knew someone saw his car, not to mention when I started it, I thought it would wake up the whole complex. As I drove, I began to think of what happened that night and a big smile came over my face. It was good, but what was he going to think? Would he try to call me when he woke up? I tried not to think about that part.

I wasn't going home. Nadia was still over Candi's. They seemed to still be sleep and Cheryl saw me pull up from her back door across the street. Cheryl was another good friend who lived across the street from Candi. I confided in her a lot when the other girls were trippin off of stupid shit. She was about six years older than me and Candi. She was married with a little girl the same age as Nadia and Kiki.

"Girl, tell me what happened! Come on in. I just put the coffee pot on the stove. You are smiling a little too hard, sweetheart. You gave that man some?"

I told Cheryl all that happened, soon after Candi was coming through the door for a cup of coffee.

"Oh, so you made it home, hoe." "Shut up, girl."

"Candi, wait until she tells you what they did girl!"

I also gave him Candi's number. That day, I kept waiting for her phone to ring. It didn't. I slept most of the day and just lied around until it was time to go home and get Nadia ready for school. So he didn't even call, huh? Figures! He seemed so sincere. I decided it was time to go.

"Hi mama."

"Hi, some guy name *Devin* keeps calling you." "For real?"

The phone rang again. She answered it. "Speak of the devil. Telephone's for you." My mom handed me the phone.

"Hello."

"Man, I've been calling you all day. Who was that, your mom?" "Yes."

"She sounds so sweet. I know she was like, "who is this fool that keeps calling my house?" You didn't think you were going to hear from me, did you."

"No, not really."

"Why, cause you left me in the bed like you stole something?" "Man, I had to go home! You messed my hair all up, I didn't have a comb or a brush or nothing. I didn't want you to see me like that. You live there with your friend?"

"Hell no! That nigga nasty. It wasn't even any toilet paper in there!"

"Yeah, I know. I had to pee real bad!"

"Oh, I'm sorry, baby. I would have went out and got you some.

I didn't know that dude live like that."

"What you mean. You said he your buddy."

"Yeah, but you know how a nigga don't clean up like they should, and he probably be over his girl's all the time, so he's never home."

"Okay then, I guess he gets a pass on that one. I could have gotten cooties on my ass!"

"So, when am I going to see you again." "Whenever you want."

"How about having lunch with me tomorrow?" "Where?"

"Downtown? I'm working on that Federal building down on I Street. I work construction."

"Oh!"

"I thought you could pack me a picnic basket." "Very funny. I could do that for you."

Whenever I was off on the weekday, I met Devin downtown, or we met after work, in different parks or playgrounds to talk. One time, I met him at his cousins and we walked across the street to an elementary school. We were sitting on the bleachers. Devin pulled me behind the school building. We started kissing and once again, his hand went straight to my ass.

What was with this man and my ass?

He picked me up against the wall and unzipped his pants. *Was he crazy? He was trying to put his penis inside me in broad daylight?*

Much as I wanted to feel it again, I kept telling him to stop. He just kept trying to penetrate while he was kissing me on my lips and down my neck.

"You have to stop! What if someone sees us? Let me down, boy."

"I just get crazy when I get around you." "I see!"

Devin continued to kiss me. Luckily, I was able to calm him down, or so I thought. His dick stayed so hard he went in for it anyway. He put my leg on his shoulder, while we were still standing. I couldn't believe we were fucking on the side of that elementary school. It felt so good though, he was so strong and big. Damn! There was no controlling him until he busted that nut. I don't even think my foot was touching the ground at this point.

"Shit, Baby! Your pussy is so good!"

He was grunting and sweating. Whew! When he let my leg down, I almost fell over. I pulled my dress down and he fixed his clothes. I was so scared to move. *I know someone got they eyes busted!* And what made it worse, I had to drive off in Juelz' Drop! Shit! He could not stop kissing me. We walked back across the street.

"Let me get the hell out of here!"

"Yeah, don't want anybody to spot you in your man's Drop." "Shut up!"

"When am I going to see you again?" "Soon, call me."

"He had his nerve. He was living with someone, too.

CHAPTER FORTY-THREE

S ummer was ending and Juelz would soon be home. I had befriended my instructor, Regina. I shared stories about my life with her and we became close. On my birthday, I received unexpected gifts from my classmates. That made me feel real special. Everything seemed to be going so well. After we graduated, Regina helped me land a receptionist job at a hair salon.

Juelz's car couldn't make it through that everyday commute to Sunrise, so I had to catch the light rail and three buses to get to work. When it was my Saturday to work, Devin always took me, because I had to be there at eight and there was no way I was getting up at the crack of dawn for that trip! I thought I was getting the hang of it. I never knew there was so much involved in being a receptionist of a salon. This was not any normal salon it was "*The* Salon."

As the weeks went by, it didn't get any better; it basically got worse. My resume looked better than my performance. One thing I *did* like was the fact that I didn't have to work every Saturday.

The salon had very demanding owners. Their daughters worked in the salon, one as a stylist and the other was the receptionist. She trained me, because she would be leaving for Clark Atlanta University in the fall. Her name was Danielle too. She was a real sweetie pie. It was a very pleasant atmosphere, but sometimes it was stressful, because the clients were on the high end of society. They tend to be very rude and manipulative to new employees in order to get their way with their appointments. Some wanted to be squeezed in, even after they have canceled their standing appointment for that week.

Juelz got out. Of course, after I picked my man up, we went straight to a motel to get our swerve on. It wasn't the same, though. My body was different and there was no real chemistry like before. I guess I had a lot on my mind... like Devin. I had hooked back up with April, and she did a mini makeover on me. She hooked me up with some MAC makeup and some cute short summer dresses.

She stole almost everything she owned, so I was grateful it didn't cost me anything. I spent most of my money at Macy's, buying my Steve Madden's. I was looking for a house to rent, and I found the perfect place, away from the hood, that would be hard for anyone to find. I wanted to make sure Juelz liked it before I agreed to rent it. My mom had said it would be okay for Juelz to stay at her house until our place was ready. I took him to check out the rental. Of course, his cousin Jamal came with us.

"This is the spot, mama. When can we move in?" "So, you like it?"

"Hell yeah!"

It was a cute two-bedroom, two-bath, two-car garage, with a fireplace. It had new carpet and paint, and the house was less than ten years old. It was perfect for us. It also had an alarm system. We were able to move in the first of the month.

We hung out at the park. I hated going to work. I wanted to spend every minute with Juelz. One night, everyone was meeting up at the park to have a drink to celebrate him getting out. I put on some short shorts, with a cute top to match, and some Carl Kani high heel tennis shoes. I was looking real cute.

Marquise was there, and of course, Evelyn wasn't. Marquise didn't want Evelyn hanging out like that. He reported back to Evelyn though.

"Danielle was looking cute, she and Juelz seemed really happy together."

"Oh for real? That's good. You know she hella happy he home."

"Yeah, it's all good! I'll be home in a minute, Hiff." "Okay. Bring me something to eat."

"I'll hit you when I'm on my way, so you can tell me what you want."

We still couldn't spend any time with each other, but we found ways to talk when he was nowhere around.

Evelyn started working at the salon with me. We never worked the same shift and we worked opposite days. She fit right in, but she didn't like it. She said she'd hang in there until something better came along. I was just too edgy, or ghetto, for the environment. I really had never worked anywhere, so it took a lot for me to learn. I spoke well and dressed nice, though. Evelyn was just all around prettier and always wore the latest fashions. So they fell in love with her.

I was on the schedule that day. I hadn't seen Juelz, but I needed some gas. When I went to the hood, no one had seen him. I started to head back towards the south side of town, when something told me to check by Jamal's house. I thought for sure he wouldn't be there, but I went anyway. Juelz thought I was at work, so he hooked up with another bitch he was messing with while I was locked up!

When I rode past, it looked as if I was trying to creep up on them, and I was so I rode by without stopping. Then all of a sudden, something told me to stop. I busted a U-turn and parked one house down. I knocked on the door. When I did that, I heard them inside.

When Jamal opened the door, I asked if he had seen Juelz. He knew not to lie to me, so he couldn't. When I peeked over his shoulder, Juelz and that bitch were sitting on the floor. She jumped up and tried to hide in the kitchen. Juelz tried to get up to explain to me what was going on. I didn't want to hear one word! I stepped in the house and walked into the kitchen.

"Bitch don't worry. You ain't even worth the trouble!"

She just stood there, looking as dumb as she was. *Illiterate ass hoe!*

I looked at Juelz.

"I hate yo ass. You stay right here with this bitch. You ain't got to worry about me at all mothafucka!"

I always knew to trust my intuition. I was so upset that I felt like going back in there and beating her ass, but I told myself I could never hurt anyone like that again. *Just to let it go!* When Juelz came running out of the house to stop me, I tried to run his ass over.

"I hate you, you mothafucka!"

I sped off and bent the corner. I instantly started to cry. That was the same bitch he was with at the market when I got out of jail. He made sure he kept her around. I couldn't stand to be second. I was furious! I couldn't do anything but scream. I ended up back on 33rd, at my grandmother's house, where my uncle now lived, trying to get it together. I was supposed to go to work that day, but I damn sure wasn't going. I had my uncle to call my job for me and tell them I was not coming.

"Nigga, you betta get yo shit together. What you crying for?" "I just caught Juelz at Jamal's house with that other bitch!"

"So mothafuckin what, nigga! You do yo shit and these niggas gonna do theirs. It's a part of the game. You chose this shit, nigga. You's a *gangsta'* baby. Fuck that bitch! Who that nigga come *home* to? Who got that nigga Drop top? You do. A mothafucka *always* gonna have a side bitch, but she can't be the number one bitch. Shake that shit off nigga, and go about yo business. I'm done talkin!"

That was LeAnn's dad. That nigga don't play. *I heard what he said and I shook that shit off!*

I rode right downtown to see Devin. *How could he be working up so high? I would be scared to death!* I was trying to find a parking spot across from the building. *Do I even have any quarters for this damn parking meter?* A construction worker. He fit the bill too, with his big, fine sexy ass! He could always spot me from the street. Sometimes his buddies would spot me before he did.

They would start yelling and whistling, and when he'd look down and see me, he'd have the biggest smile.

"Be right down!"

I had a new look.

"I almost didn't recognize you. You are looking good girl. Where have you been?"

"Juelz came home a few weeks ago."

"So what are you doing here? Don't make me have to shoot nobody."

"Shut up! He's with his other bitch he was with when I was locked up. I told you it was a long story."

"So what does that mean for me and you?" "Whatever you want it to mean."

"Well, you know my situation, but I'm tryin to get out of there.

We can get a place together."

"No, we can't. We're renting a house in the South Area." "Damn, so are you living with this nigga? So what are we supposed to do?"

"We'll figure something out, but until then, we can just see each other whenever. So far, he's never home. I'm always there by myself. I don't care what he does at this point. As long as I have some money and transportation, I don't care."

Devin pulled me close and gave me a big, wet kiss. Then he held me so tight that I didn't want him to let me go. I felt safe with him.

"I'm sorry baby. I can tell you hurtin'."

CHAPTER FORTY-FOUR

They scheduled me less hours at the salon for some reason. I remembered one of my aunt Chellie's closest friends coming in for an appointment. I didn't think anything of it when I first saw her. As I spoke with her, I reminded her I was Chellie's niece.

In recollection, they started treating me funny after that appointment. When I would call for my schedule, they would keep me on hold for twenty minutes at a time. I was naive to the fact that they were being rude, so I would just hang up and call back.

Finally, Juelz objected.

"Fuck em! You ain't got to *go* back, tell them to mail you your check. You ain't no sucka!"

I was fine with that, but I really didn't want to quit. It was cool, though. I hung in there as long as I could. It was Friday. I got off at seven and headed straight to the hood to meet up with Juelz. Of course, he wasn't there. I hung around on 33rd, but nobody was at the house. I wondered where everybody was, and then they pulled up.

"Did you hear what happened at the big park?" Tarsha asked as she got out the car.

"No, what happened?"

"Said Marquise passed out and they had to take him to the hospital."

"Which Marquise?"

"I don't know. Probably Jordan."

We had a Marquise Michaels and a Marquise Jordan in our hood. I kept trying to page Evelyn but she never called back. I thought nothing of it, so we just figured it was the other Marquise and everything was probably okay. I knew her man didn't like me, so I didn't make a fuss to get in touch with Evelyn. By the time night fell, everyone was coming by the house saying it was Marquise Michaels, he had had a heart attack and died.

"Oh my God!" I immediately called my aunt. It was true! He had a heart attack. He was dead. When I hung up the phone, I just collapsed on the lawn, screaming.

"What about Evelyn? What about the baby?"

Evelyn had just given birth to their son. He was only six or seven-months old. They tried to help me up. More people came by looking for me. Evelyn was at the hospital and had been asking for me. I hopped in the car and they took me to the hospital. When we arrived, there were so many people there, I couldn't get in the door. I tried to make my way through the crowd. When Darwin spotted me he grabbed me.

"Where have you been? Evelyn been asking for you!"

He walked me to the back, and there they were. Marquise was dead on the stretcher and Evelyn was standing over him in a daze, with her hand on his stomach.

"Evelyn!"

As I walked toward her, her face was so pale, her eyes were bloodshot red and swollen. I could see the trail of dried up tears on her face as she looked up at me.

"What am I gonna do, Danielle? What am I gonna do?" I grabbed Evelyn and just held her.

"You're going to be alright. We are here for you. It's going to be alright."

Evelyn just cried in my arms. LeAnn was there right beside Evelyn. We looked at each other in disbelief. Marquise was actually lying there dead! We could see where his heart had contracted. His left side had collapsed. So many things were going through my head. I never disliked Marquise. If anything, my feelings were hurt because he didn't like me. However, *I never wanted things to end like this! This was crazy.* He was gone.

It was time for the coroners to take the body. They told everybody to leave. We had to pry Evelyn from his side. They basically took him away before she even moved her feet. LeAnn had been dropped off as well so we rode back together to 33rd. She drove Evelyn's car. I sat in the back with Evelyn, still in disbelief. Evelyn was quiet, still sitting in a daze. We had to find out what she wanted us to do. She said we had to go to his house. By the time we got to my uncle's, Juelz and everybody was there. I hadn't seen him since the day before. When he saw me, he asked how we were doing, and he asked Evelyn what was up.

"Juelz I want y'all to ride out to Marquise's house with me." We loaded up in the car with Juelz and rode out there. "Damn, girl! How far did you guys live? In another city?"

It was a long ways to travel every night.

Once we got there, Evelyn began to cry again. She was scared to go inside.

"Juelz, you go in first."

He was always like a big brother to her. We walked in behind him. The house had been ransacked already.

"That is a damn shame that nigga ain't even been dead a good four hours, and they came and stole his shit. I know it was his stupid-ass brother."

Marquise had jars and jars of quarters, dimes and nickels. They were gone. All his clothes and hats gone! Shoes! They were gone too!

"I know what they were looking for, but they will never find that. Yeah, they won't find that shit at all."

It was a long night. We stayed up as long as we could to watch over Evelyn. She was too scared to stay alone, so we all slept over Juelz's cousin's house which happened to be LeAnn's mother-in- law. Every now and then Evelyn would wake up out of her sleep crying. We got up early and went to my aunt's house. Evelyn had recently moved back home. I hadn't been in that room for years. I was in Georgia when she had the baby. I left in August and she had him in November, and then I returned that next month.

Those next few days would have a lot going on. I couldn't wait to call the salon Tuesday morning to let them know neither one of us would be returning. I explained to them what happened, and that was that. The salon sent Evelyn a big, beautiful plant. That was nice. After the whole ordeal was over it was time to move on with our lives and be there for Evelyn as much as we could. For the most part, Evelyn held up pretty well.

Juelz and I had to go to the mall to find something to wear to the funeral. I was first, then with whatever I chose, he would follow my color.

We went to Banana Republic. I felt like Pretty Woman, where she was trying on all kinds of dresses and Richard Gere was sitting in the chair telling Julia Roberts which one looked good on her. Well, that was me that day. I went through about six different dresses, and then Juelz finally liked one gray piece. It was cute actually short, fitting my body close. It was sleeveless and had a skinny belt around the waist. The material wasn't metallic, but it was some sort of shiny charcoal gray. The neckline was closed.

"That's the one I want. You like this one?"

"Hell yeah, mama! You lookin good in that! I can bend you over and fuck you in your butt." He said laughing.

The store assistant heard him and started laughing. I was so embarrassed. I took it off and she took it along with Juelz to the register.

"Two hundred and eighty five dollars!" I got to the register and squinted. "You worth it mama."

Then he leaned over to whisper in my ear.

"But you know you gotta suck my dick for breakfast, lunch and dinner!"

"You are so stupid! But okay, I will!"

We both fell out laughing and walked out the store. We bought him the simple black. Shirt, pants, shoes, with a gray tie to match my dress.

The funeral was well-organized, and everything went smoothly, but you know them hoes came out the woodwork, showing Evelyn no respect at all. But either way, she had the last say so, she was their son's mother, and she ran the show.

Of course, Juelz was drunk as a skunk, and that bitch tried to show up and take a moment to chop it up.

"No, bitch! Not today. I will beat yo ass!"

He sat his ass in the car and fell asleep. He slept through the whole procession and the burial and all the way back to the house! *Damn, Nigga!*

Things didn't get any better between Juelz and me. I was constantly trying to keep tabs on him, letting everybody know that we were together. Those bitches didn't care, but they made damn sure I didn't find out about it. With everybody coming out, they were just more hoes not to trust around Juelz. And what was done in the dark would soon come to light.

Tamika Brown had come back. She had been in Atlanta too. She became part of the crew again, and she always seemed pretty cool. She was quick to sell some dope and get her hustle on. *Those them bitches that get down and dirty!* That's not my style, but if you like it, I love it!

Juelz tried to spend as much time with me as he could. He gave me some lame excuse about him not caring for that bitch, that she was just a dummy who was going to hold his dope at her house for him and not to be trippin, that I knew I was the one. I believed him, for what it was worth, and I tried to act like nothing bothered me, but we kept bumping heads.

I was feeling that new Chanté Moore. I lit some candles, put them in the fireplace and turned on the CD, waiting for Juelz to come home.

I wanted to make love like we used to. When he got there, he came in the door, turning on all the lights.

"What the fuck you doin' man? Having a séance in here or some shit? What you listening too? Put in some *Scarface*, Nigga don't nobody want to hear that love shit."

What the hell just happened? It was like a needle sliding across the record.

Hold up! No, this nigga *didn't* just say put in some *Scarface*! And he took my CD out and put *Scarface* in? I knew right then I had outgrown that shit. I was ready for a family, someone who was going to be home at night, and knew how to sit they ass down! We ended up having sex, but it was not like it was when I was nineteen. Either my pussy got bigger or his dick got smaller. I knew I couldn't do that scene much longer, especially, after having Chase's oral sex, and having Devin's big dick inside me. *No, this was not going to work, Boo-Boo!* I had become more of a woman, and he still wanted to be a thug with no benefits.

We still didn't have any furniture in the house. The only thing Juelz bought was a big refrigerator and different accessories for the house. I had to make sure each bathroom was decorated from top to bottom and that I had everything I needed in the kitchen. I had to use excuses to buy new stuff.

The convertible was out of commission. I forgot to put oil in it, and one day it just wouldn't start. Oops! *Did I do that shit again!* So we didn't have a car. Juelz was always driving someone else's car or someone was picking me up.

"What the fuck was you doing, man? You didn't put any oil in my shit? What, it cost two dollars to buy some fuckin oil and pour the shit in! *You* was just driving my shit! Bet your ass won't be driving nothin else of mine! You better call a mothafuckin cab if you want to take your ass somewhere!"

We argued and cursed at each other all the time, but now I wasn't so cool with it anymore. I felt it was totally disrespectful. It was like I was getting on his nerves! He never had anything good to say, or when he did, he was on the way out the door. He more or less tried to pacify me with money.

"If you need some money, page me."

I had gotten used to being home alone at night. Finally, he broke down and let me go get a car. Nothing fancy I was just happy to get a car. I picked out a used Honda Accord. It was gold, and the upholstery was like new. It could have used

256

a paint job, but I didn't care. It was the only thing I could find for fifteen hundred dollars.

He still found a way to leave me stranded. He would take my car and have someone else give me a ride or drop me off. When it got late, Juelz called to let me know he would be home in an hour or so. I tried to wait up for him, but before I knew it, I would fall asleep and woke up when it was morning. He never came home.

I started cleaning out our closet and hanging Juelz's clothes. There was a card in his shirt pocket containing the instructions to his pager voicemail and the access code. *Yes! Big dummy he didn't even change his pass code.* I picked up the phone and called the pager. I began to listen to all the messages and write down all the numbers.

One particular number kept repeating. I couldn't catch the girl's voice on the message. All I knew was that he was fuckin around. I kept the list of numbers and started calling them to see if I would recognize any of the voices before hanging up.

There were only two numbers that he called frequently. One time, I thought I recognized the voice. Was it *Tamika*? I matched the number up with a late call from the previous night. The next morning, Juelz didn't come home. First, I paged him. No call back. I called back a few times and left a message for him to call home. When he didn't call back, I dialed the number off the list I had. My heart started beating fast as I dialed the number and asked if Juelz was there. *It was Tamika!*

"Hey, let me speak to Juelz."

Tamika had no idea who I was. She probably thought it was somebody wanting to buy some dope.

"Hello?"

"What the *fuck* you think you doing?" "Hello?"

"You heard me, Nigga! Why you didn't bring your ass home last night."

"Oh! Wassup?"

"Not a god damn thing! I just wanted to make sure you knew I knew where you was."

I hung up the phone.

The phone rang right back. "What you want?" "Nothin!"

I hung up again. Juelz called right back. I wouldn't answer. I let it go to voicemail. He hated when it did that. He would always tell me to take it off the phone, because if you left a message, you had to call in to retrieve it, so whatever it is you were saying no one could hear it anyway. He left a message though. I called and retrieved it.

"Bitch, if you don't answer the mothafuckin phone, I'm gonna come home and kick your mothafuckin ass!"

The phone rang again. This time I answered. "Hello."

"What the fuck you call me for?" "No reason at all."

"Then what the fuck you want?" "Nothing!" I screamed in the phone.

"I'm gonna come kick you mothafuckin as for playin wit me!"

He hung up. I knew by his tone he was heated and he *was* really coming home to kick my ass. I called Evelyn and told her what happened.

"That nigga ain't gonna do nothin."

"Yes he *is*! I know his voice when he's mad!"

I started to cry. I had no car and nowhere to go. He was coming all right, and I knew it.

"Well, just stay on the phone with me. If he comes home, I will call 911 from here."

"Girl, that shit ain't funny. I'm telling you he is going to come and fuck me up!"

No sooner that I said that, I heard the garage door opening. "He's here! He's here! Oh *shit!*"

Lying in the bed, I put my head under the covers. I started whispering to Evelyn.

"He's coming through the door. Evelyn! Oh shit!"

The kitchen door flew open, slamming into the counter. My heart was pounding. He couldn't kick the bedroom door open, it already had a hole in it from the last time he put his foot through it. The door flew open.

"Bitch, where you at?"

He yanked the covers off of me. I had hid the phone behind the pillow so he wouldn't know I was on it. He started punching me in the head as I tried to cover my face with my arms. One blow after the other, but I kept my face covered. He threw me on the floor and started kicking me in my back.

"Didn't I tell you to quit playin with me, mothafucka?"

By that time, I just wanted it to be over. I kept my eyes closed so tight, thinking that would take some of the pain away. Juelz grabbed me by my hair. I was on my knees when he started choking me. He choked me so hard that I passed out.

When I came to and looked up, I didn't know what was going on. All I saw was Juelz, yelling at the top of his lungs in my face. I couldn't even hear him. He grabbed me again. He threw me back down and started punching me again.

I had on a burgundy sports bra and Lem's matching boxers, with no shoes. He dragged me out the house by my hair and threw me in the car. Then he sped off and started riding around, cursing at me for calling over Tamika's house.

After he drove to a park and stopped the car, he started telling me how he was sorry and that we had been tight too long to be going through that shit! I sat there, tears rolling down my face, staring out the window at the green grass in the park. As he continued speaking, I continued staring out of the window. He started the car and drove to his cousin's house (LeAnn's mother-in- law's home).

Why we went there, I did not know. He got out the car, acting as if nothing happened, like he was just stopping by. They were outside. She spoke to me from the door and then started walking to the car. *Please don't come over here!*

"Hey girl, how you doing?"

She took a second look and knelt down at my window. I immediately started crying. She saw I had no clothes or shoes on.

"What happened?" She whispered.

"He jumped on me. He drug me out the house and has been riding me around so I won't call his parole officer."

"Girl, are you serious? That is not right! You know he's not going to listen to *me*, so you be careful. Call me if you need me."

"Okay."

The tears kept flowing. Juelz finally came back and got in the car.

"You alright?"

I still did not say a word.

"Come on, man! I said I was *sorry*! You just can't be fuckin with me. I'm trying to get my money back right. Shit! I'm under a lot of pressure!"

"What the fuck that got to do with me? You are never home, and I don't call or bother you unless I need some money either, do I? Isn't that what you told me? Call you if I need some money?"

He just shook his head and we ended up pulling back into our driveway. I got out the car, went right into the house and got back in my bed, putting the covers back over my head. As I walked in the room, I saw that the phone was still off the hook. I could feel him walking behind me to our bedroom. He was standing at the foot of the bed. What did he want? I didn't move a muscle, but it was hella hot under that damn cover.

"Here go some money to go get your hair done. It's on top of the speaker."

He left. I heard him go through the front door and lock it. I waited until I heard him pull off, *in my damn car!* I slowly peeked from underneath the covers. I was still scared to move, but I ran to our bathroom and peeked out the window, where there was a clear view of the driveway. He was gone.

I looked in the mirror at my face. Thank God nothing! I had to keep it covered. I'm too damn cute for black eyes and shit. My face was intact. I was touching it as if something was going to fall off. I went to the speaker. Two hundred dollars? And *that* is supposed to make it all better? I threw the money on the floor.

I hung the phone up and called Evelyn.

"Girl, what the fuck happened? I heard everything! I didn't know what to do. I forgot I didn't have your damn address. Where he take you?"

"Riding me around with no clothes or shoes on so I wouldn't call his parole office or the police! Hell!"

"Oh my God! Are you okay?"

"Yeah, I'm fine. I covered my face the whole time, so I'm cool.

He left me two hundred dollars to get my hair done.

"What? No, he didn't. Your hair is messed up? You just got it done."

"Hell yeah! He drug me out the house by my hair, not to mention he was punching me and kicking me!"

"He was kicking you? What the fuck!" "Can you call Tavia for an appointment?" "Yes, I'll call you right back."

The phone rang. I had walked in the kitchen, looking out the window. Every bump or noise I heard scared me to death.

"Okay, she said you can come now. I'm on my way. I can drop you off, but I can't pick you up."

"That's fine. Someone will come and get me."

Tavia's shop was close to my house, right next to the Seven Eleven.

"Hey Tav."

"Hey Dan, come on. I can get you. So, do you know what style you want?"

"Yep, cut it off."

"Cut it off how? You want it shaved like...?"

"Yes, shave it off in the back, and leave some on the top with some blonde pieces, like T-Boz."

"For real, Dan? Are you serious? You're cutting all your hair off?"

Tavia was laughing at the thought.

"Wait! Let me get a conference call with the gang."

She called Evelyn, Evelyn called LeAnn, and LeAnn called Moná.

261

"You guys Dan wants me to shave her hair off." "What the hell? What does her *neck* look like?" "You *know* her Eczema be having her neck be all black and shit!"

"Her neck is fine, you guys." Tavia was cracking up.

"They talkin about my neck?" I grabbed the phone. "Fuck y'all!"

They were all on the line laughing.

"I'm scared of you. What you doing trying to do, Exhale?" I hung up the phone.

"Go head Tavia, cut it off." "Okay!"

Six hours later...

"You look amazing! Oh my gosh! I love it!"

Tavia turned me around to look in the mirror. It was gorgeous. I looked like a different person. I had lost a lot of weight from my stress diet, stressing over Juelz never coming home, I wouldn't eat for days at a time. I was a size nine.

I called Tarsha. She and Kiki would come pick me up.

"We can be there in about an hour. We trying to move some shit right now."

"Okay, that's fine. I'll go next door and get my nails done." "Well, go on witcha bad self! We'll be there."

"Okay, thanks."

I went next door to the nail shop and signed my name in on the sign in sheet.

"Fi minute. Fi minute we do for you." "Okay, no problem."

I sat down and grabbed a magazine to read. "Danielle?"

A voice called out from the dry station. I looked up. "Toni?"

"Girl, yeah! How you doing? You cut all your hair off?" She said laughing.

"Yes, I just got it done. What are you doing in Sacramento? When you get out? Oh my God! I can't believe we are sitting here in the nail salon. Is that your baby?"

"Yes, that's her big behind. You know I got out six months ago. Mark's mom had got custody of our baby. He still locked up, girl. So I'm down here, living with his mama. You still with Juelz? Girl, you loved you some Juelz!"

"Yeah, we still together. We got a house up the street. It's so good to see you."

"You too, girl! Well, let me get out of here. My ride just pulled up. You take it easy."

"Okay, you too."

That was Toni. We were locked up together and she had gotten pregnant by one of the dudes up there. She was a skinny string bean with a big old belly. You couldn't even tell she was pregnant from the back. That was her second pregnancy while being locked up. It was a small world! She was from LA. Who knew I would run into her two years later.

By the time my nails were done, Tarsha and Kiki pulled up. I was walking back and forth, looking at my reflection in the window. I *did* look like a different person with my hair shaved, and I was skinny too I hadn't realized how much weight I had lost. I remember Amiria and I went shopping one day and I bought a bunch of shorts, thirteens and they were too big.

"Amiria, give me these in an eleven. They're too big." She brought me another pair.

"Girl what size are you getting? These are too big too!"

"It says eleven."

"Are you serious, girl? Shut up then give me a nine!" A few minutes later.

"They fit perfectly. Oh shit! I am a size nine! I've lost weight and didn't even realize it. I had been in an extra large dress.

"Hand me a dress in a medium, please. It fits. I can fit a medium dress! Let me come and pick me out some more."

I picked out four more dresses, tried them on and it was a go. I was excited. Yeah, *that's* from not eating. I was never hungry and Nadia ate at my mom's. Juelz had me so nervous I always had to expect the worst. Every time we were together, he asked me if I had eaten, and I would always say *no* that I wasn't hungry.

263

"When was the last time you ate?" "I don't know."

"Man, you gotta eat, man. Just quit trippin."

"I ain't trippin. I don't bother you, I don't call you. I'm cool."

Of course I was being sarcastic. He knew why I was stressing. He never came home and I knew he was up under that bitch, but I ain't had nothing to say.

"What you wanna eat, Nigga?" "Chicken!"

"*Besides* that!' "Nothin!"

"All you fuckin eat is chicken! Yo ass gonna fly away some mothafuckin where!"

He killed me, tryin to act concerned. Nigga, kick rocks!

I rode with Tarsha and Kiki to 33rd. I guess I could see if my car was there. When we pulled up, my car was parked across the street, and so was that red one. What the fuck was *that* all about? We got out the car. I walked straight in the house and that bitch was sitting on the couch.

"What the fuck is she doing here!" I yelled through the house.

I kept walking down the hall to the bathroom to get my composure. Monique was in there, putting on her make-up.

"What the fuck is *that* all about?"

"Girl, that some scandalous shit! We already *told* Juelz that shit ain't cool. He didn't think you was gonna find a ride out here."

"Did he tell you he *beat* my ass this morning?"

"Stop lying! For real Danielle? What the fuck he do that for?" "Because I called over to Tamika's to let him know I knew they was fuckin around. So he got mad because I kept hanging the phone up in his face, and came home and whooped my ass!"

"Ooh! Uh uh! That's a damn shame!"

Don't trip! You still looking cute, mama. He couldn't have did too much."

"No, he did I just made sure he didn't hit me in my face. I kept my head covered up."

"Fuck that nigga! That shit is way too foul."

264

My mood immediately changed from glad to sad to frustrated. I walked back into the living room, headed out the front door. Monique followed behind me.

"Girl, you look too cute. I love that haircut on you! What made you cut your hair off?

"Tryin to exhale" before I fuck a bitch up!"

Juelz pulled up with Steve, just as I walked outside. I didn't have any words for him, remembering the day's events of him beating my ass.

"How you get over here?" He hesitated.

"Tarsha and Kiki came and picked me up from the shop." "Oh, is that right? You need the car?"

"*That* would be nice." I said sarcastically.

"Here you go!" He said as he handed me the keys. "I'll find a way home."

"I'm sure you will." I said as I walked straight to my car. I got in and left without saying another word.

That mothafucka right there! I wasn't crying anymore. I had something for his ass.

CHAPTER FORTY-FIVE

I grabbed the phone to page Juelz. My stomach had butterflies.

It wasn't the first time he had done this. The phone rang. "It's Monday. Are you comin to take Nadia to school?" "I'm way in the North Area."

"What are you doing out there? You told me last night you would be home in an hour."

"I started fuckin around with this dope and shit, and I lost track of time."

"So what are you sayin? You're *not* coming to get your daughter to take her to school?"

"Man catch a cab."

"Hell no! I'm not catching a cab. Your ass is gonna come pick her up and drop her off, and she better not be late for school!"

He knew I didn't have no way to take her. "Hello? Hello?"

He had hung up on me. Bastard! He always hated for me to call him that, because he never knew who his Dad was until he got grown, and someone had to tell him who he was.

I called LeAnn.

"Does Aaron have my car? Juelz is with that bitch, Justice, and he left me here without a car. He's going to tell me to catch a cab!"

"A cab? That nigga know that baby has to go to school! Let me call them. I'll call you right back."

I couldn't believe he actually told me to catch a cab! That was it! I was leaving! He showed me once again that he didn't care anything about me. He put another woman before me and my child.

The phone rang. "Hello?"

"Danielle, I called and cursed them out. Aaron has your car and I told them they better get over there and take that baby to school."

"Alright, thank you."

"You call me if they don't get there in fifteen minutes, or I'll come take her myself."

"Okay. Bye."

"Bye, talk to you later. Nadia are you ready?" "Yes."

"Okay, your dad will be here in a minute to pick you up."

I pushed the garage opener. I wanted to see what car he would be in when he pulled up. Last time, he parked down the street and walked to the house. He was in a red Ford Escort. At that time, I didn't think anything of it, but I knew if he pulled up again in the same car that he had been with Justice. I never said anything. I was just waiting.

I tried to run her down a few weeks back, when she had the nerve to come to the park where we were. She wanted me to beat her ass then! I had spotted her riding through the hood and jumped in the car after her. She tried to cut me off by pulling in front of me, but when I jumped out the car, she backed up, took off and drove right over to Juelz. When I got close, he tried to snatch me out of the car.

"Bitch, what is your problem? Do you want your ass to go back to jail? Take your punk ass home man!" He yelled.

"Ain't that a bitch! So I have to go home and *that* bitch gets to post up here? Fuck you, Nigga!"

"Fuck you, bitch!"

I heard those words as I sped off. I looked in the rear view mirror and saw that he tried to throw a beer bottle at my car.

"That son of a bitch! You see what the fuck I have to put up with. Fuck that! I'm leaving his ass! Watch!"

"Ah bitch, you ain't going nowhere. His ass gonna sweet talk you, and you're going to forget all about that bitch." Evelyn said. She had been riding with me all day.

"Whatever!"

Juelz embarrassed me, so I wanted to go home. Once I got over Evelyn's, I paged Devin. I could always count on him to make me feel better. He called right back.

"Where are you? Come see me at my home boy's house." I drove over to his friend's place.

"Let's go someplace where we can talk." "Okay, I'll follow you."

I didn't know where he was going. I just knew the road was long and dark.

Where is this man going? Is he going where I think he's going?

To a fishing hole this time of night? *That's exactly where he's going!*

Juelz had dragged all of us down there to go fishing once. He even bought Nadia her own pole and tried to show her how to fish.

It was a warm night and the moon was shining bright through the trees. After we got out of our cars, I walked over to Devin.

"Hi baby." He said as he pulled me close to him and gave me one of those wet kisses I loved so much.

I loved the way he kissed and squeezed my body. He was like an octopus when he got around me. We leaned against the car and Devin held me in his arms from behind as we talked about a future together.

"Where's your man at?" "Where else?"

"So what do you want to do? We could look for a duplex to rent."

"What area do you want to live in?"

CHAPTER FORTY-SIX

J uelz had pulled up in the garage. I opened the door. All I saw was that red ass car. *Bastard!* My heart sank to my stomach. I kept my composure, but he was the one looking white around the mouth. He was scared to look me in the eyes. I stared right into his face.

"Nadia come on your daddy's here."

He walked in the door.

"I need the car. Me and April have to go to take a drug test for Pacific Bell."

"No shit!"

"Yeah. They said we need to be there at eleven o'clock this morning."

"So you think you got the job?" "Yep!"

I did not have to take any drug test. I was just trying to find a way to get my car back. I had a plan, and it was going down that day.

Juelz got the phone. He was calling LeAnn's husband, Aaron. "Yeah, Nigga where you at? Danielle needs the car."

"Okay."

"Come on with it, Nigga. She has to go take a drug test at eleven."

"I'm comin Nigga. I'll be there in a couple hours." The voice sounded on the other end of the line.

"Okay baby. He said he'll be here at around ten." "Uh huh!" I said as Juelz made his way out the door. "I don't get a kiss good-bye?"

"Oh yeah, sure mama."

I leaned out the door and kissed Juelz on the lips. Nadia had already been waiting in the car.

"Bye baby. Have a good day at school."

I waved to the both of them with the biggest smile. I knew Juelz was saying, *What the fuck is up with her? And I was saying, "Yeah nigga that was your good-bye kiss for real!"*

As soon as they pulled off, I hit the button to close the garage. I called Shelise in Los Angeles.

"Can I come stay with you?" "Why? What's going on?"

"I'm tired of this nigga. I am ready to get away from here completely."

"You can't stay at Candi's until you guys make up?"

"No, and no we ain't makin' up. He doesn't even know I want to leave. He is never here. He stays gone two, three days at a time. All he says is, *call me if you need somethin'.* So I'm leavin. Fuck him! He's still messing around with that same girl from when I got out of jail. Ain't nothing changed with him. You'd think I'd get some respect by now! Please! He doesn't give a fuck about me, and nobody else for that matter. Hell, I got shot and he or Chase ain't stepped to nobody. Fuck that! I'm ready to go."

"Well, what are you gonna to do here?"

"I want to go to Georgia. Yeah, call daddy for me and ask him can I come there. Please? I have to get out of here, today!"

"Okay, I'll call you right back."

I didn't want to ask my dad, because I didn't want him to know what was going on. I had gone to Atlanta once I realized there was nothing in Sacramento for me. I just felt bad about leaving Juelz while he was locked up, and he was the one who begged me to come back.

As I stared out the kitchen window, tears began to roll down my face. I couldn't believe all the shit I let happen in my life behind this one nigga. I wished I had never met him. How could he do me like that? It was seven years later. Huh, seven years bad luck. If God got me through this, I was surely going to take a good look in the mirror when all the dust settled.

The phone rang.

"Daddy said you can come, but he's on vacation and he won't be back for two weeks."

"Two *weeks*? But he said I can *come*?"

"Yes, but he said you better get there the best way you can, because he's not helping you and he doesn't want to get in the middle of you and Juelz's mess."

"For real?"

"That's what he said."

"So can I stay with you until he gets back?"

"Sure you can stay, but I don't have any food and I don't get paid until Friday."

"Oh, we just went grocery shopping the other day. I'll pack that shit up like it came straight from Albertson's."

"Okay, what time you leaving?"

"As soon as I can pack and pick up Nadia from school, I'm coming."

"You remember how to get here?"

"No, but I know to take I-5 and go through the Grapevine. I'll call you when I get into LA for directions to your house. What exit do I take to get to a phone booth where I can call you?"

"You're going to take the Santa Monica freeway and get off on exit 356."

"Okay, I'll call you. Let me hurry up and get out of here!"

I finished telling Shelise what had happened that morning and how I had borrowed some time to get away. If he thought I was taking care of business away from the house, he had no reason to come home. Plus he thought everything was cool, since I didn't act a fool when I saw that car. That's exactly what I *wanted* him to think. When I got off the phone with Shelise, I called Evelyn.

"Girl, can you come over and help me pack?" "Pack for what?"

"I'm leaving his ass. I'm moving back to Georgia!" "Girl, how yo crazy ass gonna get to Georgia?"

"I'm going to drive."

"Shit, all the way to Georgia?"

"Hell yeah! As a matter of fact, just stay with me on the phone while I get all this stuff together."

"Where's Juelz? With that bitch?" I ran the whole story once again. "Girl, you crazy!"

"I'm gonna pack up what I can in this car and come over there and sort it out, so Nadia can fit in the car."

"Okay!"

"Okay, I'll call you when I am on the way. I can't do this shit and pack. I'm too nervous!"

My heart was beating so fast. I began to shake at the thought of him actually coming home while I was packing. Let me pull this car and the trash can in the garage and close it, so I can throw his shit in it. I pulled the switch to put the garage door on manual, just in case he came home. I could stall until I let him in the house.

The first thing I did was throw all our clothes in the trunk. Then I packed up both bathrooms in bags and threw that in the trunk. I took down all the pictures and packed up all the dishes, setting them on the floor of the car. I packed up the three TVs one from every room ,the microwave and the CD player. I threw all the CDs and cassettes in a box and threw them on the floor. I was shaking so badly. I thought I was going to pass out. I was running from room to room, making sure I hadn't left a thing.

When he did come home, there would be no sign of me anywhere. I pulled open his side of the closet. All those new clothes that I had bought I grabbed them off the rack and threw them in the trash can. Trash day wasn't until Thursday but so what.

I went and got the bleach and the jar of bacon grease from the counter. I poured all of it into the trash can on top

272

of his clothes. Then I set the can out on the curb to be picked up.

I was still running from room to room, looking from wall to wall. I ran to the kitchen! I forgot to take the stuff out of the cabinets. Damn! Lord please don't let this man come home! Please, he will kill me! Jesus! I was so scared I started crying.

When I hopped on the counter to look on the very top shelf, I saw a stack of money and all Juelz's jewelry. There were gold chains and ropes, a watch and two rings. Oh damn! I grabbed *all* that shit! I hopped of the counter so fast to count it that I almost busted my ass.

They were all one hundred dollar bills. One, two, three, four, five, six, seven, eight, nine, ten, eleven, twelve, thirteen, fourteen, fifteen, sixteen, seventeen, eighteen, nineteen, twenty... I couldn't believe money was stashed way up there all that time. The cabinets were so high that I never bothered to put anything up there, let alone look up there. I counted fifty one hundred dollar bills. Thank you, Jesus!

I hadn't even thought about money. Damn, what was I thinking? All I had on me was two hundred dollars and a gang of groceries. I took one good look around the house. It was empty, all right. I stood in the doorway, between the kitchen and the garage. The car was so packed that you couldn't see out the back window.

I grabbed the phone and called my friend, Lena, to let her know my plan. I told her she could come get the refrigerator that Juelz had just bought. It was an all-white, side by side, with automatic water and ice.

"Are you for real, girl? You gonna *drive* your ass to Georgia? I know that's right. I wish I was bold enough to do some shit like that. My dumb ass just gonna stay here and let my baby daddy keep beating my ass till he kill me or I kill him."

"Girl! Now you crazy for that! I'll leave the garage unlocked on manual, so if you get a way, you can have it. If not, fuck it! I'm out this bitch."

"I love you, girl. Call me as soon as you get to your sister's." "I will. Love you too."

I hung up and called Evelyn. "I'm on my way!"

"Okay."

I hopped in the car with my burgundy sports bra and Lem's burgundy paisley boxers on, with tennis shoes and no socks the same shit Juelz beat my ass in. I started the car, opened the garage and I took off down the street. God, I hoped no one saw me.

The first thing they would say would be, "I saw Danielle flying down Mack Road with her car so packed you couldn't even see in the windows." Or worse what if I got stopped by the police for not being able to see out my back window?

I was just praying to make it to Evelyn's. It was a straight shot down Meadowview, and I was able to come up the back way to Florin Rd. When I made it, I ran to the door and asked Evelyn to open the garage so I could rearrange my stuff for travel. I folded the clothes in the trunk and put them in bags. Then I placed most of the bags with the kitchen stuff in the trunk. I had to leave the groceries in the back seat on the floor along with the TVs. I put the microwave on the floor of the passenger seat.

Nadia would have to share her seat with one of the TVs and prop her feet on the microwave. The car was still packed, but at least I could see out the back window enough to where I wouldn't get stopped. It was one o'clock. Evelyn drove me to pick up Nadia from school. When we arrived, I checked Nadia out completely and requested any paperwork I needed to take with me to register her in another state.

"Mama, where are we going?"

"We are going to go back to Georgia to stay with Papa. Or do you want to stay here with your dad?"

"No, I want to go with you." "Okay, then let's go."

"We get to ride with Evelyn?" "Yes."

"Where's our car."

"At Evelyn's house. She was just giving me a ride because the car is packed with all our stuff."

"We're going to *drive* to Georgia?" "Yes."

"Oh! I thought we were going to fly, like last time."

"No, this time we are driving, and we need to drive really fast." "Okay."

Evelyn looked at me and laughed. When we made it back, I said my goodbyes to Evelyn. I told her I was going up the road to the Shell gas station and get the car checked out, to make sure it would make it to Georgia.

"Okay."

"I almost forgot. Let me call Shelise and let her know I am going to be on my way in about an hour."

I planned on leaving around four o'clock. I figured it would take me another hour to get the car checked out and get Nadia something to eat. That would put me on the road at five.

"Well, let me get on the road." "Are you going to be okay?" "Yeah!"

"I wonder what he is going to say. I would love to be a fly on the wall when he gets home."

We both laughed.

"I know, right? Love you! Let me get out of here."

I got in and headed around the bend to the Shell they still had full service. Once I arrived, I asked the question burning in my mind.

"Will this car make it to Georgia?"

He lifted the hood checked all the fluids and then checked the tires. I told him to put four new tires on the car and do whatever else it needed. The only thing it needed was an oil change and a full tank of gas and I was on my way.

One person I did call was my Aunt Chellie. She lived right up the street, but I didn't have time to stop to deal with her in person. I told her I was going to Georgia. I hadn't said anything to my mother because I didn't want her to jinx my trip, but I wanted someone else to know what I was doing.

"Well, you should be okay."

"I'll be going to stay with Shelise for two weeks in Los Angeles until my dad comes back from vacation."

"Then you'll be fine."

"How long does it take to get there?" "You should get there in six hours."

"Okay, then we better leave. It's almost five." "Call and let me know you made it."

"Okay, I will."

"Love you, Danielle." "Love you, too."

I got on the road. I was scared someone would see me going down the I-5. I was speeding, trying to make it out of the city limits. Before I knew it, I made it to Stockton. I kept looking in my rear view mirror, thinking Juelz had found out I left and would try to catch me on the freeway.

If the speed limit was 75mph, I was going 95mph. My heart raced and raced. I was shaking. I didn't know what to think. I just wanted to get out of town fast. I couldn't help thinking that if Juelz caught up with me, he would kill me.

The freeway was one long stretch. It went from five lanes to two lanes. Once I started seeing mountains, I knew I was well on my way. It started getting dark at around 7:30, and once I reached the Grapevine, it started to rain. I remembered what they said about how you will only be able to go only so fast because of the grade.

When that happened, I knew I was on the Grapevine. But it was only going on eight o'clock, after Aunt Chellie had said it would take six hours. Once you cross the Grapevine, you are almost to LA. When it became nine o'clock, I saw the sign for the Santa Monica freeway. What in the world? Was I already in Los Angeles? I started seeing different signs for freeways and cars. *This must be LA!* I had made it. I couldn't wait to get off the exit to call my sister.

I stopped at the first pay phone closest to the freeway. I didn't want to get lost. I jumped out of the car and pulled out the piece of paper with her address and phone number. My heart was still pounding.

"I made it! We're here."

"You're where?" My sister asked in amazement.

"In LA! We are on the corner of Manchester and La Cienega." "Oh my God! How fast were you driving? Are you crazy? You driving that fast with my baby in the car? Girl, I'm going to kill you when you get here."

"I was scared. I was just trying to get out of town."

"Oh my God, Danielle you got here in fuckin four hours, shit!

Nobody does that!"

"Just tell me how to get to your house."

I got the directions, and when I hung up, I called Evelyn. My aunt Lynn answered the phone.

"I see you made it. Evelyn told me what happened. It takes guts to do what you did. Have you called your mom?"

"No, I wanted to call her after I got here. You know *her,*so negative. I didn't want my car to break down or something if I told her what I was doing."

"Well, I'll tell Evelyn you made it."

"Okay. I'll call her tomorrow. I'm on my way to my sister's now."

"Okay, you take care. Keep in touch." "I will."

I got to my sister's with no problem. We had to unpack the car right away, or else someone would have broken into it by morning. We unpacked all the groceries.

"Dang, what did you do? Just go shopping?"

"Yes, that's what I told you we had just went so I just packed it right back up in the same bags."

After we finished putting everything up and in its place, I plugged up the microwave my sister's wasn't working. When I settled in, I began to run down the story of how Juelz jumped on me, about how my *Waiting to Exhale* moment made me cut my hair off, and about how I was running through the house like a mad woman, trying to pack everything in the car to get out of there.

One of her male friends was over, and he was soaking up the whole story as I acted out, play by play. They were laughing, but at the same time they were telling me how crazy I was.

"Shoot! It wasn't funny when I was getting my ass beat, and it wouldn't have been funny if that nigga came home while I was trying to leave his ass. We can laugh now because I'm gone!"

That next morning, Shelise left for work and Evelyn ended up calling me. No one had talked to Juelz since I left. He obviously hadn't been home or called to even know I was gone.

"That is a damn shame!" Evelyn said.

"I told you he wouldn't come home for days at a time, and I wouldn't talk to him unless I called him."

I left on a Monday, Tuesday passed, and it was three days later. I was on the phone with Evelyn, as usual. At that point, we actually *were* in different cities.

Still no word from Juelz. We called over to our cousin's to see if anyone had seen Juelz. I moved out and he hadn't even been back to the house to know.

"That is a damn shame. Well, I guess we'll just sit back and laugh at his ass when the shit hits the fan."

I forgot to turn off the utilities. Evelyn called SMUD on the three-way, and then we called Pacific Bell. That did it. That night Juelz called Evelyn.

"Hey, man you talked to that girl?" "Yeah, I talked to her earlier."

"I was trying to get a hold of her. I been calling the house but her ass ain't been home."

"Oh well, I don't know where she is now." "Well, if you talk to her, tell her to call me." "Okay, I will."

"Boy I can't wait to hear what he has to say once he goes to that house." Evelyn laughed to herself.

Evelyn called me to tell me about the phone call. The house phone hadn't been turned off then, but by morning it was.

That next day, like clockwork, Juelz called Evelyn. "Man, where Danny at?"

"I don't know. I ain't talked to her today."

"I called to the house and the phone off. I just gave her money to pay the mothafucka. When you talk to her tell her ass I said meet me at the house with my mothafuckin car."

278

"Okay, I will."

She was laughing so hard she could barely dial the number to call and tell me.

"Hello?"

"Girl, Juelz just called and he is hot!" "What did he say?"

"He said if you call, tell you to get your ass to the house, cuz he needs the car."

I was like, "Okay, tell him I am on my way." We both laughed.

"I wish I was a fly on the wall when he walks through the door," Evelyn added.

We waited that evening to call over to 33rd. Evelyn got a call from Juelz, ranting and raving. Assuming I was still in Sacramento, he told Evelyn to tell me he was going to kidnap Nadia from school until he found me.

How dumb did he think I was? Like I would really do all of that and be bold enough to stay in the same city. Tarsha was on the line, and sure enough, he was over there, raising hell. They were on the phone whispering about what was going on.

"Girl, this nigga is having a fit. What happened?" "Danielle left his ass."

"What? Where are you?"

"I'm in LA on my way to Georgia."

"What? Are you serious? How did you get down there?" "I drove the car."

"Oh my goodness! This nigga is talking about shootin up yo mama's house. He said you stole his money."

"I did. I moved everything out the house, took his money, poured grease and bleach all over his clothes and put them on the curb in the trash can."

"Is Nadia with you?"

"Yes, we're stayin at my sister's for a few weeks. Let me call my mama."

I clicked over to call my mother. I never told my mother I was leaving. I explained to her what happened and that Juelz had threatened to shoot her house up.

"I wish he would. I'll put a cap in his ass if he comes anywhere near *my* house."

We all started laughing.

"He knows better than to come over here, fuckin with me." "Okay, I just wanted to tell you what was going on."

"I always have to worry about you you always have something going on."

'Don't worry about me, Mama. I'm gonna be fine." "That's easy for you to say. Call me later."

We laughed as Juelz kept cussing everybody out. Tarsha said Aaron told him, "That's what you get!" He told him he was wrong from out the gate, after all I had been through behind him.

The next person I had to call was Devin.

"What you doing in LA. I see that 323 area code?" "I left. I'm at my sister's."

"What you mean, you left?" "I'm moving to Georgia." There was silence.

"What are you doing that for."

"Juelz jumped on me, so I had to get out of there. I couldn't deal with all that."

"Baby, come back. I can get us a place. Fuck that nigga! Bring yo butt back to Sacramento."

"I'm sorry, I can't. I'm scared."

"I got you. You don't need to be scared with me. I need you with me. I already got my situation in order. Just come back."

"I can't."

He hung up the phone in my face. "Hello?"

CHAPTER FORTY-SEVEN

I was scheduled to leave Thursday morning at 5 am. I was scared, but I figured my dad wouldn't allow me to drive alone if he thought I wouldn't be all right. He told me to take I-20 all the way, that it was a straight shot. I wondered what it would be like.

Well, we got on the road while it was still dark out. I said a prayer for me and Nadia and we headed on our way. I went down the street to the light, made a right and hopped on the freeway.

"Well Lord, here we go!"

By daylight I had reached Palm Springs. Nadia was awake, and she had her own little playroom in the backseat. There were coloring books, puzzles and crayons. I stopped at a gas station to fill up. I also decided to buy a map. We searched and searched for a road atlas in Los Angeles, with no luck. At the gas station, I found a good one that was easy to read. Nadia and I looked it over to check out the road ahead.

"Here we are. So it took us five hours to make it to Palm Springs."

Crazy as it may have seemed, we used the finger method to track our time and distance.

"If it took from here to here." Nadia said, measuring distance with her index finger and thumb. Then she put her index finger and thumb on the last mark where her thumb was, to measure the next set of miles.

"Okay, so in five more hours we will be here. So how long will it take us to get to Texas before dark?"

I didn't know how long or how big Texas actually was, but I soon found out.

We got back in the car, Nadia situated in the backseat, and we were ready. Only one thing the car didn't start. I checked the gears, turned the ignition again, and no sound. It was dead.

"Oh my God! What's wrong? The car won't start."

I popped the hood and looked at the battery, which seemed new. I checked to make sure the cables were tight.

"Excuse me, my car won't start. Do you think you could check my battery for me?"

The man looked at me and didn't say a word. "Hello? Excuse me."

He got in his car and drove off, so I asked another man. "Excuse me, my car won't start. Can you help me?"

The man didn't even look my way. He stared straight ahead and walked right on into the store.

My heart started to race. No one is paying me any attention. *Don't tell me I'm stuck in a town full of prejudice ass people!* I sure as hell didn't see any other black people. Oh God! Help me, please! I went into the store and told the cashier my car wouldn't start and that I didn't know what was wrong.

"Is there anyone who knows about cars, or a tow truck that might take a look at it?

"There's a guy that works on cars who stays around the corner. He usually checks up here around lunch time. I could try to page him for you."

"Oh, would you please? Thank you so much." "Can't say when he'll call back, though." "Okay, just go ahead and call. I'll wait."

No sooner than the man picked up the phone, the guy was pulling into the gas station.

"There he goes right there. His name is Tommy." "Thank you so much."

When I approached the primered Cutlass, the driver was a young guy, tanned skin, no shirt on it was hanging from his back pocket. The hair on his chin indicated he was in his mid to late twenties.

"They told me you are the mechanic around here."

"Yes, I try to check up here every day to see if anyone needs any work done. What you got?"

"Well, I don't know. I went to turn my ignition and it wouldn't start. It's the gold Honda over there."

I was so embarrassed. I left the hood down to make it seem as if I had just pulled in to get gas.

"Pop the hood for me." "Okay."

He wasn't under the hood five minutes before he figured out what the problem was.

"It's not your battery. It's these wires right here looks like the rubber has burned off and they are not connecting, so you're not getting any juice. Turn the ignition for me."

I smiled with relief, hoping it would start. "Okay."

When I turned the ignition, it started, but when he let the wires go, it quit.

"That's it. Let me get you some electrical tape. I'll wrap the wires good, and that should hold you for a while."

"Wow! That's *it*?"

He went to his car and grabbed the tape from his trunk, wrapped up the wires and played with the ignition, starting it over and over.

"You should be fine."

"Thank you so much! How much do I owe you?"

"Not a thing. That wasn't any trouble. You have a safe trip."

"Thank you so much."

I hopped in the car and I told Nadia to do the measuring again.

We marked each stop with a dot.

"Okay, you ready? Do you have to go to the bathroom?"

"No."

"Okay then let's go."

We were on the road again. Daddy was right, as it was a straight shot. We tried to hurry to get to Georgia. I drove at an average of ninety miles per hour, calculating we would get there the next night if I drove nonstop. I ended up getting stopped by the police for speeding.

"Sorry Officer."

"Can you tell me, what's the rush?"

"Well I'm just trying to make it to Georgia with my little girl. I never traveled this far and I'm just a little scared."

The officer could tell from our plates that we were from California. All our stuff stacked in the car, with Nadia in the back seat.

"Well, just be careful and slow down. Have a safe trip. You'll be fine."

"Thank you, sir." "Take care."

Whew! He scared the shit out of me! I just knew he was going to give me a ticket.

I forgot that I had promised my Aunt Laura I would stop and sleep in a hotel. I went to visit her with Shelise before I left, she even gave me fifty dollars. I drove all day until I got tired. I didn't know where I was. I just kept driving. By nightfall, I drove through what appeared to be a desert. I saw fields of windmills. I figured that if I could make it to the next city, I would stop and rest there.

I stopped at what I thought was a store or gas station. I parked on the side of the building and made sure all the car doors were locked. It was ten o'clock. I let my eyes close and fell asleep.

Loud noises and smells woke me up. I had parked in the middle of a truck stop. I saw a sign, *Welcome to El Paso*. I didn't notice it until the trucks came. My car was surrounded by trucks full of pigs. Oh my God! I guess I *was* in the wrong spot. It was eleven o'clock. I had slept for an hour. Nadia was still asleep.

"I'm not that sleepy. I'm going to keep driving."

I hopped back on the road and continued my drive, barreling along all night on a two-lane highway. It was pitch black. I started thinking about all my past events all that had happened in my life and what was to come. I never thought about any plan that God had for my life. I was paranoid, adrenaline pumping through my veins. I was wide awake. I could drive all night.

It was so dark I couldn't even see Nadia in the back seat. I just held tight onto the steering wheel, sitting straight up, and drove until the sun came up.

It was six in the morning, and I had to get a few minutes of rest. I pulled into a convenient store and parked off to the side. Nadia was awake. I told her that she was going to be the lookout.

"Okay Mommy. What am I *looking* for?"

"If anyone comes close to the car, honk the horn first so that you will scare the hell out of them. Then wake me up if you don't scare the hell out of me first."

She laughed and entertained herself with coloring as I went to sleep. Three hours passed. It was nine o'clock.

"Oh shit! It's already nine? I must have been sleeping good Nadia, you okay?"

The store started getting busy. I thought we better get on the road. I had only wanted to sleep for an hour.

"You have to use the bathroom?"

"Yes."

"You want some orange juice? We can find a McDonald's." We went into the store to use the bathroom.

"What state are we in?"

"You are in the state of Texas."

"Texas? Still? I was in El Paso at 11 PM last night, and I'm still in Texas?"

"Yes ma'am. It takes a whole day to drive through Texas."

I got back on the highway and made it to Dallas by three o'clock. I called my mother to let her know where I was, and I told her I needed my dad to wire me some money. When he passed through Los Angeles, I gave him my money, because he said it wasn't safe to travel with that much cash. I didn't realize how much money I would have to spend on gas. When I reached my dad, I told him I needed him to wire me some money.

"I will be in Louisiana at seven o'clock tonight, so I can pick it up there."

"Where are you now?" "I am in Dallas."

"Oh, you won't make it to Louisiana." "Yes I will, trust me."

"You don't know those roads. You are still a ways from Louisiana."

"Just wire the money and I'll get it. I'll call you when I get there. Thank you, mama, love you."

I got off the phone and got back in the car. "Too bad I couldn't stay in Dallas."

"I know it's some dudes in this city. Wish I could ride around some neighborhoods."

But I didn't know anyone or which way to go. It was just a thought, so I was on my way to the highway. We arrived in Louisiana at seven o'clock. I looked for a Western Union and for a pay phone to call my father.

"Okay, Daddy, you can send it." "Where are you?"

"In Louisiana. Sir, what city is this?" "Shreveport."

"I'm in Shreveport, Louisiana."

"Girl, you were humpin it, weren't you!"

"I told you I would be here. Me and Nadia are timing everything on the map. We should be there tomorrow sometime right?"

"Your sister is having a baby shower tomorrow. Mama is up at Michelle's. Why don't you stop by there."

"Okay."

I thought about stopping by, if I could remember how to get there. But did I really want to stop, with all my drama? And with everything I owned in my car? I just wanted to get to my destination and breathe.

"Okay, Daddy if I remember how to get there, I will."
"Okay. See you tomorrow. Drive safe baby."

"I will. Thank you, Daddy."

I didn't like my surroundings much. The store was dirty and men were hanging out drinking. It just wasn't clean. I hurried and got back in the car, locking the doors. I didn't know who saw me getting money, so I didn't want to take any chances. You can never be too careful. We got back on the road of course, found a McDonald's and got Nadia a happy meal. I hopped back on the highway.

"Mama, can we please sleep in a bed tonight?" "I thought you were okay?"

"No. I want to sleep in a bed. I'm tired of sleeping in this back seat."

"Well it's a good thing you said something. It's almost 11 o'clock."

I drove to the next state I saw Mississippi. "Wow! Two more states and we're in Georgia!" "Okay."

I drove another half hour, until I saw a suitable motel room and stopped at the one that looked like it was still open, and clean.

"Well, Aunt Laura I'm keeping my promise."

I planned to send back the receipt in a card. We parked around the back and grabbed a bag from the trunk. I hoped no one would steal the microwave or the TVs. I tried to cover them with the blanket. We settled in the room and took a hot bubble bath. I laid out our clothes and made sure I had everything together. I did not want to forget anything. I set the alarm for 6 a.m., wanting to get an early start back on the road.

Morning came fast, but we had a good night sleep. We woke up at 6 a.m. without the alarm clock. Nadia found some cartoons to watch while I got dressed. I loaded everything back in the car and got on the road by seven. We checked the map, using our finger method, and we determined that in four hours, by eleven o'clock, we would be in Birmingham, Alabama, where we could probably catch McDonald's for breakfast. We made it there four hours later, like clockwork. I forgot that McDonald's stopped serving breakfast at 10:30. The breakfast menu was unavailable, so we had to settle for lunch.

We went through the drive-through and headed right back to the highway, Georgia bound.

"How long will it take us to get to Atlanta, Nadia?"

Nadia had the map, measuring with her finger, and she said we were just two hours from Atlanta. My father had told me Tifton our final destination, was three hours from Atlanta. So that would put us in Tifton by four o'clock.

"Okay, then let's get it."

I decided we wouldn't to stop at Michelle's. I wanted to get right to Tifton, *Don't pass go, Don't collect two hundred dollars!* I wanted to get straight to my final destination, safe with my father.

"Why hasn't she called?"

My mom picked up the phone to check the dial tone, and then she decided to call my father, to see if he had heard from me.

"No, I thought she was in touch with you."

"No. I haven't talked to her since we were on the phone in Texas."

"Well she hasn't called here. I've been looking out for her. She should be here sometime tonight."

"Okay. make sure she calls me as soon as she gets there."

I never saw a sign that said "Tifton," but I knew I was on 75 South. I was scared I was going the wrong way, but I kept driving even faster, hoping to see a sign at some point. I knew it had been almost three hours, and it was almost 4 o'clock.

It was three-thirty when I finally saw a sign that said Tifton was thirty-seven miles away. Nadia was sleep.

"We are almost there!"

I pulled out the directions my father gave me so I wouldn't pass up the exit. The exits were so spaced out in Georgia that it would be a good 10 minutes before you came up on another one.

"We're *here!*"

Nadia looked out the window. "Yay!"

I got off on the exit. *Turn left off the freeway. After the traffic light, make the first right on Carolina Drive. Come down two streets to Texas Drive and make a left. The house is on the right.* On Texas Drive, I looked to my left and saw my dad's red 356 Porsche.

"There's the house."

We were excited and I was relieved. I pulled into the driveway, relieved to have finally made it safe. They didn't have a garage just a carport, attached to the house. It looked like a garage with no door. As I knocked, I couldn't wait to see my father, to see the look on his face.

"Thank you, Jesus!"

That was the first thing he said when he opened the door. He hugged me so tight.

"Thank you, Jesus! Thank you, Jesus! Girl, you was humpin! I didn't expect to see you until sometime tonight."

"Not at all. I was trying to get here. I was scared, so I was just trying to hurry up."

"Come on in and sit down."

"I need to go to the bathroom."

"Come on let me show you where it is. Then I'll show you around. Nadia, come give Papa some sugar. Look at *you* just growing like a weed."

When I finally sat down, I told my father the whole ordeal with Juelz. I shared with him what led to me leaving and the details about how I left. I told my father everything that was on my heart. We laughed, and then we cried. We prayed and put our heads together to come up with a plan for my days ahead.

The first thing I had to do was get Nadia into school Monday morning. Then I would look for a job. I was still on welfare, so my mother would continue to deposit my checks in my account. That would help with my rent for when I found an apartment. I didn't know how long I would be allowed to stay with my father, but my plan was to get my own place as soon as I could. I was safe. My stepmom was staying in Atlanta, helping Michelle get prepared for her baby and for her six weeks.

"Oh, call your mother and tell her you made it." "Oh, yes. Let me do that."

"Little girl, you had us worried."

"I'm fine. I was just trying to get here." "Why didn't you tell me you were leaving?"

"It was spur of the moment. I had to get out of there, and I didn't want you to talk me out of it or jinx me. Because if you had told me not to go and I did, my car might have broken down or something. You know how you think so negative I just didn't want anyone to know. I was scared, and I just didn't want to keep living like that. If I had stayed, he wouldn't have let me go. I'm in good hands here. I'm ready to start over with my life. I will call you every day."

"Okay. I just worry about you."

My father talked about the town he lived in and about how the Lord had blessed them the entire time they had been there. He also thanked me for the money I sent while they were making their transition. They received money from all of the children who could help. That was during the time I was stashing Chase's money. I wished I had taken more than I did, but I was glad I was able to come through for my father when he needed me.

Later, after I got settled in, my father took us out to dinner. When we returned, we walked around the neighborhood while he explained how the Lord showed him the house they had acquired. When they arrived two years earlier, the plan was to move to Albany, but God showed them this town called Tifton. He said he looked it up and began to scope it out. When he found a building to rent, he said he went down every day, but he couldn't operate until his license was approved in Georgia.

"It was a blessing. I was obedient to the Lord's word. Albany had just had a horrific flood, so if we had moved to Albany, we would have lost everything."

The town seemed quiet. I hadn't seen any black people so far. I thought I was going to have to come with a big plan, or I was going to be bored to death. The next day when I woke up, my father was gone. He must have gone to church and didn't want to wake us. I had hoped he didn't ask us to go, because I didn't want to.

When he got home, Nadia and I were dressed and ready. He was taking us to see the rest of the town, and he wanted to take me down to see his office. We went out to eat first. He said a lady from the church told him the hospital was hiring for Registration Clerk. That next day, I got Nadia registered for school and went straight to the hospital to put in an application.

As we rode around, my father drove over to the south side of town. Down the main street, who would have thought it was named South Central! And there were black people there! I got so excited. *Now this is what I'm talking bout!*

There were crowds of people hanging out on the corner, at a car wash. People were walking up and down the street. I knew I would be right back over there, trying to see who I could meet, once I had time to get out on my own. The last time I came to Georgia, I didn't have a car and had to depend on Michelle to take me around, but not this time. I was free to go wherever I wanted, and I didn't have to depend on anyone this time.

I waited to hear back from the hospital. Within two weeks, they called me for an interview. I was nervous. I met with the supervisor of the department. After the interview, they said they would call me back for a panel interview and they would go from there. I hated the thought of a second interview, not to mention a panel. That made me even more nervous.

I waited and waited to hear from the hospital for the second interview. No call. That next week, they called.

"May I speak with Danielle Manning?" "Speaking."

"This is a Marsha with Tift General. We wanted to offer you the position in our registration department."

"Okay."

"We want you to come to our personnel office and take a drug screening and fill out consent for a criminal background check."

"Okay. What day should I come?"

"If you have time today, we would love for you to get that taken car of today. That way, we can get you started in our next orientation."

"I can be there shortly. Thank you again."

"Do you know where our personnel office is located? We are the right across the street from the hospital with the blue coverings."

"Okay. Thank you."

On the way to the lab for my blood test, I ran into a guy who worked there.

"Are you lost?"

"Well, no. I just came from the lab." "Oh, are you starting here?"

"Yes. I start orientation Monday."

"Oh, okay. Congratulations. I'm Ricky." "Hello. I'm Danielle. Nice to meet you."

"You too. Well, you should like working here. I've been here almost five years."

"You have a pen?" "Yes."

"Take my number. If you need someone to show you around, just call me."

"Okay."

I put his number in my pocket. When I got home, I put his name and number in my phone book. I never used the number I forgot I even had it. I worried all night about the background check. I remembered being told to always tell the truth about my felony, because if they found out, they could fire you for giving false information on an application. I figured that maybe they couldn't check that information from another state. Either way it went, I was off of parole, *and I wasn't telling nothin!*

They wanted me to start the next orientation on Monday. Had the criminal background check come back already? No one said anything. Orientation was held in a small classroom. I was the first of person there. I was nervous as I watched everyone else enter the room. There were two black guys and one other black girl. She would be working in the same department as me. One of the black guys ended up sitting right behind me. He was tall, kind of skinny and dressed real neat. I didn't pay him much attention, but during the two-week orientation, we all became close enough to laugh together, eat together and hold conversations.

By the end of orientation, it was evident that he liked me.

"Girl, what are you going to do?" "About what?"

"About that *man*! You know he likes you don't act like you don't know."

We both laughed as I blushed. He had made it pretty obvious. His name was Brian. He sat behind me during the entire orientation, always commenting on my every word. And if he stepped out to grab a drink, he made sure he brought me back one too. Every day, after orientation, he showed up at my desk.

"You going anywhere for lunch?"

"No. I was just going to the cafeteria." "Do you mind if I join you?"

"Sure. I mean, sure I don't mind."

I actually liked him. He was tall and very well built. He was on the slender side, but he wasn't skinny. He still could have been every bit of 230 pounds broad shoulders, chocolate skin and a nice bald head. He had dark features and a light thin mustache. I noticed he had earring piercings in both ears. He was a former Marine, which was impressive. He was hired in the MIS department. He could actually disassemble a computer and put it back together. I was very impressed. I looked forward to his company and I couldn't resist his charm.

I planned to get my own apartment sooner than I thought. My father took me around, looking at different properties. I found an attractive complex, not too far from him. One apartment seemed to be under renovation. The walls were freshly-painted and the floors were cement, which meant new carpet and new tile would have to be put down.

"This is the one I want. Everything will be new."

We went over to the property management company down the street to inquire about the particular unit. It could be ready by the 15th of October. That would be perfect. I could use the rest of the money to move in and buy furniture. I would have my first paycheck by then, and I had already got my welfare check from the 1st, which was five hundred and ninety-five dollars.

The rent was $525 for a two-bedroom, one-bath. I didn't have any rental history I could use, so they required an extra month's rent on top of the first, last and deposit. I was happy to pay it, as long as it got me in the apartment. I was so excited to have my new place apartment A-1, first of the first.

And before I got off work, I asked Brian if he would mind helping me clean the apartment before I moved my things in. He said he'd be happy to help. He didn't have a car, so he usually rode with his sister, who also worked at the hospital in Central. I agreed to give him a ride home after we finished. The carpet was new, and so was the flooring in the kitchen. I loved that new smell. Brian did most of the cleaning.

Georgia was known for having huge roaches. I think they have another name for them here. He swept a few from the cabinets. Everything seemed to be in order. That weekend, my father gave me a mattress set and rails, and we went to the Goodwill to find a twin set for Nadia. I had my bathroom and kitchen stuff all together. I bought a few sheets sets, and that about did it. I had the basics. I was just happy I had my own place.

During the time I stayed with her father, my stepmom kept her bedroom door closed and locked. I didn't think anything of it. I never knew the door was locked, until one day my father came home for lunch and went to open it.

"Is Mama here?"

"I don't know. The door is always closed. If she is, she hasn't come out."

Before I started working, I would get dressed and leave the house, without even saying a word. I didn't want to disturb her, in case she was still sleeping. I got the feeling that my stepmom didn't care for me to be there. I wasn't trying to follow my father. I just wanted to come back to Georgia. There was nothing in California for me any longer.

After that incident, my father was upset to hear her morning routine. Then I figured it must have been a problem with me staying there, but she didn't have to worry about it any longer. Because God had blessed me with a job and an apartment in less than thirty days!

When I went over to the mall to look for work attire, I ran into a girl named Annie. She seemed very sweet. She was real short, with a tiny frame. We ended up hitting it off. She already knew my father.

"What is there to do in this town?"

"Nothing too much. On Sundays, everybody just walk the road."

"Walk the road? What is that?"

"You know, when you just walk up and down the main street on South Central?"

Oh, I knew where that was, but walking up and down the street seem real boring.

"Albany is having their homecoming. You like football?"

"No."

Well, Homecoming is a big deal. The clubs are usually packed. We have a real good time. I know a girl I can introduce you to. I will give her your number and see if she can take you around, and maybe you can go with her.

I did hook up with some other girls, but I had no fun. I didn't get home until three in the a.m. When I woke up the next morning, my father was extremely upset. I didn't know at the time why he would not speak a word.

When I said "Good morning" he just mumbled. It wasn't until later, over dinner, that he complained about me coming home at that time of morning. In that case, my stepmom made a good point that I was grown, and it was my first time out. I thought nothing of it, but my dad was pissed that I came in that late, or that early.

Brian and I started eating lunch together every day. He would just pop his head in my cubicle and ask if I was ready to go to lunch? Of course I couldn't refuse. We went at the same time every day. We talked about everything and found out that we had few things in common, mainly our tastes in music, but not much else. Still, he was very interesting to me. There were never any of those awkward moments of silence. When we talked, he kept me laughing , with all his jokes and charm, not to mention the way he smiled, looking into my eyes.

We both knew something was there. I just wondered how far it was going to go. After work, we started leaving together and would go to my house after picking up Nadia from school. On a few occasions, Brian would stay over for dinner. One particular night, he decided to cook for me. He told me to just sit back and relax. Brian helped Nadia with her homework and fixed her plate for dinner. After dinner, I told Nadia to take her bath and get ready for bed.

When she had gone to bed, Brian fixed dinner for the two of us. He turned out most of the lights and we sat in the kitchen, holding hands at the table. Brian always kept a smile on his face, he began to feed me. *I wondered what was going on.* That had never happened to me before. He cooked dinner, cleaned the kitchen and helped my daughter with her homework. I thought it was not real. Was that what I finally deserved, after years of nothing?

The next few weeks felt like months. We grew closer and closer. Almost four weeks had gone by. Brian came over after work for dinner every night, and I let him take my car home. Then he would be there in the morning to pick us up. He dropped Nadia off at school while I finished getting dressed. I felt comfortable with him. The way he treated me was special, like I was the only one that mattered. How could I have been so lucky to have found someone so sweet and thoughtful? He had just got out the Marines and I snagged him.

Thanksgiving was coming up. Brian asked if I would come meet his family. I said yes, but I was nervous about the idea. Annie also called me, to see if I wanted to come to her family function.

"Hey girl, how have you been?" "Fine. How have you been?"

"Good. Workin just workin. What are your plans for Thanksgiving?"

"Well me and my daughter are going to go over to Brian's to meet his family."

"You're going to meet his *family*?"

"Yes, he asked me to spend Thanksgiving over there." "Girl, quit lying."

"I'm not lying. He asked me for real." "Whatever, girl. I'll talk to you later." "Okay."

I was shocked. What was *that* all about? Did she really think I needed to lie about something like that? Needless to say, I didn't talk to Annie again.

Everything went well. His family was nice. They made me feel at home, especially since Brian threw me to the wolves. I had to fix my own plate.

"Naw, baby you family. Go on and fix your plate."

That next month, Brian moved in with me, two weeks before Christmas. We were a great couple. Michelle had had her baby boy, and their family came down for Christmas. I had loved that little baby. I was happy for my sister.

At Christmas dinner, I ate so much I couldn't hold my eyes open. Brian took my car to visit his family, while I stayed at my father's and enjoyed my family. I loved when we were all together. I had really missed Michelle, even if she did piss me off for how she treated me when I stayed with her.

"BaeBae!" Brian called me.

I had never had anyone to call me that or any other pet name. "Nigga" and "mama" didn't count as terms of endearment. Names like that didn't roll off my tongue. I just called him Brian.

"You know we've been getting busy a lot lately, with no interruptions."

"What you mean?"

"I mean, I ain't had to run to the Winn-Dixie, to buy you your little friends."

"What are you talking about?"

"You're cycle baby. You haven't had one in a couple months." "Dang! I hadn't paid any attention to that!"

"And you have been eating enough for three grown men. You know you inhale your food? I don't believe you even know what it tastes like."

"Shut up, boy!"

"I'm just sayin' baby."

I *had* gained a few pounds, and I gave most of my dresses to Brian's niece. When I was at work, I went to the lab and had a pregnancy test done. There was a lady who worked over in that department who took a liking to me. Well, when I got the results back, I put them in an envelope, called Brian and asked him to come to my desk.

"I have something for you." I told him over the phone. When he arrived, I handed him the envelope.

"Call me when you get back to your desk."

The phone rang not a minute after the sentence left my mouth.

"Baby, is this for real?"

"Yes, I'm pregnant."

"Geesh, baby. I don't know what to say."

"What you mean, you don't know what to say."

"I don't know. I'm just at a loss for words right now."

I didn't know what to think. We decided to talk about it when we got home. My mind was going one thousand miles to nowhere. Did I want another baby? The answer would have to be, *no.* By the time we got home, we were anxious to let reality

298

sink in about the baby, but we decided we weren't ready, and we didn't want to have any children right then.

"Is that *wrong* of us?"

"No, baby. We just have to be careful. I didn't know your butt was so fertile." Brian said as he winked at me. He pulled me close. "Come here baby. Everything will be all right. We're just not ready."

I agreed and I didn't give it a second thought. Brian got in touch with his cousin later that week to find out where he and his wife had gone for their abortion. When he got the information, he passed it to me and we made an appointment in a nearby city. It would be the second week in January.

After that, we made it through the Christmas holiday. Brian took extra tender-loving care of me. On the scheduled date, we went to our supervisors and requested the day off. On the morning we arrived at the clinic, I couldn't eat or drink anything. I was starving and nervous. I really couldn't believe I had gotten pregnant again. *I had been pregnant every year for the last three years!*

"Okay, Ms. Manning let me get some information about your medical history. How many pregnancies have you had?"

"Four."

"So you have four children?" "No."

"How many living?" "One." "Miscarriages?" "One."

"Abortions or still-births?"

"Two abortions, this one included?"

"No."

She finished up with the questions and prepared me for the procedure. Brian had to stay in the waiting room. He was so nervous he just kept kissing on me and rubbing my face. When I went back, he was pacing the floor.

"Lord, I know this is *wrong* of us, but can you please watch over Danielle? I love her, and if you get us through this, I will let her make me an honest man. I know that's not how the saying goes, but Lord, you know what I mean someone to keep me straight. I haven't always been the best person, but

I try. I know I have a bad temper, but Lord, just help me with that, and I promise to treat her right."

Brian kept going to the desk. "How's Ms. Manning?"

"I believe she's fine, sir. They will call you when she is ready.

She'll need to remain in recovery after the procedure." "Okay, thanks."

Brian kept checking the time on his watch.

"Damn this is taking forever! Every twenty minutes seems like two hours!"

"Mr. Jackson, you can pull to the back of the clinic to pick up Ms. Manning."

"Okay. Thank you sweetheart."

Brian went around the back, but I had not come out yet. He pulled a cigarette from his sock. I didn't know he smoked, and he wanted to keep it that way, but right then, he was a nervous wreck. When the door opened, he threw the cigarette down. The nurse wheeled me out, and Brian ran around to open the car door and help me in the seat.

"Baby, you all right?" "Yes." I mumbled.

Brian put the seat belt around me and gave me a kiss on my forehand. I slept all the way home, which wasn't but an hour drive. Once we arrived at the apartment, Brian carried me to our bedroom.

"Baby, I'm hungry."

"You want me to run and get you something?"

I slept for another two hours, with Brian sitting at the edge of the bed holding my hand.

"What do you want?"

"You can just get me a cheeseburger happy meal with no pickles, and a chocolate shake instead of a drink."

"Okay sweetheart. I'll be right back. You sure you're going to be okay while I'm gone?"

"I'll be okay."

I drifted right back to sleep. When I woke up, he was bringing my food to the side of the bed. I bit into the cheeseburger, but it had no cheese.

"Brian, it doesn't have any cheese on it. I can't eat it without cheese. I don't want it."

I took the fries out and put the hamburger in the bag. Brian looked at me like I was crazy. I caught a glance of that look and thought I'd better chill out. He still had to go get me some pads from Winn-Dixie. I waited a minute before I told him that, but he was a good sport. He went and got them.

I took off work the next two days and then it was the weekend. I would return to work on Monday. Brian went back to work the next day.

We had a good routine down. He gave me his check, keeping twenty to put in his pocket, and then I would buy whatever we needed for the house, along with groceries. I paid the rent with my welfare check from California, and Brian's work check paid the utilities. We kept the money in one account. If we needed to go anywhere or buy something extra, we had it to spend.

Nadia started playing basketball for the city recreation center. Each time Brian dropped her off, I stayed in the car while he walked Nadia into her practice. I never really knew how good she was. I never attended any of her games, because Nadia never wanted me to come. I never thought anything of it.

Nadia became friends with some girls from the team who lived around the corner from Brian's mother. So on the weekend, they asked if it would be okay if Nadia spent the night.

"Sure, if you don't mind, that would be fine. I have an early hair appointment. Would you mind if I picked her up after that?"

"Of course, that's no problem."

So Nadia stayed overnight. I looked forward to being home alone with Brian. Our chemistry was so strong. We loved to kiss and make love every chance we got. Always a quickie before work, and definitely once we got in bed before we went to sleep. Every day! I didn't think his sexual appetite ever got satisfied.

Once we made it home, Brian wanted to hear some Maxwell. I turned out the lights and jumped in the shower. I always knew when we kissed and he caressed my body that he would soon make his way between my thighs. His tongue was so soft that he could make me reach that point of ecstasy over and over again. He tasted me, like I held the sweetest taste he ever had. At times it was so good to him that he couldn't help slipping his tongue inside me. I continuously climb the walls. That's when he loved to hold my arms down at my sides, so I couldn't move. Having so many orgasms was torture, and he loved to count them. One night he counted eight.

I came out of the bathroom with my towel on. He grabbed me, not letting me slip on anything else. We danced in the middle of the living room, kissing and holding each other, with the rhythm of *When the Cops Come Knocking*. I couldn't believe anyone could make me feel so special and so good to love.

Everything was happening so fast. It was like we had been dating for years, instead of just three or four months. I thought I finally was getting what I deserved. He even took me to get my nails and feet done on payday, and he would sit there with me. As we danced, my towel fell to the floor.

"Leave it."

He started kissing my breasts, then his hand rubbed gently between my thighs, his fingers making circles around my clit. He kissed me again, slipping his tongue inside my mouth. He lifted one of my legs by my thigh and guided me to the wall. He kneeled down and began to lick between my thighs. I knew what that meant, and if *that* was going down, I needed to be in the bed, on my back. I didn't want to waste that sensation on my feet.

"Wait, wait let's go get in the bed." "Okay."

We both went down the hall to the bedroom and fell on the bed. Brian was right behind me, spreading my legs to get right back to the tasting. After I had about four orgasms, I wanted to feel my man deep inside me. As we kissed I could taste my pussy on his lips. Hell, I didn't care. He tasted so good. I just wanted to take it all in.

We lied beside each other. The light was still on in the room and we talked. In the heat of the moment, my purse got pushed to the floor. After I went into the bathroom, Brian had sat up on the edge of the bed. Glancing at the floor, he noticed my purse, where my phonebook had fallen out next to it.

He went to pick it up off the floor, but something inside him led him to examine it, instead of putting it back in my purse. He skimmed through the pages. It was empty as far as the phone number section showed, but it didn't stop him from seeing one number: *Rick 229-382-1568.*

Brian felt his heart racing and his mind thinking back to our conversation. *She told me she didn't know anyone else in Tifton. She lied!*

He waited for me to come out of the bathroom. When I returned to the bed, Brian was putting on some shorts in the doorway of our walk-in closet.

"BaeBae,you know anyone in Tifton?" "Nope!"

"And you haven't met anybody since you've been here?"

"No. I haven't been anywhere to meet anyone. You're the only person I've met, and that's because we started at the hospital together."

"So you haven't met any guys?"

"No! Why do you keep asking me that?" "Who's Rick?"

"I don't know a 'Rick'."

"You don't know anybody named Rick?" "No, I don't know anybody named Rick."

I had forgotten about the guy from the hospital, until Brian showed me the name and number in my book.

"I don't even remember *writing* that! I don't know who that is!" "You know who it is!"

Brian jumped on me so fast I didn't know what hit me. He sat on top of me, with his knees on my shoulders. He grabbed me around the neck and started choking me.

"Who is Rick? You're going to lie to my face and tell me you don't know who the Nigga is!"

I couldn't say anything, but he kept yelling at me asking me the same questions. I tried to buck him off of me, but it didn't work. I tried to be still, in the hope that he would stop, but he didn't.

I couldn't believe what was happening. How was I going to get him off of me? He started putting his fingers up my nose, as if to puncture my membranes. I shook my head from side to side, but I couldn't move my body at all. When he moved his knee off one of my shoulders, I bucked my body to try to get loose, but he still had my wrists.

"Please let me go!"

He refused. I understood why he was mad, but had taken it to the next level.

"Get the fuck off me, Brian!"

I screamed for help. I knew the neighbors upstairs had to hear me screaming. Brian grabbed me and put me in a head lock. He had my arms behind my head and pushed my face down in the pillow. *Oh God! He's trying to kill me!* When I tried to resist, it felt like my arms would break or come out of the sockets.

He lifted my head, just in case I couldn't breathe. I couldn't fight him off. I used all my body weight to throw him off, causing the mattress to slide off the box springs. Our bodies slid into the corner, behind the bed. I was stuck again, because he still had my arms behind my back. If I moved my neck, it would have snapped. I stopped screaming and decided to lie there still.

When he let me up, that was all I needed to charge at him. We wrestled to the floor. I could give him a run for his money, since he was no longer using military tactics to restrain me. I kicked and slapped him as much as I could, but he locked on me again and pinned me back on the bed. I was crying by then, and I was tired.

"Please stop! Please!"

He tried to poke my eyes out and bit my arm. If I moved, the bite got harder. All I could do was cry.

"Get off of me! Get off! You're hurting me, Please let me go." When he let me go I tried to get to the phone to call my dad or

911, but he had snatched the phone out of the wall and locked the bedroom door.

"Please stop, please!" I cried.

Brian grabbed me again. I was tired. We were sweating and my heart was racing. I wouldn't give up. Every time I got the strength, I tried to break away from his hold. I couldn't grab him my hands were too sweaty. I bit his arm like he bit me, but he was biting me in the back.

"Ouch! You're hurting me! Please stop!"

I had to let him go or he would have bit a hole in my back. His teeth were so sharp. He tortured me until five o'clock in the morning. My nose had started to bleed after I tried to head bunt him in the face.

He stopped! He got off of me, opened the door and went into the hallway to the living room. I ran across the hall into the bathroom and locked the door. On the other side of the bathroom, I fell to the floor, holding onto the toilet.

"Oh my God! Oh my God!" I screamed. He banged on the door.

"Danielle, open this door!" "Leave me alone."

"Open the door!"

"Fuck you Brian! You motherfucka! Leave me alone!" "Danielle, open the door!"

He grabbed the door knob.

"I'm sorry. Let me talk to you. I promise I won't touch you. I've called JC and he's on his way to get me. I've packed my stuff. I know I was wrong."

"Wrong! You son of a bitch! You tried to kill me? You are crazy!

I want you to get out. Get all your shit and get out!" I cried.

I stayed in the bathroom until he left. I heard the door close, and it was quiet. I peeked out the bathroom door and didn't hear anything. I walked into my bedroom and went to the closet. All his things were gone. I peeked out the window. No other cars were there but mine. I crept into the living room no sign of him.

I walked to the front door, and it was still unlocked. I locked the door and walked toward the kitchen. His key was on the ledge of the kitchen counter. He was gone. I walked to the window once more and peeked out. Was he really gone, or would he come back? It was six o'clock in the morning. My hair appointment was at ten. I went back to my room and cried. I tried to clean up and make the bed. I threw the phone out the back door. He had yanked it out the wall, and the wall would have to be repaired.

I sat on the floor and stared at the bed. I replayed the whole scene in my mind. He could have killed me. *Who the fuck is Rick anyway?* I couldn't believe that shit! It was daylight outside, so there was no way I could go to sleep. I sat there, and tears began to roll down my face.

I left California because I didn't want to go through what I just left. How could I have been so fooled? Who was he? What happened to the man I met and made love to every day? He was crazy! I knew it was too good to be true, and I thought I loved him. Oh, and I was carrying his child. No! I'm glad I didn't give the abortion a second thought.

I went to the closet to pick out something to wear, and then I ran the shower and got in. I wished I had never met him. I let the water run down my face, along with my tears, down the drain. I was tired and weak. I had to go straight to my father's house. I had to tell him.

When my father opened the door I started to cry. "What's wrong? What's the matter?"

"He tried to kill me." "Who Brian?"

"Didn't you feel me calling for help in your spirit? Daddy, he tortured me all night until five o'clock this morning."

"I've seen him riding by the, house back and forth. Where is he now?"

"I don't know he packed all his stuff and left. I told him he had to leave."

"Well now, you see what type of man he is. Leave him alone and don't take him back."

"I'm not."

I explained to my father everything he did to me how he pulled the phone out the wall and locked the bedroom door and wouldn't let me out. I told my father I was on the way to a hair appointment and that I would stop by when I got back. As I rode down the highway, a little red car appeared out of nowhere. It pulled up beside me, and when I looked, it was Brian. My heart started to race. What the fuck did he want?

"Pull over, pull over!" He yelled out the passenger window.

I kept straight ahead and didn't stop. Certainly, he wouldn't follow me out of town, so I kept driving.

I finally get my hair done, and after the previous night, it was a mess. I started to cry again. I had to sit in the car until I could get myself together. I made it upstairs to the shop. I had enough of those spritz up-dos that I couldn't comb through.

While I was in the chair, my back stayed turned to the mirror. The beautician wouldn't let me look in the mirror at all while she styled my hair. I couldn't wait to see it. I was just getting a few colored tracks sewn in, like I did back home. When she was finished, she turned the chair around. I couldn't wait.

When I looked in the mirror, I couldn't believe what I thought I saw. What the hell did she do? I was instantly upset. What was she thinking? All I wanted was a cute style with a few highlighted pieces. My whole head of hair was blonde, and it was as high as a bee hive. What the hell was that? I was upset and I had to pay eighty-five dollars for something I was going to take out as soon as I got home.

I was so furious, I couldn't even speak. Everyone in the salon kept saying how cute it was. The hell it was! That shit was ugly!

"How much do I owe you? Eighty-five?"

I gave her the money and left without so much as a thank you. All the way home, I couldn't believe I wasted my money and my time, because it was almost four o'clock. As soon as I got back in town, I went to pick up Nadia, hoping not to run into Brian. I made it! No sign of him anywhere while I picked up my daughter. After we made it home, I tried to figure out what I was going to do with my hair. I had to call home and tell Candi what happened.

The next day Brian called and asked if he could come over and talk. I agreed. When he arrived, we sat out back on the porch. I listened to his long speech and after he was done, I had questions to ask.

"Who were you that night? Why did you do that to me?"

"I don't know." Brian confessed. "I just clicked. I don't know what happened. I love you. I never meant for that to happen and it will never happen again."

I felt sorry for him. Clearly something was wrong, and I thought maybe I could fix it. He asked if he could bring his stuff back. He vowed to me that it would never happen again, and if there was ever anything that even resembled an argument, he would leave, no questions asked, and the relationship would be over.

I allowed him to come back. He had no place to go. A few weeks went by and I was out of my MAC makeup. He rode up to Atlanta with his cousin, JC. It would be perfect he could go to Michelle's while he waited on his cousin to handle his affairs, and they could go over to the mall and pick up my makeup. Everything seemed to have gone as planned.

Brian made it home and I got my make-up. When he walked through the door, he grabbed me and led me back out the door.

"What are you doing?"

"Come go somewhere with me." Nadia and I jumped in the car. "Where are we going?"

"You'll see."

We pulled up into my father's driveway. "What are we doing over here?"

We went into my father's house. "Hey, Daddy!"

"Come on in. How you guys doing?" "Fine. I don't know why we're here."

"Mr. Manning, can we all just sit down for a minute?" "What is wrong with you?"

I didn't know what he was talking about. He started talking directly to my father.

"I love your daughter. She is an incredible woman, and I have just been blessed to have met her."

Brian took my hand and looked me in my eyes.

"Danielle, you're the best thing that's ever happened to me. I may not have much money, but I have a whole lot of love to give."

"Will you do me the honor of being my wife?"

I looked at my father. He nodded. Then I looked at Brian. "You for real, aren't you?"

"Yes. Don't make me ask you again." "Yes, I'll marry you."

My father was pleased. He just admired us with a smile. I guess he figured we worked through whatever mishap and got past it, which we had.

Weeks went by and we tried to start planning a wedding, but we realized we weren't going to be able to afford a wedding. We didn't even have wedding rings. We decided to get married on Valentine's Day. I liked that idea, so I would always have a date. It seemed kind of crazy to think of it like that, but I was a hopeless romantic. Every year, when Valentine's Day rolled around, I was always single.

Brian's mom took us to the pawn shop to buy us some wedding bands. When the big day rolled around, we were both at work. We had planned to get off early to go and do our blood work and get our marriage license. As soon as it was time to get off, it started thundering, with lightning.

One of the clerks in my department, the oldest white lady there. She had to be seventy and refused to retire told me that the thunder storm was a warning that our marriage would be full of arguing. I didn't think anything of it.

"I'm sure we'll be okay." I replied.

"Okay, but don't say I didn't warn you. I mean, it's none of *my* business..."

We were all pretty close in our department, so it really wasn't out of place for her to give me advice. We shared so much with each other every day. Brian worked in the MIS department, and he was always servicing the system in our department. So they built a rapport with him as well. He was a real charmer.

Brian arrived at my department. "Good morning, ladies."

"You know, Brian, I just told Danielle that this isn't a good day to get married. Thunderstorms means the marriage will be filled with arguing and confusion."

"No, not me and *my* baby! Ain't nothin gonna stop me from marrying this woman!"

I smiled and said my 'goodbyes,' as Brian led me by the hand out of the department.

I DON'T LOOK LIKE WHAT I'VE BEEN THROUGH

I spent the next month dating myself. It looked like it was going to be a long winter. Every Friday night I went next door to block Buster and rented their date night special, two movies, popcorn, candy and a drink for ten dollars. Yep, that was my routine for the next six weeks. I snuggled up every Friday night with my movies and snacks and cried myself to sleep. I watched the same movies again all day Saturday without even getting out of bed.

The Perimeter office had scheduled their new Holiday hours. We would be closed for the week of Thanksgiving to return for one week and closed for the whole month of December. I had no plans for the Holiday. Kelly dropped in to check on me for Thanksgiving and brought me a plate. I thought that was so sweet of her to think of me.

It was time to get back on the grind. Every morning I still woke up at 6 am to watch Creflo and out by 6:25 with earmuffs, scarf, hat and gloves with my black wool Trench coat I was out the door like clockwork in the freezing cold praising God for my life, health and strength and to get through this breakup with Brandon. Several nights I would sit in the staircase in the dark waiting to see if he would get dropped off by some chick or if he would stay out for the night. Well if you look for it you will find it. I made sure our paths never crossed. We hadn't seen each other since the night of our Kings of Comedy date. Well that silence was broken. A car pulled in the parking lot and Brandon came out of the next building with his overnight bag. My heart dropped to my stomach and it was pounding. I ran in the stairwell so the light wouldn't reflect on my figure in the dark as the car backed up out of the parking lot. I went back to my apartment; I walked in the bathroom and starred in the mirror. It was really over and he had moved on. I could feel the tears surfacing. I tried to hold back as I put in Kirk Franklin. Lord, I can't take it. I laid on the floor crying...

Look for the sequel to

"Lukewarm"

"I Don't Look Like What I've Been Through"

Order and follow Angela Marie Holmes at

www.amazon.com/author/angelaholmes.itsmystory

Made in the USA
Columbia, SC
18 April 2018